A DANGEROUS DANCE

Twirling her smoothly onto the floor, Northcliffe held her several inches closer than the accepted twelve. Zel's muscles were clenched so tightly she feared she would shatter.

"Relax."

"Relax," Zel hissed. "Relax? I'll relax when this dance is over and you decide to leave."

He chuckled. "But you enjoyed our waltzes only days ago."

"I do not enjoy this waltz, nor do I enjoy your company."

He circled rapidly, drawing her close, until the tips of her breasts brushed against his chest. Despite layers of cloth between them, she felt her breasts warm, the nipples harden. How could her body betray her so? How could she respond to such a scoundrel? She must learn to guard herself well around him and discover any means to avoid him.

Northcliffe loosened his clasp on her waist, the distance between them nearly respectable. "If I apologized on bended knee, would you forgive me?"

Her back stiffened. "I would doubt your sincerity."

His mouth curved into the boyishly crooked grin that so disarmed her. "As it is useless to apologize, I must find another way to thaw your cold heart."

"Does my heart really have anything to do with this?"

He laughed too loudly then whispered close to her ear. "I wouldn't know, madam. Does it?"

THE
WEDDING
CHASE

REBECCA
KELLEY

BANTAM 🐓 BOOKS

New York Toronto London
Sydney Auckland

THE WEDDING CHASE

A Bantam Book / June 1998

All rights reserved.

ISBN 0-553-57870-7

Published simultaneously in the United States and Canada

Bantam Books are published by Bantam Books, a division of Bantam Doubleday Dell Publishing Group, Inc. Its trademark, consisting of the words "Bantam Books" and the portrayal of a rooster, is Registered in U.S. Patent and Trademark Office and in other countries. Marca Registrada. Bantam Books, 1540 Broadway, New York, New York 10036.

PRINTED IN THE UNITED STATES OF AMERICA

WC   10 9 8 7 6 5 4 3 2 1

First I have to thank my family, and not just because they'll draw and quarter me if I don't. They have been a tremendous support through this fine madness. A special thanks goes out to my incredible critique partners: Robin Anderson, DeAnne Imatani, Misuzu Shima, Pam Schlutt, and Cindy Preece, without whose threat to break into my house and send out my manuscript themselves, I might never have found the courage to submit my work to Bantam.

PRELUDE

A performance introducing the principal theme

"BY SATAN'S POINTED TAIL, what's all the ruckus?" Wolfgang Hardwicke, earl of Northcliffe, slammed a fistful of cards on the table. "Can't even concentrate on my game. 'Cuse me, gents. I'll only be out a hand or two." Standing suddenly, he upset the rickety chair and strode from the dimly lit main salon toward the offending noise. He threw open the door of the private gaming room, almost knocking the flimsy thing off its hinges.

Inside, he noted a tall, disheveled young man swaying near a scowling, well-muscled giant. Two tough-looking men hovered near a table across the dingy room, one small and wiry, the other short and squat. Instinctively, Wolfgang felt for the dagger tucked in his waistcoat pocket.

"Bloody cheat!" The young man slurred, his balance off kilter as he lunged for the much larger man.

Wolfgang intercepted the young man neatly, swinging him into the nearest empty chair—which promptly crumbled, tumbling both of them to the floor.

"Lemme at him." The young man, at least ten years shy

of Wolfgang's thirty-two years, struggled to rise, impeded by Wolfgang's heavier form firmly ensconced on his chest.

"You're foxed." Wolfgang stood, pushing long black hair, freed of its usual queue, from his eyes. Turning from the young man, he glanced around at the coarse men lining the dirty, smoke-filled room. "What happened here?"

"Fleeced me." The young man still tried unsuccessfully to stand. Wolfgang extended a hand, yanking him to his feet.

"Won fair 'n' square, guv." The giant, big enough to tower over Wolfgang's own considerable height, folded his beefy arms defiantly over his chest. "Fleetwood 'ere is so drunk 'e wouldn't know 'is own pa, let alone an ace from a king."

"And cheating?" Wolfgang's blandly spoken inquiry met stares from three sets of sullen eyes.

"A gent don't accuse a gent of cheatin'." But the fellow with the beefy arms was obviously no gentleman, and the odds being what they were, Wolfgang felt it unwise to question his claim.

Young Fleetwood was not so wise. "You're no gennleman, you're a cheat."

The big man took a step forward, clenching hamlike fists at his sides. Wolfgang took a diplomatic step backward. Fleetwood, however, straightened his tall, slender form, and took a wobbly step forward. Wolfgang felt the tension in the squalid room swell, tightening around him like the skin around a sprained ankle. If he had any sense, he'd turn and walk away, leaving the youthful fool to deal with his own stupidity. But he paused too long, and the time for sensible inaction passed. Fleetwood somehow connected his fist to the fleshy cheek of the huge brute with a sickening thud, and the fight was on.

One of the smaller ruffians, wiry and surprisingly strong, launched himself at Wolfgang, who took one punch to the stomach before collecting himself and landing bone-crunching hits to his assailant's face and neck. When the third man, the squat one, circled around him, Wolfgang knew this was not the right moment for a fair fight. He disposed of the wiry man before him with a hard, sure kick to that most sensitive spot between the legs.

Reaching under his jacket, Wolfgang withdrew his dagger. A swift twist of his torso and a snaking of his wrist, and the squat man stumbled back, howling and clutching an open gash on his cheek. Lunging forward, growling low in his throat, Wolfgang sent the man careening into the hallway.

One down. One out.

Wiping sweat from his forehead, Wolfgang spun back to the one-sided battle being waged on the other side of the shabby gaming room. The beefy man gripped Fleetwood by the throat. Still wielding the dagger, Wolfgang sliced through shirt and skin. With a savage shout the giant loosed Fleetwood and turned on Wolfgang. Wolfgang slashed at the broad chest, leaving behind more torn clothing streaked bright red. The giant lurched back, raising both hands. Wolfgang grabbed Fleetwood's arm and edged toward the door.

Fleetwood stumbled, striking a glancing blow to Wolfgang's shoulder. "You'll not cheat me and walk away."

"Don't be stupid." Wolfgang gripped him tighter. The young fool didn't know a friend from an enemy.

The beefy man, heedless of his wounds, came toward them again. Wolfgang released Fleetwood's arm. Switching his dagger rapidly to his left hand, he met Fleetwood's jaw firmly with his right, then caught the now limp form under the arms.

"Sorry. You'll thank me later." Wolfgang dragged Fleetwood swiftly into the hallway. "Don't try to follow," he barked, kicking the shaky door shut behind them.

"Maven! Where is that demon from hell?" He yanked Fleetwood down the narrow hall into a small, sparse office and dropped him into a chair, shouting to a skinny youth peering through the doorway. "Get Maven now!"

The grubby boy dashed off in search of the gaming hell proprietor. Maven, tall and hawkish, appeared in moments, looking down his nose at the unconscious Fleetwood. "Young fellow's cut from the same cloth as his father. He'll meet a bad end. But it won't be here. Don't bring him back, Captain." Maven smiled thinly. "Oh, excuse me, *Lord* North-cliffe."

"I didn't bring him here." Wolfgang ignored Maven's slur of the unexpected title he'd assumed a scant year ago. Actually he preferred Captain himself. "I haven't a damn clue why I came to his rescue." He paced the tiny room. "I should have left the chuckleheaded pup to fend for himself."

"You carved up a few of my best regulars." Maven's mouth cracked in a very dry, condescending imitation of a smile.

"Best? You're due for an upgrade in customers." Wolfgang sighed, long and loud. "Give me his direction. Settle with my card partners and order my coach, then help me carry him out."

Despite the cool, bumpy ride back into the more fashionable residential districts of London, Fleetwood still lay unconscious when they reached a modest town house on Brook Street. The first rays of dawn streaked across the gray sky, providing enough light for Wolfgang to see the young man's face. He was scarcely more than a boy and as green as the rawest recruits he'd seen fight for glory against Boney, only to die on a mud-soaked Spanish battlefield.

Pulling Fleetwood out of the coach, he swung him over his shoulder, grimacing at the strong odor of whiskey on the man's breath. Before he'd reached the bottom stair of the house, the front door inched open and a round face illuminated by candlelight peered down at him.

"The young master's home," Wolfgang called out,

climbing the steps to the entryway. "Where should I deposit him?"

The servant pulled the door open and, glancing nervously up and down the street, gestured them inside. As Wolfgang moved to lower his charge to a chair in the hall, the man cleared his throat. "Could you please carry him upstairs?"

"Do I look like a footman?"

"Forgive me, sir." The man's round face took on a distinctly reddish cast. "Could you please carry him into the salon?"

"Do you have a footman?" Wolfgang shifted his weight, Fleetwood still dangling over his shoulder.

The pudgy retainer shook his head, eyes aimed at the floor.

"Lead on, I'll take him to his room, although I'm sure if I refused it wouldn't be the first time he bunked on a sofa or the floor." Steadying his grip on the drunken cub's knees, Wolfgang followed the servant up the stairs.

At the top of the stairs Fleetwood suddenly jerked. Struggling to maintain his balance, Wolfgang lurched into the wall, slamming his shoulder and Fleetwood's backside into a portrait.

"Bloody spawn of the devil." Wolfgang regained his footing, as his little guide waved the candelabra before him. The door across from him swung wide, and a figure in white with a cascade of dark hair stepped into the hall.

"Robin?" her husky voice questioned.

"Master Robin's a little under the weather, coming home with a friend," the servant told her, then clasped Wolfgang's arm with a surprisingly firm grip, directing him toward the nearest doorway.

Wolfgang cast one last look at the woman in white, his connoisseur's eye assessing her tall form, noting the slender hips and full breasts not quite hidden by the thin cloth of her night rail. He hurriedly laid Fleetwood out on the indicated bed, returning to the hall as the door across the way softly shut.

Sauntering down the stairs, he grinned. Wolfgang Hardwicke, lecher and Good Samaritan. Brushing off his hands he exited the house and jumped into the waiting carriage. In heaven's log of good works, this deed would cover him for the next six months of debauchery: a little wine, a little gambling, and a lot of women. Clean, married women from whom he'd be unlikely to contract syphilis or matrimony. And if she met his criteria, maybe he'd start with that shapely apparition upstairs.

CHAPTER 1

PIZZICATO

Plucking the strings instead of bowing them

THE THREADBARE WALL hangings rippled. Robinson Crusoe Fleetwood blinked at the light shifting through the thin draperies and covered his ears in an effort to protect them from the thundering pianoforte notes. Zelly was launching a full-force Beethoven assault. And it couldn't even be noon yet!

Lord, his head felt like shattered glass. Why did he do this to himself? Maybe it was time to listen to Zelly, to call halt to the fast life. He massaged his throbbing temples. Damnation! His stake! He'd lost his last chance to turn things around. He'd been so sure, his luck so strong. He couldn't lose. But lose he did—quickly, surely, miserably.

He'd been playing with a crude hard-drinking crew, sure that he could outclass them . . . and there was a tall, dark man, not a denizen of the streets, but skilled with knife and fists.

Robin yawned, rubbing his tender jaw. That tall, dark man punched him! He eased up gingerly. It was all coming back to him now. The man had cheated. His gaming partners caught the man and he drew a dagger, cutting the gamesters. Then he turned on Robin and landed a facer. Maven must have sent him home, but that damn cheat had his money.

He stood shakily, straightening yesterday's pantaloons and shirt. A splash of cold water cleared his head a little. Time to leave town. Put the creditors off his scent, till he had a new plan. He hadn't been to the country seat in months. Moreton-in-Marsh would be a welcome sight. But first he had to face his father and Zelly . . .

The dining room was empty, sideboards bare. He made for the kitchen and charmed a biscuit and some flat ale from his aunt's housekeeper. If Sir Edward Charles Fleetwood, his father, was about, he'd be in the study pretending to peruse ledgers while he tippled a little brandy and read about the horses at Newmarket.

Robin knocked softly, entering the small dark-paneled study without waiting for a summons. The elder Fleetwood sat motionless at the shabby cherrywood desk as expected, clutching a glass partially filled with amber liquid.

"Father?" Robin shuffled across the faded Aubusson carpet, his voice low and uncertain.

"Robin, my boy." Sir Edward reached for the decanter. "Join me?"

"Could use a little hair of the dog." Robin took a small glass off a tiny corner table, passing it to his father to fill. He muttered, "I'm done up."

"You lost it all?" The older man handed him the half-filled glass, accusation in his voice. "But you told me you had the perfect game. How much did you drink?"

Robin took the brandy, downing it in one gulp. "Had a couple of pigeons ready for the taking, but a high-flyer cleaned me out. When I cried cheat, he attacked me, knocking me cold. Knifed the other men. Don't know who he was, but I'll find him."

"And what in the devil's name will you do when you

find him? You've no skill with pistol, sword, or fists, Robinson." Sir Edward scratched his head, mussing the thinning, gray hair. "Challenge him and you're a dead man."

"I'll find a way to deal with him. Besides, I'd as soon be dead as in debtor's prison." Robin threw himself into the nearest chair, burying his face in his hands.

"Zelly will find a husband who can settle your debts."

"But she don't want to marry." Robin's tone was obstinate. "A man takes care of his own affairs."

"She'll marry." But his father's expression belied the surety of his statement. "We've tried everything else. No banker or cent-per-center in London will touch us. And at the mention of money even my oldest friends disappear."

"More talk of money and marriage?" Zel paused in the doorway, staring hard at her father before striding into the room, her huge red-brindle Irish wolfhound at her heels. Her mood softened when she saw her younger brother sprawled in the chair before the desk.

Robin rose, and she embraced him warmly. Spotting the bruising on his jaw, she grasped his chin. "You have been hurt! What happened?" She continued in a sharper tone. "You were doing more than drinking last night. You were fighting, and one of your friends had to carry you home."

"I got caught up in a fight." He looked at the floor. "Not my fault."

"You have been in the hells." She clenched her fists, pushing aside the image of Robin's friend, his handsome face etched in candlelight. And that wicked grin when he spied her in her nightgown. "You were gambling again. What can I do to make you stop?"

Robin's voice echoed hollowly in the tiny room. "I was trying to win enough money to pay my debts, so you wouldn't have to marry. Would have done it too, but I was cheated by some *gentleman* who doesn't even need it. I'll find a way to get it back." He touched her hand briefly, moving to the open door. "I have to go. Won't be back for dinner. Tomorrow I'm off to the country."

Zel frowned fondly after him, as her dog nudged her elbow with a damp nose. Turning to her father, she could feel her face heat in anger, but she kept her tone cold. "I suppose I cannot expect you to control him, when you cannot control yourself."

"Damn, girl! Don't fight me!" Her father rose, facing Zel eye to eye, glare to glare. The dog growled softly.

"Mouse! Sit! Remus, I said sit!" Her voice escalated with her temper. "Why should I be the one to pay the price for your vices?" Zel rubbed eyes suddenly moist with tears. She wanted to hit him, throw things, but instead she concentrated on fighting back these stupid tears. Lord, she hated feeling so powerless and weak.

"Wouldn't ask for myself. I can't stall the creditors much longer. They want the blunt now." He lowered his voice, pleading. "Robin needs you, girl. Don't let him go to prison."

"Stop calling me girl." She ignored his begging as her hand twined in Remus's wiry coat. "You let this happen again!"

"No, I told him he was playing too deep."

"What about you, your debts?"

He evaded her eyes. "My debts aren't the problem."

Zel sank into a threadbare chair, Remus's head following to her lap. She was tired, weary to the core of a battle that never ended. "Maybe I do need to marry, settle for you both this last time, then leave you to your own devices."

"I know you can do it. Gir . . . woman as bright and lovely as you should be able to land a wealthy husband. Could have done it long before, if you'd a mind to." His lighter tone echoed his victory. "The problem's those bloody women's reformer ideas."

"Father, you know my feelings about marriage." She

sighed, massaging her neck. "After all, have I not had your example of what a husband can be?"

"Don't bring your mother into this." Sir Edward bristled.

"I spoke of you, not Mother." Zel scowled at his ruddy face. "She was a better wife than you ever deserved."

"Zelly, despite what you think of me, your brother needs you." The begging crept back into his voice.

Robin. Of course it came back to Robin. The thought of him in prison horrified her. She could never let it happen. Her shoulders sagged. "Finding a suitable husband may be more difficult than you realize." She rubbed her eyes. "You may require only wealth, but I require that he neither attempt to control my life nor interfere with my work."

"Husband has the right to tell his wife what's what." His mouth curled. She felt sickened by his triumphant gloating. "Unless you can find some man-milliner who'll be happy to let you run his life."

"You forget several important points." Zel was determined to quash that victorious smirk. "I have never gone out in London's fashionable society. I am too old for the marriage mart. I know nothing of flirtation or pleasing a man." She fluttered her lashes, laughing harshly. "I am far from the conventional standard of beauty. I am too tall, too blunt. I value utilitarian over frivolous pursuits." She pushed a stray strand of hair behind her ear. "I will appear as a post-horse among Thoroughbreds and will never receive a single offer."

"You've got more brains than any of them. You've got your mother's looks, though you don't make the most of them." Papa's smirk had not diminished. "Spend some time on your appearance. Keep your mouth shut or use it to flatter."

He gave her an appraising look. "You could stand with the best of them. If the young bucks are fools, you can easily catch a rich old widower who needs a mama for his children or a little comforting in his dotage. You know my sister will be happy to help. Diana has friends in the best circles." He finally met her eyes. "You have to do it, girl. Robin's depending on you."

"I am not a girl. You also seem to forget that no man will care to burden himself with in-laws running from debtors' prison." Zel dropped her eyes, her voice low and quiet. As much as she would like to defy her father, she would not abandon her brother, no matter how futile she believed this plan to be. Besides, she had no better ideas. "I will do what I must, for Robin."

"ZEL, we cannot hurry this. One does not jump into a season. It must be planned . . . every detail made just so, just so." Diana Marie Fleetwood Stanfield patted her gray-flecked hair as she paced from the window to the door in the bright, floral-papered drawing room. Most of Aunt Diana's house was well worn, the furnishings long past their prime. But her aunt's careful budgeting had preserved this room along with the dining room and small salon. "You have no clothes, your hair . . ." Zel squirmed on the pianoforte stool as Aunt Diana surveyed her with a critical eye. "You need vouchers for Almack's, invitations. . . . Invitations will not be a problem. With so many in Paris celebrating Napoleon's defeat, the hostesses are looking for anyone to fill their ballrooms. But we must do this right."

"Aunt Diana, I cannot afford to wait. The creditors are pounding at the door. Robin is truly done for this time." Zel laid her fingers heavily on the keys, feeling as taut as the instrument's inner strings. Remus hovered at her side.

"Oh, Zel dear, I am so sorry." She stopped and spread the thick drapes, looking out the window. "I know you wish to remain single. Now you face the uncertainties of marriage. If I had the money . . . if only I did."

"But you do not. Father is certain I can land a wealthy husband." Zel went to her aunt's side, frowning at the spring blossoms in the tiny courtyard below. "I am not so certain. And if I do get an offer, how can I be sure he will not be like my father?"

"Or my late husband." The old bitterness touched Aunt Diana's voice. "Child, pick carefully . . . and well."

"How can one know? Stanfield was so charming." Zel forced a smile. She dearly loved the older woman and knew her aunt looked on her as the child she never had, despite only ten years difference in their ages. Even with little to share—the bulk of her husband's estate having passed to a distant cousin—she always welcomed her brother's family into her home. "Forgive me. I know you hate to think of him."

"We need to think of you. I wish you would wait, but if you cannot . . ." Aunt Diana's handsome face brightened. "I know just the thing. My friend Julianna, Lady Selby, you remember her . . . her house party. But it starts in a few days." She tapped lightly on the windowpane. "It would be perfect for you to practice a little flirting, polish up your manners." She turned to Zel, frowning again. "But your—your clothes. . . ."

"I know my clothes are not at all the thing, but I can afford nothing better." Zel swirled and curtsied, laughing as she nearly tripped over Remus's inert form. "I shall be the Dandyess of Dowd."

"Now, Zel, my sweet, do not fun me. We must think of something. You know clothes dress the man . . . are the man. Oh, whatever that saying is, you know what I mean. Clothes are important." She resumed pacing, her tall form moving with a compelled grace. "Zel, my coming out clothes, in the attic. I saved them all these years. They are scarcely worn, as my husband kept me in the country. They would only need a few tucks to fit you to perfection."

"Aunt Diana, they are nearly fifteen years old. They must be moth-eaten and the style completely outdated."

'No, no, they are well cared for. I take them out some-

times. . . . I like to remember the days before I married."
She looked at Zel, excitement overtaking the sadness in her
eyes. "I was nearly as slender as you, and so carefree. . . .
The simple elegant lines would flatter you so. The thin silks
and muslins cling to the natural shape of the body."

"Aunt Diana." Zel stared at the older woman. "I do not
wish to appear a loose woman."

"We will try not to offend your modesty." Aunt Diana
chuckled. "You may wear a shift and a petticoat, as I did."

"I will not wear a corset." She frowned. "Nor do I like
yards and yards of ribbon and lace."

"There is no lace and little ribbon, and they will require
almost no remodeling. But the whites and pastels will be all
wrong for you . . . as they were for me." Aunt Diana
rubbed absently at her jaw. "I know, we shall dye them.
Bright jewel colors. Sapphire, emerald, aquamarine to accent
your eyes. Ruby and garnet to bring color to your cheeks."

"But such bright colors are frowned upon for unmarried
women." Zel was not at all sure about this whole scheme.

"Posh, you are old enough to carry them off." She gifted
Zel with a brilliant smile. "No one will blink an eye. We'll
leave just a few white or pastel for the most formal occasions."

"Can they be ready in two days?"

"Two days?" Aunt Diana fluttered about the window.
"It will take several dyings to get the colors right. Nothing
will be ready for the house party."

"Then I shall wear the best of my old gowns."

"Oh, you should wait. But I know how you are when
you have made up your mind." She stopped abruptly. "There
is a lovely, classically styled riding habit. . . . With a few
tucks it should fit admirably. At least you would look presentable atop a horse."

"If I ride."

"You must ride. Lord Selby keeps a fine stable."

"I would like to ride. If I remember how." Zel resolutely

faced her aunt. "Please write Lady Selby and tell her to expect me. Will you come?"

"I must stay here and prepare your wardrobe." Aunt Diana patted her arm. "I will probably have more fun. The guests may be very dull."

"I will check on the coach times." Zel's voice was businesslike, with the plan now agreed upon.

"Zel Fleetwood. You will not take the public coach. Julianna's sister will attend. You shall ride with her."

"Aunt Diana, I cannot thank you enough, for all of this." Zel put a hand on her aunt's shoulder and kissed her cheek.

"You may run roughshod over me on most everything, Zel, but there is one other thing on which I will stand firm." Aunt Diana rose to her full height, ready to do battle. "That monstrous hound of yours will remain here. He would surely intimidate even the sturdiest suitor, and Julianna would never, never allow a near horse in her house."

"But Mouse will miss me. And he will obey no one but me." Remus stirred, thumping his tail against her skirts.

"No, dear, Smythe will learn to control him, and the dog will carry on without you, for a few days."

"I suppose you are right. Remus would frighten to death the type of husband I seek." Zel laughed, but a vision of a well-favored face half-hidden by tousled black hair and a tall muscular form hoisting her brother's body hovered in her mind. She squashed it. "After all, I am looking for the richest, oldest, most mild-mannered and most easily controlled man in England."

RAFAEL OWED HIM for this one. How would a dull country house party further his acceptance by polite society? Unlikely to advance his political career, it was more likely to place him irretrievably in that most deadly of spots, the marriage mart. Wolfgang shuddered as the borrowed valet tied his cravat. Satan's misbegotten! The thought of those matchmaking mamas turned his skin cold. A wife! The last thing in the world he needed or wanted.

He'd missed dinner but hadn't timed his arrival well enough to miss what would surely be an excruciating musical evening. He pushed aside the valet's hands. "Stop fussing. This will do."

As he descended the stairs two at a time, the first lambent strains tickled his ears. The music swelled as he strode down the long hall. This was not the fumbling amateur recital typical of a country retreat. Lady Selby must have hired a professional musician.

Slipping into the crowded music room, he leaned against a silk-hung wall, absorbing the ebb and flow of the melodious tide of notes. Too soon the music stopped, applause forcing him to reluctantly bring his attention back to the gaudy room. A husky female voice informed the audience they had heard a selection of Bach's preludes and fugues. Next she would play Beethoven's Sonata in C-sharp minor, recently named the *Moonlight Sonata.*

Beethoven, he sighed, ready for the music to consume him, but first to discover the maker of the astonishing sounds. Wolfgang edged along the wall toward the pianoforte, watching the pianist's slim shoulders sway, as if buffeted by the very tones she produced. Moving until he stood nearly beside her at the piano bench, he leaned against the pier table, observing her delicate profile. Her face was flushed, her full lips parted, her large, ever-so-slightly slanted eyes glazed in sightless concentration. Strands of errant sable hair dusted her smooth brow.

Her breathing came fast and shallow, her hands alternately caressing, coaxing, and compelling the pianoforte until it became an animate object, quickened to do her bidding, alive at the touch of her long, slender fingers. A grimace passed over his face as he found himself blessing his mother. She gave him precious little in his life, but she had given him this reverence for music. Nothing else stirred him so, yet gave him such peace.

The last note resounded throughout the room. The musical sorceress sat motionless, waiting while the applause played out. The crowd silently followed the hostess, Lady Selby, through the carved door, bursting into chatter upon reaching the hall.

Wolfgang found his progress arrested by a hand on his arm. "Gadth, man, odd to thee you here," Jeremy Crawley, Lord Melbourne, drawled, his irritating childhood lisp increasingly exaggerated as the man advanced further into adulthood. "I'd have thought you'd be in Parith thelebrating Napoleon'th defeat."

"I have no desire to join the revelers. My tour in the army showed me all I wish to see of the Continent for years to come."

He glanced over the shorter man's shoulder. The pianoforte's bench lay empty. Devil it! He scanned the room. Was she the brunette passing through the door? The woman's face was averted, but she was too short.

Wolfgang walked beside Melbourne, his usual pace hampered by the deliberate cadence of the crowd. "The entertainment tonight was a cut above average." Wolfgang's voice projected the proper hint of boredom. "Did Lady Selby judge the talents of the company so meager as to require importing a musician?"

"Oh, that'th Mith Fleetwood." Melbourne's padded yellow shoulders shrugged. "Her aunt'th a friend to Lady Thelby."

Fleetwood? He'd heard that name, and recently—the young fool several days ago at Maven's. Stepping into the drawing room with Melbourne at his heels, Wolfgang again surveyed the crowd. Did the lovely body and seductive flow of hair of his apparition belong with the passionate face and manner of the pianist? This dull house party got better by the minute.

"I'd like an introduction," Wolfgang announced, twisting to view the rest of the room.

"Introduction? Oh, to her. Why the devil would you want to meet her?" Melbourne eyed him with suspicion. "A bluethtocking. A dyed-in-the-wool thpinthter. And too bold at the pianoforte to be much of a lady."

"Exactly."

Melbourne grinned stupidly and gestured across the room. "That'th her thanding bethide Lady Thelby, over there."

Wolfgang nodded his thanks and slipped over to stand beside Lady Selby and the woman Melbourne had indicated. Was this the impassioned pianist with whom he had shared a paean to the gods only moments earlier? She was brunette and very tall, with a delicate, pointed bone structure and a mouth too large for the accepted standards of beauty. He would be tempted to call her looks feline or even elfish except for her height and quiet dignity. But where was the spirit, the fire? And those spectacles and that shapeless mud-brown gown, where in Lucifer's flaming realm did they come from?

Turning with exaggerated politeness to where Lady Selby spread herself on a brocaded sofa, Wolfgang lightly grasped the proffered hand. He brushed the woman's fingers, plump sausages encased in kid gloves and golden rings, with his lips.

"Ah, Northcliffe, you decided to grace us with your presence." Her jowled, turbanned head bobbed a greeting. "Never tell me you are here to peruse the latest batch of debutantes?"

"My lady, would I tell you such a tale? I am interested in establishing political, not family, ties." He released her hand, lying effortlessly. "Forgive me for coming late but I had business in town." He glanced at her silent companion. "If the rest of the week is equal to tonight, I shall breathlessly await your every entertainment."

"My dear sir, if compliments are due, they are surely owing to the musical interpretations of Miss Fleetwood." Her generous bosom quivering, she turned to the young woman standing at her side. "Zel, dear, have you met the earl?"

He regarded the object of Lady Selby's inquiry. A faint coloring washed over her cheeks as her eyes darted away from his close scrutiny. A touch of feminine modesty as she remembered their first meeting?

"No, my lady," she murmured, the low pitch rumbling gently as a cat's purr.

"Miss Fleetwood, may I present Wolfgang Hardwicke, earl of Northcliffe." Lady Selby shot him a look of warning. "Northcliffe, may I present Miss Grizelda Fleetwood."

As he raised her gloved hand to his mouth her eyes lifted, her gaze dancing across his face. A faint scent of spice hovered about her. Now he could see beneath the thin lenses of her spectacles. A spark, a flash of golden fire illuminated her large sea-blue almond-shaped eyes.

"Charmed, Miss Fleetwood." He held on to her long, slender fingers, his eyes capturing hers. "Your playing tonight was superb, and how brave to play the daring Herr Beethoven."

"Brave, my lord?"

He focused his gaze on the laughter barely contained by her full lips. Did she think him a prude, offended by her ardent rendition of Beethoven? No, her embarrassment had fled at the mention of Wolfgang's name—turning to amusement. But what right had she to laugh with a name like Grizelda?

"Miss Fleetwood, you need not stifle that giggle." He lowered his thick eyebrows in his best fierce look. "My name has always been sorely abused. I hoped that one of your musical nature would have more compassion."

"My lord, please excuse my rudeness." The glint in her

eyes held no contrition. "But you see, I suffer also from the curse of Mozart. My second name is Amadea."

His mouth twitched and spread open in a wide grin he knew exposed that annoying boyish dimple. He clasped her hand again. The covering of smooth, cool kid thwarted direct contact, but he was rewarded by the return of that touch of color to her pale high cheek bones.

"We are destined to become the best of friends." As his thumb grazed over her palm, her color deepened. "We are blessed with the love of music and cursed with a name made for jest."

Lady Selby took Zel's arm, pinning Wolfgang with a protective glare. "You must reprimand Northcliffe severely when he becomes too familiar. He is a most incorrigible, ah, flirt, you know." She pulled more forcefully on Zel's arm. "Come along, dear, we must introduce you to the other guests."

Wolfgang flashed a ghost of a bow. "Miss Fleetwood, we *will* speak again."

Lady Selby steered her away from him as if she were a green debutante. Certainly she was well into her twenties, too old to be considered an innocent needing to be spared a little flirtation, even from such a known rakehell as he.

His eyes moved lazily over her departing figure. Her ill-fitting, hideous gown made a nearly effective disguise, but after the view of her in her night rail, his practiced eye could see the very appropriately placed curves and infinitely long limbs that moved with feline grace. Her scraggly chignon, pale complexion, and wire-rimmed spectacles made it equally difficult to ascertain the charms of her countenance. But he had seen her glow as she played Beethoven, and he had seen the flash in her eyes when she concealed her laughter.

There was a mystery here. Why would an unmarried woman fail to capitalize on her beauty? Unless she had no interest in dangling after a husband. Perhaps the intriguing

Miss Fleetwood remained a miss because she had no more interest in marriage than he. This house party could certainly be enlivened by a little flirtation. Or more than a flirtation if the impassioned pianoforte recital correctly reflected her other inclinations.

Zel took a steadying breath as Lady Selby drew her across the room. She was unused to the company of men, except for her family, and Lord Northcliffe's presence overpowered her, to say the least. It was not just his size, although that was considerable, nor his piercing silver eyes, nor his long sensual face. He had an air about him . . . something uncompromising and untamed.

She shook her head to clear her thoughts. He was not the type of man to suit her purposes, but his forward manner confused her. Her face heated again. He had looked at her as he had that night in her upstairs hall, when she had worn nothing but her night rail. She should coquettishly rap him with her fan as she had seen more sophisticated women do, or, better yet, discourage any fancy he may have for her by slapping his handsome, insolent face. Zel nearly laughed aloud at her conceit. A man such as he would have no real interest in her, but perhaps she could practice some flirtation with him, prepare herself for London.

No, wisdom dictated she was out of her depth and should stay far away from him. She found herself tempted to turn, wanting to know if his eyes followed her, or if he quickly found other diversion. Straightening her shoulders, she directed her eyes to her hostess and the tiny gray-haired woman on Lady Selby's other arm, whose name she failed to catch.

The evening was a blur of faces and polite conversation. Zel felt like a baby chick under the plump, protective wing of Lady Selby. Aunt Diana's introductory letter had done its work too well. She must have been presented to every unattached man in the county.

Between spells of watching the intricate plasterwork on

the walls, Zel found herself responding demurely to comments on the weather, fashion, and the prince regent's latest exploits. Several times she felt herself the subject of pointed observation. When she glanced around she discovered Lord Northcliffe nearby, a black-haired, silver-eyed wolf, regarding her intently. She chuckled softly at her flight of fancy, receiving a sharp look from the stout older gentleman who had been describing modern sheep-raising techniques.

"Lord Astin, I believe your wife is looking for you." Northcliffe's deep voice resonated near her ear. "I last saw her in the library."

As Astin made his excuses, Zel, skin tingling with the blush moving up her throat and cheeks, turned to Northcliffe. She felt far too aware of how broad his shoulders were in his perfectly fitted midnight-blue evening coat and how he stood so tall her eyes barely met his chin, she who looked down on most men's brows or hairlines.

"Your knight errant, mademoiselle, at your command." He winked broadly. "Specializing in rescuing fair damsels from the evil dragon of boredom."

Her laughter stopped abruptly as his long fingers wrapped around her upper arm, directing her to the door. She grudgingly smiled her thanks for the rescue, then dug in her heels, tugging at his hand. "Where are we going?"

His reply was low and intimate. "I thought you might like to accompany me to the terrace and indulge in a more stimulating conversation."

Before she could answer, they passed through the French doors, entering a terrace lit only by the graying rays of the setting sun. He guided her to a stone bench, sinking down beside her, the warmth of his leg inches from her own. Was he sitting too close? He must be, but should she move to the edge of the bench or stand indignantly? Wishing she had experience in these games men and women played, she shifted slightly.

"Who was the Mozart lover who named you?" As he

turned toward her, she could see the muscles bunch in his thigh. His knee nearly touched hers.

Zel controlled her voice. "My grandfather." She watched as the twilight play of shadow and light flickered over the lines of his face. "I suppose I should be happy Beethoven was not a famous composer when I was born, or I might be Grizelda Ludwigia."

He laughed, a musical growl coming from somewhere low in his chest. "That would be quite a mouthful indeed. My mother insisted on Wolfgang." The gray of his eyes clouded slightly. "She loves music but was more concerned with countermanding my evangelical father's choice, John Wesley, after the nonconformist religious leader. My full name is Wolfgang John Wesley Hardwicke." The bright silver glint returned to his eyes. "I fought over that name so many times as a boy I've actually developed a perverse pride in it. But with your musical prowess, I'm sure Beethoven and Mozart would be honored for you to use their names."

"My lord, your flattery goes too far." The barely respectable distance between them diminished further. Zel slid to the edge of the bench to widen the gap, focusing on a previously unnoticed tiny streak of gray zigzagging through the glossy black hair above his right temple. Hair unfashionably long and tied with a ribbon at the nape of his neck.

Northcliffe narrowed the space. " 'Tis not flattery, Miss Fleetwood. You play with incredible passion." His eyes refused to release hers. "Your whole body is possessed by the music."

"My lord, I do not believe this is proper discourse." Zel flashed him what she hoped was a scathing look. Part of her knew she should leave him alone and return to the dull conversations in the drawing room. Another part of her longed to stay, unaccountably intrigued by his charm and flirtatious manner.

"I'm not known for my polite discourse, but I shall try to behave myself. The earlier piece by a Mr. Bach . . ." He tapped long, tapering fingers on his thigh. "I pride myself on familiarity with all types of music, but he's unknown to me."

"He is not widely known in England. My old German music master introduced me to his preludes and fugues, regarding them as great teaching tools. I found them extraordinarily beautiful." Zel cleared her throat, watching his hand as it stilled, then rested on his leg, very near her own thigh.

"Would you play more of them for me?" Northcliffe's eyes gleamed in the soft twilight.

The air, fragrant with spring blooms, was cool, but Zel felt a warmth seep slowly through her body. "They are intended for the harpsichord or clavichord." Her voice faltered as she contemplated a private recital. "Either are unlikely to be available."

They sat in silence for several moments. Not an easy, companionable silence, but a silence filled with discomforting sensations, strange tingles in her legs, cool shivers along her back, heat flooding her abdomen. Zel could feel his eyes touching her, lingering where her skin lay exposed. Her hand darted to her bodice, smoothing over the fabric, making certain the cloth was still in place. She looked down at her feet, incapable of returning his gaze, then opened her mouth seeking anything to break the spell surrounding them.

"Are you one of my brother's reprobate gambling friends?"

He laughed. "No, I am not his friend, reprobate or otherwise. He was drunk and I delivered him home as a favor to a friend."

"And your friend was the gaming hell proprietor?"

He shifted about, rubbing his arm against hers. "Yes."

Zel held her ground. "How did he get injured?"

"Injured? I thought he was drunk."

"His jaw had a nasty bruise."

"I never saw a bruise." Northcliffe suddenly grasped her

hand in his while his other hand snatched her spectacles from her face. "Why do you wear these things?"

She sat stunned, watching as he peered through the lenses, then scanned her face. "You hide lovely eyes. Inside they appeared a blue green, but now they are green—"

"Sir, return my spectacles and my hand." Zel tried to pull away, but his grip held firm.

"—with flashing golden flecks." His face advanced to within inches of hers. "The eyes of a cat. What is the color?"

"Ordinary hazel." With a note of command in her voice, she attempted to wrest control of the interchange once more. "My spectacles and my hand, please. It is time to go inside."

His lips twitched. "I'll return you to the drawing room." Turning her hand, he placed the spectacles in her palm, and released her. "I warned you, I rarely behave." His lips spread into a wide smile, the single dimple hanging at one corner.

"Northcliffe!" A trilling flutelike voice followed them onto the terrace. A stylish, beautiful blonde well beyond the first blush of youth looked past Zel. She might have stepped off a fashion plate, with her filmy, pastel muslin gown clinging to her boldly full figure. "Come inside, you naughty boy. I swear I will die of boredom without you."

"Isadora, I had no idea you were in need of me." His murmur was the texture of raw silk, but his eyes were cold steel. "Have you met my new friend, Miss Fleetwood?"

"I heard her performance, but we haven't met." The woman's eyes brushed over Zel, returning quickly to Northcliffe.

"Then I shall do the honors." Northcliffe stood, gazing from one woman to the other. "Lady Horeton, may I present Miss Grizelda Fleetwood. Miss Fleetwood, may I present Isadora Morganton, Lady Horeton."

"I am pleased to meet you, Lady Horeton." Zel felt awkward beside the petite, graceful woman.

"Call me Isadora, dear." The corners of her mouth curled ever so slightly upward. "I would love to call you Grizelda."

Coughing an unwilling assent, Zel turned away from Northcliffe's intent look. An image filled her mind of two cats fighting over a canary. Zel blinked to clear the vision. She was not a cat, and Northcliffe resembled no canary she had ever seen. He was undoubtably handsome, but not a picture of masculine beauty for women to fight over. His nose was a bit too long. His mouth was too wide and his jaw too prominent. In all, entirely too rugged to be considered beautiful.

"Your gown is most unusual, Grizelda, dear." Lady Horeton rubbed against Northcliffe. "Was it made especially for you?"

Nodding again, Zel scanned the voluptuous woman before her. "I dress for comfort and utility, not for style."

Lady Horeton's laughter tinkled, high and sharp, like a tiny bell. "How wonderfully wise of you."

Northcliffe laughed, a short bark. "Odd as it seems, some women do value wisdom. Where is Lord Horeton?"

The petite blonde gave him an oddly hard look, then smiled again. "You know the poor old dear would never survive a trip longer than five miles from London."

Rising beside Northcliffe, Zel towered over Lady Horeton, who quickly grasped Northcliffe's arm. He reached for Zel with his free hand, but she pointedly ignored his offer, escaping through the French doors. She had foolishly begun to feel she could joust with Northcliffe, but Lady Horeton, and her smooth, coy manner, made Zel feel gauche and coarse. Her sophisticated clothing further served to emphasize Zel's dowdy appearance.

Zel did not speak to Northcliffe during the remainder of the evening, but she again found herself surveyed by his keen eyes and felt an uneasy mixture of irritation and pleasure. A flush heated her cheeks as the quirk at the corner of his mouth indicated he was aware of and amused by her response to him.

•   •   •

DESPITE THE STRANGE BED, Wolfgang slept deeply, awakening uncharacteristically groggy and muddled. A vague image clouded his thoughts. A dream image of a sleek, sable cat with glittering golden fire in its sea-hued eyes and an elfin grin on its very uncatlike lips. He stretched into the pillows, frowning, surprised at the vision hovering in his mind. The frown slowly transformed into a wide smile as he realized Miss Grizelda Amadea Fleetwood would be even more astonished than he to find herself the object of his dreams.

He sat up abruptly, decision made. She would be a pleasant distraction at an otherwise monotonous house party. A mild dalliance, and if it built to more—fulfilling—activities, so much the better. He would not normally pursue an unmarried miss, but she was surely no innocent fresh out of the schoolroom. She was old enough and intelligent enough to understand the ways of men and women and make her own decisions. If she declined his advances, he'd cut his losses and return to London to seek a new mistress among the bored wives of the ton.

Wolfgang flung off the bedclothes. Blazing lakes of brimstone! Within the week he would press his lips to that slender, graceful neck and warm himself in the fire flickering in her eyes.

CHAPTER 2

CANZONET

A graceful song in parts

STANDING BEFORE LADY SELBY'S ornate basin and mirror, Wolfgang splashed cold water on his face and neck. Lucifer and his cat! He'd wet the damn dressing again! Frowning, he ripped the bandage off his shoulder. A narrow scab came up with it. The scurvy footpads who attacked him three days ago outside Brooks's Club had barely scratched the skin. Rank amateurs! He dabbed at a few drops of blood with the gauze dressing. The runner he'd hired at Bow Street should be responding with a report, detailing the identity of the assailants and the reason for the attack. Maybe it was just a simple robbery.

Deciding the wound didn't merit a new dressing, he quickly donned attire of which even his valet would approve: buff pantaloons, white shirt, pale blue waistcoat, and black Hessians. Finishing off a simple cravat knot, he slid into the snug morning jacket. He felt a little lost without Jenkins's attendance, but the staunch retainer deserved a few days off. An adult male should be able to dress himself on occasion.

Wolfgang rooted through the pile of last night's cloth- ing for a hair ribbon, finally finding the black strip tangled about a rumpled waistcoat. He'd had a week his friend, Freddie, would be proud of, first the fight at the gambling hell and the next night the footpad attack. What did Miss Fleetwood know about the fight? He'd evaded her questions, but he knew the issue hadn't died. Frowning at his reflection in the glass, he brushed his hair, tied it in a queue, then set out in search of breakfast.

The sideboard in the bright breakfast room was filled with rashers of bacon, kidney pie, salmon, eggs, jam tarts, dried fruit, toast, coffee, and tea. He loaded a plate, joining the sparse gathering around the table. As conversation ran equally sparse he ate rapidly, excusing himself to wander the house.

Eventually, Wolfgang found himself in the music room. He hadn't practiced in months but, inspired by Miss Fleetwood's performance, he couldn't resist trying his hand. First the pianoforte, then its player.

A smile brushed his lips. Her sweet blush contrasted so intriguingly with her bold behavior. She followed along with his game of cat and mouse, allowing him to sit far too close, moving away only a bit to encourage rather than discourage him. Yet when faced with competition, she deserted the field, leaving him in Isadora's clutches despite his silent plea for aid.

He sighed, seating himself on the bench. If he wished to be an honorable gentleman, any doubts dictated that he leave her alone. But why should he allow a few scruples to interfere with his amusements? And she did amuse him.

He would proceed with flirtation, moving ever so skillfully into seduction. Smiling, Wolfgang rifled through the sheet music arrayed on the pianoforte. Finding a familiar Mozart sonata, he began to softly finger the hardwood keys.

He was thoroughly destroying the piece when he sensed another presence in the room. A spicy scent. Wolfgang turned to see Grizelda Fleetwood, in another dowdy gown, hesitating at the door. He stopped abruptly, surprised at his embarrassment.

"Discovered! The foul deed uncovered!" He smiled, eased the bench back, and stood with a flourish. "I confess my guilt. I've murdered Mozart."

She laughed, a throaty sound of full, easy humor that struck a chord within him. Her laughter bore no resemblance to the rehearsed titter affected by the ladies of the ton. "I wouldn't call it murder, my lord, maybe a little unintentional mayhem. You have a fine hand, but it's clear you rarely practice."

"The truth is indeed revealed. I seldom, almost never, practice. Lacking discipline, I have become a much better listener than player." Wolfgang took a step closer, drawing her eyes to his. "You are quite beyond my touch."

That faint blush appeared again, as she set a well-worn portfolio on the table. "Do you sight read?"

"About as well as I play."

"That will be fine. I have a few Bach pieces my music master arranged for four hands on the pianoforte." Her low voice softened. "The easier part was for my brother. My part acts as the counterpoint. Would you like to try?"

"I would be honored to take instruction." He bowed, sat back on the bench, and patted the seat beside him. "But please be kind to your humble pupil, Madam Music Master."

An answering smile lit her face as she opened her portfolio. She pulled out some tattered papers before sitting a respectable distance from him on the bench. He took the music, scanned it quickly, and laid it out where they both could see.

Miss Fleetwood removed her eyeglasses, pushed back a wisp of dark brown hair, and ran bare fingers lightly over the keys. "Are you ready? My part joins in after the first few measures."

Wolfgang began to tentatively tap out the notes. The piece was easy, and his confidence rapidly increased. Soon she joined in, the notes prancing, circling, interlacing playfully. They both reached to turn the page, his hand met hers, skin to skin. A thrumming—a contralto's lowest note—reverberated through him. Their gazes crossed and locked. Suddenly he wanted to touch much more than her fingers. As if he'd spoken the thought aloud, she looked away, stumbling over the next measure. She seemed to draw herself in, her slender form compact and contained, and continued the piece. He inhaled slowly, breathing in her scent, and found his place in the music, barely missing a note.

As they finished the arrangement, she turned to him with what might have been a smile had her mouth not been so tight. "I believe you could be quite good if you applied yourself."

The corner of his lips twitched as he restrained an answering smile. "I'm always good when I apply myself, Miss Fleetwood." The threatening grin broke through. "But speaking of good, you should see me ride. Do you ride?"

"Ride? What do you . . ." She hesitated slightly. "I ride, but not well."

"Good. I've played your student, now you'll play mine." Wolfgang stretched contentedly. "In all modesty, my girl, my skills on a horse exceed yours on the keyboard. This afternoon?"

Her husky tone moved a shade higher. "I am not your girl, and the gentlemen were to engage in a billiards tournament."

"Billiards is not my game, my lady." He scanned her briefly. "In the name of equality you must permit this lesson. How else will my masculine pride survive?"

She met his eyes squarely. "I am also not your lady, as you well know, but I accept the lesson. For equality."

ZEL LAID HER SPECTACLES on the tiny corner table, in the relentlessly feminine pastel-and-lace bedchamber. She squinted at her reflection in the cheval glass. Her heavy hair was twisting out of the chignon, before the ride even began. The dark green riding habit had belonged to her Aunt Diana, and made over it felt like a second skin. She frowned, almost relieved the rest of her new wardrobe was not yet ready.

Striding down the stairs, she tugged at the jacket, trying to pull it free from its close hold on her breasts. The house was quiet, with the female guests in the drawing room gossiping as they attended to their stitchery and the men in the far wing telling tales as they competed at billiards.

Northcliffe would be lounging in the music room, as arranged. Zel hoped she would not shame herself with her lack of horsemanship. Good riding horses rarely lasted more than a few weeks around the Fleetwood house before they were lost in the next bout of gambling.

As he stood to greet her, Zel couldn't ignore his lengthy perusal of her person, but glaring at him when the inspection paused overlong at her bodice didn't stop the heated flush from rising in her cheeks.

"I prefer this ensemble over any I've seen you in yet." The corner of his mouth quivered dangerously.

"You are guilty of the most counterfeit flattery." Her tone aimed at severity and missed completely. "I am certain you know this is horribly out of date."

"My dear, what does fashion matter when the fit is superb." The twitch in his lips spilled over into a boyishly crooked grin. "And the color compliments your eyes."

Zel tossed him a warning look. He smiled wider, tucking her hand in his elbow, guiding her out the door and down the hall.

The mare selected for her was a small even-tempered gray. Northcliffe lifted her effortlessly into the sidesaddle. When he turned to mount a chestnut stallion, she ran her palms down her sides to rid herself of the lingering feel of his hands.

As they rode slowly away from the stables it became obvious Northcliffe held back his enormous steed.

"If I am too slow for you, please ride ahead at your own pace." Zel surveyed horse and rider who moved as one.

"It won't damage Ari to practice restraint. Besides, if I galloped off, your mare would likely attempt to follow."

"Ari?" She gripped the reins tighter. "Is he your horse?"

"Yes, Aristophanes would never forgive a country outing without him." He ran tapering fingers through the thick mane.

"Aristophanes? Are you an admirer of Greek drama?"

"My guilty secret." He studied her face, as if expecting a reaction.

"I too enjoy Greek drama and philosophy."

"Ah, mademoiselle is a bluestocking?" His smile spred deep enough to summon up the lone dimple.

"I've been called that." She felt herself bristle. "I find it a title of honor."

"I meant no offense. Women have few ways to use their minds." Northcliffe gave her an accusing look. "I've offered my equestrian expertise to one who needs it little. More experience will increase your confidence. And your seat is excellent."

He might be a master horseman, but he could use educating on the uses of a woman's mind. Yet the day, replete with birdsong and wildflowers, was too lovely for dissension. She held her tongue, watching his hands lightly enfold the reins. Long, slim, graceful hands contrasting with his hard masculine body.

After a long canter past meadows and furrowed fields, they reached a narrow stream and dismounted, allowing the horses to drink. Zel pulled off a glove, stooping to dip her hand in the rocky brook. The cool water ran through her fingers, the force of its flow pressing against her palm. Cupping her hand, she lifted the liquid to her lips, swallowing what didn't run down her chin and throat. She rose and met his eyes, challenging his pointed stare as she wiped her sleeve across her mouth.

"I remembered where I've heard the name Grizelda." Northcliffe lounged against a tree, a mischievous grin playing about his mobile mouth. "Chaucer's *Canterbury Tales*. Griselda, the virtuous wife. She who endures all manner of testing by her husband but remains loyal, ever willing to submit to the domination of her lord and master."

Zel grimaced, settling on a large, flat boulder. "That horrid little story." She bit her lip. "Unfortunately, society would not only permit but applaud the husband's actions."

"Forgive me, I've dug too deep and uncovered a reformer."

She felt her color rise at the smile in his voice. "I am indeed proud to be a women's reformer, sir."

"Your cause isn't well supported by those in power."

She snorted. "But as an earl, you are part of that group."

"Touché. I'm a member of Parliament." Northcliffe strode the short distance between them and laid a hand on her arm. "But my time and energy are consumed with tenants' rights."

She leaned sideways, away from his hand, and pulled on her glove, but she couldn't stop herself from looking at him in surprise. "You are a tenant advocate? Astonishing for a landowning peer."

"I've been a peer long enough to know my tenants are my responsibility. If they can't feed their children, the blame is mine, by my mismanagement or greed."

"I am pleased to hear such views coming from one in the House of Lords." Zel watched, mesmerized, as the bright sun reflected off the lines and planes of his face.

"I'm not totally alone, Grizelda." He smiled. "What does your family call you? Surely a woman so lovely must go by a prettier name than Grizelda."

"Zel." She returned his smile, the compliment somehow offsetting his familiarity. "Sometimes Zelda or Zelly."

"Zel." Holding her gaze, he climbed onto the boulder, scooting closer until his body connected warmly with her own.

She twisted away abruptly, shoving him hard with her shoulder. Unbalanced, he toppled off the rock, hitting the ground with a thud and a groan.

"Oh, Lord! Did I hurt you?" Zel slid off the rock, kneeling at his prone form, stroking his forehead and closed eyelids with her fingertips. "Are you injured?"

Strong fingers grasped hers. His lids popped open. "You pack quite a force in that slim frame." Northcliffe pulled her hand to his chest. "Was I such a bad boy you had to beat me?"

"Do not be silly. I never meant to hurt you." She frowned at her fingers splayed over his chest. "Should I go for help?"

He sat up, wincing, keeping her hand at his chest. "There's nothing wrong with me your sweet touch wouldn't cure."

Zel yanked her hand free, jumping to her feet, trying to hide the quaver in her voice. "If there is nothing wrong with you, then we may return and dress for dinner."

Northcliffe maintained a light banter as they remounted and rode back to the house. He stopped in a clump of trees just short of the stables, sliding smoothly off Ari's back. His hands clasped her waist, lifting her from her mount. "Thank you for the splendid afternoon." He lowered her gently to the ground, then eyes focusing on her mouth, he pulled off his glove. Raising a finger, he softly traced the curve of her lower lip.

Zel jumped back, stung, her lip tingling from the caress, pushing against him with the hand still braced against his shoulder. He flinched and stepped back, releasing her abruptly. Her hand dropped. It felt warm, sticky. She gasped, watching a stain widen on his jacket.

"My God! You are bleeding."

She thrust aside his neckcloth and jacket. Ignoring his protests, she quickly unfastened the top of his shirt to examine the wound. "My God! Did I do this?"

"Of course not. It happened several days ago."

"This needs to be thoroughly cleaned and bandaged." She lectured him to assuage her guilt. Despite his disclaimer she was sure the fall off the boulder had caused the bleeding. "You should be in bed. Not out riding."

"With all your other talents I can't believe you're a nurse too!" She rewarded his attempt at humor with a stern glare.

"I will accompany you to your room and let you observe my nursing skills firsthand." Zel signaled a groom to handle the horses and hooked Northcliffe's arm, leading him to the house.

"I'd normally not deny you entrance to my chambers, but I don't need a nurse." His smile was obviously forced. "If you insist on mending my hurts, it would be better done downstairs."

Zel blushed at her lack of propriety and ordered the footman at the front door to usher them into an empty salon and send for hot water and bandages.

Pulling Northcliffe into the indicated gray-and-white room, Zel yanked off her stained gloves and helped him slip out of his jacket and waistcoat. She pushed him down on the sofa and removed his neckcloth, then unfastened the remaining buttons on his shirt so she could poke at the wound.

"Bloody devil's spawn!" He growled, shoving her hands away.

"This looks like a knife cut, and it should have been stitched. Why didn't you seek a physician?" She stopped. Lord, she was reprimanding him like a despotic schoolmistress.

"I saw a doctor, but I told him it didn't need stitching." He sucked in a breath when she prodded the wound again. "It's a flea bite. I've had worse." As he tried to sit she leaned over him, a hand on his uninjured shoulder, the other on the opposite arm. His lips curled as he settled into the cushions.

Zel released him and took a step backward. "You will stay put and allow me to clean the wound. Lady Selby's physician was at the musicale last night and may still be here."

A maid entered with water and cloths. Zel took a cloth and ordered her to fetch the doctor.

"This may hurt a little." She wet the cloth and began scrubbing blood off the wound.

He stiffened, hissing. "By Lucifer's scaly skin, woman, have a little care. You're taking off hide with the blood."

She pinched back a smile at his colorful language, but gentled the strokes. "Now, my lord, may I hear how a respectable gentleman came to have a knife wound at his throat?"

"Miss Fleetwood, you're sadly mistaken in thinking me a respectable gentleman. But if you must know about my little adventure, I was set on by footpads several nights ago outside my club." His look oozed studied masculine insouciance. "And I'm not bragging to say they came out of the affair in much worse condition than I."

Zel scowled at him as she rinsed the cloth. "Violence is nothing of which to be proud."

"Ah." Northcliffe raised his thick black brows. "Have I hit on another cause?"

"Do not take the focus off yourself." She squeezed the water from the cloth. "You undoubtably were not taking precautions to avoid the incident." This was none of her business, but she continued to act like a guilty, meddling fool.

"This little speech sounds well used." He winced when she again rubbed too hard. "Your brother?"

Warmth touched her cheeks. "Excuse me, please. I had no right to say what I did. I am certainly not your mother."

"Ahem." She whirled about as Dr. Lyndon shuffled in.

He slowly approached the sofa then quickly took stock of the situation, eyes bright under thick eyeglasses and grizzled brows.

"This wound is several days old and should have been stitched, my lord." The doctor turned to Zel, handing her a leather case. "We need to get him to his room. Could you bring this while I help him up the stairs?"

"I'll manage on my own." Wolfgang rose to his feet.

"I'm sure you can, young man, but you will take my arm all the same." Dr. Lyndon did not wait for an argument but grabbed Northcliffe's good arm and moved out of the room.

When they settled Northcliffe on the massive dark wood four-poster in the incongruously lavender room, Dr. Lyndon turned to Zel. "Miss Fleetwood, you seem to have a level head and a strong stomach. Can you assist?"

"She'd be happy to." Northcliffe's smoky eyes met hers. "She can hold my hand, if nothing else."

Zel did hold his hand and his shoulder when he stubbornly refused laudanum for the stitching, claiming he had no head for the stuff and Lady Selby would never forgive him if he slept through dinner.

As her usefulness ended, Zel felt uncomfortably aware she was in a man's bedchamber and the man's state of undress was decidedly advanced. She tried to reassure herself there could be nothing wrong with Dr. Lyndon beside her, but her eyes kept returning to Northcliffe's torso. Never had she seen so much bare skin on a man other than her father or brother, and neither of them looked much like Northcliffe. She found she had a peculiar fascination for the curly black hair powdering his firmly muscled chest. Following the dark line down over his flat stomach, she stopped suddenly at the waistband of his riding breeches. The room became too close. Too warm.

"Everything seems under control." She felt pleased that her voice sounded calm although she knew her color rose higher. "I need to leave to dress for dinner."

"I'll see you there." Northcliffe gave her his disarming grin. "Thank you, Nurse Fleetwood."

"You should rest." Zel inwardly chided herself for even glancing at the small male nipples hiding under the dusting of hair. After all, the man had just been stitched and bandaged.

"I'll be down for dinner." He caught her eyes, and she knew he was pleased to be the object of her wayward attentions. "You can lend me your shoulder and hold me up during dinner."

With one last scolding look she darted out the door, nearly colliding with Lady Selby's ample purple mass in the hallway.

"Zelda! That's Northcliffe's room. Why is Lyndon in there?" Lady Selby's eye for scandal was as sharp as a hawk's eye for a field mouse supper. "Why were you in there?"

Zel took the puffy old hand in hers, hoping to slow the woman down. "No need to worry, Northcliffe is fine. A wound reopened and needed to be stitched. I assisted the physician."

"You assisted Lyndon?" Her jowls and voice quavered. "Are you sure Northcliffe is not badly injured?"

"Several days ago he was set on by footpads and not properly attended to afterward. He swears he is well enough to come down for dinner."

"Oh dear, I am so pleased he is well. I would not want anyone taking ill at my home." She clasped Zel's arm and whispered conspiratorily. "Zelda, you shouldn't be in his room."

"I was assisting the doctor," Zel repeated firmly.

"Zelda, this isn't really the time—" Lady Selby hesitated, "but Northcliffe is not the type of man for you. Your aunt will never forgive me. . . . His reputation is dreadful. He is not accepted in the best circles." Her voice lowered further. "He could not be truly interested in you, not in a respectable way. He usually consorts with married women. If you don't watch out, you could end up broken-hearted and ruined." When Zel tried to break away she held on tighter. "It is said he has vowed not to marry. And when he inherited his title less than a year ago, there were stories about his family and how he got the title." Lady Selby looked about, whispering, "Mysterious deaths, sudden illnesses, carriage accidents."

"I know nothing of stories, nor do I put faith in gossip and rumor." She looked at the door she had just exited. "If he is such a scapegrace, why did you invite him?"

Lady Selby pulled Zel farther down the hallway. "His dear grandmother is my friend, and I would never snub her kin. He is also a close friend of the duke of Ridgemont."

Zel jerked her arm free and faced the woman. "And you wish to curry favor with the illustrious duke."

"My dear, you know I have granddaughters entering the marriage mart, and any connection with His Grace—"

"You tolerate Northcliffe to cultivate Ridgemont."

"My dear, you are such an innocent for one of your years. Northcliffe is exciting but dangerous. You must avoid him. He is not suitable company for naive, unmarried females."

"As a mature woman of six and twenty, I know my own mind. If I choose to be a friend to Northcliffe, I do so on my own assessment of his character." Zel lifted her chin. "And if I choose to have a mild flirtation with the man, it will not go beyond what I can control."

"WHAT'TH THE MAN DOING?" Melbourne's whining drawl moved higher in query. "Dangling after Mith Fleetwood, and what'th thith about a knife wound?" He crossed his orange satin-covered legs, settling in the plush chair.

Wilmington John Wilborn Hawthorne, earl of Newton, allowed a slight smile to touch his lips. "Lady Selby claims he was attacked by footpads several days back. As for Miss Fleetwood, I would never have given her a second glance."

He bent his thin form before the library window, but he barely saw the terraced garden below. "Northcliffe has singled her out, and as his taste rarely errs, I believe a second glance may be warranted."

"Newton, you are becoming positively shortsighted. The woman is a dowd, and as tall as a man." Isadora's normally smooth tones carried an unaccustomed edge. "Wolfgang must be bored to be playing with her. This country life's too tame for his blood." She ran her tiny fingers along a row of books, the movement too rapid to be seeking reading material.

"If he'th bored, why ithn't he theeking your company, Lady Horeton?" Melbourne twittered.

"He will be." She pulled at the top of her gown revealing more of her full white bosom. "We'll be back on old terms."

"Such a dreamer." Newton stared at her and barked out a hard-edged laugh. "Perhaps our Miss Fleetwood is a libertine. She is known to be outspoken on the rights of women, and some of that mind do not have conventional views on morality."

"A libertine?" Melbourne's vacant smile matched his drawl. "I don't think tho."

"We will attempt to solve this puzzle or scatter its pieces." Newton ran his nails down the pane of glass. "A sure remedy for the ennui of a country retreat."

"I'll distract Northcliffe." Isadora grimaced, watching his hand at the window. "And allow you to pursue Miss Fleetwood."

Newton smiled, tracing the line of his mustache. "I was certain you would volunteer your services." He glanced toward the open door of the library. "Here is your victim now."

Isadora dashed to the door just as Northcliffe entered and grasped his arm, her voice dripping honey. "Wolf, dear, you are avoiding me. Dinner has been delayed to accommodate your little injury. We'll take a turn about the garden. You can tell me all about it."

AFTER CONSUMING his postdinner port, Wolfgang led the other men to the drawing room. He could hear Isadora's irritatingly high voice ring out before he entered the room.

"I shall scream, if I have to hear one time more about what a Trojan Miss Fleetwood was. It is not at all ladylike to be around blood without fainting." Isadora turned to the door, her smile sweet and welcoming. "Ah, gentlemen, we were just praising Miss Fleetwood for her bravery."

Wolfgang edged toward Zel but was hindered by Isadora's hand on his sleeve. She pouted. "Come sit with me."

Determined not to make a scene, at least not immediately, he reluctantly sat beside her. But he looked to Zel, frowning when Melbourne and Newton flanked her as they had at dinner. Their interest must be piqued by his own. They had not observed her closely enough to see her true value. True value? He nearly snorted out loud. What by the rosy fires of hell did he mean by that? Whatever her value, it was greater than that of this waspish piece of flotsam sharing the sofa with him.

What had he seen in Isadora? He scanned the woman beside him. Her figure held no appeal. The overabundant curves seemed vulgar next to Zel's slender suppleness. He watched Zel juggle the attentions of Newton and Melbourne. Satan's small clothes! Zel Fleetwood's value, with all that passion buried in her long, sleek body, would be discovered soon enough, when she shared that body with him. Wolfgang smiled at the immediate response of his own body. He was ready, but how would she respond? Would it be with abandonment? Or would she shyly smile at him, a soft blush suffusing her skin from head to toe?

Isadora tapped his arm, effectively terminating his little

fantasy. Their affair ended months ago but she was unwilling to release him, even following him to this house party. Her pride couldn't allow her to face his continuing rejection much longer.

He moved his legs farther from Isadora, catching Zel's eyes just as Melbourne commandeered her as his partner at whist. Her lips curved in a silent plea for rescue. He would be happy to come to her aid, freeing himself and her of unwanted companions, but not yet. A little more of Melbourne's company, and she would be begging for relief.

Wolfgang followed the progress of the whist game as he pretended to listen to Isadora's conversation. He watched Newton hovering over the card game, a patient scavenger. Chuckling, he glanced around at Melbourne, Isadora, and Newton. A mismatched trio of bloody jackals, waiting to pounce. But who was their intended victim? Zel? Or, having noticed his interest in her, could they be using it to get to him? If so, he had difficulty being frightened.

But maybe he should be frightened. Maybe they were involved in the attack on him several days before. The attack he claimed was a simple footpad strike, although he felt nearly certain it was more, certain enough to hire an investigator. He looked again at the trio. Newton and Isadora might be capable of anything. But Melbourne? A most unlikely villain.

Excusing himself from Isadora's company without prelude, Wolfgang approached the card table. Zel threw herself into the game, winning most hands despite Melbourne's poor showing. He stood beside Melbourne, addressing the table at large. "I believe Miss Fleetwood is deserving of a partner such as I might provide."

Melbourne surprised him with a blush. "Thaying I'm not an adequate player?"

"I'll wager five hundred quid that with me as partner we'll take every hand."

"You're on." Melbourne, predictably, was intrigued enough to dispense with a little of his pride.

Wolfgang played a bolder, faster game, and Zel seemed to unconsciously follow suit. Her color rose in tandem with the stakes, and the gold in her eyes shimmered. They couldn't lose.

Winning hand followed winning hand until she suddenly froze, face pale, eyes lowered. Zel dropped the cards and stood, almost toppling her chair, dashing from the room without a word.

Promising to settle later, Wolfgang bolted after her. She was still in the hallway when he caught her arm, compelling her to a tiny salon.

He pulled her onto a divan in the dimly lit room. Her eyes were bright with unshed tears. Taking her fine-boned hand in his, he curled his free arm lightly over her shoulders.

"What is it?" His grip tightened around her trembling fingers. "What's wrong?"

"I am sorry." Her husky voice broke. "I . . . I am acting foolishly."

"Something has obviously overset you. Something about the card game?" He searched her face for an answer.

"It's the damned gambling. . . . I never should have done it. . . . My family has been decimated by it." She went on hoarsely. "We even had a special entail granted so the main estate cannot be gambled away. . . . But I was gambling, I was loving it. . . . God, it frightens me. I will not be like my father or brother." The tears finally streamed out. "My brother is on his way to debtor's prison . . . if I do not find a wealthy, old husband."

Wolfgang's other arm circled her, pulling her close. She clung to him, sobbing. He patted her hair, attempting to comfort her. Zel pushed in closer, her arms moving up over his shoulders and neck, her soft, full breasts sinking into his chest. He forgot his restrained efforts to soothe, and the embrace turned instantly sensual. Stroking her back, he molded her to him. He pushed aside her hair, seeking her face, her lips.

Her hand accidently rubbed against his bandaged wound. Wolfgang flinched at the stab of pain. He felt her stiffen and wrenched himself away, surprised by the degree of his arousal. His timing was deplorable. Not very sporting to seduce a woman in tears. And not very safe to seduce a fortune hunter, even if she did voice a preference for wealthy, *old* men.

"I'm sorry." He took her hand again. She was shaken but recovering quickly. He spoke casually, "I don't see you as being done up by gambling. Take a moment to contain yourself, then we'll return to the drawing room."

THE WOLF STALKED in ever narrowing concentric circles. His glossy coat illuminated by the moon. His brilliant silver eyes locked onto hers. Paws reached for her, only they were not paws but hands, long, elegantly tapered hands, gentle and strong, stroking and teasing.

Zel woke, shivering, to rays of moonlight pouring through the window, filling the room with a pale silver glow. It wasn't until dawn changed that glow to a soft gold that she finally found sleep again.

CHAPTER 3

CAPRICCIO

A lively composition in free form

ZEL EASED into the Selbys' cavernous mahogany-paneled library, hoping for a little time to herself before she faced Northcliffe. He must think her mad, furiously gambling one minute, then weeping in his arms the next. Throwing herself at him like a complete wanton. Mad or wanton, she grimaced, so much for her little flirtation. But she had known from the first she was out of her depth. What could she hope for but disaster with a man who ran in Robin's circles?

She heard a low mumble and turned toward the fireplace. Northcliffe's long, lean form was draped across an overstuffed chair, his dark head bent over a letter, reading in a very slow, deep tone. Zel cleared her throat and his head jerked up.

He crumpled the vellum in his fist, a flush creeping over the sculpted lines of his face. "Miss Fleetwood. I didn't hear you come in."

"Lord Northcliffe, forgive my trespass. I will leave . . ." She couldn't pull her gaze from his high-boned, reddened cheeks.

"Stay. There's nothing I desire more than your company,

except to have you call me by my given name, Wolfgang. As I will call you Zel." His eyes gleamed the bright silver of her dream. His jacket and waistcoat lay open, the kerseymere of his trousers stretched taut over muscular thighs.

Zel swallowed hard, averting her eyes, but she knew he was aware of where her glance had fallen. She must learn to exercise more control over her wandering eyes. "I, ah, came for a book."

"As good a reason as any to visit a library." His grin had a feral curl to it, and a glow came from behind his eyes. This was no tame house pet, but a wolf as far removed in the animal kingdom from her well-trained dog as an Indian tiger was from a domesticated cat. It took all her meager will-power to stand in place when every nerve in her body screamed to turn and run from his potent presence. Only the lingering touch of pink clinging to his cheeks, that hint of vulnerability, kept her there.

She found her voice. "Please return to your letter."

A scowl skimmed over his features. "You know, I hired a runner to find the footpads, but he's turned up nothing."

"The footpads?" Zel paused, then caught his chain of thought. "The attack was more than a simple robbery?"

His face hardened, his tone turned harsh. "Why would you say that?"

Surprised by the vehemence of his response, she stumbled over her words. "No reason, I meant . . . I am sorry. I only thought you would not bother with a runner for a simple robbery."

"You think I wouldn't seek justice after being stabbed?" Northcliffe stood and stared at the carved fireplace.

"Is there any hope of finding a few footpads among all the criminals in London?" Zel tucked a strand of hair into the knot at her neck. "You were hurt, but your own neglect made it worse. Did they take something of great value?"

"No, they took nothing. My men and I drove them off." He turned, stalking slowly toward her.

"Did you describe them to the runner?" She held her ground.

"They wore masks and hooded cloaks."

"Then how do you ever expect to find them?" Looking up at him, she paused before plunging in. "You must have some clues to warrant hiring a runner."

Tempered steel eyes met hers. "Must I?"

"You are being evasive. There is more to this than you admit." Certain he was not telling her the whole story, Zel felt equally uncertain as to whether she should seek more answers.

Northcliffe gripped her arm, the lines of his mouth tight. "This is not your concern."

She glared back at him. "You brought it up."

His frown softened to a crooked smile as his hand loosened on her arm. "Forgive me. Perhaps my years of military service have made me look for enemies under every bush and hedgerow."

"You were in the military?" Zel tried to stifle the astonishment in her voice.

"That surprises you?" A grimace pinched his face. "I served as a captain under Wellington until an injury sent me home. I decided to sell out after I healed."

"You must have stories to tell."

"None worth the telling." Northcliffe sat on a small sofa, patting the space beside him. "Come sit with me."

Zel moved away, striding purposefully toward a book-lined wall. "I planned to read before the picnic." Browsing through the volumes, she selected a book at random. Taking a seat across the room from Northcliffe, she opened the book. Sensing his movement, she looked unseeing at the words until he sat on the arm of the chair, taking the volume from her hands. He smelled of the outdoors, of horses, saddle leather and green things.

Northcliffe flipped back to the title page, then stared down at her. "Do you have any idea what you're reading?"

"Of course I do." She lifted her chin. "It is a collection of poetry."

He chuckled. "It is poetry. By the famous, or should I say infamous, Lord Rochester. A friend, I might add, of the first earl of Northcliffe." He scanned slowly through the pages. "My ancestor was titled by Charles II for service to the crown against the Roundheads." Smiling broadly, he pointed to a passage. "Read this. Aloud."

Taking the leather volume, she found the requested lines.

" 'O that I now cou'd, by some chymic art.' " Zel gulped as her eyes caught the next words before her mouth could utter them. Did he know what he asked her to read? Looking through her lashes at the smug smile curling his lips, she knew he did. She lifted her chin higher.

" 'To sperm convert my vitals and my heart.' " She coughed, raised her voice and continued.

" 'That at one thrust I might my soul translate,/ And in the womb myself regenerate.' " Her face must be glowing scarlet, but Zel would not stop and give him the satisfaction of knowing the level of her chagrin.

" 'There stee'p in lust, nine months I would remain;/ Then boldly dash my passage out again.' "

"Dash? Where does it say dash?" Northcliffe leaned over, running a finger methodically along the page.

"Right here." She traced the tiny line.

"Do you know the word that belongs at that dash?" Laughter danced in the eyes that held hers.

Zel fought to appear sophisticated but knew the battle was falling to her embarrassment. She bravely looked up into his eyes. "I am not sure."

"You don't know." His grin showed miles of white teeth. "If you think about it, I'm sure you can guess its meaning." He closed the book. "Thanks for the recitation. But I believe Rochester is a little fast for you."

"I choose my own reading material." Zel reached for the book.

Wolfgang slid off the arm of the chair, standing at his considerable height, Rochester's poetry held high over his head. "How badly do you want it?"

Zel lurched out of the chair and jumped for the book, landing flush against his chest. His arm slipped around her, steadying her, holding her for one impossibly long moment.

"Oh, Lord!" She shoved him away, heart thudding in her throat, and flew from the room. His laughter followed her into the hall. Rushing up the stairs, to her little room, she slammed the door, bracing it with her back.

Whatever possessed her to leap at him like some crazed bedlamite—after stubbornly reading that lascivious poem? He had the strangest, most disconcerting effect on her. If she could not get a better hold on herself, she would have to abandon this absurd flirtation. But exchanging witty repartee without wishing to feel his lips pressed to hers and his arms about her should be easy.

Zel sighed noisily. The sensible thing would be to let it go now, stay away from him and look for suitable husband material. Robin needed her. A tiny smile crept over her lips. There were a few more days before she returned to London and to the usually sensible, calm Zel Fleetwood.

ZEL WATCHED from the shade of a topiary castle spire as the carriages lined up in the long drive tracing the front of Selby Hall. The guests were beginning to pair and saunter toward the phaetons and landaus. She spotted Northcliffe climbing down the entry steps just as she felt a hand at her elbow.

"Miss Fleetwood. I would be pleased to have you accompany me to the picnic site in my curricle." Lord Newton's thin-lipped half smile had the unerring ability to send a small unpleasant flutter down her spine. "My new cattle are a lively pair, I promise you an enjoyable ride."

"I would be honored, my lord." She forced herself to return his smile, allowing him to usher her to a brown-and-gold carriage. Much as she disliked Newton, she did not feel very brave, and it would be less dangerous spending the day with him. There was absolutely no possibility she would be tempted to throw herself into *his* arms. She caught sight of Lady Horeton attaching herself to Northcliffe and purposefully directed her attention back to Newton.

Newton handed her into the curricle, speaking softly in his bass voice with just the hint of a nasal twang. "They do make a striking couple. He so large and dark and she so petite and fair. Were you aware that most men favor only one type of woman?" He smoothed his mustache, seemingly oblivious to Zel's lack of response. "I prefer variety, but Northcliffe is clearly partial to petite, blond voluptuaries like his wife."

"Wife?" The word broke through her lips before Zel could stop it.

"Yes," Newton's tone lowered. "His lovely, faithless, dead wife."

Zel sat, quiet, stiff. Dead wife! Curiosity and propriety warred in her. Propriety, augmented by apprehension, won, and she did not ask the questions burning in her throat. She did watch Northcliffe toss Lady Horeton onto the seat of a shiny black-and-silver high-perch phaeton and take the ribbons to the perfectly matched grays. She unclenched her fists, staring straight ahead. How like him to have such a flashy and bold conveyence.

WOLFGANG BARELY SUPPRESSED a groan as he settled on the seat beside Isadora, Lady Horeton, her childishly small hand at his arm. He would tolerate her company for the ride to the picnic, as Zel sat ready to depart in Newton's carriage. Once there he would quickly abandon this plaguesome piece of female flesh.

"Your little pet seems to have deserted you for Newton." Isadora studied his face, clearly waiting for a reaction.

"My little pet? I'd hardly call Miss Fleetwood little, a pet, or mine." Wolfgang shifted his weight on the plush silver squabs, disengaging her hand. "I find it fascinating you watch her with such interest, Isadora."

"I have no interest in her," she replied too quickly. "I only wonder about your interest. She's not your type."

"You have no claims on me. Our liaison, such as it was, ended months ago." He slid over the last few inches to put as much distance between them as the narrow seat allowed.

She started to reach for his arm again, then seemed to think better of it. "You know, your little innocent may not be as innocent as she appears."

"Oh? And what makes you believe I give a damn if she is an innocent or not?" He gripped the ribbons and pulled the phaeton out to join the line of carriages wheeling down the drive, alarmed by the mixed feelings Isadora's words stirred in him.

"She may have an innocent air but I'd wager she's as experienced as any streetwalker. And you were never one to seek the company of whores."

"You're sadly mistaken. I fear I'm well known to associate with whores." Wolfgang's voice came out little more than a growl as he directed his attention to keeping his spirited horses within the confines of the plodding caravan.

"Why do you treat me so badly?" He could hear the phony tears in her voice and twisted to see her bat damp eyelashes at him. "I only want to be your friend."

"We both know bloody well what you want from me."

"Whatever do you mean?" She dabbed at her eyes with her lacy handkerchief, the picture of injured innocence.

His eyes veered back to the road. "We have been over this ground before."

"Yes, you are willing to use my body but not offer your name or protection."

"Blessed flames of hell! You entered into our agreement with eyes open and hands out. I made it clear what I offered and what I demanded in return. You were only too eager to comply." He stared at the tears glistening in her reptilian eyes before turning his attention back to the pair of grays. "You seem to have forgotten your husband is still alive."

"Not for long. He's old and sickly." Her voice softened to a breathy whisper. "I never expected to fall in love with you."

"Beelzebub's bootblack!" Wolfgang laughed harshly. "Do you think I'm a babe in the nursery? You love only yourself." He glared at her. She wasn't worth losing his temper.

"Wolf?" Isadora inhaled till her breasts nearly popped the seams of her dress. "Do you forget how our bodies fit together?"

"You bore me, *Lady* Horeton. You no longer have permission to use my Christian name. This conversation is over." She pouted but to his relief made no further attempt to engage him in conversation. But he knew she hadn't given up yet.

The mismatched bevy of conveyences clambered along beside the stream that cut gently into the curving hillside. They soon reached a grassy, tree-laden spot halfway to the summit.

As vehicles emptied, the revelers scattered, exclaiming over abundant rhododendrons and fragrant wild lilacs. Wolfgang watched, amused, as Zel made an escape.

Following silently, he slipped behind her and laid a hand lightly on her shoulder. As Zel whirled about, his hand played along her back, coming to rest on the opposite shoulder, and Wolfgang slid his other hand around her slender waist. "Bored of Newton so soon? I would never bore you."

"I prefer to be alone." She removed both hands, placing them back at his sides.

His lips twitched as he watched her walk rigidly toward

a meadow sprinkled with buttercups and daisies. He would enjoy taking some of the stiffness out of that straight spine.

He caught up to her, matching his stride to hers. "You never wear a corset."

"And you, sir, are forever saying the most improper things." Zel's voice rang out a little higher than its usual throaty tone.

"I haven't felt one when I've touched you." He scanned her as they walked, sure he'd raised a blush, if only he could see her elfish face beneath the faded chip-straw bonnet. "And there's no telltale line beneath your gowns, loose as they are."

"What I wear beneath my gowns is no concern of yours." Her stride lengthened as they emerged from the trees.

Wolfgang chuckled with devilish delight as he admired the sway of her hips. "Oh, but it is. Sometimes I think of nothing else for hours on end." He moved close by her side. "I'd place odds you possess strong opinions on the merits, or should I say demerits, of corsets."

Zel attempted a stern look, then grumbled. "Point to Lord Northcliffe. The corset was designed to restrict a woman and make her appearance more desirable to men."

"But today's fashions allow a freer look. I'd wager as many men as women wear the things. And don't they afford a barrier to a man's touch?" Wolfgang stood close enough now that he could distinguish her spicy scent from the floral perfume surrounding them.

"Not to anywhere he truly wants to touch."

"And you call me improper!" His mirthful crow stopped her short. He grasped her arm to keep from crashing into her.

"You started this conversation. I am only making polite response." He could imagine the little hairs along the nape of her long neck bristling like the quills of a hedgehog.

"I would have a little impolite response then." With one hand Wolfgang tugged free the ribbons under her chin and hurled the ugly bonnet to the ground. With the other, he pulled off her spectacles and pocketed them. His eyes crept over her face, he could almost feel the smooth coolness of her skin. His mouth brushed hers, a soft question she answered with parted lips. Countering with his tongue, he tenderly outlined the opening of her full mouth, arms pressing her gracile form to his. His senses filled with her pungent spice, tart as gingerbread. Zel's arms circled his shoulders, fingers tangling in the hair drawn loosely at the back of his neck. He inhaled sharply, her warm breath flowed over his lips and tongue.

A branch crackled behind them. Releasing her, he spun about as Melbourne appeared from the grove of trees beyond the meadow. As he neared, Melbourne was obviously taking in Zel's flushed skin, Wolfgang's hand still at her waist, the chip-straw bonnet lying among the buttercups.

He cleared his throat, struggling to suppress a grin. "Luncheon'th ready, if you thtill have an appetite for it."

Zel bent to retrieve her bonnet, but Wolfgang grasped the hat and placed it on her head, fastening it beneath her chin.

"My eyeglasses, please." Her voice was a mere husky breath.

Wolfgang lodged the bridge of the glasses firmly at the top of her straight little nose as she reached to wind the temples through her hair and over each ear. She marched past Wolfgang, tucking a hand into Melbourne's elbow. The foppish man walked her back to the picnic speaking in a stage whisper Wolfgang knew he was meant to hear. "Thtay away from him. Man'th got the motht awful rep. Dangerouth. Not for a thweet thing like you."

Wolfgang scarcely registered Melbourne's remarks. He walked several paces behind Zel, focusing on her slender form, the regal set of her head, the narrow, straight back, the unconsciously graceful flow of her hips and legs.

In her venomous stupidity Isadora had stumbled onto

the secret to Zel's appeal, a heady mixture of passion and innocence. A mixture he should have recognized this morning when she brazenly read Rochester's poem, then ran away at the impromptu embrace. And yesterday when she, without hesitation, undressed him to examine his wound, yet earlier jumped when he touched her lip. Zel was not a libertine, nor was she a naive miss. And, on top of it all she bluntly admitted to being a fortune hunter. The lovely Zel Fleetwood was a hybrid to be cultivated and nurtured, sure to bear a rare fruit. His for the plucking.

Wolfgang slowed as they reached the trees, falling farther behind Zel and her determined escort. Didn't he deserve a hybrid, in a life populated by weeds? His wife had been a weed, deceptively lovely, yet nothing but a weed. If she had lived, she would have choked all the life and love of beauty out of him.

Gwen, his sister, had been a hybrid. Alive with contrasts he could never understand. She could be so passionate, gay, and fun loving and still so pious, wise, and restrained. How such extremes survived in one body, one soul, he could not fathom, especially in one so young. He had adored her and still felt the pangs of sorrow and guilt he had never been able to bury. If only it had been him that day, instead of her. If only . . .

He tossed his head violently, as if he could shake off the memories as easily as an animal emerging from a stream could shake off the water clinging to its coat.

WILMINGTON HAWTHORNE, Lord Newton, lifted his nose and stiffled a yawn, barely listening to the chatter of Melbourne and Isadora, as he surveyed the occupants of the gilded drawing room.

But Melbourne's next lisping words, even in an undertone, drew his full attention. ". . . and she was kithing him back. No little peck on the cheek either."

"Who was kissing whom?"

"Newton, you haven't heard a word. You ignore us cruelly." Isadora simpered from her perch on a spindly legged sofa.

"Don't try your wiles on me, I've known you too long." Newton emphasized his affected nasal tone. "Now kindly repeat your gossip."

"Mith Fleetwood kithed Northcliffe in the woodth. They were wrapped up tight and their mouth were open." Melbourne's fawning grin looked positively moronic. "He even played her lady'th maid, tying her bonnet and replathing her eyeglatheth afterward."

"We are due a little more fun." Newton spotted Miss Fleetwood sitting across the room with Lady Selby, her gaze straying frequently to her side where Northcliffe stood, restless as a pendulum, switching his balance from one foot to the other. "Which would be more amusing, to facilitate or interfere? Or throw in a complication and watch the results."

"But what complication?" Isadora's eyes followed Newton's. "He is acting like a fool over that slut."

"Tut, tut. Jealouthy ith not becoming." Melbourne twittered. "Hard to call one a thlut when one'th rigged out like an aging maiden aunt."

"Ah, Melbourne, you have unwittingly hit upon a plan." Newton stroked the silk wall covering as he continued to stare at the couple across the room. He scarcely saw Miss Fleetwood, so focused was he on Northcliffe. Northcliffe who took any woman he wished, on his terms, leaving others the remains. "The masquerade. Miss Fleetwood is deserving of a costume that clearly reveals her charms. My valet will call on Lady Selby's butler and help him find the *only* costume that will possibly fit her."

THE BORROWED MAID applied the finishing touches to the plumed headdress and the ringleted, powdered wig.

"Look in the glass, miss. You're a princess, straight out of a fairy tale."

Zel turned, afraid to face her reflection. She felt naked despite the yards of rich cloth. Picking up the skirts, she gingerly approached the glass. Lord! She was naked! Pulling at the chiffon-and-lace stomacher was futile, it barely covered her nipples, and the corset pushed her up so high she could almost lay her head down on a pillow of her own breasts.

"I cannot go out in public in this."

"Miss, there's nothin' wrong with showin' a bit of bosom."

"But not the whole thing. What a disaster. There must be another costume." Zel blinked back the threatening tears. "I picked out a shepherdess gown just yesterday." She had been excited as a child, anticipating this masquerade, and now . . .

"There isn't another, miss, I asked the butler. This is the only one left that'll come close to fittin' you, you bein' so very tall and slender and, ah, full on top. And there's no time before the ball to be takin' in or lettin' out seams and hems." The plump maid curtsied. "Now, miss, I have another lady to dress and the first dance only minutes away."

"Go ahead." She sighed, hands brushing over the sleek fabric. "Thank you."

Zel stood before the glass again, fearlessly taking stock of what she saw. The dress was beautiful. The tight, open bodice and overskirt were of a brilliant aqua watered silk. The ecru chiffon stomacher and underskirt were lightly laced and flounced, trimmed with gold ribbon and underlined with the aqua silk. More of the ribbon-trimmed lace circled her neck and the hem of her sleeves. She did look like a fairy-tale princess, down to the low-heeled brocade slippers on her feet. That neckline—Zel Fleetwood would never wear a gown cut so dangerously low. But Madame Pompadour would, without a single qualm.

Could she play the part? Could she masquerade as

Jeanne-Antoinette, marquise de Pompadour, just for to-night? Be the mistress to King Louis XV?

Zel lifted the aqua demimask to her face. She did not even recognize herself, how would anyone else? With the additional guests from throughout the countryside attending this event, she would be lost in the crowd. She could whirl among the masked and costumed throng, coy and flirtatious as she had never been.

Inhaling deeply, she straightened her shoulders and pulled at the bodice quickly, fearful her breasts would escape the confines of the stomacher, but the gown stayed in place. She bent in a deep curtsy and still the gown clung firmly to her skin. At least exposing herself completely was one less thing to fret over.

She fastened the mask securely, planning not to remove it, even for supper, and strutted out the door.

The orchestra readied to play the opening minuet as she hesitated at the threshold of the enormous Ionic-columned ballroom. Heavy, leafy garlands and huge sprays of spring blossoms assaulted her eyes and nose. She stood her ground as the footman announced, "Madame Pompadour."

More attention focused on her entry than she would have desired, but her courage did not falter as she skimmed down the staircase. When she reached the bottom a soldier and a pirate vied for the pleasure of her company for the dance.

"You are both so dashing, how can I choose? I must however admit a tendre for pirates." Did she say that? Smiling, she emphasized the low timbre of her voice. "You, Sir Buccaneer, may have the first dance, the major may attend me on the second."

As the tall pirate whisked her onto the floor, she found herself searching for another more familiar tall man. Would she recognize him in costume? Zel smiled at her partner. What did it matter? She was determined to have a wonderful time with or without *his* presence. Turning her attention on the pirate, she resolved to charm him completely.

Zel danced with the pirate, then the major, smiling flirtatiously, gay and confident, as if she were indeed the courtesan to a king. Although she had sipped only one glass of champagne, she felt intoxicated. Dizzy and giddy with the combination of music, lights, and ardent male attention.

As she twirled to a reel with a viking, she glimpsed a somber puritan, his long, broad-shouldered body propped against a column. His eyes were obscured by a black mask, but she knew they followed her, shimmering, luminous as molten silver.

When the dance ended, her partner escorted her back to her growing court. The puritan stood slightly apart from the others. A roundish man in a monk's robe stepped toward her.

"Sorry, Friar, the lady has already been claimed." The puritan stepped forward and held out his arm. "Madame?" When she moved too slowly, he grasped her arm, leading her out on the floor to the strains of the evening's first waltz.

His gloveless hand clasped hers, his other rested at her waist, as he launched into the elegant steps. She felt weightless, floating on a cloud of sound and movement, aware only of the pressure of his hands, the warmth of his body, and the scent of woods and horses.

Zel knew they danced dangerously close, but she did not care. She wanted to press her body against his and forget anyone was in the ballroom but the two of them. The music ended, and too soon she returned to her chair beside the eager monk.

The puritan raised her fingers to his lips, his breath warming the silk of her gloves. "The supper dance is mine."

Her next partners blurred in a colorful montage of costumes, flattery, and smiles. She played her part well, never forgetting she was Madame Pompadour, employing the wiles of a courtesan, playing the coquette, whispering, laughing, making clever conversation. Tonight was as distant from reality as a dream. Tomorrow she would be ordinary Zel Fleetwood again.

She should be thinking of her brother and the husband who would and could pay his debts. Zel loved Robin dearly but this time belonged to her, her fairy tale, her ball with the prince. But tomorrow there would be no happily-ever-after. Her charming, reckless prince was not the marrying kind. And even if he were, she wanted an older, milder husband, one she could control.

"Jeanne-Antoinette, my dance." Her puritan-prince's deep voice vibrated through her body as she placed her hand on his arm and allowed him to lead her to the floor.

Zel was grateful for the country dance, fearing her senses could not withstand the full-force assault of another waltz. When the dance ended, they joined the crowd promenading to the supper room. He ushered her to a corner table, then juggled plates loaded with lobster patties, roasted pheasant, stewed mushrooms, asparagus in butter sauce, and fruit tarts.

"A feast for the palate to accompany a feast for the eyes." He laid out the plates and pointedly scanned her from the top of her feathered headdress to the sharp tips of her slippers.

Flicking her fan coquettishly, Zel attempted to cover the blush she knew tinged her, from stomacher to wig. "Yes, it all looks delicious."

"But *you* are the most delectable. Your eyes are a storm at sea, your skin moonglow." He smiled crookedly. Tonight he would indeed play her prince.

"I am not one to be swayed by pretty words." She tapped him with her fan. "I demand proof of your devotion."

"The proof lies beneath this plain puritan dress." He paused, sweeping his hand down his long torso. "Where my heart beats for you."

Zel paused, confused, he could not be saying what it seemed he was saying. But Madame Pompadour would never be flustered, so she gamely proceeded with the charade. "Such insignificant proof you offer me."

"Madame, I assure you my proof is far from insignificant." His eyes and low inviting tone flashed a challenge. "Would that I could reveal it to you."

"One cannot show the trueness of the heart." She tried to avoid his intent gaze so at contrast with his playful words.

"The heart can only be guessed at, but other signs may be more readily observed." His eyes beneath his black mask never left her mouth. "Meet me later in the garden, and I'll offer you such proofs, that the most doubting would be convinced."

"Oh sir, such sweet temptation. Dare I accept?"

His eyes lifted to hers. "Dare you refuse?"

When supper ended, Zel returned to the ballroom, already knowing she feared joining him in the garden. After that interrupted embrace at the picnic she was no longer sure she was the party in control. What would have happened if Melbourne had not happened on them?

As the ball progressed, she found herself courted by gentlemen in all manner of dress. With those of the house party, she guessed their identity quickly, but they were obviously unsure of hers. When Lord Newton, outfitted as a devil, leered at her chest and claimed a dance, she almost refused, but convinced herself she was being unnecessarily rude.

Zel regretted doing the polite the instant she realized the set was a waltz. The unpleasantness of such close proximity to Newton contrasted with the memories of the earlier waltz. The music faded, and before she realized what he was doing, Newton pulled her through the leaded glass doors, out onto the terrace. She tried to break away but he only pulled her closer to his whipcord-slim frame, his grip unbreakable.

"Release me."

"My dear, I don't believe you wish to draw unnecessary attention." His low, breathy tone crept down her spine.

"What do you want?" She held herself completely still.

His harsh laugh held a note of cruelty. "Such an innocent."

The music had ended, others would be entering the terrace. She pushed at his chest. "Let me go."

"The lady made a request, Newton." Zel could have wept with relief. Her puritan-prince. Her rescuer.

Newton released her, a tight smile passing over his face. "And neither of us would ever deny a lady anything." He pivoted on one foot and was gone.

"Devil's begotten," Wolfgang spat, whirling to follow.

Zel grasped his arm. "Let him go. Nothing happened." She smiled into his tightly drawn face as he turned back to her.

The stiff lines around his mouth eased. "Walk with me a few moments, before we go indoors. I could use a little cool air."

She nodded, aware of the hardness of his arm beneath her hand, the warmth of his body brushing against her.

He stopped before a carved marble bench and pulled her down beside him. She did not resist when he took her gloved hand, studying its shape with his long, bare fingers. His hands, so slender and perfectly formed, were almost too beautiful to belong to a man, but were clearly masculine in size and strength. He turned her arm, running his fingers up the inner length to the top of her long glove. Zel shivered as his fingers traced their way down, pausing at intervals marked by tiny buttons. Each ivory ball was in turn eased free until the glove rippled from her arm. He swept the silk off, finger by finger, stroking the warm flesh beneath.

"Zel." Wolfgang's breath hummed across her palm, lips whispering up her arm. His hand crept over her shoulder, following the line of bare flesh from ruffled collar to sleeve. She moaned as he shifted to face her, hand flowing up her throat, coming to her mask. He pulled at the fastenings, sliding it to his lap. She smiled in tune with his compellingly crooked grin. Of their own volition, her hands brought his mask rustling down to join hers.

His hand returned to her face, cradling her chin, soft as a

lullaby. In the pale light from the moon she could feel more than see his eyes on her lips.

"I . . . should we . . ."

"Sssh." His finger pressed lightly against her mouth.

Zel closed her eyes, leaning back into the curve of his shoulder and arm. His lips played across hers, softer than the softest pianissimo, then slid over her cheek to her eyes. She sighed and he returned to claim her mouth, the gentleness spending itself rapidly as demand grew. She sat passively absorbing each new chord as he serenaded her lips, her teeth, and the smooth, sensitive tissue of her inner mouth.

The serenade became a spirited duet as her tongue twined with his. Wolfgang's hands swept over her body, awakening melodies hitherto unknown. Her hands matched his rhythm as she learned the hard lines of his muscular back. His lips pulled away from hers, leaving both starving for breath as he scaled down her throat and chest, tongue tracing the valley between her breasts. His fingers plucked gently at the silk and chiffon of her bodice, bringing the nipple beneath to taut awareness. Sensation sang through her body, invisible strings strummed by his touch.

Breaking away abruptly, he stood. He clutched her arms, drawing her up to face him, studying her intently. "Not here, not now. Later when the ball is over."

It was not a question, but she answered with a breath. "Later."

She walked, clutching his arm, back to the ballroom, the harmony between them still tight, almost palpable.

Zel danced through the night, helplessly caught up in the power of her own masquerade. Her dark puritan-prince, always nearby, took one more dance, a forbidden third dance, but she was beyond worrying about what anyone thought as she swirled around the floor in his arms. When the waltz ended he leaned over and whispered into her ear.

"Later."

As the ball drew to an end and the guests wandered off,

she waited for him to spirit her away for the last few promised kisses, but he did not approach her again, and now with the orchestra closing down he was nowhere in sight.

She tried to ignore the disappointment flooding over her, the night had been enchanted, she had no right to ask for more.

BY ALL THE DEMONS in hell, he hadn't wanted a woman like this in years. Maybe he'd never wanted a woman like this. He'd been close to taking her in the garden, barely able to pull himself away and suggest this rendezvous.

She was not a classic beauty—he'd had his fill of them anyway. But she was surprisingly lovely in that outlandish costume. And his desire for her went deeper than her outward appearance. . . . No, he wasn't in a mood for examining the whys and wherefores. He only wanted to continue the sensual magic they had already begun.

Wolfgang pulled the dressing gown over his bare chest and tied the belt. Slipping into the hall, he watched carefully for signs of other nocturnal wanderers.

Empty. He smiled in anticipation, rapidly covering the distance between their rooms.

Should he knock? He paused before her door. No, she was expecting him, and he didn't wish to risk discovery. He sucked in a breath and tried the handle. It opened easily. He exhaled unevenly and entered the room, closing the door behind him.

One candle burned at the table near the bed. Zel lay asleep, breathing softly, her hair flowing in a loose circle about her head, in stark relief against the white of the pillow. His hand shook as he untied his dressing gown, allowing it to slid off his skin to the floor. Should he wake her now with her name on his lips? No, he'd wake her *with* his lips, and hands. Pushing back the sheets and counterpane he crawled into her bed.

His weight on the mattress unbalanced her, rolling her against him, her body warm beneath the thin lawn of her night rail. She stirred slightly, then settled back into the bed, her arm, hip, and thigh pressed into his naked length.

Wolfgang ran one hand beneath her head, locking his fingers in the thick, silky mass of hair. His lips sought hers as his other hand found the ties at the front of her night rail. Zel stirred again and he deepened the kiss. Suddenly she came fully awake, thrashing about in his arms.

"Quiet, Zel," he whispered into her mouth. "It's me."

She pushed him roughly away, rearing up to her knees. The night rail tore in one hand, strands of hair ripped off in the other.

"Zel." He jumped to his knees, facing her across the narrow bed. Their eyes met and held, hers glazed. Was she still half-asleep, did she recognize him? His gaze fell to her rent nightgown, one perfect breast glowed pale in the candlelight. He reached out, reflexively, cupping smooth flesh and puckering tip.

She cried out, clenched her fist, and struck him hard in the stomach. As he doubled over, her other fist met his eye. He howled in pain and outraged surprise, leaping off the bed.

"You bastard." Her voice rasped, low, gravelly. "Get out."

"Zel?" His look searched, asked.

"Get out! Now!"

He yanked on his dressing gown and strode from the room.

CHAPTER 4

SOTTO VOCE

Softly, not to be overheard

DAMN THE WOMAN! Damn her straight to the fiery depths of hell! What kind of game did she play? Wolfgang rubbed his eye, wincing as he marched down the dark hallway. It hurt like the devil. He needed to put a cold cloth on it. Or a beefsteak from the kitchen. Maybe it wouldn't look so bad by morning.

How in the name of Old Clootie would he explain it? He could claim he fell and struck his head on a piece of furniture. His reputation would take a more severe blow if anyone discovered a supposedly willing bedmate had landed him a facer worthy of the champion boxer, Gentleman Jackson.

What was wrong with the woman? She behaved like a courtesan all evening, even inviting him to her bed, then became a horrified virgin when he accepted her offer. Zel had said yes with body and word, her door was unlocked, a candle lit . . .

Wolfgang probed again at his eye as he rounded the corner and bounded down the stairs to the kitchen. Time enough to analyze Zel Fleetwood tomorrow. Right now his eye was throbbing and his stomach was queasy from the combination of the champagne and her punch. He needed that beefsteak, then his own bed.

THE SLAM of the door still reverberated through Zel's shuddering body. Her breathing came in short, fierce gasps. She tried to inhale, deep and slow, but the quick gulps and shaking would not stop.

She massaged her bruised knuckles. What if he came back? Jumping off the bed, she ran to the door. Of course the latch still would not work. She moved a chair against the door—not the most effective barrier, but at least she would hear him coming if he returned.

Zel flopped onto the bed and dropped her head into her hands. The warnings were clear. She chose not to listen. The man had been in her bed, naked, and ready to take her. She rubbed her eyes vigorously but could not erase his shadowed image from her mind. The candle flickered before her. He was a rake of the worst order. Did he think her masquerade as Madame Pompadour real, or was he so accustomed to taking what he wanted that he never considered she would refuse? She pulled the torn nightgown tight around her neck.

A little flirtation! Lord, she was miles out of her league. Northcliffe made an assignation with her, but she had been too naive to recognize it. Now he had ruined everything. Her magic, fairy-tale night lay in shreds. Her fairy-tale prince was a frog at best, more likely an ogre.

Zel pulled the bedclothes up to her chin, tucking them around her shoulders. He was a villain. She twisted onto her side, curling her feet up in her night rail. But in all honesty, she had allowed him unimaginable liberties. He kissed her, touched her, as only a husband should, and she enjoyed it, encouraged it. He must have thought her completely brazen and behaved toward her exactly as she deserved.

Northcliffe would have no interest in her now. He probably thought she was an escapee from Bedlam, kissing him one minute, punching him the next. With the crowds diminished by so many still in Paris, it was inevitable that she would see him in London. But she must find a way to avoid him, as he would surely wish to avoid her. If or when they did meet, she would never let on how his embrace had shaken her.

WOLFGANG ROLLED onto his side, tangling the cover as he gently stroked his aching eye and massaged his tender stomach. Bloody horns of Satan! If he couldn't have her as a lover, maybe she'd agree to hire on as his sparring partner. His pugilistic skills would improve drastically, but would he survive?

He needed a good, hot soak. Lifting himself gingerly out of bed, he fumbled for the bell pull. Within seconds a timid knock was followed by a wrinkled face peering around the door.

"Fetch me a hot bath, and quickly," Wolfgang barked.

He surveyed the damage in the glass. Oh, she'd certainly done fine work last night. Luring him like a siren and dashing his head on the rocks. Leaving him with a lovely shiner for remembrance.

He scratched at his hand. Scratched at it again and raised it before his face. Laced tightly through his fingers were several long, dark strands of hair, Zel's hair. He closed his eyes and breathed deeply. Hair, soft and thick, velvet to the touch, suffused with that faint scent of spice. Until last night always pulled back in that disordered but maidenly chignon.

Had he misread that pause, as they faced each other, kneeling on her bed? When her slumberous eyes and full, lustrous breast had beckoned. Had he misread her soft "later" in response to his suggestions earlier in the evening? Had she misread his suggestion, not realizing it was a request for much more than a few kisses on the terrace?

From the first he had been intrigued by her contrasts. Who was Zel Fleetwood? Bold reformer or shy girl, passionate pianist or naive bluestocking, dashing courtesan or frightened virgin? Wolfgang yanked a dark green jacket, striped waistcoat, and buff breeches from the armoire. Where were his damn linens?

By all the denizens of hell! A gnawing in the pit of his stomach told him he had made a mistake of gigantic proportions. The passionate responses to his kisses and touch were certainly real, but they were not the schooled rejoinders of an experienced woman. The dashing courtesan was a role performed for the masquerade with naive enthusiasm. Zel pretended at flirtation, having no inkling what the stakes were. Wolfgang knew this, had known it from the beginning, but had chosen to ignore it last night. He had chosen instead to believe that as a radical thinker and avowed fortune hunter, she must also be a fallen or eager-to-fall woman.

Finding a clean neckcloth and shirt stuffed in the bottom drawer, he shook out the worst of the wrinkles and laid them on the bed. Jenkins would refuse to take another holiday if the efficient valet ever saw the condition of his wardrobe.

Walking to the window, he parted the curtains a sliver. The sun rode high in the sky. He would seek Zel out and declare himself all manner of fools and villains, throwing himself on her mercy. She would have to listen. She would have to agree to remain his friend. His friend? Damnation, what he wanted from her, even after a black eye, had little to do with friendship.

A scratch at the door announced the arrival of his hot water. Wolfgang bathed quickly, ignoring his throbbing eye. He dressed himself, then hurried downstairs, still buttoning the waistcoat under the uselessly dangling cravat.

No sign of her in the breakfast room, music room, or library. He sidled up to the stolid, sour-faced butler.

"Has Miss Fleetwood come down yet?"

"Miss Fleetwood, my lord? She was up and off hours ago."

"Off?"

"Yes, my lord." The man looked through him in proper, irritating, butlerish form. "She took a ride with Lady Ashley. She must be halfway to London by now."

"The devil and his demon spawn!"

"Pardon, my lord?"

"Nothing, absolutely nothing." Satan take the infuriating female. What was she thinking, turning tail and running back to London? Miss Grizelda Amadea Fleetwood couldn't even stay put long enough to receive his apology. He'd make a proper call, and she'd bloody well allow him in her salon and hear him out. She'd probably glare at him, stiff as all hell, perched on the edge of a chair, her spine never nearing its high back. Wolfgang smiled grimly. Or maybe she'd scream at him and blacken his other eye.

"Late breakfath before the trip back to London?" Melbourne was developing the most aggravating habit of appearing at inopportune moments. "Gadth, man, your eye!"

Wolfgang pushed Melbourne aside, scowling into his stupid, grinning face, then grabbed the butler's rigid arm.

"Send for my horse. I'm leaving now!"

"OH DEAR, it could not have been so horrible." Aunt Diana nibbled on a cold slice of roast beef, pushing the tray to Zel.

"It was much worse than horrible." Zel scooted her high-backed chair closer to the sturdy mahogany table and played with a piece of ham. "What am I going to do?" She inhaled deeply, the dining room smelled more of beeswax and lemon than of cold meat. It was one of the most used rooms of the house, and Aunt Diana kept its dark furniture shining, its drapery and carpeting spotless and bright. The silver, crystal, and china were, of course, impeccable. Dinner guests would never reconcile it with the shabby parts of the house only the family saw.

"I have already responded to invitations and several gowns are ready. It is not like you to lose your . . . courage," Aunt Diana murmured. "What happened?"

"Aunt Diana, I cannot talk about it." She looked down, slipping a piece of beef to her dog. Remus swallowed it in one unchewed gulp and rewarded her with a wet nose in her palm.

"Zel, what happened?" Zel fell silent a moment, but she knew she was not about to elude her aunt's questions. "Are you feeding that dog under the table again?"

"No, Aunt Diana." *That* dog licked her hand, begging for more. "There was a man. I, ah, had a little flirtation."

"A little . . . flirtation? You do not flirt, dear." Her aunt's stare caught and held her. "What happened?"

"I allowed him to kiss me. He thought . . ." Zel paused, remembering clearly what he thought and what he did, then blurted out. "He came to my bed and I hit him, in the eye and stomach."

"Oh, Lord . . . for goodness' sake!" Aunt Diana chewed hard on a piece of meat. "No one saw . . . did they? Did anyone see?"

"No, I am sure no one saw." Zel was surprised to hear her aunt sigh loudly.

"Who was it?" Aunt Diana asked, a little too eagerly. "Anyone I know?"

"Do you know the earl of Northcliffe?"

"Northcliffe!" She choked, trying for a delicate swallow, but a grin spread over her face. "You hit Lord Northcliffe?" The grin broke into a chuckle. "You refused Northcliffe . . . hit him?" The chuckle grew until her aunt clutched her stomach, rivers of tears running down her cheeks.

"This is not funny." Zel's voice sharpened in amazement at her aunt's reaction. "I was nearly assaulted, my reputation may be in tatters, and you are hysterical."

"Zel, dear, I am so sorry." Aunt Diana regained a modicum of her composure. "Lord Northcliffe is a rake of legendary proportions. Women throw themselves at him. He must be quite beside himself to be refused . . . in such a manner. He is not marriage material, but I believe he is not a gossip either, so I doubt you will be ruined. As long as you were discreet."

"I behaved with the utmost discretion." Zel felt her cheeks heat with her lie, and she looked down at her hands.

Her aunt chuckled again. "Well, at least now you have some, ah . . . valuable experience, and we can go back to our schemes to land a husband. The worst-laid schemes of rats and men, no, not rats, mice." She scratched at her chin. "What a strange saying. Why would mice be scheming with men, even badly?"

Zel smiled warmly at her aunt, muttering under her breath. "Robbie Burns be rollin' in his grave." Remus barked softly.

"Did you say something, dear?"

"Only that we should finish our luncheon and attend to my wardrobe, which I hope to be a better part of our schemes."

"I'll ring for Sally and we'll undertake a fitting now, before I go out this afternoon. Are you sure you will not come with me?" Zel shook her head and her aunt continued, "You will be amazed at the gowns. . . . They turned out ever so much better than I dreamed. You will make quite the dash, a leader of fashion. And you will let Sally cut your hair." She ignored Zel's horrified look and went on reassuringly. "No, no, not one of those awful bobs. They are not the thing anymore. But your hair is so long and heavy and it falls so shapelessly. When you don't have it pulled back in that dreadful knot. Just a little off around your face . . . a few curls around your forehead and temples, then a loose cascade at the crown."

"The ultimate sacrifice for my brother." Zel grimaced.

"I suppose I will not expire from a few curls, but no ringlets."

"Most certainly not, my dear." Aunt Diana patted her arm approvingly. "The Mattinglys' ball is tomorrow night."

"I shall begin, in earnest, my search for the weakest and wealthiest representative of the male animal in the British Isles." She smiled with false gaiety. "Then I shall proceed to marry him and pick the guineas and sovereigns from his pockets."

Remus licked at Zel's hand, then bounded to the doorway and stood attentively looking back at her.

Robin's raised voice carried through the closed door. "Damn, Father. I said I'd take care of this my own way."

"And I said to drop it."

Zel grimaced at her aunt. "They are at it again." She pushed past Remus and flung wide the door. "Father, Robin. Come in and get a bite to eat." She ushered her father to the empty chair beside Aunt Diana, motioning Robin to take the seat across the table. "What are you two bickering about now?"

"It's nothing that should concern you ladies." Sir Edward glanced at Zel, then flashed a warning look at Robin.

Sparing only a slight frown for her father, Zel sat beside her brother. "Robin, what are you taking care of your own way?"

"Lay off, Zelly. It's not your affair."

"I expect it is, or soon will be."

Father jumped in before Robin could respond. "He's still after that man who took his money at Maven's. He'll get killed."

"Maven's? The gambling hell?" Zel grasped Robin's arm. "For once Father is right. Let it go, Robinson. I would much rather be married to an ogre than have you dead. Besides, you don't even know the man's name."

Robin stared at her, his face set in hard lines. "Made it my business to find out."

Sir Edward pulled the cold meat tray before him. "Don't tell her, she'll only interfere. Make it even worse."

"All of you leave me alone." Robin jerked away from Zel and stood. "I'm dealing with this myself."

"Robinson Crusoe Fleetwood. Do not do anything foolish." Zel reached for him again but he was almost at the door.

"He'll find out he's not trifling with a fool."

"YOU'RE A TOTAL MESS, Captain, if you don't mind me saying so." Jenkins walked around the lacquered dressing table, tripping over the huge charcoal-gray furry object sprawled on the floor. "Blasted cat."

"And when did my minding ever stop you?" Wolfgang bent to pick up the cat and grinned at the tiny, white-haired man. It was good to be back at Hardwicke Hall where Jenkins could take care of him.

An answering smile cracked the leathery face, lending a touch of the absurd to the ragged features. Jenkins's rough youth lived on his face, his oft-broken nose, his crooked jaw, his uneven eyes, his missing earlobe. But his teeth, by some miracle, had endured, straight and radiant white.

"Hecate, did you miss me?" Wolfgang scratched the cat's fluffy head, then ran his fingers lightly over the offered throat.

Jenkins brushed more dirt off Wolfgang's jacket. "It won't take but half an hour to repair you right."

"I don't have half an hour. It's long past the proper hours for making calls now." Wolfgang took a quick glance in the glass. He looked like the wind had blown him in, and indeed it had. He had ridden Ari hard, leaving his groom to bring in the phaeton. And his eye. Let her see it and feel bad, guilty, maybe even sorry for him.

"Then make your call tomorrow." Jenkins assumed his

tone of propriety. "Your eye might look a bit better by then."

Jenkins hadn't shown the least surprise over his eye, and Wolfgang found himself more than a little irritated. He was no longer a little ruffian fighting his way through Eton. And when he did fight, he was skilled enough to rarely be injured.

"It can't wait. By Mephistopheles! I can't wait." Stalking into the bedroom, he pushed aside the nearly sheer bed hangings and sat on the silken cushions of the low, wide bed. He extended his legs to allow Jenkins access to his boots, with Hecate still draped indolently across his arm.

"What scrape are you in now?" Jenkins's voice changed to piously indulgent, as he brushed the dirt off the black Hessians.

"Why I allow you to talk to me like this I'll never know. Do you realize no other employer would permit the liberties I do?" He continued to stroke the rumbling throat of the giant feline, purring back into her ear. "Would he, little witch?"

"But Captain, you're not any other employer." The boots were nearly back to their usual mirror shine.

Wolfgang laughed, deep in his chest. Jenkins had been with his family over thirty years, through childhood and youth, military career and marriage. It was not an exaggeration to admit that without Jenkins's wisdom, courage, and unusual skills, he would never have survived childhood, let alone the later years.

"Jenkins, I need to call on a lady. A lady to whom I have given grave insult." Wolfgang frowned, toying with the tassel dangling from the pillow beside him. Hecate batted at the tassel with a deceptively quick paw.

"Can we expect her family's seconds to call?" Jenkins's tenor voice was firm and steady, he didn't miss a stroke as he brushed off the dusty breeches.

"From what I know of her family, she would be more

likely to fight a duel for them than vice versa." His lips twitched. "But I am the villain of the piece and I must apologize to her today. If I leave it for tomorrow, she'll never speak to me again." He set down the complaining cat and pushed up from the cushions. "My phaeton won't arrive for hours, so I'll take the town coach. Could you see that it's ready while I raid the kitchen?"

Minutes later Wolfgang jumped into the coach for the short ride from his elegant graystone mansion on Berkeley Square to the little brick house on Brook Street. He could have walked, but the call warranted the coach with the earl's crest. She wouldn't be impressed, but maybe her family would.

The speech he'd rehearsed on the neck-or-nothing ride to London seemed increasingly inadequate the closer he got to her home. How in hell did one apologize for attempting to bed a woman and at the same time soften her up for the next attempt? In all his experiences with women this was a new one for him. If he had a shred of decency . . . Lucifer's misbegotten! He'd been over that argument before. No, he wanted Zel Fleetwood. And she wanted him. Those kisses in Lady Selby's garden were proof of her desire. The coals had been stirred in that banked fire. All he needed now was to add more fuel, and he'd have a roaring blaze.

And if he didn't have her soon, she could easily become an obsession, a symbol of unattainable passion, that he would be compelled to covet. The best way to kill the hunger was to taste the fruit. And this particular hybrid promised flavorful fruit, but just fruit all the same.

The town house seemed smaller than he remembered from the night he brought her brother home. The knocker was up and no one was in sight. As he stepped down from the carriage, the front door was opened by the short, round man who had escorted him up the stairs to Fleetwood's bedroom. Wolfgang handed the man his hat and card, watching as recognition spred over the ruddy face. "I would like to see Miss Fleetwood."

"Miss Fleetwood?" The butler stifled an exclamation and ushered him into a small front salon to await his prey. "I shall bring her straightaway."

As soon as he disappeared a high-pitched attempt at a whisper carried easily through the open door. "It's him."

"I know," came the butler's lower-pitched reply. "It's the man who carried Master Fleetwood upstairs—how did you know?"

"No, not *that* him. Look at the earl's crest on the coach. And he's got a fresh shiner." The woman lowered her tone. "It's Miss Zel's rake."

Prince of darkness! Had Zel told her servants, and what had she told them? Soft footsteps echoed down the hall.

He walked to the window, scanning a tiny garden, a tangle of wild blossoms, strange greenery, and untrimmed flowering shrubs. He spotted what appeared to be herbs and vegetables tucked in among the other foliage. The garden was practical yet unusual and lovely, like Zel herself.

"She won't see him." The loud, shrill whisper resumed. "Says to tell him she's not home."

"Hmmpff." The rotund butler appeared in the doorway. "My lord, Miss Fleetwood is not in."

"Then I'll wait until she is." Wolfgang flashed his teeth.

"But my lord." The little man backed up a step. "She is not in, to guests."

"I repeat, I'll wait until she is." Settling onto a comfortable brocaded sofa, Wolfgang watched the butler's florid face turn a deeper shade of red as he bustled out of the room.

"He plans to wait." The butler's deeper tones were still audible, although they didn't carry as well as the maid's.

"He can't wait." The high voice squeaked. "She won't see him."

"Go talk to her. I can't throw him out!"

Wolfgang chuckled quietly at the thought of the little, fat butler tossing him down the front steps.

Footsteps clattered down the hall and within moments clattered back, stopping outside the door. "She says to make him go, she won't see him."

"How can I make him go? We haven't even a footman." The butler's voice rose in pitch to match the maid's. "Does she wish for me to take his arms and you his legs and carry him out?"

With his face a brilliant scarlet, the butler stepped back into the room. "My lord, Miss Fleetwood is not and will not be home tonight. She asks that you leave."

"Then I'll see Mrs. Stanfield. I'm sure she'll receive me," Wolfgang replied amiably.

"Oh no, my lord, Mrs. Stanfield is attending a committee meeting and dining with friends afterward. She will not be back until late." A thin sheen of perspiration highlighted the red on the butler's face.

"Then I'll see Sir Edward Fleetwood."

"My lord, he is not in town."

"What about Mr. Fleetwood?"

The short, round man sighed. "I will see, my lord." The door shut silently. "Now he wants the young master."

"Master Robinson?" The high voice pealed. Footsteps trailed down the hall, paused, and returned. Wolfgang counted steps, fifteen total, seven there, eight back. "She thinks he went out hours ago. Heaven knows if or when he'll be back."

The butler poked his head in the door, huffing in a few breaths. "Mr. Fleetwood appears to be out for the evening."

"I begin to see." Wolfgang spoke patiently, as if to a child. "Mrs. Stanfield is out. Sir Edward is out. No one really knows whether Mr. Fleetwood is in or out. And Miss Fleetwood is in but out."

"Yes, my lord. I am so pleased you understand." The

little man begged, sweat circling his eyes, outlining his nose and upper lip. "I'll show you to the door."

Wolfgang followed him into the hall, pivoted, and moved in the direction of the earlier footsteps.

"My lord, you can't . . ."

A light-filled doorway beckoned from the end of the short hall. Before Wolfgang could take the last strides to reach it, a large—no, gigantic—dog padded quietly from the room, facing him, teeth bared, hackles raised.

He put out a hand. "Nice doggie."

The shaggy-coated dog growled, a low rumbling sound Wolfgang could feel vibrating through his own chest.

"Miss Fleetwood? Zel?" His voice lacked its usual assurance. Why didn't she answer? He wasn't about to be defeated by a dog, even if it was the size of a small horse.

The growl shook him again, and he found himself backing slowly down the hall, the dog matching him step for step, teeth still bared, hackles still raised.

"Miss Fleetwood?" Curse the woman! She was in that room, silently laughing at the big, bad earl, frightened off by a goddamn mangy beast from hell. Wolfgang took one step forward. The cur looked at him as if he were very stupid dog food and growled again.

"You win for now, my furry friend." He crept to the front door, easing out and slamming the heavy wood behind him.

His military experience told him retreat was often the wisest course, but having met the cannons of Napoleon head on, Captain Wolfgang John Wesley Hardwicke felt like a fool backing down from a dog. Time to fall back and analyze his foe, and plan a new strategy to induce her surrender.

MELBOURNE PEERED around the brightly lit gaming room. Newton usually frequented the whist tables at Brooks's but obviously not tonight. He finally ran the earl down playing faro, of all things. He watched Newton win the next two hands and gather up his counters, then tapped the older man on the shoulder. "Let'th have a bit of thupper."

Newton gave him a half smile, more a sneer, and stood. They moved to the dining area and summoned a waiter.

"Give us the beefsteak and whatever fowl and vegetables the cook had the urge to boil tonight, and keep the brandy coming," Newton ordered, leaning his tall frame back into his chair.

"Playing faro?" Melbourne was truly puzzled, a too frequent occurrence in this friendship. "You alwayth win at whitht, why bother with faro?"

"The whist tables were slow tonight and I was feeling extraordinarily lucky. So I changed my game and won a tidy little sum." Newton ran cold, dark eyes over Melbourne, that slim smile again twisting his lips. "But come, sir, you're positively brimming over with something. Spit it out."

"I wath arranging for one of my footmen to watch Northcliffe, like we planned, when another thervant told me he thaw him come out of a house down the thtreet, looking motht unhappy." Melbourne paused for dramatic effect. "Mith Fleetwood livth there with her aunt."

Newton's icy chuckle was all the reward he desired. "Ah, Melbourne, you've done well. I'll warrant she refused to receive him, and the arrogant cur couldn't believe it."

"I thought thomething like that too." Melbourne's pride could have burst right through his chest. Pleasing someone as clever as the earl of Newton . . . well, it didn't happen every day.

"It warms my heart to see someone refuse him. The chit's got spirit." Newton scratched his mustache. "But she's no match for him. I fear her capitulation is inevitable if he continues his attack. Shall we help her fortify her defenses or shall we sadly watch her defeat?"

"Man like him can get any gel he wanth." Melbourne sat up eagerly. "Let'th help her."

"We could help by spreading the word that she blacked his eye." Newton pushed a lock of brown hair off his high forehead.

"Do you think it'th true?"

"Whether she did or not is beside the point." Newton's tone was sharply impatient. "The point is to make people believe she did, thereby taking Northcliffe down a notch or two."

"But won't that hurt her too?" Melbourne hedged warily.

"A little. We won't say he got away with anything or that she was to blame in any way. Just that he tried and she defended her virtue." Newton smiled reassuringly. "It might even enhance her standing, give her an air of adventure, mystery."

"I gueth that won't hurt her."

"We can take it slow, just a few words here and there, an amusing anecdote whispered in the right ear."

"Thupper'th here." Melbourne inhaled hungrily as the plates, platters, and cutlery were laid.

"Such as it is." Newton snorted. "Brooks's isn't known for its fancy fare. But that's not why we come here." He speared a bite of boiled potato. "I believe I'll place a little wager in the betting books after we eat. I'd like to be the first."

"The firtht?" Melbourne spoke through a mouthful of steak.

"To place a bet on our lovers."

Dinner, brandy, a bit more gossip, a few hands of cards and a few shakes of the dice later, and Melbourne was ready to call an end to a satisfying evening. He stopped to check the betting books on his way out.

Frowning, he read Newton's bold scrawl.

"Match all comers. Earl of N. will bed Miss F. before the season is out." Signed, "WJWH."

CHAPTER 5

COLORATURA

Ornamental trills and runs in vocal music

"I CANNOT go through with this." Zel watched through the back window of the hired hackney as the house disappeared and they rattled their way toward the Mattinglys' Richmond mansion.

"Yes, you can." Aunt Diana took Zel's hands. "Yes, you can."

"But I know he will be there." She looked down, grateful for her aunt's firm hold on her. "I cannot face him, but how can I avoid him if he seeks me out?"

"And he will. . . . He will surely seek you out." Aunt Diana's conclusion reassured much less than her warm hands on Zel's. "He is persistent. There were orchids with no card, delivered this morning. And he called again this afternoon, did you know? Smythe said he did not even make it through the door this time before that hound of yours came after him."

Zel's first smile of the evening broke through. "I know. I saw his carriage drive up and I set Remus on him."

"Goodness' sakes, dear, I know you do not wish to see the man, but do you need to attack him with that . . .

monster?" Aunt Diana's scolding voice held a soft peal of laughter. "The poor soul must have been frightened near to death."

"The dog or the earl?" Zel's smile spread. "Nothing would frighten his lordship, but he has enough sense to be cautious." She held on to her seat as the hack lurched forward into a break in traffic, her smile dimming. "Still I fear he may have a temper and I would not like it directed at me or Remus."

"Well, tonight he will not get near you for all the hordes of suitors surrounding you."

"Aunt, I do love you, but you need not flatter me." Zel laughed softly. "I look a cut above my usual dowdy self but I am hardly a beauty."

"Dear, you do not credit yourself enough. You are a lovely girl. Woman." She corrected quickly, studying Zel thoroughly. "Your new little maid did wondrous work with your hair. The wisps around your face and the long upswept waves are most flattering, and not a single hated ringlet in sight."

"Maggie is a treasure. So sweet and resourceful." Her smile disappeared completely, her mouth suddenly tight. "Her bruises are healing, but the pain and fear inside . . ."

"Will her husband seek her, do you think?"

"Most men do not release their *possessions* easily." Her voice crackled, brittle as paper clenched in a fist. "He will look for her. But London is large and I will not allow her to leave the house alone. He will not find her."

"She is very, very grateful for your help, Zel, dear."

"I should do more, society should do more." Zel coughed to clear her voice. "Hundreds of years ago Eleanor of Aquitaine gave her support to a refuge for beaten wives. Today, royalty would not recognize the problem if it slapped them in the face with a leather glove." She sighed, toying with the window curtains, scanning the carriages as they jostled for position on the narrow street. Not a single shiny black equipage with an earl's crest in sight. Unconsoled, she continued her tirade, aware that nothing she said came as new information to her aunt. "The nobility and the church are no better. If not for the Methodists and Quakers, these women would receive no help at all."

"Your speeches and writings do much good. And your home has taken in its first women."

"I suppose you are right, but the work is so slow. I fear I will never see any real changes."

"Dear, you do all you can. Now we need to think of this evening . . . your search for a husband." Aunt Diana took her chin in hand. "Your looks are not in the classic style, a little elfish, I suppose." She smiled in response to Zel's scowl. "But your face is very pretty and your figure superb, now we have it out from under those horrible gowns. Combine those with your clever mind, and you will have no difficulty bringing a suitor or two up to scratch. You need, however, to let your confidence and spirit show through. Throw your best pearls to the pigs, no, I think it is jewels to the swine. Oh well . . . you know."

The hack pulled up to the Mattinglys' gracious manse. Zel and her aunt stepped down, climbed the exterior staircase, and passed through the front doors. After mounting another flight of stairs, Zel paused to straighten her gown. Then, head held high, she entered the brilliantly lit gold-and-cream ballroom as the footman pronounced their names to the hostess.

Lady Mattingly pushed her husband toward another guest and drew Aunt Diana to her side. "Diana, I am most happy to receive you and your lovely niece. Why have you never brought her to my little gatherings before? Such a striking gown, most unusual." Her stare bordered on rude. "It looks a bit like what we wore around the turn of the century, of course the colors were never so rich. But somehow it suits her." Her little eyes narrowed, yet her smile held some warmth. "I will make certain you have all the appropriate introductions. The crowd is so slim, but there are still several desirable men in attendance."

Zel felt her cheeks heat and gave her aunt a hard look. Did everyone in town know she was husband hunting? Aunt Diana directed her to a strategic sofa near the dance floor. Lady Mattingly, as good as her word, brought several gentlemen to sign her dance card. Lords Newton and Melbourne made an appearance with several leering friends in tow. All signed her card, but after their departure she fervently wished to raise the neckline of the revealing sapphire-blue gown. Her hand went to her bosom, she should have at least stuffed in a piece of lace.

She whirled through a country dance, cotillion, and ecossaise, becoming more hopeful by the minute that Northcliffe would fail to appear. Her hopes were dashed when her partner returned her to her sofa to find the villain conversing easily with her aunt and Lady Mattingly. Aunt Diana smiled stiffly. She would never show the slightest impropriety in public. Northcliffe was in his element, playing the charming man-about-town. . . . His eye, oh Lord, Smythe was right, she had done fine work. It had the loveliest shades of blue and purple, with just a touch of green. Spirits suddenly lifted, she advanced to her aunt's side and smiled radiantly as he raised her fingers to his lips.

"*Enchanté*, Miss Fleetwood." The deep, full resonance of his voice rippled across her skin, raising the tiny hairs on her arms and nape.

"Lord Northcliffe," Zel murmured, purposefully coy. "Your poor eye, however did you do that? It must hurt awfully."

"My eye is well enough to see how divine you look." He smiled, smoothly changing the subject. "That gown was designed to display your charms to their fullest advantage." His eyes held that familiar sensual gleam as he scanned the wide expanse of skin exposed by her neckline. If he dared to pull out a quizzing glass, she would stuff it down his throat.

"Ah, my lord, still the consumate flatterer." Zel tried to hold his eyes with a cool look, but as the image of his long-fingered hand cupping her bare breast flashed through her mind, she lowered her head to hide her flaming cheeks. Thank God the candle had been behind him, merely outlining his naked form, or she would have a more disturbing image with which to contend.

Damn the man!

Northcliffe took her card, signing for the remaining dance before she could respond. He caught her eyes, his challenge clear. Would she boldly refuse him? How would it feel to wipe that gleam from those insolent silver eyes? Aunt Diana's light touch on her arm brought her whirling back from certain folly.

The strains of a waltz sounded. Zel looked for Melbourne to claim his dance.

"I fear your partner has abandoned you for the lure of the card room. I'd be happy to assume his place." Pouncing before she could respond, he led her toward the dancers. His fingers curled around her arm, knuckles grazing the outer curve of her breast. Zel gasped, nearly pulling away, but he tightened his hold, forcing her to walk rigidly beside him. She would not make a scene, though she would dearly love to blacken his other eye. She glanced back toward her aunt. Melbourne stood watching them, mouth slightly ajar.

Twirling her smoothly onto the floor, Northcliffe held her several inches closer than the accepted twelve. Her muscles were clenched so tightly she feared she would shatter.

"Relax."

"Relax," she hissed. "Relax? I'll relax when this dance is over and you decide to leave."

He chuckled. "But you enjoyed our waltzes only days ago."

"I do not enjoy this waltz, nor do I enjoy your company."

He circled rapidly, drawing her close, until the tips of

her breasts brushed against his chest. Despite layers of cloth between them, she felt her breasts warm, the nipples harden. How could her body betray her so? How could she respond to such a scoundrel? She must learn to guard herself well around him and discover any means to avoid him.

Northcliffe loosened his clasp on her waist, the distance between them nearly respectable. "If I apologized on bended knee, would you forgive me?"

Her back stiffened. "I would doubt your sincerity."

His mouth curved into the boyishly crooked grin that so disarmed her. "As it is useless to apologize, I must find another way to thaw your cold heart."

"Does my heart really have anything to do with this?"

He laughed too loudly, then whispered close to her ear. "I wouldn't know, madam. Does it?"

They finished the dance in silence, and as the music finally ended, Zel quickly took his elbow. She would control where those long, wicked fingers landed.

The next dances were with men she had just met but they hovered too close. One let his hand drift over her hip, another murmured an unknown word in her ear, his lips nearly touching her. She made it clear to them that their attentions were undesirable, but by the supper dance she was thoroughly shaken. Had these men seen her waltz with Northcliffe and assumed they could take similar liberties? But he had pulled her close for only a moment, no one could have seen. So what was she doing to encourage these attentions?

Zel's supper dance partner was the youngest Mattingly son. He could not be a year over twenty, and she sighed with relief when he treated her as a respected elder. Being something of a scholar, he engaged her in a lively discussion on the classics. Northcliffe and his partner sat across the table. She could feel his eyes on her and kept her head turned to the youth beside her.

The evening improved as Northcliffe kept his distance

and her next few partners behaved. When she complained of thirst after an energetic reel, she was not surprised to hear Northcliffe's even baritone offer to fetch her punch.

He turned, snagging a glass from a footman's tray. "Regent's Punch, for the lady's refreshment." He put the glassware into her hand, his light touch lingering on her fingers.

"Thank you, my lord." Zel drank deeply, choking on the potent mixture. Removing the goblet from her hand, Northcliffe tapped her gently on the back until she ceased to cough. Putting her hand out for him to return the punch, she watched in mortification as he deliberately turned the rim of the glassware until the faint smudge made by her lips lay directly before his own. He drank slowly of the citrusy liquid, leaving one sip in the bottom of the glass bowl.

"Your punch, my dear." He placed the stem into her still-outstretched hand, carefully positioning it so the smudge of both their lips faced her mouth, his eyes again offering challenge. Zel met his eyes and his challenge, calmly dropping the goblet to smash against the hard floor below.

His eyes glittered, a flash of surprise followed by amusement, laughter rising from deep in his chest. Startled, she tried to draw away, but his fingers circled over hers. Several of the men near enough to witness the exchange joined his laughter. Northcliffe raised her hand to his lips, his voice low and welcoming. "Well met, Miss Fleetwood."

Zel disguised a sharply in-drawn breath with another little cough. Oh, the man certainly had nerve. He must have made a formidable, if wildly reckless, captain. But who would have feared him more, the French or his own men?

Lord Newton stepped forward for his dance, happily, this time not a waltz. But she never felt comfortable in his company, and the expression in his eyes told her clearly that he had observed the preceding interaction with cold amusement.

The dance with Newton heralded the evening's complete collapse. When her next partners were improper to the point

of insult, she cravenly hid in the retiring room, feigning a
headache until her aunt summoned a carriage to take them
home.

WOLFGANG REINED in at the little town house on Brook
Street, handing the phaeton's ribbons to his groom. A curtain fluttered in a second-story window. By the great horned
demons, he'd blundered again. He was far too predictable.
Without thinking, he'd come at the same time as yesterday
and she would set her dog on him again.

He jerked about at the rumble of another carriage, then
flashed his teeth at the aged dumpling inside. His luck was
in. Mobilizing his best manners, he handed Lady Selby
down, escorting her to the door. The clairvoyant little butler
answered as usual before he could knock, and ushered them
into the small front parlor. No dog in sight. His smile widened to a full grin. Zel must have seen Lady Selby and called
in the hound. He graciously—yes, he felt quite gracious—
assisted as Lady Selby settled her carmine-clad self on a sofa
with legs entirely too thin for her voluminous bulk.

Distant, sharp vibrations of a harpsichord twined about
the endless stream of words flowing from Lady Selby's
mouth. The complex melodies and rapid runs surrounded
and bounced off the droning conversation in a strangely
agreeable counterpoint. Zel was playing that fellow Bach. He
listened to the music, nodding frequently to Lady Selby,
thinking of the private performance Zel had promised and
never delivered.

Moments after the music stopped, his quarry appeared
with aunt and dog in tow. Shouldn't the hunter have the
hound, rather than the fox? And what a lovely, intriguing
fox she was. Whoever dressed her now certainly knew their
business. The clinging sea-green muslin gown hid not a single curve. The cloth looked so soft, so smooth, that touching

it would surely feel like stroking bare flesh. He stretched his fingers, itching to massage the skin lurking beneath.

Wolfgang shook his head. That thought and similar others had filled his mind and dreams since the Mattinglys' ball last night. He could still see her as the goblet shattered on the floor, a barely leashed storm-at-sea shimmering in her eyes. He had taken her hand when what he wanted was to pull her to him, kissing and caressing away the chains that bound her passion.

Now he moved quickly to her side, again taking her hand, and before the dog could so much as bare its teeth, shoving Jenkins's special treat into its gaping mouth. As he kissed her fingers, the beast plopped onto the floor at their feet, chewing noisily.

Zel looked down, then swiftly back to Wolfgang, her voice a fierce, husky whisper. "Did you poison him?"

"I'd never punish an animal for his mistress's temper." He met her glare with a triumphant smile. "What's his name?"

"Remus. I sometimes call him Mouse." She seemed to soften, albeit unwillingly.

"Raised by wolves, like his Roman predecessor?"

"No, by dog breeders." Humor? She must be softening.

"What breed is he?" Wolfgang led her to a sofa near the window. What was behind this agreeable manner?

"He is an Irish wolfhound." Pride echoed in her voice.

"I've never seen his like." The dog gobbled the last of the dried meat and followed them to the sofa. Wolfgang watched him uneasily, but he sat docile and quiet by his mistress. How long would it last?

"The wolfhounds were a popular breed centuries ago, too popular in fact." She reached over to scratch the beast's curly haired muzzle. "Kings and nobility gave them so freely as gifts to foreign royalty and diplomats they all but disappeared."

"And are they bred to a particular function?" Wolfgang wanted to keep her on the subject to which she'd warmed.

Zel smiled broadly. "As their name implies, they were bred to hunt wolves."

Wolfgang jerked, then contained himself. Her voice sounded so matter-of-fact, but there was a glint of cool metal in those eyes. Was she warning or teasing him? He asked a bit stupidly, "Remus is a hunter, then?"

"He comes from a long line of superlative wolf hunters." She raised the dog's head, brushing the hair from its eyes. "The Irish wolfhounds were so successful in ridding Ireland of wolves, they actually furthered their own decline."

"How unfortunate for them." He aimed a tentative grin at mistress and hound. "And fortunate for any remaining wolves."

"Northcliffe, Mrs. Stanfield says you have been pestering Miss Fleetwood." Lady Selby's stentorian voice carried clearly across the small room.

"Dear lady, how could a few posies and calls brand me a pest? I'm hurt to the quick." He turned to his hostess. "Mrs. Stanfield, tell me the problem so I may amend my behavior."

Mrs. Stanfield spoke with obvious reluctance. "I suppose it's not just you. Zel received several bouquets this morning and refused to show the cards. She was embarrassed and upset."

"But my flowers had no card." He stood, the hound raised his head, eyed Wolfgang lazily, and dropped his muzzle back on his paws. "Not being even an adequate poet, I planned to deliver my message in person. Miss Fleetwood would you kindly explain. I'd like the chance to clear myself."

Zel blushed crimson, shaking her head. Wolfgang glanced from woman to woman, surprised at Zel's lack of rejoinder, but Lady Selby and Mrs. Stanfield resumed their conversation, seemingly content with Zel's refusal to comment. Being unused to acquiescing to stubborness, unless it was his own, he determined to pursue an answer. He settled back down beside her, placing his leg over a portion of her skirt where it lay draped across the sofa.

"About those cards." He kept his voice only slightly above a whisper.

"There is nothing to speak of, and it is not your concern anyway." She matched his volume, her tone sharp.

"You're upset."

She tried to rise but was well trapped. The fine cloth would rip if stretched further. "Get up."

"I'm very comfortable where I am, thank you."

"You are on my dress." She was hissing at him again. Her voice made a very pleasing hiss, low and sibilant. He found himself beginning to like it.

Wolfgang smiled blankly at her. "Tell me about the cards."

"You win." The hiss subsided but her eyes still flicked green venom. "Several of the men I danced with last night wrote . . . questionable remarks on the cards accompanying their flowers. Not what I believe a lady would expect, but then I do not have vast experience in receiving flowers."

"Did you do anything to give them cause?" If it had been possible for her to spit venom at him, she would have. "What did the notes say?"

Zel's renewed blush proved the perfect antidote to the earlier poison. "I cannot repeat them."

"Give me an idea, did they praise your hair, your ankles?" Wolfgang felt his patience thin. "You haven't been reticent about risqué conversation before."

"Maybe I need to be." She paused a moment more then plunged in. "They praised my bosom . . . legs and . . ." She shook her head. "Two requested a tryst."

"Satan's small—!" When the other two ladies looked daggers at him, he lowered his voice again. "Who were they? What kind of woman do they think you?" He was ready to call the scoundrels out! He quashed the protective surge.

Damnation, what right had he to feel protective with one breath and plot her seduction with the next? He was worse than the worst of them, with no plans to alter his course.

"You thought the same thing." Her face was drawn and pale. She looked away quickly, but he thought he saw a sheen of moisture glaze her eyes. He wasn't about to feel guilty. Protective was bad enough, but guilty? Never. Besides, just his attentions, no matter how persistent, couldn't be causing all this reaction. Something else was up. Maybe he could even help her discover and deal with the problem, worming his way into her good graces.

Her tight voice echoed his thoughts. "I must be doing something dreadfully wrong to be attracting this attention."

"Do you talk to other men as freely as you have me?"

"I do not . . . maybe I do." Now confusion warred with distress in her eyes. "I have always been blunt, but I am certain I have said nothing really improper."

"Many equate views," Wolfgang tried to put it delicately, "such as yours on the rights of women, with general moral laxity."

"Good Lord!" Now it was her turn to lower her voice as eyebrows across the room raised. "You cannot be serious."

"You're the strangest mixture of sheltered miss and worldly woman." His mouth twitched. "And, yes, I am very serious. Are you going out tonight?"

"No, and it is no business of yours."

"You should go out. Be seen, accept callers, act the model of decorum. The Melbourne ball tomorrow, will you be there?"

"I suppose, if I should."

"That's my girl."

"Woman." A little spirit popped back, quickening her voice.

"Woman, then." He grinned. "Your aunt and Lady Selby are looking daggers at me again. I believe I've overstayed my welcome." He stood, and bowing formally made his farewells.

Wolfgang strode through the front door and down the stairs, flinging himself onto the plush leather squabs of his waiting coach. Beelzebub's bootblack! What was he doing? Maybe his behavior had something to do with the questionable suitors. But how could they know he had her halfway on the road to ruin, with no intention of stopping? Hellfire! This continual debate with himself, this confusion about his motives, this strange concern about her feelings, only cluttered up his mind. One thing was clear: he desired her, she desired him, and he was not in a habit of subverting his desires for a little pricking of a conscience he had decided years ago he no longer possessed.

"MAGGIE, do not fuss so, just finish it."

"But, miss, it should be done right." Maggie worked to artfully arrange the wisps of hair around Zel's face.

"Please, I have asked that you call me Zel." Zel smiled into her dressing table mirror.

"Miss, Zel, you have been so kind to me." Maggie's voice quavered. "I hope you will not regret taking me in."

"I could never have turned you away. Now I do not know what I would do without you. And you will be safe here." Zel touched her hand, then tugged at the neckline of the sky-blue silk gown. "I wish the same could be said for me." She smoothed the filmy skirts. "You have a flair for fashion—could you convince Aunt Diana to raise a few necklines and starch a few fabrics?"

"But you are out to catch a husband." Maggie pulled at a wayward curl. "You seem to have attracted one devoted admirer."

"Northcliffe?" She snorted her amusement. "He is the most unlikely husband material one could imagine. These last two days he has called each afternoon and has been almost a gentleman. Although he still sits too close, holds my hand too long, and some of his remarks I would never dare repeat. I suspect better behavior is not in his repertoire."

"He is handsome," Maggie ventured.

"Handsome. I would rather he was not." Her expression softened as she remembered today's call. "He spoke of his family. He said little, but his was not a happy childhood. His grandmother . . . I would like her. And I do enjoy his company, his wit, humor, and charm, much as it pains me to admit it."

"There, you'll do."

Zel studied her reflection. "I barely recognize myself. And I am not sure I like it." Closing her eyes, she tried to envision herself waltzing in the shimmering blue gown. She opened them quickly when her imaginary partner emerged as Wolfgang, the earl of Northcliffe.

She covered her too-bare shoulders with a lace shawl as she rushed down the stairs. Her aunt and Lady Selby were having an intimate coze when she entered the drawing room. They looked up, as guilty as if she'd caught them smoking cigars and tippling port. What were the two plotting? And would she need to extricate herself from the results?

The distance to Melbourne House on Grosvenor Square was so short it seemed foolish to ride, but no one of fashion took useful walks, so they made their way to the ball in Lady Selby's antiquated carriage. Wolfgang must have been watching for her, as he was at her side the instant their names were announced, insisting on the opening and supper dances.

He led her out in the first country dance, hand appropriately at her elbow. His voice was low, scarcely a murmur. "Your new wardrobe suits you admirably. The blue makes your eyes translucent as the sky, and your skin glows like moonlight on new fallen snow."

"And your tongue is slippery as an eel."

"Madam, an eel? I believe I've been grossly insulted."

His thumb lightly stroked her arm. "You know you could start a rage, but I don't believe most women have the figure to carry off that form-draping style, especially with no corset."

"You are thoroughly impossible." Zel feared her blush revealed her mixed feelings. How could he keep her so confused?

"I aim to please."

He continued to hover near her, directing a careful eye to her partners. Most behaved. The few who held her too close or caused her to blush with off-color remarks met with Wolfgang's scowl, and thereafter kept a safe distance. While helpful in the short run, would this only damage her further in the long? She took a deep breath. The evening was developing well enough. She need not interfere with success, no matter how tenuous.

When Wolfgang held her at the appropriate distance for the supper waltz, she felt a twinge of disappointment—no, it must be relief. Instead of expending energy doing battle with him, all her efforts could be directed at finding the perfect husband. She rewarded him with a sugar-candy smile.

"I'd like you to meet some of my family," he whispered without returning her smile. Taking her arm, he led her to the supper room.

"Oh, is your grandmother or mother here tonight?" She was delighted he wanted her to meet his family. A gentleman did not introduce an intended mistress to his mother.

"My aunt and cousin are taking a table." He hesitated. "We could join them."

"Yes, I would like that."

"She is a bit in love with herself, but I think, well meaning enough." He smiled a bit too broadly as if attempting to convince himself when they made their way to the indicated table.

"Aunt Dorothea, I'd like you to meet a friend of mine." Wolfgang bowed over his aunt's hand. "Mrs. Dorothea Clayton, this is Miss Grizelda Fleetwood. That fellow by the buffet table is my cousin Adam Clayton. May we join you?" Without waiting for an answer, he seated Zel. "I'll fetch our food."

Zel watched Wolfgang step up to a smaller, tamer version of himself filling plates at the supper table. The hair was the same jet black, but without the streak of silver, and cut in a short, stylish Brutus. Adam Clayton's face was both the same and different. The general look was there, but the features seemed rounded and boyish, not in the least hard or dangerous.

"Lady Melbourne must be devastated. Such a poor showing." Mrs. Clayton's bell-like tones advised all the neighboring tables of her opinions. "Last year's affair was a positive crush."

"The crowd is right for the size of the room, any more and one could not walk, let alone dance," Zel commented.

"But that is the idea. Grizelda, is it?" She looked at Zel as one would a household pet, smoothing her elegant gray silk skirts. "You live in the country then?"

"Oh no, my family has a home in Moreton-in-Marsh, but I spend most of my time in London."

"Yes, I see." Zel could not be sure exactly what she saw, but it was clearly not favorable. She would try to be cordial. Mrs. Clayton examined her closely. "You are not his usual. But then Hardwicke does not introduce his usual to me." Mrs. Clayton laughed, high and shrill. "His women do not do credit to the earldom. But then, neither does he."

"His lordship, I'm sure, makes a fine earl." She surprised herself by jumping so quickly to Wolfgang's defense.

Mrs. Clayton stared at her and laughed again.

Zel fought an urge to cover her ears. "Do you divide your time between town and country?" Cordiality to this woman was proving most difficult.

"No, I find the country annoying." Mrs. Clayton must get an awfully stiff neck from holding her chin so high. "I stay in town year-round, except for a short trip to Brighton during the hottest part of summer."

"I have heard Brighton is lovely." Zel glanced behind the haughty creature. What was keeping Wolfgang? Surely placing a few tidbits on a plate did not take so long.

"You have never been to Brighton?" Mrs. Clayton didn't wait for a reply when she so obviously knew the answer. "It is charming enough. But one does not go for the scenery."

"I am surprised you are not in Paris." Zel wished the odd, arrogant woman there now.

"Oh, we were in Paris," she sighed theatrically. "But with prices what they are in France, we could not afford a lengthy stay. Hardwicke is miserly with my allowance."

"Did your son accompany you?" Zel feigned an interest she did not feel. The woman's rudeness and reference to Wolfgang by his family name rather than his title were strange. Perhaps she had not yet grown accustomed to Wolfgang holding the title.

"Of course, I would never leave London without him."

Zel barely contained her relief when Wolfgang returned with his cousin. She concentrated on her food while he exchanged awkward pleasantries with his relatives. Why had he wished to join them? There was clearly no love lost in either direction.

Melbourne stood up with Zel for the first dance after supper. The reel seemed a bit too energetic for him, and he pulled her aside, red-faced before the piece ended.

He leaned against a column, catching his breath, eyeing her appraisingly. "You know, you look dathed lovely, you could do better than a man like Northcliffe. You thouldn't allow him to run tame, 'cauth he ain't."

"Whatever do you mean?" Her eyes met his squarely. His were the first to lower.

"'Cuth me for being blunt, Mith Fleetwood." Melbourne's lisp became more evident with his increasing nervousness. "But people are thinking you might be the type to permit thertain libertieth. I don't think tho, but you thouldn't encourage him."

Zel would have liked to glare him down, but he did not lift his eyes to hers again. Without another word she started walking back to her aunt.

Melbourne lightly took her elbow, keeping pace with her long steps. "Mith Fleetwood, I didn't mean to give inthult." He hesitated. "But I thought you thould know."

Zel nodded a dismissal and strolled absently back to her aunt. It was unfair to kill the messenger. Maybe he was right, she had wondered if she was doing something wrong, but could the whole problem be her association with Wolfgang? She suspected earlier that his obvious attentions would not be entirely for the best, yet how much harm could he do? No one had seen more than a too-close waltz and a broken goblet several nights ago.

Could people be so ruled by gossip and rumor? But Zel couldn't help beginning to feel that his reputation undermined her own. She asked a servant for directions to the retiring room, and she walked along the indicated hallway. Footfalls sounded behind her. She started to turn as a long-fingered hand gripped her arm and another pressed lightly against her lips.

"Zel, I wanted to see you alone." Before she could reply, Wolfgang whisked her into a small anteroom, shutting the door behind them.

"What did you—?" She never finished the question. His lips feathered over hers, his hands locked tight on her arms. "Wolfgang . . . ," she whispered as his mouth left heated patterns across her eyes and cheeks.

"You talk too much, kiss me." His lips found hers again, with a force soft yet binding as a spider's silken web. She could not move, think, or breathe, trapped by his firm, mobile mouth. Her lips parted, absorbing the seductive deliriant he exhaled. Intoxicated, helpless to resist, she entered his embrace. Wolfgang drew her mouth into his own, twining her in his arms. His hands stroked her back and shoulders, cocooning her, insulating her from the outside world, holding her so she felt only his touch.

Liquid fire swept through her veins, incinerating all willpower and self-control in its path. Her arms circled his waist. Zel pressed her body against his, molding herself to his hard, angular lines. A rough, guttural sound escaped from deep within him. His hands grasped her derriere, molding her to him. He bit at her lower lip as he rocked her, hip to hip. A thin fiber of fear spun through her chest, she slipped one hand between them, pushing at his stomach.

He groaned, rocking her faster, harder. "By Mephisto, Zel. What you do to me. . . . Do you feel it too?"

She felt it, distinctly. "No!" The filament of fear expanded to thread, rope, cable, heavy and binding in her chest. She tried to struggle but she was only a tiny moth, caught in his net. Zel pushed at him again. "No!"

Wolfgang stilled. His mouth left her lips, his arms lightly circled her waist. "Ssshh."

She snatched free a hand and scored her nails down his cheek. Wolfgang sucked in a breath and dropped his arms, staring at her, dazed, as his hand smeared blood across his cheek and jaw.

The knot in her throat strangled her cry, as she whirled about, bolting through the door. Zel skirted the edges of the ballroom, vaguely aware of the need to avoid notice. He followed. She knew it and could think only of escaping him, the ballroom, the house. Upon reaching the entryway, she stopped, sending one footman for her aunt, another to summon a hack. She slid into a corner, but he found her and moved to touch her.

"No!" Zel shrank back from his hand, her voice low and hoarse. "Do not touch me."

Wolfgang stopped, inches from her. "Zel, I'm sorry," he whispered. "No, I'm not sorry. . . . Devil it, I don't know. But there's something between us. Why do you fight it so?"

"Leave me alone."

"No. I want an answer." She felt trapped, wedged securely in her corner, immobilized by his long, muscular frame.

"You know my situation." She paused, moistening her lips. "I must make a good marriage and you are ruining everything."

His eyes rose from her mouth to her eyes. "I'll help you."

"How can you help?" Zel forced a thick layer of scorn into her wavery voice. "I know you have no interest in marriage."

"I'll help you find a goddamn, old, feeble husband."

She heard a gasp. They both turned to the sound to find her aunt, Lady Selby, and Lady Melbourne and her son circling them, their eyes riveted on Wolfgang's cheek and her bloodstained gown. How much had they heard? By their faces, more than enough. She might be a naive fool, but she knew they would interpret his last remark as a plan to marry her off to gain free access to a bored wife or widow.

Zel looked to her aunt. "I want to go home."

Aunt Diana moved to her side, placing a firm arm around her shoulders. "Julianna, may we take your coach?"

"Of course, my dear." Lady Selby gave Wolfgang a cold look. "My coachman may return for me later."

Wolfgang's eyes were on her, hard, searing, but Zel did not back down. She held his stare, her voice harsh when she spoke. "Go wash your face. You are bleeding everywhere." She stood tall, walking into the cool evening air on her aunt's arm.

By the time they reached the carriage for the ride home, she was shuddering with the effort to hold in her tears, shaking from the center of her chest. Here was the violence that terrified her. This attraction was too wild, too passionate, too uncontrolled. It embodied the very same lack of control that led to the violence in marriages like that of her parents, her aunt, and her maid.

Sinking into the carriage cushions, she tucked her feet up beneath her legs. She had been as consumed by the kiss as he, but her fear had erupted when he wouldn't let her go, when he was so lost in desire he did not recognize her struggle. Zel had felt completely overwhelmed by his size and strength.

But then he stopped.

He stopped.

Oh, God. Her hand went to her cheek. She scratched him, drew blood, like some rabid alley cat. After he stopped.

Zel wrapped her arms tight around her ribs, a vain attempt to contain the wild swirl of emotions inside her. Fear, she easily identified. But fear was only one of those hurricane force emotions. And whom did she fear more? Wolfgang or herself?

CHAPTER 6

DUET

A musical composition for two vocal
or instrumental performers

HE MUST LIKE PAIN. Wolfgang paused before the stairs. There could be no other reason to be at her door.

He must want a broken bone or two to go along with the black eye, the scratch, and the ache in his groin. The black eye maybe he deserved, but the scratch was another matter. He had felt her stiffen, heard her say no, and he'd stopped. Damnation, he'd stopped and she'd scratched him anyway. If he had any sense at all, he would walk away and never seek her out again. Sighing, he put a foot on the bottom step. He wasn't known for his good sense, was he? Perhaps he should do as he'd threatened and help her find just the husband she wished for. In a year or so he could look her up. When she was ripe with boredom and dissatisfaction. He took another step. Lucifer's scaly skin, it shouldn't be so difficult to think of her with another man.

He sighed again. If she agreed to see him today, would he try to make amends or continue his mad pursuit? Damned if he knew.

Wolfgang's fingers were at the knocker before the door

swung open. The little butler's clairvoyant powers were slipping. No, today's guardian of the inner sanctum was a tiny redhead.

"My lord, she's not in." Wide green eyes furtively scanned his face. "No one is home unless young master Fleetwood is still abed."

"I'll wait."

"My lord, Miss Zel and Mrs. Stanfield are walking the dog in Hyde Park." She looked hesitantly up the street, then pulled farther back into the house. "I don't know as you should try to see her. She's still angry."

"Angry?" Wolfgang smiled innocently. "At me?"

"Oh, my lord, please stay away, at least for a few days." He noticed the faint yellow of an old bruise on her jaw and cheek and tried to catch her gaze.

"I'll take a turn in the park." He handed her his card. "If I happen to miss her, please let her know I came by."

The sky was dotted with clouds, the air had that just-washed freshness only a spring shower can bring. A pleasant day for a walk in what would be a nearly deserted park. Clearly Zel walked for the exercise, as it was far too early to be seen. And much of the fashionable crowd would still be in Paris. He fingered the dog treats in his pocket. Thanks to his valet, when he met up with that beast she called a dog, he'd be prepared.

After an hour of circling the park he had not spotted her. Wolfgang leaned against a tree, closing his eyes. He could still envision her as she'd looked last night, her supple form draped in liquid blue, her eyes effulgent with gold flame, the exposed upper curves of her breasts softly translucent. He'd played the gentleman as long as he could, but he wanted to touch her and he chose not to deny himself. When she parted her lips under his mouth and pressed the length of her body into his, desire had burst over its banks. Carried away at flood tide he had moved too far too fast and terrified her. But damming up the passion, a mighty struggle, had still not calmed her.

He rubbed the raw abrasion scoring his cheek. The sleek, sable feline had claws. Pushing off the tree, he strode for the main path. Satan's small clothes! He'd seen enough of Hyde Park to last a month.

Thunder roared from a nearby stand of trees, followed instantaneously by a soft buzz as pain seared his right temple. Wolfgang stumbled to his knees, pitching forward into the soft mud. Dazed. Sticky liquid running down the side of his face.

He lay there, minute after minute, conscious of his own breath moving in and out, keeping cadence with the arrhythmic thud of his heart. That part of his mind trained by war listened but heard only bird cry punctuated by the chatter of squirrels. The shot had come from the trees on his right. The oak he had leaned on was the only cover in range, and it was a good ten paces away. He'd never make it, and the little dagger in his waistcoat was a feeble defense against a pistol or rifle.

Every muscle in his body tensed, ready for battle, as he forced himself to lie quiet and motionless as death itself. The minutes lengthened. Mud oozed damply through the layers of his clothing, chilling his skin. He supressed a shiver. The park was quiet save for the rustling of leaves in the breeze and the soft, soothing calls of animals.

Wolfgang ran his fingers surreptitiously up the side of his face, through the trail of blood. The wound seemed slight, a parting of the skin over the right temple. Remembering how copiously the mildest head wounds bled, he pushed up to his knees. His head felt suddenly light, his vision spotty. He knelt, in silence, still nothing but the usual sounds of the park about him. The dizziness passed. Raf would be back from France, his home only blocks away. Wolfgang stood, yanking out his handkerchief, wiping blood off his face and mud off his jacket and waistcoat. He made his way through the park, drawing a few curious looks, but the scowl on his face kept at bay any offers of help.

When he reached Rafael's town house, the perfect, never ruffled butler escorted him to a small salon. "His Grace will be down shortly." Crompton spared a short look at his face. "Do you require a physician, my lord?"

"No, just send in Mrs. Saunders to help me clean up."

He flung himself on the nearest sofa, lowering his bleeding head into his hands. Mephisto, he felt tired, dulled. Was he injured more than he realized? His brain refused to work.

"What kind of muddle have you gotten yourself into now?" Rafael Langford, the duke of Ridgemont, stood beside Wolfgang, his cultured voice more clipped than usual. Raf's deceptively slight form bent smoothly over him while thin, immaculately groomed fingers pushed aside his matted hair to examine the wound. "You look like the devil himself, but it's not much more than a flesh wound. I thought you had given up dueling."

"You know I haven't even thought of dueling in years." A frisson of anger constricted his throat. He swallowed it. Rafael, his friend since schooldays at Eton, was only trying to help in his sardonic manner. "Someone shot me in the park."

"A stray bullet?" Ridgemont's golden brows rose.

"No, Raf. I believe someone is trying to kill me."

The brows edged higher, but the sculpted face remained cool as marble. "This isn't the first attempt?"

"No, the first was nearly two weeks ago. I was attacked by footpads outside of Brooks's."

"I've always told you those Whigs at Brooks's are nothing but trouble, Wolf."

Mrs. Saunders entered, intrepidly sure of her place. Both men were quiet as she made quick work of cleaning the wound and wrapping a bandage around Wolfgang's head. After she tucked in the edge of the cloth, Raf ushered her out the door, thanking her for her labors.

"You believe the footpad attack was not a simple robbery?" Rafael seated himself gracefully on a carved ebony chair.

"Between my coachman's cudgel and my dagger, we convinced them that flight was the most judicious course." Wolfgang rubbed at the bandage. "But as they fled, one complained that they'd better get the promised pay for the night's work."

"I see your point, footpads are normally paid by the proceeds of their work. You think they were hired assassins?" Raf's excessively handsome face revealed none of his internal cognition, but Wolfgang knew he was rapidly piecing together the puzzle, placing it into an ordered pattern.

"I was suspicious enough to hire a runner, but as he turned up nothing, I began to doubt my assumptions." Wolfgang swung an ankle up to rest on his knee. "Now this, Raf, the park was deserted. A stray bullet is too much of a coincidence."

"I agree, Wolf." Rafael scratched his head, sending his carefully ruffled Brutus into wild disarray. "I'll bring in a few of my best men. You can meet with them tomorrow, tell them all you can of both attacks. One will stay with you, install him as a footman. And alert your ex-army staffers." He paused a moment. "Whom do you suspect?"

"I've given it a lot of thought. The list is longer than I care to admit." Wolfgang rose, stalking to the fireplace. "There are, of course, my relatives, who aren't too happy that I'm head of the family. There's Rosalind's brother. He never approved of our marriage." He traced the elaborate scroll-work along the mantel with his forefinger. "He was the first to accuse me of her death."

"And we can't forget the cuckolded husbands, spurned lovers, and bested rivals." Raf's sarcastic tone had a bite. "Who would bear a serious grudge, and be capable of murder?"

"The devil and his hellhounds! This is worse than I imagined. I haven't been careful or kind."

"Then perhaps you deserve to be shot."

Wolfgang turned from the fireplace, glaring at him.

"That scratch looks evil, and is that the remnant of a black eye? I hear you've been tangling with more than foot-pads and assassins. Now you're taking on virgin bluestock-ings." Rafael gave him an appraising look. "Tell me the whole story."

"There's nothing to tell." Wolfgang sighed broadly. He'd never win against Raf's relentless questioning, so he might as well surrender now. "I suppose you'll torture me if I don't confess. I met her at the Selby's house party, you know, the one you insisted I attend. The one to start me on the path of improving my standing in society."

Rafael sat a little straighter in his chair. "Am I to blame then for trying to help you reenter polite society, for helping you build your career in the House of Lords?"

"Stop, I don't need the lecture. I understand more laws are passed in drawing rooms than in the halls of Parliament." He slumped into the chair opposite his tormentor. "I do appreciate your efforts on my behalf."

"What about your bluestocking?"

"Our association started on a high note, but has been at the bottom of the scale ever since." He slouched further in the chair. "Every time I touch her, she hits me."

"That's simple to deal with. Stop touching her. One line of gossip claims she's your mistress, another that she rejected you, but you won't give up."

"How the devil did you hear anything? You haven't even been in England." Wolfgang jumped to his feet. "She hasn't really rejected me. She wants me, she just refuses to admit it. And she isn't my mistress, yet."

A tiny smile touched Raf's carved lips. "Wolf, this isn't like you to pursue an unmarried woman, and an unwilling one."

"She isn't unwilling." He turned to the window, squirming under Rafael's stare. "Well, she's sort of unwill-

ing, but not for long. There's something between us and I
want it. She does too. Once she admits it everything will be
fine."

"Are you as confused as you sound?"

"I know what I want. You'd understand if she kissed you
the way she kissed me."

"You need to leave her alone." Raf's voice took on that
paternal tone Wolfgang hated. "You're looking for trouble
seducing an unmarried miss."

"I won't be trapped into marriage again. But I can't
leave her alone." Wolfgang rubbed at his head. It throbbed
and the blasted cloth itched. "I tell myself to stay away, but I
don't. I haunt her house. I follow her to parties."

"It's the chase. You're not accustomed to being refused."

"At first, I thought so too, but it's more than that.
There's a spark—no, it's more like a lightning bolt—between us, and I'm drawn to it even knowing the dangers."

Rafael's voice went very soft. "Marry her."

Wolfgang choked. "Marry her? I'm barely surviving
now. Marriage would kill me." He lowered his tone. "I won't
marry again. Rosalind more than convinced me how unex-
alted that institution can be." He left the window, approaching Raf's chair. "But I've made a mess of Zel's reputation. I
introduced her to my aunt, but I don't think that will help."

"Your aunt would be no help." Raf laughed, a harsh
bark. "Bring in the big guns. Introduce her to your grandmother. No one would cut her under Lady Darlington's patronage."

"Perfect!" He pounded Rafael's shoulder. "I'll write
Grandmama today. She'll be in town soon anyway to repre-
sent me at some of the celebrations." Wolfgang paused,
frowning. "Smoking brimstone! I think they'll like each
other."

"Sounds like you're in even deeper trouble than you
think."

"You need to arrange for Zel to be presented to Grand-mama."

"Shouldn't you make your own introductions?"

"Zel won't talk to me."

"Wolf, this makes no sense." He ran his finger across his lower lip. "Or perhaps . . . What does her refusal to talk with you have to do with those fresh nail tracks down your cheek?"

"I pushed her too far last night. We made a scene."

Rafael moaned faintly. "How big a scene?"

"No one saw us kissing." Wolfgang lowered his head. "But several people saw us afterward finishing the fight."

"I don't think I want to know more." Raf leaned back in his chair, regarding Wolfgang through cool brown eyes. "Maybe bringing in your grandmother won't be enough."

"MISS FLEETWOOD, may I introduce your dinner partner, His Grace, the duke of Ridgemont." Lady Netherby presented a man of Zel's height with pale brown hair and facial features so handsomely chiseled as to be almost beautiful.

"Charmed, Miss Fleetwood, forgive my late arrival." His bow over her hand was effortlessly graceful. Ridgemont tucked her hand into his elbow, walking her to the dining hall with the other couples. "I hope you didn't fear you'd be seated alone."

"Your Grace." Why was she, probably the lowest-ranking female at the gathering, paired with a duke—even if this duke, according to Lady Selby, was a friend to Wolfgang? She hoped she had not been a subject of their confidences, but suspected she had. Her suspicions were confirmed when Wolfgang, whom she'd studiously avoided, seated his partner across the table and the two men exchanged a veiled glance. The hostess had obviously not chosen Zel's dinner partner. But what could Wolfgang and His Grace be plotting? Wolfgang's companion hovered about him, leaning in so close she might as well be serving her mostly exposed breasts to him on a platter.

"Miss Fleetwood, I believe you are acquainted with my friend Northcliffe and his dinner partner Lady Canning?" Lord Ridgemont gestured across the table.

Zel nodded, thankful they were on the opposite side and she would not be required to engage them in conversation. Lady Canning was welcome to him.

"And the gentleman on your left is Northcliffe's cousin, Mr. Adam Hardwicke Clayton."

She turned to Clayton, offering her hand as she sat. "We have met. Good evening, Mr. Clayton." Here again was the soft miniaturized version of Wolfgang. A tame puppy to his feral beast, bedecked in padded jacket and shirt points to his cheeks.

"Miss Fleetwood." He took her hand, raising it to his lips. She supposed the look he bestowed on her was a leer, but she did not feel at all threatened. Could a puppy leer?

"Mr. Clayton. How is your mother?"

"She is well, but had a previous engagement. She'll regret missing you." He belatedly released her hand. "A most unusual. Not in the common mode, old-fashioned, but enchanting on you." Adam Clayton smiled at her chest. The Hardwicke family seemed cut from a similar mold, physically and morally.

Zel looked to the duke of Ridgemont for rescue. He gallantly obliged. "Yes, I believe Miss Fleetwood will revive a previous fashion, with a new flair." He smiled at her. "But your true flair is your music. I have it on the best authority that you are accomplished on the pianoforte."

"I do play with some skill." She smiled, Wolfgang's comments to his friend could not have been totally negative.

"Good, no false modesty. After Lady Netherby's tenor has assaulted our ears, will you heal us with a few melodies?"

"Happily, if our hostess so desires." Zel looked into his

beautiful shuttered eyes. The eyes of a man who allowed the
world to see only what he wished it to see.

"Miss Fleetwood, I understand you've become a *dear*
friend of my cousin?" Mr. Clayton made a suggestive nod
toward Wolfgang.

"We are barely acquainted. I would hardly call us
friends. Let alone dear friends." She glared across the table
where an eavesdropping Wolfgang gagged on his drink.

"True, he seldom makes friends of women, especially
lovely ones." Clayton looked as though he might wink. Zel
looked away, her eyes drawn to Wolfgang. He turned fully to
her, watching her with the keen gaze that never failed to
unnerve her.

The scratch lines were red and ugly. He had made no
attempt to cover them with bandage or cosmetics. There was
also a new wound above the scratch, beginning at his right
temple near his eye and disappearing into his thick black
hair, just below the streak of silver. Her shock must have
been obvious. He smiled, nodding slightly, as if to say, "See,
you are not the only one who injures me."

Zel turned back to his cousin, confused, wishing she
could hold on to last night's fury. She feared the anger but
found herself fearing the emotions that might replace it
more. Was it this war of anger, fear, and desire that fueled
her parents' marriage? She tossed back her head. No, she was
not like her mother. And she would never be trapped in such
a relationship, never entangle herself with any man, never
marry at all, except for Robin's debts. Robin's debts. That
thought must be kept at the front of her mind.

The duke's sardonic humor made dinner pass quickly.
But afterward Zel sat alone in the drawing room until
Ridgemont led the men in to rejoin the women. He sat next
to her on a bright gold divan. "I need to speak with you,
privately." The smooth murmur drifted inches from her ear.
"There will be a brief intermission. Meet me on the terrace."

She twisted on the sofa, ready to archly refuse. But the

coolness in his eyes and the ironic smile on his lips were strangely reassuring. She nodded her assent.

The tenor's voice was pleasing, his program Mozart, mostly from the *Magic Flute*. When the music ended she moved quickly to the terrace. Ridgemont joined her, settling them both on a stone bench, overlooking the garden.

"I'm here on Wolf's behalf." She stood to leave, but his steady voice stalled her midstep. "Please, hear me out. This is important to both of you."

Zel looked at his face, dimly lit by the sconces lining the terrace wall, and sat, surprisingly sure he was sincere. He might be Wolfgang's friend, but for some unfathomable reason she trusted him. "I will listen to what you have to say."

"Wolf has always been impetuous. He got in more scrapes at school than any other five boys combined. But he never meant to hurt anyone." Ridgemont laid a hand lightly, briefly on her forearm. "His intent wasn't to harm you, but he does not think clearly where you are concerned."

"I am not sure I understand you."

"You have confused him, and he has smudged your reputation. He is sorry and would like to call a truce."

"A truce?" She laughed. "A little late for a truce, Your Grace, when the battle is over."

"The battle isn't over. If you disengage now, you'll be the loser." Ridgemont sat still, for all the slightness of his frame as solid and immovable as one of the statues dotting the grounds. "He has no reputation left to lose, you do. Wolf has promised to behave as an older brother and has invited his grandmother, Lady Darlington, to town to meet you."

"I do not want to meet his grandmother." Despite her earlier trust, her anger grew at this man, so restrained and so accustomed to command. "And how could it possibly help?"

"She is a respected member of the ton. Association with her will ensure that no one will completely spurn you. If you and Wolf behave." His expression softened as he blocked her protest with a wave of his hand. "I wish we could prevent the raised noses and subtle insults. You'll have to plunge through them. With Lady Darlington's patronage you may emerge unscathed."

Zel sighed, defeated. "And when will I meet this paragon?"

"You'll cooperate?" A flash of warmth flickered in his eyes.

"Yes. I have no better idea." She smiled hesitantly, then looked down at her gloved hands.

"Lady Darlington should arrive in town within a few days. You will attend minor functions with her, and when the war heroes arrive you may be ready for the upper levels of society." Ridgemont wrapped a finger about his chin. "You and Wolf must appear as cordial, physically distant, brother and sister."

"That insufferable, self-serving—" Her anger broke through and she hissed at him, jumping to her feet. "Physically distant! As if I wanted anything else. If he thinks I'll—"

"My dear, I realize you're at daggers drawn." He grasped her arm with strong, slender fingers, pulling her back beside him. "But you're an intelligent woman. Forget your anger and use that intelligence on your own behalf."

"You are undeniably correct." Zel contained herself, shrugging her shoulders, as he released her. "I will try to behave towards Lord Northcliffe as if he were a human being, perhaps not a brother but a far-removed cousin. And I will graciously accept his grandmother's patronage."

"Good. You will talk with him tonight and arrange to be seen with him in a casual setting tomorrow."

"I said I would see his grandmother, not him."

The duke's voice was clipped with impatience. "You're acting nearly as stupidly as he is."

"Fine." Zel slumped against the cold bench back. "But not tomorrow. I have an important meeting at my club, several guests may make substantial contributions to my women's home."

"Perfect. Wolf can make an appearance and a contribution."

Zel stared at him in complete disbelief. "This will never work." Wolfgang loose in her club? She couldn't stop the image of a helpless herd of sheep circled by a shaggy-haired, silver-eyed, two-legged predator.

"It will work, have faith in yourself." Ridgemont stood, clasping her hand to help her to her feet.

"Oh, I have faith in myself, but I gravely doubt your friend Northcliffe."

Ridgemont laughed. "The music has resumed, we must return. It has been a distinct pleasure making your acquaintance, one I hope to further."

Zel returned to the music room before Ridgemont. But the attempt at stealth had been worthless, as Lord Newton arrived in her absence and eyed her entrance with his usual ravening gaze. He, of course, noted Ridgemont's entrance a moment later and pinned her with a twisted half smile.

After the last aria was sung and refreshments served, Zel observed Wolfgang picking his way across the room, eyes intent on her face.

"Miss Fleetwood." Lady Netherby touched her arm. "Would you do us the honor of playing?"

Wolfgang was only steps away. "The honor is mine, Lady Netherby, to be privileged to follow such a distinguished musician." She looked toward Wolfgang, gifting him with a tiny smile, then walked briskly to the pianoforte. Nothing formal tonight. Perhaps a popular song or an Irish ballad?

Zel played, captured as always by the melodies, harmonies, and lilting refrains. Even the simplest song could hold great beauty. Only as she completed the last measure did she become aware that Wolfgang and Ridgemont both stood near the pianoforte, regarding her closely. Wolfgang tapped his friend's arm and grinned broadly, as if he were bragging, taking credit for her accomplishments. She gripped the edge of the bench, needing to physically hold her anger down.

"Beautiful, my dear." Lady Netherby moved behind her, skirts rustling noisily. "I have heard that you also have a lovely voice. Would you favor us with a song?"

"A fine idea." Lord Newton appeared beside her, that cold smile still clinging to his lips. "But would not a duet be twice as sweet? Northcliffe has a strong baritone."

"Oh, please, Miss Fleetwood, Lord Northcliffe?" Lady Netherby pleaded.

"How can we refuse?" Wolfgang sat on the bench, a good six inches away and much too near. He shuffled through sheets of music, then bent toward her, whispering, "A ballad? A drinking ditty? A song of unrequited love?"

"Quiet." Zel breathed harshly. "I will pick the songs." She snatched the sheets. "You sit silently."

"Yes, ma'am."

"Here." She stuffed three sheets in front of his face. "You must know 'Annie Laurie' or 'Oh, Youth Whom I Have Kissed' or Robert Burns's 'Bonnie Lesley.' "

"Must I?"

"Do you know them or not?" Small wonder she had blacked his eye and scratched his cheek.

"I know them. We'll sing the 'Oh, Youth' one and 'Bonnie Lesley.' Would you like to sing melody or harmony?"

"I will sing the harmony."

He arranged the music before her and positioned himself near the edge of the bench. She played quickly through to familiarize them with their parts, then signaled to Wolfgang and they launched into the Irish love song. " 'Oh, Youth, whom I have kissed, like a star through the mist./ I have given thee this heart altogether.' "

The gleam in his eyes told her what a big mistake this song was going to be, but she could not stop now. She would ignore him and continue playing and singing.

" 'At first to steal the bliss of a maiden with a kiss . . .' "

Wolfgang sang louder, overpowering her softer voice. She looked up from the pianoforte keys to catch him licking his lips.

" 'To deceive her after this and to leave her.' "

Zel concentrated on the sheets of music, willing her fingers not to stumble over the keys as he continued even louder.

" 'Preferring sheep and kine and silver of the mine./ And the black mountain heifers to me?' "

She heard him cough and refused to raise her eyes.

" '. . . the riches that you love, have chosen,/ Who would come to me and play by my side every day/ With a young heart gay and unfrozen.' "

The blasted man was winking at her. Had he no sense at all?

" 'But when the sun goes down, I sink upon the ground,/ I feel my bitter wound at that hour.' "

She glared at him as he cleared his throat.

" 'And all my friends not dead are casting at my head/ Reproaches at my sad undoing.' "

She met his eyes, smiling sweetly.

" 'And this is what they say, 'Since yourself went astray,/ Go and suffer to day in your ruin.' "

Wolfgang was quiet, his restlessness betrayed by long fingers running silently along the pianoforte keys. She nearly chuckled at his discomfort. Had she finally gotten the best of him? The song was not such a bad choice after all, if it could prick his conscience even a little.

"Are you ready for 'Bonnie Lesley'?"

He started, quickly recovering. "Play on."

Zel felt his eyes on her as they sang Burns's Scottish ballad. His voice was rich and resonant, blending well with her own contralto. She dared to meet his eyes, he neither winked nor licked his lips. He steadily met her gaze, his expression soft, almost tender.

" 'To see her is to love her,/ And love but her for ever,/ For Nature made her what she is,/ And ne'er made anither!' "

She left her hands resting gently on the keys, unwilling to release the lingering vibration, stirring when his hand brushed her arm. His crooked smile warmed her, the long, single dimple seemed to ask for her touch. She allowed a ghost of a smile to drift across her lips, then stood to acknowledge the applause.

He rose beside her. "Another?" Had she noticed before that his voice even in speaking had a melodious core?

"No, I believe we have done enough damage."

"I'll get you a lemonade." Wolfgang took only one step. His face hardened in lines of tempered steel. "Simon Bedford."

"Northcliffe, is that what you're now called?" A slender young man of medium height with flaming red hair blocked Wolfgang's path. "You're daring to reenter society?"

"Simon, don't start." Wolfgang's voice stretched taut, like a thread before it snaps. "This isn't the place or time."

"And what is the place? When is the time?" The smaller man blustered, chest puffed out, face red. "The field of honor you would never meet me on?"

"My God, man! You were a grief-stricken child. It would have been murder."

"And it wasn't murder with my sister?"

"Simon, we've been over this ground before. My wife's death was an accident." Zel placed a hand on Wolfgang's arm. He glanced at her, features frozen, eyes narrowed and clouded. She opened her mouth to speak, to reassure or detain, but he brushed off her hand and with shoulders rigid stalked from the room and the party.

·   ·   ·

WOLFGANG LOOKED furtively up and down the street before entering the unmarked oaken door leading into Zel's women's club. He assured himself there was nothing wrong with a man entering this holy of holies. And it wouldn't bother him in the least if anyone saw him.

Leaving his hat with a servant at the door, he poked his head into the designated room. Had there ever existed a single location inhabited by so many respectable women? Wolfgang feared to open his mouth, envisioning their reaction if he cussed or said something even mildly risqué. They would attack him with their reticules. He would go down under their blows, unable to defend himself. That devil, Ridgemont, owed him for this one.

Where in the fiery lakes of hell was Zel, anyway? He paced off a few steps, looking over heads for her. She would stand out, a blue jay among the sparrows. No, there she was across the room, back in her own sparrow garb, loose, dirt-brown dress, hair pulled back from her brow and temples.

Even the spectacles, which he'd barely seen in the past week, were back, in place on that impish, little nose. She should know it was far too late for disguises, enough had been revealed for him to imagine the rest. Wolfgang shook his head to clear his thoughts. A brother did not visually undress his sister.

Lucifer's cloven hoof! This was never going to work.

And what demon had inspired that bloody song last night? His fists clenched, unclenched. Wolfgang had no idea he could feel so guilty. Zel was bringing out things long buried. Things that his father's hatred, his sister's death, and his wife's betrayal had destroyed in him. Things too long dead to be safely revived. Buried they would remain. Yet he owed her something. Her reputation was badly mangled. It might not be entirely his fault, but if he didn't help her, it would soon be beyond repair. And a woman such as Zel, strong and resourceful as she was, could not thrive without her reputation intact.

He would play out this little masquerade, play the doting brother, put Grandmama to work. Grandmama would adore Zel, he could already see that matchmaking gleam in her old eyes. Wolfgang tugged at his suddenly too tight collar as he edged toward Zel. He would need to be slippery indeed to escape Grandmama's snares. She was getting older, slowing down a bit, maybe he would be lucky, but somehow he knew she would fight harder for this one. Maybe he should—

Wolfgang stumbled over a wrinkle in the worn carpet, grasping a chair back to steady himself. Satan's horns! This was all that bastard Simon's fault. If he hadn't come to the musicale last night reviving old memories of Rosalind and their brief, ill-fated marriage, he would never be thinking this way. He should run, hard and fast, as far as his legs would carry him. Australia probably wasn't far enough.

Zel was speaking to a small circle of women, fire burning bright in those crusader eyes.

". . . that hallowed institution is nothing more than slavery. The woman moves from the tyranny of a father to the tyranny of a husband." She paused for a breath and rushed on. "If marriage is to be tolerable it must be entered as one would a business contract, a merger of equal partners."

He smiled as she continued. "Terms would be outlined on both sides, agreements hammered out regarding societal, family, and personal duties and responsibilities."

"But what of romance, love, trust?" Wolfgang regretted the question the moment it passed his lips.

"Oh, the gentleman asks of love and trust and *romance?*" Her voice oozed sarcasm. "Fine emotions. They look so appealing in sonnets and novels. But where do they get a woman in real life? Bruised. Beaten. Living in fear of her life under the thumb of a man who regards her as merely another possession. The best a wife can hope for is a benevolent lord and master."

"Are these the only options for a man and a woman,

Miss Fleetwood?" He moved to her side, close enough to inhale the spicy warmth that contrasted so with her cold, harsh words. "Are there no good marriages, no friendships across gender lines?"

"I suppose they may exist, my lord, but I have yet to see them. Excuse me, ladies, my lord." She tried to move away but was stopped by an attractive, small, plump brunette.

"Zel, please speak with Lady March. She may donate a tidy sum." The woman spied Wolfgang, scanned him appraisingly, and smiled. "Oh, I'm sorry. Who is your handsome friend?"

"Emily, this is Lord Northcliffe. My lord, my friend Mrs. Emily Carland." Zel glanced briefly at him. "Please excuse me." She pushed her friend ahead of her, through the crowd.

Wolfgang leaned against a high-backed chair, watching Zel's slim hips sway as she walked purposefully across the room. A few women tried to pick up the thread of the conversation Zel had abandoned, but without her zeal it seemed to unravel. He paused a moment longer, then sauntered after Zel with studied nonchalance.

". . . these women are terrified. They have nowhere to go. They must make a choice between the uncertain life on the streets of London and the certain horror of life with their husbands." Zel spotted him and cast a thinly veiled warning with a golden green flash of her eyes. "We try to offer them a third choice, with Aquitaine House. But that choice takes money, Lady March."

"I would like to see the establishment before I commit to its patronage, young lady." The elderly woman patted Zel's arm familiarly.

"Of course, I would be happy to escort you there, but remember, most of the place is not yet fit for habitation and we have only a few women living in the rooms that are now ready. I could take you there tomorrow morning."

"It is not on the premises?" Lady March raised her bristly brows.

"The club only provides a sort of sponsorship for the home and this location is too well known." Zel lowered her voice. "We keep the location of the women's home secret for their protection."

"May I join your tour? I'm considering contributing to, what did you call it, Aquitaine House?" Wolfgang's generous offer was met by a metallic glare as he sidled up to Zel.

"I am sorry, my lord, but men are not allowed within its doors. It is too difficult for some of the women. It brings memories they would sooner forget."

"How can I give my money to a cause I haven't seen for myself?" His lips curled slightly at her crestfallen expression. At least she believed his proposed patronage as real as he was surprised to find it was. "But I don't wish to frighten your women. I'll send my man with a bank draft tomorrow."

Her answering smile was worth every pound he would commit. Perhaps he'd become a regular patron of women's causes. "My lord, your support is appreciated, thank you." She extended her hand, he took it, squeezing gently.

"May I ask why you call it Aquitaine House?"

Zel pulled away her hand, but her smile remained. "Eleanor of Aquitaine was a patron of Fontevrault, an abbey founded by Robert of Arbrissel. The abbey was known as a haven for battered and ill-used wives."

"So you pay homage to Eleanor, but what of Robert?"

"Clever, Lord Northcliffe." Mrs. Carland patted his arm. "We honestly did think to honor Robert, but to call our home Robert's Place would repel more women than it would draw. Sounds a bit like a tavern. Fontevrault House raised more questions than it answered. People seemed to accept Aquitaine House."

"You see, my lord, we do not despise all men." Zel shared a laugh with her friend. "I must attend to my other guests. Emily, please see that Lord Northcliffe is served refreshments."

Wolfgang turned his attention to Mrs. Carland, favoring her with his best womanizing smile. She met his eyes, humor dancing in hers, and returned his smile, full measure. "We have nothing stronger than ratafia, my lord."

"A cup of tea will do nicely." He lowered his voice. "I'd sooner have rat poison than that nasty concoction."

Mrs. Carland chuckled. "Ratafia is unpleasant. I can't think why so many ladies drink it. I prefer a good port."

"I'm disappointed, Mrs. Carland." His answering smile was real, comrade to comrade. "I'd have laid odds on you being a brandy drinker."

"I do like a little of Napoleon's best, now and then, late at night when I can sneak it out of my butler's pantry." She grinned widely. "But don't breathe a word to Zel, she'd probably have me drummed out of the organization."

Wolfgang drew Mrs. Carland's hand through the crook of his elbow. "Lead on to the liquid refreshments, dubious as they might be."

Her laugh reached out, solid and warm. "Dubious tea for his lordship."

He joined her laughter, inordinately pleased that Zel would have such a friend as Emily Carland.

THE CAT CROUCHED, still and patient, the only sign of life an occasional twitch of her whiskers or tail. The tiny gray mouse ambled by, oblivious to his fate, unaware of his mortal enemy's sable coat gleaming in the thin scratch of moonlight filtering through the open window. The rich fur shimmered as muscles bunched, preparatory to the deadly pounce. The mouse squawked, caught, rib cage securely wedged under one velvet paw, while the other paw, claws extended, batted playfully at the now blood-soaked snout.

Devil's fangs! Jerking upright, he rubbed the sheen of

perspiration off his nose and mouth. Wolfgang took a few deep breaths to slow his racing heartbeat. He should buy back his commission today. Somewhere in the world there had to be a war with England. Yes, the conflict in the former Colonies. They must need good officers to fight the Americans, and it had to be a damn sight safer than London was right now.

He pushed out of the bed, pacing to the mullioned window, flinging the curtains wide. The sun was just beginning to brighten the morning sky. Ari could use an unfettered gallop through the park as surely as he could. Maybe he'd be lucky and someone would take a better-aimed shot and save him from the misery sure to come if he didn't extricate himself from the reluctant clutches of one Zel Fleetwood.

CHAPTER 7

POLYPHONY

A musical piece wherein two or more
independent but integrally related melodic parts
sound against each other

"COME HERE. Take those spectacles off and let me look at
you, gel."

"Lady Darlington, please do not call me 'gel.'" Zel
walked slowly into Aunt Diana's bright drawing room, offering her hand to the elderly woman seated on the sofa. "I am a
grown woman, not a child."

With a chuckle, Lady Darlington took Zel's hand,
squeezing her fingers. The eyes scanning her were keen, a
familiar silvery gray. "A disciple of Mary Wollstonecraft?"

"I admire her writings, but if I considered myself a disciple of anyone, it would be Catherine Macaulay or Mary
Astell. Their opinions are every bit as succinct, their lives a
clearer example to other women." Zel signaled Smythe to
bring the tea.

"You think Wollstonecraft a hypocrite or a weak soul?"
Lady Darlington's lips curled, a startling echo of another
crooked smile.

"I would not judge her quite so harshly." Zel smiled

back, charmed in spite of herself by that smile and her guest's blunt conversation. "But one must admit her behavior diminished the respect accorded her. To throw herself so relentlessly at a man so obviously unworthy of her, does not advance the notion that women are thinking, rational beings."

"Reputation is everything, in this society." Lady Darlington tapped her carved ebony cane against the table leg.

Zel felt her skin warm. "Unfortunately it is."

"Miss Fleetwood, may I call you Zel?" She continued without waiting for the answer. "Zel, I'm not one to shy away from the delicate or unpleasant. May I speak frankly?"

"Please do."

"I know my grandson's attentions have done you harm. He has admitted so and requested my help." Zel squirmed under her close scrutiny. "You are not his usual. What are his intentions?"

"He has no intentions." Zel's face went from warm to hot. "I mean, you should ask him. . . . I mean, he sees the damage done and wishes to make amends, so we both may get on with our lives."

Lady Darlington grunted, her look turning speculative as she smoothed her aqua skirts. "Has he said anything that would make you think he might be contemplating marriage?"

"Good heavens, no!" Zel coughed the words out. "Whatever would make you say that?"

"It's not like him to care much about a woman's reputation, but then he has never pursued an innocent." The elderly woman leaned her tall, slender form forward in her chair. "You are an innocent, aren't you?"

Zel swallowed hard, speechless for perhaps the first time in her life, and grateful when Aunt Diana bustled in, Smythe and Remus close behind.

"Smythe, set down the tray. I will pour. Lady Darlington, I am so pleased to welcome you to my home, it has been such a long time." Aunt Diana moved to take the older woman's hand, nearly tripping over the dog. "Remus, sit." He looked up and wagged his tail. "Zel, do something with him."

"Mousey, come. Sit." Zel smiled indulgently as the beast eagerly complied, throwing himself at the foot of her chair.

"Fine dog." Lady Darlington studied the hound. "I haven't seen his like in years. My grandfather had one when there were still a few wolves around." She turned back to Aunt Diana. "It has been too long. I'm afraid I don't get out as much as I did formerly." She took the offered tea. "I'm happy in the country with my books and music and the occasional guest. But with all the to-do of the Czar and such coming, I have to show myself, attend a few balls and soirees."

"Oh, yes, it will be only a matter of days before London will be abuzz with activity. You spoke of your music. . . . If I remember, you play the violin." Aunt Diana pivoted to address Zel. "Your tea, my dear. You would love to hear Lady Darlington. . . . The two of you must perform a duet sometime."

"My grandson speaks highly of your abilities, Zel. Perhaps we can arrange a musical evening." Lady Darlington sipped at her tea, then straightened in her chair. "But we must return to the business at hand. May I speak freely before your aunt?"

Zel nodded, hoping the brazen woman would refrain from any further unanswerable questions.

"When you came in, Mrs. Stanfield, we were speaking of your niece's reputation and the harm my grandson has done it." Zel stared at the woman, willing her not to say what she was surely about to say. "He normally does not pursue innocents, is she one?"

"Of course she is." Aunt Diana replied absently, as if she fielded such questions daily. "I assume you have a proposal?"

Zel looked in amazement from one woman to the other. "You cannot blithely discuss me as if I were not here."

"My dear, of course you are here. . . . Lady Darlington only wishes to help." Aunt Diana sipped her tea and gestured to their guest. "Please proceed."

"Wolfgang asked me to sponsor Zel. I am known among the ton as a bit of an eccentric, but my good name is unassailable." She smiled. "I would lend it through association. No one will shun a friend of mine."

"I appreciate your generous offer, but—"

"No buts, Zel, I insist." Lady Darlington waved aside all protests with her long-fingered hand. "Wolfgang asks so little of me. Please don't ask me to refuse. Besides, I like you."

"Zel would never dream of refusing, would you, my dear?" Aunt Diana's vacant tone belied the steel in her eyes. Clearly outnumbered and outmaneuvered, Zel nodded her consent. Remus whined, rubbing his wet nose in her palm.

"Now, as to Wolfgang's intentions, I believe we should push for marriage." Lady Darlington persisted as Zel was speechless for the second time in her life, and within minutes of the first. "You are beyond the first blush of youth, though very attractive, but you could not make a better match than my grandson." She lowered her voice confidentially. "I know about the affliction of your brother and father. Not many men would marry you with such financially troubled kin, but Wolfgang will keep them in line. And he has money to burn."

Try as she might Zel could not get enough air into her lungs to support vocalization.

Aunt Diana took their guest's part eagerly. "It would solve all our problems. But Zel claims she wants a mild-mannered man she can easily control."

"Nonsense! She'd be bored silly with such a man before the ink dried on the vicar's register." She surveyed Zel critically. "Though not a beauty in the classical sense, she's very lovely in an elfish sort of way." Zel groaned. Aunt Diana scowled at her, a clear signal to mind her manners. Lady Darlington continued, oblivious to them both, "And I'm sure my Wolfgang spotted your figure right away. He does have an eye for that sort of thing."

"Lady Darlington, please, this line of conversation is insufferable." Zel's skin burned until she felt the blush to the tips of her fingers and toes. "I have absolutely no desire to further my acquaintance with your grandson, let alone marry the man. You must know matrimony was never his intention."

"Did that wicked boy try to persuade you to become his mistress?"

Zel sucked in her breath. This woman would not get the best of her. "Not in so many words."

"I'm sorry if he offended you, but he would try that first." The presumptive gleam in her eye was unmistakable. "And as you have refused him and his interest has not diminished, we have him exactly where we want him."

"My lady, you continue to misunderstand." Zel's usually husky voice hit soprano notes. She caught Mouse's scruffy hair in her fingers. "I do not want him anywhere."

" 'The lady doth protest too much, methinks.' " Lady Darlington lowered her brows.

"Yes, dear." Aunt Diana jumped in, her eyes backlit with excitement. "You need a husband, and you would not have to sacrifice yourself to a feeble old man. How does that saying go? 'The angel you know is better than the angel you don't.' " She frowned. "That doesn't sound right. Is it the devil you know?"

Lady Darlington laughed heartily. "Indeed I am sorry to admit Wolfgang is a bit more of a devil." Her eyes narrowed on Zel. "But I sense he would make you a good husband and you may be just the wife he needs."

"How can I convince you I will not marry him? Do not press this match. You will find neither of us grateful."

"Oh, dear. It looks like I have my work cut out for me. What do you have against the sweet boy?"

"Sweet . . ." Zel snorted, then controlled her tongue as Aunt Diana launched a hard glare in her direction. "In the first place, I regard marriage as an institution incongruent with my needs for personal freedom. As for my objections to Lord Northcliffe, they are numerous."

"Despite your objections to marriage you are on the marriage mart. Now, please enlighten me as to my grandson's faults."

"He is a man who would wish to dominate, and I will not be submissive. I live a quiet, orderly life. His is anything but. I believe in virtue. He does not. I do things in moderation. He to excess." Zel smiled tightly. "I hold dear my women's work and my family. I doubt there is anything he holds dear."

"You're wrong about him. What he shows to the world is not necessarily the man inside. His life has not been easy." The lines in the older woman's face seemed more deeply etched. "I wish I could have done more for him, but his father disliked me. I was barred from their home, even though it was my daughter's estate through my brother's bequest. I saw them only on occasion in London." Her long fingers folded and unfolded on her lap. "His father was a harsh, pious man, who never understood Wolfgang's impetuous spirit. And my daughter, a cold woman, was no help. When his younger sister died . . ." She sighed. "I go on too much. Forgive an old woman's reverie." Lady Darlington pulled herself upright. "You are invited to the Warricks' literary evening tonight?"

"Yes." If only Zel could ask the questions she wished, but she sensed no more secrets were forthcoming.

"Please permit me to call for you and Mrs. Stanfield."

Zel nodded, no longer adamant in her refusal of this woman's aid. "We will be pleased to attend with you. Perhaps I can persuade my brother to act as escort."

She ushered Lady Darlington to the door, Remus trotting close behind. A footman, smartly liveried in silvery gray helped her into the fine town coach. Zel watched as the carriage rolled down the cobbled street, rubbing at the tightness in her neck. She should have refused anything to do with Wolfgang, but it seemed unreasonable to be rude to his grandmother. Besides, she found herself liking the spirited old woman. Closing the door softly, she leaned against its solid strength. Things were never simple where the earl of Northcliffe was concerned.

IT WAS NOT that he didn't like poetry. Wolfgang crossed, then uncrossed his ankles, tracing the mazelike pattern in the carpet with restless eyes. In fact he truly admired any form of literature, if it was done well. But Lady Warrick obviously had no taste. She featured the most popular poets of the day, no matter how bad they might be. And tonight's epic verse stunk. The author had never been within continents of a battlefield, had no idea how truly glorious it was to be impaled by a bayonet or hollowed out by a rifle ball. He squirmed in his seat, angling himself to better view his grandmother's party.

Zel and Grandmama sat as cozy as sisters on a small sofa, faces inches apart. His grandmother had her back to him but he could see Zel clearly, her mouth pinched with stifled laughter. They were certainly enjoying the evening more than he. Mrs. Stanfield sat quietly in the chair on Zel's other side and next to her the brother, Robin Fleetwood.

Wolfgang stretched out his legs, knocking the chair in front of him, relishing the look of surprise that would appear on the young man's face when they were formally introduced. Making only a vague reference to the night in the gaming hell, he'd allow Fleetwood to seek him out later, in private, to thank him for his help and discretion. He'd have an ally in Zel's camp.

The pattern in the carpet now committed to memory, he shifted his attention to the intricate ceiling plasterwork. Still the poet rambled on. The sofa in front of him had a wildly meandering floral design, and the drapes at his side were similarly convoluted. Lady Warrick's taste in decor was only slightly better than her taste in poetry, bad but not so boring.

When the soporific monologue finally ended, Wolfgang jumped to his feet, eager for a little wine and intelligent conversation. He beelined for Grandmama's bobbing feathers and lustrous sapphire gown. Zel stood beside her, luminous in provocatively draped emerald-green silk. Putting these two together was either a stroke of genius or idiocy. He feared it would likely be the latter.

"Wolfie, I am so enjoying your young lady's company." Grandmama's first words to him after meeting Zel only confirmed his fears. *His* young lady? Satan's tail, she had probably already begun to plan the wedding.

Zel coughed and whispered, "Wolfie?" She was so amused by the childish nickname, she missed Grandmama's use of a possessive pronoun. "My brother is about somewhere. I will introduce you to him later, my lord." She smiled and mouthed, "Wolfie."

"I'd be most pleased." Most pleased to put his hands around that long, graceful neck of hers. Better yet, his lips, tracing a line from her stubborn chin to her bare shoulder. That would shut her up. He settled for tucking his hand in the crook of her elbow. "Grandmama, Miss Fleetwood and I will fetch refreshments. Would you and Mrs. Stanfield prefer lemonade or wine?"

"A little sherry for me, dear." Grandmama positively beamed as Zel's aunt nodded in agreement.

"Two sherries it is." The old tabby had likely progressed to naming great-grandchildren by now. Wolfgang pulled Zel a little harder than he meant to and was rewarded or tortured when her breast and thigh pressed into his side. Her eyes widened, then quickly narrowed. He grasped her elbow more firmly, anticipating her move before she could jerk her arm away.

"I see you and Grandmama are getting on famously." He twisted the corners of his mouth in a parody of his usual grin. "Just as I'd feared. You both look like you stepped off with the crown jewels. Did your maids consult on your toilette? Both pretty as a picture." Wolfgang blabbered on, ignoring her smile. "Where is your brother? Did you like the poet? I found his knowledge of war most amusing."

"Oh, calm down." Her smile broadened. "You have nothing to worry about from me. I have no intention of disrupting your bachelor state. I believe between the two of us we can outflank your grandmother, no matter how determined she may be."

"You're an angel." He released her elbow, taking her hand.

"Do not kiss my hand. It would not be appropriate for our brother-sister status." Zel eyed him warily. "We have a close charade to play. We must appear a tidy little family group and still find a way to convince your grandmother we do not suit."

"You! You swine! Take your hand off my sister!" Fleetwood stepped in front of him, red-faced and sputtering.

"Robin, this is Lord Northcliffe." Zel pulled free of Wolfgang, placing her hand on her brother's shoulder. "Lady Darlington's grandson."

"I know too well who he is." Fleetwood took another step forward, inches from Wolfgang's face.

"I've said nothing to your sister."

"Oh, I'm sure you haven't, Lord Northcliffe."

What the devil was wrong with the ungrateful cur? No wonder he didn't make a habit out of saving people's lives, if this was the thanks he got. "Fleetwood, let's find a salon and continue this in private." He kept his voice even and low. The room around them had fallen far too silent.

"By God, Northcliffe, I'll say what I have to say before all London." Fleetwood's breath reeked of cheap whiskey.

"Robin, please." Zel clutched her brother's arm.

Fleetwood pushed aside her hands. "This man cheated me out of the last of my blunt at Maven's. When I confronted him he struck me and knifed my comrades."

"If memory serves me correctly, it happened a little differently." Wolfgang spoke slowly, trying to smooth the volatile situation.

The younger man was having none of it. "You bastard, you ruined me." His voice swelled. "Stay away from my sister. You won't ruin her too!"

"Flames of hell, you fool, keep your voice down or you'll be the one to ruin her." Wolfgang reached for his arm. "You'll give the gossips an unending fuel supply."

Fleetwood shoved him. "Keep your bloody hands off me, or I'll strike you down where you stand."

"Robin, stop this. Now!" Zel yanked on his hand just as he swung wildly, and off-balance, he struck her instead of his intended target.

Wolfgang sprang forward, pinning the smaller man to the wall, his voice little more than a growl. "Damnation! You idiot, we'll take this outside."

"So you can murder me like you did your wife and most of your other relatives?"

Several men hesitated nearby, readying to assist, but obviously unsure what role to take.

"Robin!"

"You should have been hung." Fleetwood pushed futilely against Wolfgang's shoulders. "Falls down stairs, carriage crashes, mysterious illnesses, laudanum overdoses. How many does it take to make an earl?"

"Enough!" Wolfgang threw him at the waiting men. "Remove this *gentleman,* now! Hire a hack to take him home."

The fight died abruptly in Fleetwood. He allowed himself to be led, almost carried, from the room, silent and limp. Wolfgang whirled to Zel, who stood rigid as the marble bust that kept her upright. He slipped an arm around her waist. She didn't move.

"Take your hands off my person." She hissed at him. "I do not know who is worse, my brother or you."

"Zel, listen to me—"

"I am going home." She moved out of the circle of his arm. "Where is my aunt?"

Wolfgang grasped her shoulders. "By the spawn of Satan, you're going to hear me out."

"Let me go." She struggled to free herself. "I will not listen to you."

"Wolfgang, I'll take her home." Grandmama touched his arm.

"No." Shifting his grip to her upper arm, he pulled Zel toward the hallway. "I've no idea what your brother was talking about. I rescued him from Maven's, nearly three weeks ago. He might have died there if it hadn't been for me. You saw me carrying him to his room."

"So you are the hero. Forgive me if I fail to believe you." She met his eyes briefly, then looked back toward the drawing room. "Lady Darlington, Aunt Diana, I am ready to leave."

"Why would I have bothered to take him home if I'd just robbed him?"

"But you never told me the whole story." Zel tried to pry his fingers from her arm.

"No, I thought to spare you from all the nasty details."

"Spare me?" Her eyes threw sparks. "I am not a child needing your protection. You admitted you were not Robin's friend, but you failed to tell me you were his enemy. You also denied knowing anything about an assault."

"Lucifer's pointed tail! I said I didn't see a bruise." Wolfgang hauled her in closer. "And I didn't. But I did knock him out so I could get us both out of Maven's alive."

She moved her lips as if to speak, then silently stared up into his face.

"You think me a cheat, a thief, a liar, and a murderer?" Wolfgang tightened his clasp on her arm and pulled her farther down the hall, out of the view of the drawing room. Hearing the outbreak of chatter, he knew the gossip was spreading like wildfire. But he wasn't about to stop until she heard him out. He would leave Grandmama to quell the wagging tongues.

"Well, do you?"

"Do I what?"

"Do you believe me a cheat, thief, liar, and murderer?" They were nearly at the stairs.

"My brother may be many things, but *he* is not a liar." Zel's chin set stubbornly, unreasoning loyalty to her brother stamped on her face.

"Zel, the deaths of my family and my wife, that's old prattle. I'm not a murderer." He loosened his hold on her arm. God, he'd probably bruised her. "But I've never been regarded as a model of decorum, so the rumors spread. And at Maven's, I saved your brother's life. If anyone cheated, it was him."

"My brother does not cheat or lie." She broke free but stood her ground, eyes fiercely engaging his. Wolfgang wondered whom she was trying to convince, him or herself. "And I do not understand why you feel you must persuade me otherwise. Now I will take my leave of you. Do not try to see me, do not approach me at any gathering. I want nothing to do with you."

"I won't accept that."

"Accept it and leave me alone." Zel turned toward the drawing room. "My family means more to me than you ever could."

Any hair of control he had left snapped. "Fires of brimstone, woman! You'll come with me to Maven's and Maven will tell you the truth." Wolfgang grabbed her hand and strode down the stairs, towing her in his wake.

She grasped the newel post at the bottom of the stairs. "You must be mad. I will not set foot in a gaming house."

"You'll walk out of this house with me willingly or I'll carry you out, kicking and screaming." He pried her off the post. "Don't you think we've made enough of a scene tonight?"

"I will walk." Zel started stiffly down the hallway. He followed, keeping hold of her hand. They cleared the front door, descending the entry steps to the drive. "Where is your coach?"

As he scanned the street, she jerked free and bolted. He caught her within a few strides, flinging her over his shoulder, dashing the last half block to the carriage. His coachman didn't blink an eye as Wolfgang threw open the door and tossed her inside. "Maven's, on Lisle Street, and quickly." She skidded across the floor, quickly regaining her feet, reaching for the opposite door. Flying up behind her, he swung her down onto the coach seat. He pulled the curtains, pinning her to the squabs with the weight of his body when she again made for the door.

"Damnation! Quit squirming, you're only making this harder."

"Then let me go, you ass."

"The proper Miss Fleetwood cussing?" But Miss Grizelda Fleetwood did not feel at all proper wiggling beneath him, her breasts soft against his chest, her long legs tangled with his. Fighting the arrhythmic rocking of the carriage, he held her arms to her sides, raising himself slightly, searching her face in the dim light. Her eyes met his and she stilled. He lowered his head slowly, eyes never leaving hers. She made no attempt to avoid his gaze or his approaching mouth, but parted her lips, her labored breathing matching his own.

Zel's lips were cool, slightly moist, pliable under the

pressure of his. He released her arms, winding one of his arms about her waist, the other snaked beneath her head, bringing her closer. She stirred against him, running her hands up his back, returning the urgency of his kiss.

Wolfgang plunged into the damp recesses of her mouth, exploring the contrasts of teeth and flesh. She nibbled at his tongue, then twined her own around his. Thrusting his fingers into her hair, he roughly dislodged pins until the thick mass fell loose into his hand. He released her mouth and buried his face in the heavy waves, inhaling deeply of the tart, spicy scent. A scent so different from the cloying floral smell many women wore. His hand at her waist inched up her side, wedging between their bodies to cup her breast. She moaned hoarsely into her ear as his thumb slid over her nipple.

"Lakes of fire, Zel." He whispered as he drew away from her hair.

"Stay." She groaned, her grip tightening around him, pulling him back. Wolfgang nipped gently at her lower lip, then layered kisses down her throat. Her sleeve had been pushed nearly off in the struggle, baring her shoulder. He trailed his mouth across her shoulder and down her chest as his hand tugged at her bodice, freeing her breast. Zel's fingers tangled in his hair as his tongue slithered over the swell of flesh, circling the budding tip. He breathed softly on the wet skin, smiling at the shudder coursing through her body.

When he drew the nub sharply into his mouth she stiffened. Wolfgang slowed, suckling more gently than any babe, kneading the smooth, surrounding mound. He could hear her faint, husky growl, feel it vibrating softly in her chest, a cat's purr. The fabric fell away from her other breast under the steady pull of his hand. He sketched patterns in the silky curves, raking his nail slowly over the point. Her unsteady fingers tugged loose his queue, scratching the nape of his neck.

"Devil's damned, I want you. Now." His lips traced a

line through the valley between her breasts, trapping her other nipple in his teeth, alternately sucking and nipping. He rubbed his chin across her, the roughness of his beard stubble catching on her velvety skin. Zel arched against him, pressing her stomach into his chest, sliding her ankle along his shin and calf.

Hellfire, she was as alive to his touch as he ever imagined she would be. Wolfgang found her hip, smoothing the slick cloth over the enticing roundness, following the curve to the firm line of her thigh. His seeking hand proceeded over her bunched skirts, discovering a stocking-clad knee. Advancing along her thigh, he pushed inside the thin lawn of her bloomers, stroking the sleek, naked flesh, higher and higher up her endless leg.

Wolfgang stopped, breath harsh, raw, lifting his head from her breasts, suddenly wanting to see her face, needing to see the desire in her eyes, hungry for reassurance that her passion matched his own. Zel's eyes opened, caught by the intensity of his stare. The passion was there but underscored with a vulnerability that seared him to the very marrow of his bones. A guileless promise lingered in her gaze, tentatively offering more than he ever dreamed to possess.

The wheels hit a rut in the road, throwing his shoulder against the lightly padded back wall. Lucifer's mater! What was he doing? He was moments away from taking her in a carriage, claiming her maidenhead on the cushions of his coach. Zel wanted him now, but the minute she came to her senses she would hate him forever. That thought disturbed him more deeply than he wished to admit. Wolfgang wanted her passion, but he also wanted the shapeless thing he saw reflected in her eyes. A portent hovering almost within his grasp.

He eased up, balancing on the edge of the seat, one hand reaching out to straighten her clothing. Something in her face splintered. She looked at him as if he'd just materialized out of nothingness. Slapping aside his hand, she sat up, shoving him hard in the chest. Wolfgang slid off the squabs, landing with a solid thud on the wooden floor. Lifting himself gingerly, he settled onto the opposite seat, riveting her with his glare.

"Cover yourself." His voice grated in his throat, low and rough. "My control is hanging by a thread and this view of your delectable body is sure to snap it." He focused his gaze on her breasts. "Now! Or I'll do it for you." He moved toward her. "But if I touch you again I won't stop."

Zel finally stirred, looking down at her near nakedness, releasing a hoarse cry. "You animal!" She yanked at her bodice and skirts, returning them to some semblance of order.

"Me? An animal?" Wolfgang laughed, a bleak biting sound. "Think again, my dear, if not for the noble beast before you and his admirable restraint, you would at this moment be rutting on the seat of my carriage, your precious virginity a thing of the past."

"You are crude." Her face was pinched, ghostly pale, even in the dim light of the carriage. The devil's satin knee breeches! She was going to cry, damn her. He couldn't deal with her tears. Anger, yes. Tears, no.

"You're not getting out of this little excursion, so don't use your bloody tears on me." His voice sounded cold and harsh, even to his ears. He softened it, but it still came out no better than a growl. "We'll be at Maven's soon. Pull your bodice straight and smooth your skirts." He bent over, running his hands along the floor, retrieving several of her hair pins. "Here, these are enough to tidy your hair."

His eyes never left her as she scrambled to make herself presentable. Zel placed the last pin when the carriage lurched to a stop. Wolfgang opened the door, jumping out before a footman could pull out the steps. He held out his hand to her. "You may walk or be carried. The choice is yours."

"I will walk." He lifted her down. "I said I will walk."

He released her waist and clasped her arm, drawing her toward a red door. "Quickly, you shouldn't be seen."

Zel smiled thinly, her voice raspy and tight. "How sweet of you to care about my reputation, what shreds may be left."

The door opened. "I need to see Maven." The doorman winked at Wolfgang, ushering them inside, directing them down a narrow, unlit hallway.

"I thought this type of establishment refused to admit women."

"They don't generally admit ladies." He paused a moment, answering honestly. "But they do allow certain women in some of the rooms."

Zel stopped, her voice dangerously high. "He thinks I am your 'bit of muslin,' I believe is the term?" She yanked free her hand. "By morning even pickpockets and footpads in the worst stews of London will refuse my company."

Wolfgang pushed her through a door and barked. "Sit down. No one saw us. The doorman is the soul of discretion and Grandmama will take care of things back at the Warricks'."

"That relieves my mind considerably." Zel glared at him, arms folded under the breasts he had just so passionately kissed. She looked around the garish gilt-and-scarlet room, a room dominated by an overlarge bed. "I prefer to stand."

Maven's long nose edged around the door frame, followed by his bright, piercing eyes. "Captain, you require something?"

"Come in and shut the door." Wolfgang slammed the door as soon as the man cleared the threshold. "This is Miss Fleetwood. You remember her brother and the incident several weeks back?"

"Yes." Maven sniffed. "I remember all too well."

Wolfgang stalked to the window and parted the curtains to watch the carriages move on the dark street outside, then turned back to Maven. "Will you kindly tell the lady what happened?"

"As you wish, my lord." Maven raised his nose another inch. "Young Mister Fleetwood was in his cups and having difficulty with a few of my rougher customers." He nodded toward Wolfgang. "Lord Northcliffe dashed to his rescue, leaving quite a mess behind, I must say."

"But what of Northcliffe cheating or attacking my brother?" Zel met Wolfgang's eyes with a fierce glare, daring him to interfere.

"I know nothing of cheating, ma'am. But I believe Fleetwood resisted help, and Northcliffe struck him to enable them both to leave the room without sustaining further injury."

"But the cheating?" She persisted.

"As I said, I know nothing of cheating."

"Maven, you know I don't cheat." Wolfgang gritted his teeth. "Tell the lady I don't cheat."

"He doesn't cheat, ma'am."

"Thank you, Maven." He walked to the door, escorting the tall, thin man out, then turned to Zel. "See!"

"I see nothing, except you perhaps failed to pay an adequate bribe." She moved toward the door. "You did not get a very credible story."

"What the hell do you mean?" he snapped. He was beside her in two strides. "How could I bribe him? I didn't plan to bring you here tonight."

"Oh?"

He wanted to shake that calm look from her eyes. "Damn you." Wolfgang gripped her arms. "You wouldn't believe the prime minister himself, would you?"

Zel smiled prettily. "Are we going to his house now?"

"I'll take you home. This was a fool's errand." He looked pointedly at the bed. "Unless you'd care to stay and finish what we started in my coach?" He laughed harshly as she hustled out of the room, then silently followed her into the hall.

The doorman nodded and swung wide the door. "Short stay, my lord?"

"We completed our business quickly. Devil it! It's Newton." Wolfgang jerked Zel around, pushing her against the wall. "Quiet. Keep your head down." He felt her squirming and pressed his body hard to hers, holding her motionless, capturing her lips with his until Newton's footsteps receded down the hall. "Come quickly and quietly." He hauled her out of the gambling hell, propelling her rapidly to the waiting coach.

Wolfgang flopped onto the seat next to her. "Imps of Satan, I hope he didn't recognize you. This isn't one of his usual haunts."

"What would he do?"

"Maybe nothing, maybe . . . I don't know." He shifted on the squabs. "But there's no love lost between him and me. He may be willing to hurt you to get at me."

"Please take me home." Zel sat very still, her voice low, jagged at the edges.

"We'll be there in minutes." He placed his hand lightly over hers where it lay in her lap, surprised when she didn't pull away. They continued to her home in silence. His behavior had certainly not been top form tonight, but at the moment she appeared too worn to judge him ill.

When he lifted her down from the carriage, he rested his hands gently at her waist, bending down to brush his lips across her forehead. "I'm sorry. My grandmother will call on you tomorrow." He watched the little butler usher her through the front door.

Wolfgang climbed back into the carriage, and the coachman smoothly entered the line of slow-moving conveyences. He rubbed at his temples. Not top form? Lucifer's misbegotten! Grandmama would have his head on a pike.

His hopes that Grandmama would have retired for the

night were dashed when his big, square Scottish butler met him at the door. "Her ladyship wishes to see you in the library."

"McDougall, tell her I got past you and went to bed."

"My lord, she is waiting." McDougall's voice boomed down the hall. He had no choice but to face the dragon.

Hecate squawked, throwing herself at his leg. "Fine protectoress you make, my feline friend."

Wolfgang strode into the library, brave as Saint George. "Grandmama. You shouldn't have waited up for me."

"I just came in myself, and thought I would have a bit of sherry." She motioned to the decanters on the lacquer table. "Care to join me?"

"Brandy's what I need." He poured a healthy dose in a snifter, sliding onto the plush silk cushions of the low divan, an easy target for the coming attack. Hecate struck first, picking her way through the cushions and landing heavily on his lap. "Does the lecture begin now?"

"Wolfie, you know I love you dearly, but you cannot continue in this vein. I smoothed things over, I hope, tonight." She sipped on her sherry, watching him over the rim of the goblet. "You may care nothing for your reputation, but the girl will be ruined."

"I know, Grandmama—"

She ignored him. "Zel will be rejected by some, I fear. The only thing saving her at this point is the fact so many of the ton are still on their way from Paris. And when they return we can only hope the gossip may shift and move on."

"You'll help." Wolfgang stroked the charcoal cat's satiny ears. "I told her you'd call tomorrow."

"I'll stand by her. I like her." Grandmama leveled her piercing pewter gaze at him. "I think you like her too. More than you care to admit. But you need to stop this madness."

"I like her well enough, when she's not making me insane." He twirled the snifter, following the path of the amber liquid as it circled the glass.

"Then marry her."

"I won't remarry." The brandy left a warm, comforting trail down his throat. "And for your information, she does not regard me as proper husband material. She seeks a hen-pecked worm who will do her bidding."

"Yes, she told me. But I know there is something between you two and you cannot deny it." She stood, eyeing him as she poured another sherry. "You would get on very well, you know."

"We would get on very well for a few months, until the fire burned itself out." He found bitterness creeping into his voice. "Then there would be nothing left except disgust, or if we were lucky, coldness. I won't go through that again."

"But it's not the same." Grandmama walked to his chair and placed her hand on his shoulder. "She is nothing like your late wife."

Wolfgang shrugged off her hand. "They're all the same, when you get beneath the fancy clothes."

"What have you done?" A slight quaver entered her voice. "Wolfgang, she is an innocent. How far have things gone?"

"Grandmama, shame on you." He took a deep drink of the brandy. "That is not a proper thing to ask of your darling grandson."

"Wolfgang, how far have things gone with her?" The quaver disappeared, replaced by pure, unblistered steel.

"Not nearly far enough." He rose and poured another drink. "She's still a virgin, but only by the skin of her teeth."

"Wolfgang!"

He gulped down the fiery liquid. "I don't need your reproaches. All I need is this bottle and a little of my own company." He picked up the decanter, balancing it with the cat and snifter. "Good night, Grandmama."

"Wolfgang, you know how alcohol affects you."

"Yes, it'll only take a few more glasses and I'll be rip-roaring drunk. Another few and I'll happily pass out on my bed."

"Wolfgang John Wesley Hardwicke!"

He ignored her, sauntering slowly out of the room.

CHAPTER 8

RHAPSODY

An irregular musical composition with
an improvisatory character

BEETHOVEN. She needed a strong dose of Beethoven. Pro-
pelled by an unusual urgency, Zel shoved open the drawing
room door. Grabbing the first sheets on the occasional table,
she flung herself onto the pianoforte stool and launched into
an early sonata. Pounding out the notes, she thundered on at
top force, ignoring any directions to soften or slow. Pianissimo and largo were not part of her repertoire today. She
struck the keys, again and again, perspiration dotting her
forehead and upper lip as she relentlessly hammered out the
rhythm.

Energy finally diffused, she collapsed onto the keyboard
with a discordant crash, head in hands. What a hopeless
bramble.

She had been up half the night, replaying the scene in
her head. Why had she allowed him to drag her to that
gambling house? She should have dug in her heels and refused to leave the Warricks'. If he had acted on his threat,
trying to carry her out of the house, there were any number
of potential rescuers. Somewhere in the back of her mind she

must have wanted to go with him and hear the proprietor's story. Why would Wolfgang lie? But if he did not lie, then Robin did.

Zel rubbed the aches at the base of her skull. She knew Robin was capable of lying. He would exaggerate or embellish his story, if it suited his purposes. And although Wolfgang might be a card shark and a brawler, she was somehow sure he was not the murderer Robin claimed he was.

And his grandmother. She really was a dear creature.

Lady Darlington should have been appalled by the goings-on last night and overjoyed to see the last of Zel. Instead she had done her best to protect Zel's disappearing reputation, making excuses at the Warricks', claiming a sudden illness had forced Wolfgang to take Zel home. But everyone there had heard the confrontation between Robin and Wolfgang, and how could they miss Wolfgang dragging her into the hallway? Lady Darlington's good name would not be enough to save her now, especially if Lord Newton had seen them at the gambling house. Yet the old woman had called again this morning and would not let go of the idea of marriage. Having gotten it into her head that this was a perfect match, nothing would convince her otherwise.

Raising her head, Zel brushed back a few strands of hair and glared at *his* tulips in the porcelain vase beside her. Yanking a red bloom from the vase, she crushed the fragile petals in her fist.

She was avoiding the worst, trying to deny what happened in the coach. When she closed her eyes, she could still feel his hands and mouth on her skin. God, even the thought still burned. Her cherished self-control had vanished like a wisp of smoke in a windstorm. Wolfgang had been the one to stop, not she. He could elevate anger and desire in her to a typhoonlike pitch she would not have believed possible just weeks ago. And she hadn't a clue what to do about it.

Maybe she should just retire to the country. But Zel would never run from any man. And where would she find a wealthy husband in Moreton-in-Marsh? There were few eligible males in the area and none with a guinea to spare. Bath had an active marriage mart, but she had no funds to rent a house and no means of procuring introductions.

London, with her aunt's house and contacts, was her only choice. Maybe Wolfgang would leave. Yes, that was the answer! She would suggest it next time they met. Damn! Next time they met! How could she face him after what they had done in that blasted carriage? Maybe she could get Lady Darlington to make him leave. Zel sighed, unwillingly remembering his gentle parting kiss on her forehead and the whispered "I'm sorry."

"Miss Fleetwood." Smythe poked his head in the doorway. "You have a visitor in the salon, a Mr. Fawkes. He asked first for the young master, but Mr. Fleetwood is out." He gripped the door. "I do not like the looks of him, and you should not see him alone, but no one else is in."

"I will see him. Wait in the hall." Zel placed her eyeglasses on her nose and strode down the stairs to the ground floor. Remus lunged up the basement stairs from his favorite room, the kitchen, and followed her into the salon.

Smythe was right, the man was positively slimy. She offered him a chair, then sat on the opposite side of the small room, speaking with as much authority as she could muster. "Mr. Fawkes, my brother is not available. May I be of assistance?"

He smiled, a very lizardlike expression. "You're the one I wanted, anyway." He eyed Remus. "Your dog tame?"

"My dog is under my control." Zel laid a hand on Mouse's curly back. "Please state your business."

Fawkes leaned forward in his chair. "I'm here representin' your brother's creditors. We're callin' in his notes. Now."

"But I thought we had more time." She pulled her spectacles off, rubbing her eyes. "My father asked for more time for me to make a good marriage."

"But you ain't doin' it."

"It has only been three weeks since that agreement was struck." Her voice stretched tight but she met his eyes. "A marriage cannot be arranged in such a short time."

"My mates are patient men, but it's wearin' thin, *Miss* Fleetwood." His little round reptilian eyes touched her. "You ain't got a marriage proposal. The way I see it, you ain't gonna pay the notes that way."

Zel crossed her arms over her chest. "What do you know about my marriage plans?"

"Just that you ain't got 'em." He scanned her from head to foot. "Been watchin' you, followin' the talk of the town. You're gonna have to work off the debts."

"What do you mean? I make little from my writing." She stood, warily stepping behind her chair, Remus close by her side.

"Writin'?" Fawkes laughed crudely. "I'm not talkin' about writin'. I mean the kinda work you do on your back."

Hands clenched at her sides, she sucked in a rough breath. "I think you should leave."

He rose and walked toward her, lips curling suggestively. "We could come to an agreement. Earn you a little more time."

Remus growled.

"Leave now!" Zel gripped the chair back as Mouse stepped forward and bared his teeth.

"You're makin' a mistake." Fawkes backed through the door, Remus sniffing at his legs. "Your brother'll be in prison by week's end." The door slammed behind him.

Zel dropped back into her chair. "Good dog, Mousey." Remus laid his head in her lap. She lowered her cheek to his muzzle, whispering, "What am I to do?" Curling her legs beneath her, she pulled the dog farther onto her lap, burying her face in his shaggy coat. Lord, she was out of time and choices. She could no longer delude herself that even with more time she had the slightest chance of marrying at all, let alone finding a man wealthy enough to pay Robin's debts. If she did not think of something now, Robin would go to prison. There was no money to pay the bribes to keep him in comfort, and she feared he did not have the kind of strength needed to survive such a place.

"Oh, Remus. I cannot do this alone." She sat there as minutes ticked away on the mantel clock, wetting the dog's hair with silent tears.

"Zelly, Smythe says Fawkes was just here." Robin strode into the room, pulling her from the chair, surveying her swollen eyes and tearstained cheeks. "Good Lord! Did he hurt you?"

"They are calling in the debts." Zel clasped his hand. "We have only days to raise the money."

"I'd flee the country, but it won't help. They'd still come after you and Father." He smiled weakly. "Suppose they'll let you visit me in prison."

"Robin, I will not let that happen."

"You're powerless to stop it." Robin stroked her hair. "There are things even you can't do. Can't take care of me forever."

Zel looked into the face so like her own. "There is one more thing I can do."

"There is nothing. . . ." He caught her look and gripped her hand tightly. "No, Zelly! You won't do it."

" 'Tis the only way."

"Won't let you. Dammit!" Robin's eyes narrowed as he lowered his face to within inches of hers. "You won't become some man's mistress for me!"

"We can be discreet, no one will know. He has enough money to pay your debts without blinking an eye." Zel laid her forehead on Robin's cheek.

He shoved her away, choking on the fury in his voice. "Northcliffe! You mean to become Northcliffe's whore!"

"I cannot let you go to prison. You would never survive."

He grasped her shoulders as if to shake her, then stopped, his eyes harder than she had ever seen them. "I'll kill him!"

"Robinson!"

But he was gone, footsteps echoing in the hall, the front door banging behind him.

WOLFGANG BURIED his forehead in his hands as the carriage clattered along the cobbled streets. Every strike of wheels and hoofs on the stones thundered through his head, still muddled and throbbing from last night's overconsumption of brandy.

Hades and Satan take the woman. He'd waited at that bloody ball tonight for hours, watching the door for her arrival, wishing desperately he carried a sword to fend off the matchmaking mamas and their pasty-faced daughters. Even with his reputation, an earldom was a prize. Grandmama's disappointment only added fuel to his growing anger.

They had stopped in at two other parties, believing Zel may have changed her plans, but no sign of her. Wolfgang grumbled continuously about needing to get away from female company, until Grandmama had wisely sent him off to Brooks's.

He had sat with a few acquaintances, gulping down a glass of Brooks's best port, feigning an interest in faro. But he had been too restive and bored with the less than stimulating company and the even less stimulating game. Newton's vaguely hostile glances from across the room even failed to amuse. Making brusque excuses, he had finally turned in his markers and called for his coach. He would call on Zel tomorrow.

The carriage ride seemed to stretch out longer than the few blocks to Hardwicke Hall on Berkeley Square. Wolfgang massaged his temples. Why this dreadful confusion? Why couldn't he decide what to do and do it? He knew he wanted

Zel, wanted to slake his desire on that long, slender body. Yet, when he had the opportunity, when she lay beneath him, half-naked and fully ready, he had stopped. *He* had stopped! But had his amazing bout of restraint been appreciated? No. She had called him an animal! Wolfgang shook his head, wincing at the sudden stab of pain. Maybe he should have been a bit more of an animal and given her real cause for complaint.

Beelzebub's tail, she had no idea how she teased and taunted him. How thoughts of her warred in his head. How thin was the thread of his control. One of them needed to leave London. It wouldn't be him. He had pressing matters in the House of Lords and with his business holdings. Zel could easily leave. He could send her off with Grandmama to Winchelsea. There had to be old, rich country squires by the score for her to marry in the Sussex countryside. Men she could happily lead about by the nose. He slammed a fist against the heavily padded squabs. And if they ever touched her, he'd break their goddamned hands.

The coach lurched to a stop. Wolfgang swung open the door, leaning halfway out to chastise his coachman. "Harris, why have we stopped? Pull in the drive."

Gloved hands roughly seized him, yanking him unceremoniously from the carriage. Stumbling, he fell headlong into the street. He rolled to his back, narrowly dodging a blow from the caped, hooded figure hovering above him. A flash of silver shimmered in the man's hand. Reflexively, Wolfgang reached for his own dagger, only to have his grasp come up empty. Raising his forearm, he deftly deflected the downward arc of the footpad's knife, then whirled from a second villain's pounce.

"Harris!" But a quick survey of the scene showed the brawny coachman had his hands full with two more assailants. Wolfgang backed to the coach, narrowly avoiding another deadly blow.

A fifth cloaked figure stepped out of the darkness, arms

upraised, brandishing a bulky, unrecognizable weapon. Wolfgang grunted in surprise when the weapon came down hard on the shoulder of the man with the knife. The accompanying yelp of pain was punctuated by the sharp clatter of the knife striking the cobblestones. The footpad jerked about, his fist smashing Wolfgang's new ally in the chest. The gasp of air leaving lungs had a decidedly feminine tone. Wolfgang eluded a thrust from the other villain, as his new companion took a crushing punch to the head. The hood of her cloak fell away as she crumbled to the ground. "Zel! My God, Zel!"

He struck out wildly, fear and rage nearly blinding him. The sound of bone crunching told him his fist had found its home. The man hadn't hit the street before Wolfgang was on the other villain, knuckles meeting face with unleashed fury. Two down. In one seamless movement he bent, hefted the abandoned knife, straightened, and hurled it toward one of the footpads assaulting his coachman. He smiled grimly when a cry confirmed the weapon had found its mark. The man would live, although for a few days as he nursed a wound to the shoulder, he would wish he hadn't.

Odds evened for Harris, Wolfgang whirled toward Zel's still form. Stooping, he placed a shaking hand to her throat. The pulse was soft and even. His arms slipped beneath her, bringing her to his chest. Wolfgang covered the remaining distance to his house in a dead run, oblivious to any weight in his arms. He kicked at the door. "McDougall! Open up!"

The front door cracked. Mrs. Soames peered out. "My lord?"

Wolfgang shouldered the door, knocking the sturdy housekeeper nearly off her feet. "Get McDougall, now!"

A booming voice preceded the big figure of his butler, and former sergeant, down the hallway. "Captain, I'm here."

"Check on Harris outside, then get Dr. Evers." He strode down the hall. "Mrs. Soames, get hot water and clean cloths."

Wolfgang thrust into the library, laying Zel gently on the silk-cushioned settee. Perching on the edge, he pushed aside her loosened hair to examine her face, running his hand over a red splotch on her jaw. She'd have an ugly bruise, but the bone did not appear to be broken. With stubbornly slow fingers, he pulled off her cloak and placed his hands on her chest, probing the rib cage for signs of fracture or serious injury. He first skirted around her breasts, then rested one open hand over her left breast searching for the heart beat.

Zel jerked, eyes snapping open, hands snatching his hand from her chest. "God, what are you doing?" Her face crinkled in pain as she tried to sit.

Wolfgang shifted his hands to her shoulders, effortlessly holding her in place. "Keep still, you're hurt."

"I feel dizzy." Her body relaxed back into the pillows and he released her shoulders.

"What in the name of Satan were you doing?" His initial fear flowed out beneath a flood of anger. "Are you bloody insane? What possessed you to attack a man holding a knife?"

She winced. "Please do not yell, my head hurts."

He lowered his voice only slightly, sustaining his tirade. "You're lucky to have a damn head left to hurt. Did you think to best him with this?" He lifted her surprisingly heavy reticule, unwrapping the ties from her wrist. "What the devil do you have in the blasted thing?"

"I always carry a book, and some writing materials."

Wolfgang ignored the breathiness in her voice and continued, "A book is no match for a knife and a man twice your size."

"He was not twice my size." Zel's voice sounded stronger now. "I can hold my own."

"You're a little fool. You may be tall but you weigh no more than a child." He leveled his voice and stood, roughly shrugging off his dark evening jacket. "Fires of hell, I don't mean to shout at you, but you scared me."

"Scared you?"

"A lady doesn't rush headlong into a fight, my dear, even armed with a deadly reticule." Wolfgang yanked out his cuff studs and rolled up his sleeves.

"Hhrrmmf." Mrs. Soames stood in the open doorway, steaming washbowl in her hands, cloths drapped over her forearm.

"Set the water here." He motioned to the nearby red lacquered table. "And you may go."

Mrs. Soames shook her steel-gray hair and slowly laid out the water and cloths before she turned to go. "Are you sure there is nothing else, my lord?"

"Nothing at the moment. McDougall will be back here shortly with the physician." Waving the housekeeper away, Wolfgang dipped a cloth in the hot water and resettled on the edge of the settee beside Zel. "Does anyone know where you are?"

"I can do that myself." She brushed away his hands as he tried to wash her face. "I am not hurt that badly."

"Do I have to sit on you to keep you still?" He brought the cloth to her face, pushing her hair back with his other hand, fingers brushing the top of her ear. "It's pointed."

Zel shook his hands loose, moaning as she tried to ward him off.

"Stay still." Wolfgang pressed his hip tight against hers and pulled the hair off her other ear. "Your ears are pointed!"

"Leave me alone." Zel tugged her hair down, freeing the last of the pins.

"Your hair is always pulled over them. You try to hide them, don't you?" He squelched a laugh, amazed at the tight expression on her face. "You shouldn't, you know. They really are quite, ah, unusually attractive. Elfish. They go with the rest of your face."

Zel grimaced. "Elves are terribly undignified and they are not inches short of six feet tall."

"Ah, sweet . . ." He stopped, reminded by her grimace

of her injuries. "Let me take care of you." He slipped a knuckle under her chin, tilting her face to look at the darkening bruise. "Does anyone know where you are?"

"Yes, I told Robin I was coming to see you." Her voice trailed off to a whisper. "But he did not know when."

"You were coming to see me?" Wolfgang grinned at her. "I'm exceedingly pleased. But so late at night? Where is your coach, your maid?"

Zel swallowed hard. "I came alone in a hired hack."

He opened his eyes wide, allowing his jaw to drop. "Am I to be forever lecturing you on correct behavior? What are you about, Miss Fleetwood, visiting a man alone, after midnight?"

"Oh, stuff it. I need to talk to you."

He laughed. "A few things first. I'll send for your brother to fetch you home. Your family should know where you are." He dipped the nearly forgotten cloth into the water and gently blotted it over her face, then tossed it into the bowl. "No cuts. Now about those ribs."

"You are doing nothing with my ribs." Zel tried to rise again, and his hands went back to her shoulders. She grumbled loudly, sinking into the cushions. "And Robin is not to come for me. I can get home on my own."

"Then I'll take you home." He removed his hands from her shoulders, leaning across her to rest his elbow on the back of the settee. "Why did your brother allow you to come alone?"

She bristled. "My brother does not dictate what I do."

"Perhaps you need someone to tell you what to do. This escapade may not have killed you, but any news of it will do further damage to your reputation."

"There you are again giving me lessons in propriety." She eyed him warily. "You need not sit on my lap."

Wolfgang laughed. "Perhaps I'll sit on your lap until I'm sure you won't try to get up."

"I will not get up."

"I'm not convinced." He pushed his hip more firmly against her hip, wedging her into the pillows. "Now, why do you need to talk to me?"

"This is very awkward." She closed her eyes, averting her face. "I need to request your help."

"Request away." He flashed her a broad smile. "I'm always at your service."

Zel opened her eyes, piercing him with a hard, metal-flecked stare. "Be quiet and listen, this is difficult enough without you taunting me."

Wolfgang met her glare silently, looking deeply into those tip-tilted eyes. Eyes that could belong to a cat or an elf. He swallowed another chuckle, certain that at this moment she would be displeased with either image.

"This is all your fault anyway." She challenged, while he continued his stoicly soulful look. "You took the last of Robin's money at the gambling house, his last chance to come about. Now the creditors are calling in his notes. If we do not find the money immediately he will be in debtors' prison before the week is out." She waited for his reply, but he continued to quietly regard her. Her voice rose half an octave. "You have ruined me. I could not make a decent marriage now if I was the queen of Egypt."

Wolfgang couldn't stop that telltale twitching at the corner of his mouth. It wasn't that he didn't understand her anger, some of it was well justified. But she looked so damn appealing when she was furious. And he wanted badly to kiss her. He sighed. He'd help her first and save the kissing for later.

"Do not dare laugh at me!" Zel positively raged now, as much as one can rage reclining on lush Chinese cushions, while trying to keep as far from her tormentor as possible. "If you had any honor at all, you would buy his notes!"

"I'll buy them tomorrow—"

"I have no idea why I ever thought to ask you for help. . . . You . . . what?"

"I said I'll buy them."

"Thank heavens, I knew you would help." She smiled, with no small amount of bewilderment glazing her eyes, and took his hand, squeezing his fingers in her own.

"Rrrowrr." Hecate appeared suddenly at his elbow on the settee back, hair on end and back arched, eyeing Zel as the mistress of the house would eye any other female who dared to breach her realm. Zel gasped and jumped, nearly toppling Wolfgang from the sofa. The cat held her balance, claws gripping the upholstery, golden eyes never leaving Zel.

"What is that?" Zel leaned into Wolfgang, eyes wide and glued to the battle-ready Hecate.

"*That* is my cat."

"Cat! That is a huge beast straight from the jungles."

"Hecate, I believe you have been insulted." He clicked his tongue against the roof of his mouth, the only call the haughty feline ever deigned to answer.

"Hecate. Goddess of the dark of the moon." Zel shifted, stiffly, still watching the cat. "Witch. Sorceress."

"Don't listen to her, Hecate, now she's attempting to turn your head with flattery." Wolfgang clicked again and the cat leaped over Zel, plopping onto his lap. Her long, gray coat had flattened, diminishing her still considerable size. Wolfgang scooped the animal into his arms, one hand stroking her silky head, her purr rumbling against his chest. "Hecate is no more ferocious than that horse you call a dog. Pet her, be friends."

Zel gingerly laid back on the pillows, raising a tentative hand, which he grasped, pulling it toward the cat. Hecate hissed, a soft, sibilant warning. Zel growled, tugging her hand free.

"Girls, excuse me, women, can't we learn to get along?"

"Captain." McDougall's form filled the doorway. He showed in the short, balding physician, whose unusually disheveled appearance bespoke his haste. "Dr. Evers."

Wolfgang rose, cat still perched on his arm, and took the

doctor's thin hand with his free one. "Thank you for coming." He nodded dismissal to McDougall. "Keep the coach waiting. Dr. Evers, this is Miss Fleetwood. She was attacked by footpads outside my home."

"Another attack?"

Wolfgang flashed a swift warning, effectively silencing the other man. "She received blows to her ribs and jaw. I believe nothing is broken."

"Miss Fleetwood, please remain on the cushions." Dr. Evers pulled a chair next to her as she settled back into the pillows. He took her jaw gently in his delicate fingers, turned her head, then rubbed roughly along the bruise. She groaned, yanking free of his hand. "Sorry, but I had to check the bone. It appears fine. My lord, you must leave. Miss Fleetwood will need to disrobe to enable me to examine her ribs."

"I'll stay."

"Indeed you will not." Zel frowned at Wolfgang, then addressed the doctor. "Please have a blanket brought, and we will dispense with this quickly."

Wolfgang put the cat down and rang for Mrs. Soames. "You need not disrobe completely. He only needs access to your chest."

"I will need you to lower your gown enough to remove your corset." The doctor looked to Wolfgang rather than Zel for an answer.

"She doesn't wear a corset." He surveyed the smaller man, unwilling to leave him alone with Zel, displeased at the idea of him seeing or touching any part of her. Wolfgang shook his head. Hounds of hell! What was wrong with him? The man was a doctor.

Mrs. Soames's square bulk hovered at the door. "My lord?"

"Mrs. Soames, bring a blanket, then assist Miss Fleetwood." The gray-haired woman tipped her head and hurried from the room.

Dr. Evers now addressed Zel. "Do you have any pain?"

"Yes, my jaw hurts, but it hurts here too." She indicated her chest below her left breast.

When Mrs. Soames returned with the blanket, Wolfgang led the doctor from the room, Hecate winding around his ankles. He glanced back at Zel. "I will send the doctor back in a few minutes." Zel nodded as he shut the door. He ushered the little man into his study. The room was dimly lit by a few candles scattered about the room. "May I offer you a brandy?"

"Yes." Evers sank into a deep chair. "Northcliffe, what really happened?"

Wolfgang walked to a carved teak side table and poured the amber liquid into a glass. "You surmised correctly. I was attacked again. Miss Fleetwood leaped to my rescue, pummeling the villains with her reticule."

"You surely jest?" A half smile hovered at Evers's lips.

Handing the doctor the drink, Wolfgang grinned. "Oh no, she fears nothing, certainly not a footpad double her size." He poured a few fingers of brandy into another glass, astonished at the note of pride in his voice.

"But she knows nothing of the other attacks on you?" Evers surveyed Wolfgang speculatively, sipping at his drink. "Who is she to you?"

"You may be my physician, but you have no business delving into my private life." He downed the liquid in one swallow.

"Did I strike a soft spot?" Evers's black eyes seemed to miss nothing.

"She's a friend. You may return and complete the examination." He splashed more brandy in the snifter, then slipped into a chair, Hecate settling on his lap. "I'll remain here until you finish."

Why had he so easily agreed to buy young Fleetwood's notes? Was it guilt, philanthropy, desire, or an ungodly combination of each? He stroked the cat, nursing the drink and his thoughts until he heard the library door open. He caught Evers in the hall. "What took so long? Is she badly injured, after all?"

"Miss Fleetwood's rib may have a slight fracture. I cannot tell for sure, so I thought it wise to wrap her chest. I'll call at her home day after tomorrow." Evers smiled. "Get her to reduce her activities for at least a week. She'll stay home until that bruise heals, won't she?" He continued without waiting for an answer. "I gave her some laudanum for the pain, but she's as stubborn a patient as you and does not seem inclined to use it. I expect you to take better care of her."

"She's not mine to take care of." Hecate jumped free, as Wolfgang escorted Evers down the hall. "I'll see you to the carriage."

With the doctor on his way, Wolfgang quietly reentered the library, eyes on Zel as she lay motionless on the settee, long, dark lashes fanning her pale cheeks, her face very young.

She stirred when he lowered himself onto the chair Evers had pulled near her. "I must go. Please call me a hack."

"I said I'll take you home, but after we talk." Leaning forward, he took her hand in his. "I'll have my man of affairs buy your brother's notes tomorrow. But first I'll call at your home to receive a full accounting."

Zel nodded. "I will have the names and amounts ready for you." She turned her head to meet his eyes. "What are your terms?"

"Terms?"

"Of course, terms." Her voice rose a few notes. "You cannot just give us money."

"I can't?" He smiled at her impatience.

"We will pay you back if it takes the rest of our lives." A small fire backlit her eyes as she pulled free her hand.

"It might." He frowned, ready for a fight over his next words. "But I do insist on handling your money."

"You wish to manage all our money?" Zel's eyes narrowed, her mouth tight.

"Yes, anything that comes in or goes out will do so through myself and my man of affairs." He had her full attention now, bruised jaw and rib momentarily forgotten. "I intend to have your brother trained in proper money management."

"But I have my own income." She moved on the pillows, gasped, and clutched her ribs. Wolfgang hovered over her but she waved him away. "Are you sure that doctor knows his business? It hurts worse now than before he examined me."

"You're noticing the pain more. You were stunned earlier." Wolfgang grasped her pointed little chin between his thumb and forefinger. "That bruise is darkening rapidly." He released her chin, winking at her with his own faintly discolored eye. "We have matching wounds. Mine's just a bit yellow."

Zel scanned his face. "And nearly gone. But I believe mine was more nobly obtained."

"Touché, Gamine."

"Gamine?" She stiffled a smile. "You are too familiar. And I told you earlier, I am not at all elflike."

Wolfgang laughed, staring at her until her pale face flushed bright pink. "I'm pleased to see your color return." He glanced about the room. "Where's the laudanum Evers gave you?"

Zel gestured toward a corner table. "I will not take it."

"You'll take it before you leave." He strode to the table and grasped the bottle. "Don't be so stubborn." Turning back to her, he pulled out the stopper, waving it threateningly. "You won't leave until you take it. You'll need it to sleep."

"I will do fine without it."

"We'll battle over the laudanum later." He dropped into

the chair beside her again. "You said you have your own income. Who handled it and the family finances?"

"I handle the family's income."

"Not effectively, if your brother is on his way to debtors' prison."

"I have done the best I can." She spoke softly but distinctly. "I have not always been able to lay my hands on the money. Most is directed back into the estate by the executor, any my father gets is gone the moment it touches his fingers." She looked fixedly at the ceiling. "Being a woman I could not ensure that the money came directly to me. Robin and I have small incomes from my mother's father. But Robin's, like Father's, goes to the gaming tables. My income has often been the sole support of the family."

"Forgive me." Wolfgang tapped his foot against the sofa leg and toyed with the medicine bottle. "I'm sure you handled the money as well as humanly possible. But as you said, a woman's monetary control can be easily circumvented. I intend to get agreements in writing that all Fleetwood money goes through me. Every expenditure will be documented and justified, and a certain amount will be earmarked to pay me for the loan."

"So I cannot buy so much as a ribbon without your approval?"

Wolfgang grinned. "Nary a chemise or petticoat."

"I do not like this."

He leaned forward. "But you'll agree to it."

Zel sighed deeply. "I suppose if Father and Robin sign over their incomes to you, you will have more control than I could ever hope to have. I cannot afford to disagree." She continued, her voice so low she appeared to be talking to herself. "This is all happening too easily. What about interest?"

"I do have one condition." He laughed at her moan. "I would request a favor of you in lieu of interest."

"A favor?" Her mouth tightened. "What favor?"

"I haven't decided yet." Wolfgang paused before meeting her gaze. "But I promise it won't be anything you can't do."

"Fine, we will work it out later." She looked oddly relieved. It was his turn to think this was happening too easily.

"Now you'll take your laudanum and I'll take you home." He stood, pushing the chair back noisily. "Do you need a little tea or brandy?"

"No, just get me a glass and I will drink it straight."

"Brave woman. I'm glad you decided not to fight me. It would have been a bit awkward to force the stuff down your throat." Wolfgang took the vial, poured a small amount into a goblet, and handed it to her. "Bottoms up."

Zel drank quickly and pushed herself off the cushions, snorting indelicately. "I do not know which is worse, the medicine or the pain."

He took the goblet, placing it and the vial on the table, then helped her to her feet. "The coach should be back now, but first we must seal our bargain."

"Oh?" She surveyed his face with narrowed eyes.

"With a kiss, of course."

Zel laughed, then groaned. "You can give me a little kiss if you keep your hands to your sides."

"Then you'll have to kiss me."

She leaned forward and pecked his cheek. "There."

"No. That won't do. I want a real kiss. Put your hands on my shoulders and kiss my lips." Seeing her hesitation, he added, "I promise I won't hurt you."

Her hands went slowly to his shoulders.

"Now that doesn't hurt, does it?"

Zel shook her head. Standing on tiptoe, she met his lips with a pressure both gentle and firm. Expecting her to pull away immediately, Wolfgang felt a wave of pleasure when she softly nibbled at the corner of his mouth. He didn't move or breathe as her hands slid up his neck and into his hair where it hung loose at his nape. A shudder coursed through him when her tongue touched his lower lip. She stopped, stepping backward, hands falling to her sides. Her voice was low and shaky. "You are impossible."

"Me?" He moaned. "You did the kissing. All I did was enjoy it."

Zel took another step back, suddenly loosing her balance. Hecate squawked. Wolfgang grabbed for Zel as she fell into a life-sized statue in the corner. She twisted in his grasp, latching onto the statue to steady herself. Hanging on to one of its many arms, she gasped. "What in God's name is this?"

Taking her arms, he pulled her gently to him. "Steady. I have you. Don't reinjure yourself." He stroked her back, whispering in her ear. "You've just thrown yourself into the arms of Kali, goddess of dreams and death."

She shivered. "Take me home."

Wolfgang released her and snatched her cloak from a nearby chair. Swinging it around her shoulders, he slipped his arm through hers. "I'd carry you to the coach, but I might hurt your ribs more."

"I can walk by myself." She held herself erect with obvious effort. "My spectacles, where are they?"

"They weren't on your nose when I brought you in. I'll send a groom out to look for them, when I get back."

The laudanum worked fast. Zel slumped against him, fully asleep before the carriage had gone a block. He slid his arm around her shoulders, drawing her securely to his chest, resting his cheek against her hair. For all her intelligence she sometimes seemed a little lacking in common sense. Tonight she showed no sense at all. Imagine coming to his rescue against a knife-wielding ruffian, armed with nothing but an overly heavy reticule. But she was accustomed to protecting others. She spent her life and energy watching over her family and ill-used women. Had anyone ever taken care of her?

CHAPTER 9

MELODY

A sweet or pleasurable sequence
of sounds

"WHAT IS HE THINKING, calling so early? Why, 'tis not even nine." Zel pointed out the unadorned blue muslin day dress. "That one will do, Maggie."

"Mrs. Stanfield and the young master are still abed." Maggie helped her out of her old lawn night rail. "You'll not be having your bath?"

"I will try to bathe later." She tugged at the bandages around her chest and eased her head through the neck of the wash-worn chemise, surprised at how sore her ribs were. Even her jaw still ached. She would not have slept without the laudanum.

Perching on the wobbly stool by her dressing table, Zel watched Maggie pull a stocking up her leg. "He needs to learn that the world does not revolve around him. You should have heard him last night, ordering me about, insisting I see the doctor. He practically forced me to take laudanum, and accept his escort home." Wincing, she tied the garter as Maggie held out the other stocking. The bottom was threadbare, but could sustain a few more wearings before requiring darning. Unfortunately, Aunt Diana's treasure trove of gowns had contained no accessories or undergarments. "He even asked if I had permission to be out on my own!"

"Men do act that way, Miss Zel. Maybe they can't help themselves." Maggie held the gown as Zel stood and carefully slipped her head and arms through the openings. Zel had given up convincing Maggie that calling her by only her Christian name was acceptable. "Miss Zel" was better than "Miss Fleetwood."

"They need to be taught differently." Zel smoothed the skirt as Maggie efficiently tied the fastenings. "Do you know he did not even thank me for coming to his rescue?"

" 'Twas probably a blow to his pride to have a woman disarm his attacker." Maggie finished the last tie. "Should I style your hair or just wind it at your neck?"

"Wind it loosely." She sat straight on the stool as Maggie quickly wound and pinned her hair. "If it looks a little sloppy that will be fine. Northcliffe knows I am no fashion plate."

The pins all in place, Maggie walked to the armoire, pausing at a lower shelf. "Your blue or white slippers?"

"The blue." Zel sighed loudly. "I wish I could stay angry at him, but he seemed sincerely concerned about my well-being." She plucked at the bodice. "I really do not know what possessed me to pounce on that footpad." She tucked a stray lock of hair under the loose knot, but it escaped back down her neck. "I saw him attacking Wol—Lord Northcliffe and I jumped in without thinking. I seem to be doing that often, of late. Jumping in without thinking, that is."

"You could have been hurt much worse." Maggie pulled a slipper on her foot.

"I know." Zel bent to tie the strap at her ankle but a twinge of pain from her rib forced her to allow Maggie to finish with her slippers. "He agreed too easily to pay Robin's debts, but I felt it unwise to question him closely." She looked at her feet to hide the warmth rising in her cheeks. Maggie did not need to know what she had been prepared to offer him. "Tell Smythe to escort him to the dining room and see that Robin, Aunt Diana and my father meet us in the drawing room later."

Zel stared at her reflection in the glass. The bruise had turned a deep purple. Even without the pain, she would be housebound until the color faded enough to be covered by powder. Frowning at herself, she felt frightened and grateful and most of all confused, certainly not ready to see him. The kiss, *her* kiss, was too fresh. Not to mention that devastating carriage ride she struggled to purge from her mind.

She could still feel the texture of his lips on her tongue, still taste the brandy that had lingered there. As she looked at her lips, her frown deepened. Lord, but she was drawn to him, dangerously, foolishly drawn to him. Now she was in his debt, tied to him irretrievably. Their bargain had also freed her and for that she owed him. But what did she owe him? He asked a favor. What it would be she did not care to contemplate. Yet it could not be worse than what she had been prepared to do.

Stuffing a carefully folded paper into her pocket, she walked steadfastly down the steps, pausing briefly before the dining room door. She took a full breath before pushing open the door. Wolfgang, pacing before the window, turned as she entered. His crooked smile warmed his lean, square features, making him disarmingly young and handsome. Another full breath failed to slow the pulse beating in her throat.

"Sorry to be so early." He crossed the room in several long strides. "But I couldn't sleep. I wanted to see you."

Zel returned his smile and without thinking clasped his outstretched hands in hers, swooping upward to kiss his cheek. Wolfgang twisted slightly and her lips brushed his. She pulled back quickly, meeting his molten eyes with a blush, envisioning what could have happened between them if the events of last night had gone differently. If she had made her rash offer and been accepted. Throat suddenly dry, she choked. "Thank you."

"To what do I owe such a greeting, my dear?" The edges of his mouth curved down as he took her chin gently in his hand. "By the Prince of Darkness, that bruise is ugly. You won't be able to appear in public for at least a week."

"Better than that, thanks to you." Her smile widened as she directed him to a chair at the table. "Breakfast is not usually served till ten, but I have asked for some tea and biscuits."

"What is better, thanks to me?" Wolfgang held her chair as she settled herself.

Zel felt his warmth and breathed in his distinctive scent, as he took the seat beside her. "Why I need never be seen in public again, unless I wish it."

"What do you mean?" As he leaned toward her, she watched his long fingers curl around the arm of her chair.

"I do not have to flaunt myself on the marriage mart."

"I still don't understand." He stroked the polished wood, back and forth along the chair arm.

"With Robin's debts paid, I no longer need to marry for money or any other reason for that matter." She smiled broadly. "Thanks to you, the ton will see no more of this happy spinster."

Wolfgang scowled, his knuckles about her chair arm turned white. "Was the idea of marriage so repugnant?"

"Of course it was." She peered up at him, puzzled by his reaction. "You know that. It was probably the one thing we fully agreed upon. Why would you ask such a question?"

"I don't know." He sat very still, eyes under lowered brows intent on her. "Maybe I thought you were changing your mind."

"About marriage? Never!"

"Most women enter into marriage without question." Wolfgang tapped a finger on the tabletop. "I know you value freedom, but I sense something more has soured you towards matrimony."

Zel turned away, looking out the window. "My parents had an unhappy marriage. I do not wish to repeat their misery." She could hear his finger still tapping at the table but continued her perusal of the garden.

"There is more you aren't telling me." His voice thrummed so soft and low, she felt compelled to shift her gaze back to him. "What is it, Gamine?"

She should correct his use of that odd endearment. Not only did she let it stand but she suddenly wanted to tell him about her parents. "It was worse than miserable." She twisted the loose strand of hair at her neck around her forefinger. "My father beat my mother. Often and brutally."

Wolfgang clasped her hand, untwining the hair from her finger. "I'm sorry."

"I was so afraid all the time, waiting for the fighting to start." Zel looked down at their hands. "I felt so helpless. There was nothing I could do to stop my father. He gambled, and when he lost at cards or any ridiculous bet, he drank. When he drank, he hit my mother. He always promised never to do it again, that things would get better. But they only got worse."

"No one should have to live through that." Wolfgang brought her hand to his mouth, softly kissing each fingertip.

She smiled tightly, blinking back hot tears. "Soon there did not need to be any drinking or gambling to get him started. He would beat her for any real or imagined slight." She closed her eyes. "When he beat her for failing to find a way to budget beefsteak into her minuscule household allowance, I learned to pinch pennies enough to buy his steaks. But he found another reason to hit her."

"I'm sorry." He held her palm lightly against his lips.

Strangely comforted by the intimate gesture, Zel didn't pull away. "He rarely hit Robin and me. I think somehow Mother protected us, took his wrath all on herself." The words were tumbling out, as if beyond her conscious control. "It finally killed her. Not the beatings directly. She just got tired of living that way and gave up. There was nothing I could do to save her. I was thirteen years old and I took over the duties of mistress of the house. I had been doing most of it anyway."

She opened dry eyes and met Wolfgang's. "My father threatened me once after her death. I told him if he ever hit me I would leave home forever or shoot him, whichever struck my fancy at the time. He must have believed me, for although he bullied me, he never hit me."

Wolfgang breathed deeply into her palm, then lowered their still-joined hands to her lap. "I see why you would never wish to be in a position where another could control your life."

Smythe entered quietly, head diplomatically lowered, and proceeded to lay out the tea service, biscuits, and marmalade.

Zel eased her hand free of Wolfgang's grasp. "Thank you, Smythe. I will pour and serve. Is Robin up?"

"Yes, miss, he is dressing and will be down shortly. Sir Edward is in the study. Mrs. Stanfield's maid is with her." The breakfast arranged, Smythe left the room.

"Do you take cream?" At his silent affirmative she added cream to the tea and handed Wolfgang cup and saucer, aware that his eyes followed every move. "Help yourself to the biscuits."

"Zel. May I call you Zel?"

"You have been doing so for some time."

"But I wanted to make it mutual. I mean we'll be almost as close as family now." His fingers rested briefly on her arm. "Would you call me Wolfgang?"

"Wolfgang." She tried the sound out loud, softly. "I suppose I could. But not Wolfie?" She teased, attempting to put aside her earlier, distressing confessions.

He grimaced comically and seemed to take her lead.

"I've tried to lose that nickname most of my life, but Grandmama does as she pleases and she pleases to call me that." He looked at her with mock severity. "I don't give you leave to use it."

"I would never dream of calling you Wolfie, Wolfie." Zel gave him a sweet smile then reached into her pocket, withdrawing and unfolding a sheet of paper. "The list of creditors and amounts owing."

"Good. My solicitor and man of affairs will start buying the notes today and meet with your brother, father, you, and myself tomorrow to sign the agreements." Wolfgang took the paper, laying it on the table without so much as glancing at it.

"I warn you." Zel paused to spread marmalade on a biscuit. "Robin is not pleased. He has an independent streak."

"Now why does that fail to surprise me?"

She frowned at him. "He may not be agreeable now, but he will come around as he realizes this is for the best."

"Will he sign over his income?"

"I can convince him to do so."

"I'll also make it very clear to him that I'm doing this for you, not him." There was a look she could not read in those twilight gray eyes. "Will that help his pride?"

"I am not sure." Zel could feel her skin warming under his gaze. "It might make it worse."

"How so?"

"He thinks there is something besides friendship in your offer to help." She bent her head and took a tiny bite of her biscuit.

"What does he think?"

She swallowed, plunging in. "He thinks I am your mistress."

Wolfgang lurched to his feet, toppling the chair and spilling his tea. "My God! He what?"

"I explained that you agreed to help because you felt bad

for the damage done us and because you and I are now friends." Zel smiled tentatively. "That is what we are, friends?"

"Of course we're friends." He smiled his boyish grin but his eyes burned her as he straightened his chair and sat.

"I believe, through all of this, we will become the best of friends." She ignored the look in his eyes, concentrating on the much safer dimple.

"Of course." Zel could feel his eyes still on her as he pulled a small package from his jacket pocket. "Before I forget, I have your eyeglasses. McDougall claims they are beyond repair. I'd be happy to replace them." She leaned over as he opened the packet, dumping the contents on the table before her. The mangled, shattered spectacles were tangled around an elegant, sheathed knife. "My dagger. I thought it was lost. McDougall didn't tell me he found it." He reached for the dagger.

Her hand closed over the hilt of the weapon first, lifting and weighing it in her palm. She slid it from the sheath, holding the blade before her, watching Wolfgang around the shining edge. "You carry a dagger?"

"Sometimes." He lowered his hand, looking away.

"This was found with my eyeglasses?" At his nod Zel continued. "You lost it last night in the fight?" He nodded again. "Why do you carry a knife?"

Wolfgang watched her quietly for several seconds. "I frequent places not known for their genteel patrons."

"Like the gambling house?"

"Like the hell, yes."

"For a weapon this is quite lovely. You have an eye for beauty." She turned away, stroking the jewel-encrusted hilt. "After falling into the arms of Kali last night I couldn't help but notice all the lovely objects from the East in your home."

"Yes, I think I have an eye for beauty." His hand closed over hers and the dagger hilt.

"You have been to India and the Orient?" Zel found

herself reluctant to move her hand from beneath the warm strength of his fingers.

"I spent several years there, wandering about, making a little money, before I inherited my title."

"Northcliffe, must you maul my sister in our own home?" Robin's cold, stinging voice rang out as he marched into the room. "What the hell are you doing with that knife?"

"Robin." Zel pulled free of Wolfgang's grip. "Lord Northcliffe has called to talk about the details of the arrangement I told you about last night." Robin glared at the dagger in her hands, and she quickly placed it on the table in front of Wolfgang.

"I was telling your sister how I had the dagger made especially for me." Wolfgang sheathed and pocketed the knife.

Pushing his hair roughly from his brow, Robin snarled. "I'll keep my eyes on you, Northcliffe."

Zel stood, yanking her brother toward a chair, her voice low and urgent. "I told you, I am not his mistress. Stop making a fool of yourself."

"Fleetwood, listen to your sister." Wolfgang jumped to his feet at Zel's other side. "She's not my mistress."

"And I'm supposed to believe that!" Robin sneered. "Why would you just hand over the money?"

Wolfgang edged Zel aside, facing Robin directly. "I admire your sister and don't wish to see her forced into a marriage that would make her unhappy."

Robin took a step forward. "Gets richer by the second. *You* concerned about my sister's happiness?"

"Yes, I am." With obvious effort, Wolfgang kept his voice even as he folded his arms over his chest. "Buying your notes is nothing to me and everything to her. But you'll pay me back, and to ensure that, I'll control your finances."

"You wish to be my warden?" Robin raised a threatening fist, the tang of bitterness in his voice strong. Zel, fearing the confrontation would turn physical, tried again to pull him into a chair.

"I wouldn't put it quite like that." Wolfgang paused, stretching to his full height. "This arrangement is to protect your sister and teach you financial responsibility."

"You! Protecting my sister!" Robin rolled slightly on the balls of his feet, his voice booming in the small room. "Isn't that rather like the fox guarding the henhouse?"

"Robinson, dear, now keep your voice down and mind your temper." Aunt Diana ordered gently as she bustled into the room, stepping neatly between the two posturing men. "Doesn't the Bible say blessed are the peacemakers for they shall be . . . ah, filled. Or is it inherit something? Oh, at least they are blessed." She took Robin's arm. "Now let us all sit and work this out like the civilized beings we are."

WHERE IN THE DEMON'S LAIR was Jenkins? An out-of-work valet must have designed this clothing. The cuff could not be fastened with only two hands. Wolfgang tugged at the thin fabric, trying to keep the holes steady with the hand inside the sleeve while inserting the stud with the other hand. The cloth slipped from his grasp. The stud skittered across the floor. Hecate watched him silently, with unblinking eyes. "Damn, you're no help." The cat blinked once and proceeded to wash her paw. He gave up his bid for sartorial independence, yanking on the bell rope.

Jenkins appeared before Hecate had moved on to her second paw. His teeth flashed white between scarred lips. "Has my lord been trying to dress himself again?"

"Don't harass me, just do it. You valets are all in league against your employers." He grumbled, picking up the stud, pressing it in Jenkins's hand. "I have no idea why I allowed you and Ridgemont to talk me into dressing formally for an at-home dinner."

"If one wishes to acquire a certain position, one must

learn to play the part." Jenkins quickly slipped the studs in place.

"I know, I know, but why can't the bloody Whigs be as radical about their dress and manners as they are about their politics?" He jerked out his arms for Jenkins to slide on the embroidered waistcoat.

Jenkins worked his way down the row of buttons. "Do you go to see your lady tomorrow?"

"My lady?" Wolfgang frowned down at the man's snow-white hair. "The devil, but you're a nosy old bastard."

"My parentage has never been in question. I was only wondering how the courtship progressed?" Jenkins lifted the finely tailored Weston jacket off the seat of a chair, grimacing as he shook out the wrinkles.

"Courtship?" Wolfgang thrust his way into the dark green superfine jacket, straining the shoulder seams. "Can I not admire a woman without wedding bells ringing in everyone's ears? For your information, *she* wants to be friends."

He twitched as Jenkins smoothed the jacket over his shoulders and back. Bloody friends, in a pig's eye! He may have rescued her from sacrifice on the matrimonial altar, but she was not free of him. She could have her little friendship, but she would soon learn that a friendship with him did not mean gossiping over cups of tea.

Great flaming fires of Hell! What did one do with a woman so wary of men? Her father should be shot and hung, then drawn and quartered. How could a man with any decency at all hit a woman? Even his own father, who thought nothing of beating his son inches short of death, never struck his wife or daughters. And after Zel's father was diposed off, her brother should be poisoned. Slowly, painfully.

He smiled grimly when he finally entered Hardwicke Hall's formal drawing room. Rafael Langford, duke of Ridgemont, was elegant, as always, in his gray-and-mid-night-blue formal attire, standing in a militarily correct pose at the mantel. Sir Frederick Ransley slouched his huge frame comfortably in a silk, cushioned settee, his black trousers and jacket wrinkled and well worn.

"So, Wolf, when is the wedding?" Raf shook his hand, the corners of his sculpted mouth turning up in a half smile.

"You're already getting on my nerves." Wolfgang growled, breaking away and pouring a substantial amount of brandy in a snifter. "And you just got here."

"Don't do it. Don't be a bloody fool twice." Freddie straightened, eyeing Wolfgang warily.

"I have no intention of being a bloody fool." He flung himself into a carved teakwood chair, the brandy swirling dangerously near the rim of the glass. "My first wife will be my only wife."

"But you're still seeing the chit." Rafael curled one slender finger around his chin. "And the rumor mill churns on."

"Don't see why you can't stay away from them." Freddie's hand dwarfed the delicate china cup as he nodded sagely. "Women bring nothing but grief."

"Not all of us wish to live as monks, Ransley." Wolfgang swung his feet onto a lion's head footstool, challenge in his tone. They wouldn't find it easy to circle in for the kill.

Rafael took a gentlemanly sip of his brandy and raised perfectly shaped eyebrows. "Oh? That's not what I hear."

"What do you mean?"

"I'm just repeating the word in my club, Wolf." Raf exchanged a glance with Freddie before returning his attention to Wolfgang. "They say you haven't been with another woman since you met her. Betting is fierce at White's. It must be unbelievable at your club."

Wolfgang muttered, kicking the footstool as he yanked his feet off its delicately painted surface. "Damn clubs, bet on every bloody thing. A man can't cross the street without a bet on whom he'll bed on the other side."

"Is it true?"

"Is what true?" Wolfgang jerked to his feet, avoiding Raf's see-all eyes.

"Do you have a mistress?" Rafael persisted.

"No!"

"Then get one." Raf smiled thinly. "Or marry Miss Fleetwood. Better yet, Wolf, do both."

"Ridgemont, leave off." Freddie drained the black coffee, laced with Irish whiskey, from his cup. "They're not betting at my club."

Rafael laughed harshly. "You don't have a club, Ransley."

"But I'm welcomed in every tavern across England."

"The ones you haven't torn up recently."

"True, but at least I'm not so stupid as to keep a mistress." Freddie pulled at his already disarrayed neckcloth. "Maybe Wolf's finally getting smart."

Wolfgang nodded his thanks to Frederick. "Right. I don't need a mistress."

"And England will sink into the seas tomorrow." Raf would allow no escape. "You obviously are not getting what you need from Miss Fleetwood."

"Satan's satin slippers, Rafael!" Wolfgang paced to the window. "She's a lady."

"So, you finally admit it. Now marry her and end your misery."

Freddie's deep bass chimed in. "Or start it."

"She'll never marry me anyway." Wolfgang pushed at the heavy draperies, staring unfocused through the windowpane. "I freed her from the altar when I paid her brother's debts. Plus she's afraid of men and marriage."

"Wolf, no woman's afraid of marriage." Raf's cultured voice enunciated very word. "So you did pay his debts? You paid the gaming notes of a man who may want you dead?"

"I thought it would put him in my debt, and he would back off." He ran his fingers over the cool, smooth window glass, trying to center his thoughts.

"But it didn't work out that way." Frederick commented so softly he barely heard it.

"Fleetwood knew Zel was coming to see me to ask for help, and was furious. He thinks she has become my mistress."

"He knew she meant to approach you before the last attack?" Raf took off like a hound after the scent of a fox.

"Yes, but it couldn't be him." Wolfgang met Raf's searching eyes. "He might be happy to injure me for touching her, but he would never allow her to be hurt."

"If he hired the men, leaving the job to them, he wouldn't know if she was there, let alone be able to protect her."

"Ha, Raf, as usual, you're too bright for your own good." Freddie eased the empty cup and saucer onto an inlaid end table. "The man's done in. Where would he get the money to hire the footpads?"

"It needn't cost him much, Freddie, especially if he has favors to collect."

"So, he's still a suspect." Wolfgang balanced on the narrow windowsill. "How the hell can I befriend the sister when I may have to arrest the brother for trying to kill me?"

"You'd better figure it out. The brother thinks you stole his money and debauched his sister." Freddie stretched his big frame, then slumped back into the cushions. "He's been in town the day of each attack. Good chance he's your man, Wolf."

"Don't jump too quickly." Rafael turned to the fireplace, studying his reflection in the mirror. "We have other suspects to consider. What of your wife's brother? It's been five years since her death. But he still blames you. I know he's threatened you, but is he angry enough to kill?"

"God, I hate this." Wolfgang pushed off the sill, stalking across the room. "Someone hates me enough to kill me." He joined Raf at the mantel, scanning his own eyes in the silvered glass. "Simon has been nursing his hatred. Perhaps he's ready to kill me, even without the duel I continue to refuse."

"That's two strong suspects." Raf's eyes converged with Wolfgang's in the glass, his voice soft and thoughtful. "And what of Newton? He's been close at hand lately."

"That rivalry's ancient history." Wolfgang turned, leaning against the mantel. "He can be vindictive and cruel, but I'm not sure premeditated murder is part of his repertoire."

"He would get an unholy joy from making you squirm." Freddie grumbled, surveying Wolfgang from behind thick, lowered brows. "But with no true aim of murder."

"Isadora has often been with him, as well as his new protégé, Melbourne." Wolfgang mused aloud. "Perhaps they're playing a dangerous parlor game."

"Possible." Raf's hand rested briefly on his shoulder. "What of your cousin and aunt?"

"They're ambitious and greedy. But what point to murder? My cousin, being the child of a sister, could not inherit the title or Cliffehaven."

"But they would inherit *your* money and the unentailed estates. And those alone are worthy of murder. You are also the last of the line," Rafael speculated. "It's unlikely but the crown may be willing, for the right price, to bestow the title through a female line."

"Quite a list we have, dear Wolfgang." Frederick's mouth almost cracked into a smile, but his eyes remained grim. "And we haven't even begun to consider all those cuckolded husbands."

"Lucifer's quizzing glass!" Wolfgang laid his forehead on the mantel. "Enough! Raf's already beaten me with that stick."

"Where do we begin? Too many bored wives." He could hear the wicked grin in Raf's voice. "And Wolf has been dedicated to pleasing them all."

"But the husbands either didn't know or didn't care." Wolfgang pleaded in his defense.

"Except the ones you winged in duels."

"Damnation, you two are ganging up on me. I haven't

dueled in years." He felt like he was sparring with Gentleman Jackson, in duplicate. "And I never killed anyone."

"Too good a shot," Freddie mumbled, "didn't need to."

"We come to an impasse, on the husbands." Raf summed up, finishing off his drink. "But we have a substantial list of suspects. My men will continue their investigations. Freddie, have some of your unsavory cronies scout out the stews and docks. We need to find some footpads." He signaled them up like an orchestral conductor. "What's for dinner? I'm famished."

"HE'S IN THE DRAWING ROOM, miss." Aunt Diana's maid, Sally, giggled, poking her head through the bedroom door.

Zel unfolded and rolled from the bed, sucking in her breath with the sharp cramp. No need to ask who "he" was. Wolfgang had called and stayed long past the proper visiting time the last two days and now was back for a third. Notes were purchased, agreements signed, plans set out. Father smiled happily. Robin frowned sullenly. But at least he seemed no longer on the attack. If only *she* did not feel so attacked.

That was unfair. Wolfgang had been a perfect gentleman, too perfect. Perhaps that was the trouble. She waited, like a pheasant in the brush to be chased out to face the hunter's gun.

She stood, brushing aside the sudden wave of pain and nausea. Straightening her skirts, she made her way down the hall. Zel quietly opened the door to find him standing before the fireplace. Did the man never sit down, except on her skirts? His thick, black hair was tied back but curled around his neck. His shoulders, broad and muscled in his close-fitting jacket, tapered to narrow waist and hips. Her fingers tingled. She vigorously rubbed them, the soft noise drawing his attention.

He whirled about, his quick, crooked grin fading to a

pensive frown. "I thought you were healing, but you look so pale and pinched. What's wrong?"

"I have a bit of the headache." She sat in a gold-brocaded settee, motioning him to sit in the chair opposite her.

Wolfgang settled himself beside her on the settee, placing a hand on her forehead. "You're not warm. Do you feel nauseated?"

"I will be fine. Do not make a fuss."

"Would you like tea? Where's the bell? I'll ring for tea." He rushed into the hall, calling for Smythe, before Zel could answer. She tried to rub the spasm from her abdomen, brows knit, body taut.

"Satan's horns, Zel, what's wrong?" He was at her side, easing her onto her back, arranging pillows beneath her. "I'll send for the doctor."

"I do not need a doctor." She surely sounded too weak, her protest would need to be stronger to stop him. "I am not ill, this is normal, nothing to worry about."

"Nothing to worry about! You're pale, almost ready to faint. You're in pain." Wolfgang knelt, cloudy eyes only inches from hers. "And you say this is normal?"

"I swear, I will be fine, in a few days."

He frowned at her, then nodded knowingly. "Your courses. I should have known."

"Please . . ." Zel's face heated. She did not know how to continue. This was not a subject one discussed with a man.

"Don't be embarrassed. I've been around women all my life."

"The tea, miss." Smythe balanced the tea tray in the doorway, eyes darting about the room.

Remaining on his knees, Wolfgang motioned to the nearest table. "Set it down. I'll serve. Miss Fleetwood is a bit indisposed. Bring a hot water bottle, very hot, and brandy."

"I do not drink brandy." Zel sat up gingerly, as Smythe silently left the room.

Wolfgang fluffed up the pillows and nestled her back down, swinging her legs gently onto the settee. "Lie still. I'll have you feeling better in no time. Now tell me where it hurts."

"My lord, please." Her voice came out little more than a squeak, and she knew her skin glowed scarlet with embarrassment.

"Now, don't start 'my lording' me again, I thought we'd progressed far beyond that." His long fingers pushed her hair off her brow and temples. He smiled as he skimmed over the tips of her ears. "Try to relax, Gamine. You only make the pain worse when you tense up. Where does your head hurt?"

"The left side, especially around the temple and eye." Zel exhaled deeply as his fingers pressed gently against her temple, then circled her eye.

"And your abdomen? Cramping?" He chuckled softly when she stiffened, anticipating his next move. "No, I promise I won't stroke you there."

Smythe returned, placing his burdens on the table near the tea, frowning bravely at Wolfgang. Wolfgang showed his teeth, and the little butler scurried out of the room.

"Let me lift you a bit." Standing, he wedged his hands under her arms, shifting her more upright on the pillows. He pressed the hot water bottle firmly above the juncture of her legs and hips. "Are you comfortable?"

"Yes." Zel nodded as he closed the curtains.

Wolfgang poured tea and brandy in a cup and raised it to her mouth. "Drink it."

She pursed her lips, wrinkling her nose. "I think that will make me feel worse."

"No, it's better for you than laudanum and it will dull the pain." Wolfgang pressed the cup edge against her lower lip. "Now be a good patient and take your medicine."

Zel sipped a little of the fiery liquid, sputtering as it hit her throat. She put a hand to the cup. "Enough."

"A few more sips, Gamine."

Reluctantly, Zel complied, feeling a warmth spreading through her chest.

"Now, I need to disturb you one last time." Urging one more sip of brandy before he set the cup aside, he then pushed her gently forward, removing several pillows, slipping onto the sofa beneath her. She tensed her back, pain shot to her head. "Relax, I'll not harm you. I can soothe the pain."

Wolfgang slid a pillow onto his lap underneath her shoulders, another under her head. "There, you're not even touching me. Now, breathe deep and long." He smiled into her eyes as she tried to relax into the cushions. His fingers burrowed through her hair to her scalp. "There are pathways of energy throughout the body. When they become obstructed we experience pain and illness. The Chinese can unblock these pathways through application of steady, gentle pressure." He pressed two spots at both sides of the base of her skull, massaging with tiny, circular strokes.

"Many practitioners use needles." When her shoulders twitched involuntarily he increased the pressure. "Close your eyes. I use my fingers, not needles. Mr. Yang, father's butler, an innocent heathen, coerced into Christianity by my missionary father, was a master, an artist."

Zel sighed as he found a responsive place, farther up her skull. "I cannot believe that—"

"Ssshh, give me your hand." Wolfgang rested both their hands on her lap by the water bottle, feeling her body relax as he squeezed with a steady pressure at the base of the V between her thumb and index finger. He moved his hand at her head up the back of her skull, rubbing again in small strokes.

"It is amazing. I am feeling relief."

"Close your eyes and your mouth. Relax into it and you'll feel even better." He moved his fingers slowly down the designated points at the back of her head, pausing at each with the tiny circle strokes. Her breathing was strong and rhythmic as he moved his hand to her ear, pushing and squeezing at selected spots on the lobe and whorls. Her hand lay in his, warm and limp. Her breasts rose and fell slowly as her breathing deepened. Wolfgang ceased the pressure, holding her hand loosely, cradling her head in his palm. In the dim light he studied the clean lines of her face. The stubborn little chin. The full, slightly parted lips. The straight short nose. The high, sharp cheekbones. The elfishly pointed ears. The silky mane of hair. Even closed, he could envision the golden flash of fire in her eyes.

The door creaked, the thin wedge of light from the hall widened.

"Zel? Wolfgang?" Grandmama hesitated beside Zel's butler, highlighted just outside the doorway, and peered into the room. Spying him, then Zel, she opened her mouth to speak. A visible warmth spread over her face. She smiled, clanging, clamoring wedding bells reflected in her gaze.

Mephistopheles's misbegotten, if he didn't hear them too.

CHAPTER 10

VIVACE

Performed in a spirited, vivacious manner

ZEL WATCHED, through the light drizzle, as Lady Melbourne twirled her umbrella and pointedly guided her young daughter across the street. The women looked through her as if she were invisible. But she did not feel at all invisible. In fact she was certain everyone on the street had witnessed the slight.

"Maggie, I believe I have received the ultimate rejection, the cut direct." Zel's legs shook as she blinked back the hot tears gathering around her eyelids and lashes. "This was not supposed to hurt."

After a housebound week sprinkled with visits from Wolfgang, his grandmother, and Emily, she had been dying to get out on any excuse and a morning shopping expedition seemed ideal. Now she wished she had locked herself away in her room. Zel shook her head. A childish act performed by a silly woman should not bother her so much. She carefully placed one foot before the other, head high. Maggie slid an arm through hers, lending a little stability as Zel's knees threatened to give.

"We will buy Aunt Diana's ribbon here." Zel pushed

into a small Bond Street shop, pleased her voice remained steady, if a trifle high-pitched. Lady March and her niece stood at the counter, pointedly looking in the opposite direction. "Then we will take a hackney home."

"Grizelda! Miss Fleetwood!" The shrill soprano that could only be Lady Horeton spurred Zel to press doggedly forward. "Come here, my dear, isn't this a luscious color?" The woman caressed a bolt of brilliant yellow silk with her tiny, perfectly formed fingers, lifting the corner to Zel.

"A perfect color for you, Lady Horeton." Zel clenched her fists, snagging a fingernail on the soft muslin of her own gown. "My complexion could never withstand it."

"How are you, my dear? You look a bit pale," she continued, oblivious to Zel's attempt to respond. "How is your dear friend, Lord Northcliffe?"

Zel choked, pulling her nail free. "I believe he is well."

Lady March and her niece stalked out of the shop, nodding slightly to Lady Horeton. Zel must have disappeared again for all the attention paid her, and this was the same Lady March who had made a donation to Aquitaine House only days before. The pretty little debutante on Lady March's arm twisted her head, wide eyes focused on Zel, obviously grappling with what foul things must have been done to earn such censure.

Zel placed some coins in Maggie's hand, whispering, "You buy the ribbon. The shopkeeper will probably refuse my money."

Maggie frowned, opening her mouth to speak. She glanced at Zel, then moved to purchase the length of lavender ribbon.

Zel turned back to Lady Horeton, who openly stared at her. Her hand flew to her face. Lord, could she see the waning bruise on her jaw? The powder should have covered the traces of mottled yellow and brown.

"I haven't seen you about of late." The petite blonde still scrutinized her face. Did she see it? Was she looking for other bruises? "Have you become bored with society so soon?"

"I had duties at home." She wondered how she could find out what Lady Horeton knew of the last week, and Wolfgang's new role in her family. If her own brother believed she was Wolfgang's mistress, would anyone among the ton think better of her? Zel shivered. Only she knew how close it came to being true. "I believe my errands are complete. Good day, Lady Horeton."

"Good day, Grizelda."

Taking a deep breath, Zel braved the damp streets, umbrella pulled low over her head, praying to find no more acquaintances perusing the shops. A walk home would be pleasant, but she could not risk any further rejection. Next time she would be prepared, next time she would steel herself, she would not care. But today . . . today there was not a rescuing hack in sight. She stalked halfway down the block before she thought to see if Maggie followed behind.

"Ned!" At Maggie's cry, Zel whirled to see a big bear of a man grasp Maggie's arms.

As Zel dashed back down the street, Ned crushed Maggie to his chest. "You'll not run from me again, woman."

"No!" Zel dove at his back as he swaggered away, people scattering from his path. Her impact barely shifted his weight, but he dropped Maggie with a roar and raised his fists.

"Run, Maggie!" Zel attacked wildly with umbrella and feet. The enormous man swung blindly, sending the umbrella flying. She ducked and twisted, coming up under him, her elbow ramming into his stomach. Ned grunted, grabbing her arm at the shoulder, wrenching her about, his fleshy red face only inches from her own. She jerked up her knee. It bounced harmlessly off his tree-trunk thigh. He seized her other arm, yanking her off the ground, shaking her like a limp rag doll.

She thought her neck would snap when she was

wrenched away from Ned and hauled into another set of muscular arms. Gasping in the scent of green woods, horses, and leather, she allowed herself to be compressed against a warm, broad chest.

"Wolfgang!"

She peered out from his solid strength to see a wiry little man facing Ned, knife aimed at his massive gut. The small man's face looked as if it had met with the service end of a meat grinder, but his bared teeth gleamed brightly as his snow-white hair.

"This isn't over." Ned growled, and with speed amazing for his size, wheeled about and lumbered down the street.

Zel felt Wolfgang lurch forward. The white-haired man sheathed the knife inside his jacket. His voice rang out, clear and cultured. "Let him go. We need to attend to the women. Where is the little maid?"

"Maggie!" Zel pushed out of Wolfgang's arms, darting off in the direction Maggie had run. A wild mop of red hair appeared from behind a shop door. Zel pulled her shivering form close. "He is gone. You are safe."

"We're drawing a crowd." Wolfgang dragged both women toward his town coach, smoothly tossing them in, then pulling the door shut behind himself and the smaller man. "This is Jenkins." He aimed Maggie at the seat with the man and drew the curtains.

Wolfgang grasped Zel's arms and hauled her down beside him as the coach swayed into motion. When she drew a sharp breath through her teeth, he released her. "You're hurt." He pushed aside her shawl, unfastening the tapes at the back of her gown.

"What are you doing?" She jerked free with another gasp, nearly tearing her sleeve.

"I'm checking your injury. Your shoulder could be dislocated. You may have reinjured your ribs."

"You need not bother. Maggie and my aunt will attend to me at home." She cast a little warning snarl into her voice.

"You're nearly as ferocious as my cat." Wolfgang grinned. "Either I check or we make a visit to my doctor. Evers would be happy to see you and chastise you for such unruly behavior with your ribs still healing."

Zel tried to glare coldly at him, but how could she be angry after he'd so fortuitously rescued them?

His silver gaze warmed her as he lowered his voice to an intimate whisper. "I've seen your breasts, and magnificent as they are, I'm more interested in your health right now." His hand returned to her arm, rotating it gently as he continued in a normal tone. "Turn around if it will preserve your modesty. Our cohorts can watch the opposite carriage wall."

Blushing, Zel faced the curtained window as he lowered a sleeve and lightly fingered her arm. She gritted her teeth, not against the pain, but against the sensations his touch evoked and the memories it stirred of his tender attentions only days ago.

"You'll have an ugly bruise." His voice was uneven. "What in Lucifer's name were you doing this time?"

Maggie answered, surprisingly brave. "He's my husband. I ran away." She paused, drawing a shaky breath. "He beats me."

"She will not go back to him. He will kill her." Zel yanked her sleeve back into place. The carriage hit a rut in the road and pitched her back into Wolfgang's arms.

"No one's asking her to go back." Wolfgang eased Zel forward and rotated her other arm before slipping the sleeve down to examine a second tender spot. "But you need to take care. If he found her once he may again."

"She will not leave the house, unless well protected." Zel peeked around to ensure that their companions still faced away from her. "Are you finished, Doctor?"

"Almost." His long fingers stroked her throat and nape. "He shook you hard. Does your neck hurt? Did he strike you?"

"My neck is fine." She swallowed, feebly batting away his hand. "I ducked fast enough to avoid his blows."

"I suppose you'll live." His hand swept gently over her shoulder. She hoped he did not feel her responding shiver. "You know, you are the worst patient I have ever attended." His hand continued down her back and snaked around her side, probing softly against her ribs under her left breast.

Zel jumped, gasping, "Stop!"

"Did that hurt?" Wolfgang released her but she could still feel his breath at her ear. "Isn't the rib healed?"

"My ribs are well enough and in no need of your assistance." She hissed a warning at him.

"Let me retie your gown and I'll leave you alone."

She sat stiff, ignoring the warmth of his fingers on her back and the smile in his voice. Arranging her shawl about her shoulders she turned back to the other occupants of the coach. The older man sat close to Maggie, her little hand resting in his rough one. Zel smiled, then directed her attention to Wolfgang. "Did we interrupt your shopping trip?"

"We were follow—"

Jenkins cut in. "His lordship's wardrobe required a little refurbishing."

Wolfgang smiled fondly at the smaller man. "Jenkins should know."

"Oh, is Jenkins your valet?" Zel realized she felt no surprise at the informalness of the relationship.

Wolfgang nodded and, reaching past her, pushed the curtains open. "We're home. But a word of caution before I return you to your aunt." He lifted her chin with a knuckle. "Please don't battle any more giants or ogres. At least not alone." His lips grazed hers, soft as fairy dust.

He lowered her from the carriage, reaching back for her mangled umbrella. "Your weapon." He eyed her quizically as he escorted her up the stairs. "I think we need to find you another physical outlet. All this fighting isn't good for your health. In the meantime, if you must go out, send for me."

As Smythe shut the door firmly behind Maggie and herself, Zel fought the urge to part the heavy draperies at the window by the door, fought the desire to watch his long, muscular form saunter down the steps and swing into the waiting coach. Zel twirled about, taking the stairs much faster than an adult should, rubbing at the little tingle on her lips. The other tingles she would just ignore.

"I DON'T UNDERSTAND what he sees in her." Isadora tossed herself daintily onto an overstuffed pastel pink chair. "He should have been bored after a few days."

"You're just too easy, my dear Lady Horeton." Newton's mouth curled, but only at the edges. "You don't understand how much men enjoy the chase."

"You think he hasn't had the slut yet?" She tried to modulate the shrillness in her voice. It wouldn't be wise to expose too much of herself to Newton's cold scrutiny.

"Sheath your claws, Isadora." Newton stretched his tall frame, sipping on his port. "I'm sure the chit's intact."

Isadora snorted. "Then you're as big a fool as he!" She spread her skirts, knowing the rose of her gown coordinated flatteringly with the color scheme of her drawing room. Why this infernal preoccupation with Grizelda Fleetwood?

"No, your dear Northcliffe is no fool, but he is obviously confused." Newton stroked the stem of the goblet. "I don't think he knows what to do with a virgin."

"You screw her, like anyone else." Isadora nearly shrieked.

"What, you . . . what?" Melbourne rubbed his eyes, stretching his heavily padded shoulders.

"Isadora, your crudeness has awakened Melbourne." Newton placed his glass on the sofa table and strode to the ornate liquor cabinet. He poured another drink, handing it to Melbourne before resuming his seat. "Perhaps he knows what to do with a virgin."

"Virgin? What are you thpeaking of?" Melbourne downed the liquid quickly. "Bah!" He spat. "You know I hate port, Newton!"

"You see, Isadora, Melbourne doesn't know what to do with a virgin either."

"Regardless of how innocent she may be, she has no better reputation than a whore." Isadora flashed her teeth. "I may be one of the few ladies of the ton to receive her."

"Her? Are you talking about Mith Fleetwood?" Melbourne's bright yellow form clashed so horribly with her rose settee, Isadora had to stifle an urge to forcibly remove him.

"Yes, she was shunned by Lady March as well as your own dear mother at the shops on Bond Street this morning." Isadora patted her golden curls. "But I talked to her anyway. Afterwards she was involved in some sort of ruckus in the street."

"Oh, tell us more." Newton maintained his fashionably bored tone, but she knew she'd piqued his interest by the sudden gleam in his hard mahogany eyes.

"I didn't see the start of it, but a crowd gathered and Northcliffe was there." Isadora paused, wanting to prolong this bit of power over Newton. "He nearly carried her to his coach."

"What was it about?" Newton's haughty, demanding tone stirred a streak of rebellion in her.

"I already told you, I didn't see the start of it." She sniffed and raised her nose as high as his. "I thought you'd be pleased I was so kind to dear Grizelda."

"It wath very kind of you." Melbourne grinned vacantly.

"Yes, indeed, Isadora is renowned for her kindness." Newton laughed harshly, pressing the tips of his long fingers together. "Poor Miss Fleetwood does need our support. Society can be so cruel."

"Yeth, and Northcliffe can do ath he will and no one will cut him." Melbourne's lispy whine was so annoying, why did Newton encourage his hanging on? "But how can I openly thupport her, after my mother thnubbed her?"

"But think, my dear friend, of the fun of defying your mother." Newton smiled, his voice low and intimate. "She needs to understand she can't keep you her minion forever."

"Do you have any plans to help the young couple, Newton?" Isadora batted her eyelashes at him theatrically, grasping for his attention.

"Thtop, pleathe, you are creating a whirlwind." Newton stood, looking down his patrician nose at her, batting his own lashes and patting his carefully disarrayed Brutus in imitation of her earlier affectation. Somehow, with Newton, even when she was party to the joke, it still seemed to be played on her. "You'll muth my hair."

Melbourne stared silently at Newton.

She tittered a bit uncertainly. "You are so droll, Newton."

"Yes, I am, ain't I?" Newton's cold, dark eyes glittered again briefly before icing over. "I don't believe our friends require our help at the moment. They seem to be doing a fine job all on their own." He paused, fingering his dark brown mustache. "But the second they appear to need our assistance, I'm sure I can count on you both to lend a hand."

"ARE YOU CERTAIN this is the correct thing to do?"

"Oh, Wolfie, I'm pleased to see you concerned about Zel's feelings." Grandmama smiled wide enough to catch flies, and any of the tiny pests that missed the smile would surely be trapped by the honey in her voice.

"I just don't want her hurt." Wolfgang made a production of helping the elderly but still physically strong woman into the carriage, his voice barely a whisper.

"Don't fuss so." Grandmama snapped, tapping his leg with her cane, while still not completely losing her smile. "I'm not helpless yet." She settled into the squabs. "That week Zel spent housebound only served to convince the gossips they were right and she was hiding in shame."

"But you know it couldn't be helped." Wolfgang signaled to the coachman and hopped in, slouching down across from Grandmama.

"Is she healed? And what about the new bruises?"

"She seemed to be healed. Evers told her it would be acceptable to go out. So she went shopping and jumped into a fight with another man twice her size." He prodded the opposite seat with his boot as the carriage lurched into the flow of traffic. "But the bruise on her jaw is barely noticeable, and with a little powder, completely invisible." He sat straighter. "Has there been any mention of that night in front of my house?"

"No, the scandal-broth was so filled with your previous antics, there wasn't room for more." She leaned forward, tapping his knee. "And don't you provide more."

"I don't intend to." Wolfgang frowned, not needing chastisement in addition to the guilt he'd already laid on his own head. "Jenkins found out from her maid that she was snubbed yesterday. I think she was surprised at how much it bothered her. She prides herself on not caring what others think of her. But reality was a little different."

"Poor dear." Grandmama narrowed her clear gray eyes. "She must rely on my credit tonight. There are many who will not seek her out but none will dare give her the cut direct when she is in company with me."

"You can't be with her all the time. It's unfair." He yanked on the window curtain. "Why don't they just slight me?"

"But dear, you know, you have no reputation to lose, and the woman is always the favored target." Grandmama grasped his hand. "Now stop worrying that curtain. You'll have it in shreds."

"Zel seems to think she can survive this, but society has

a long memory. I'm going to make it right for her." He muttered under his breath, "Even if it kills me."

"Don't tease an old woman." Grandmama's hand tightened around his fingers, her eyes intent on his face. "Are you saying what I think you're saying?"

"I suppose so." He pulled his hand free, rubbing at his shoulders and neck. "I feel like I'm tied up in knots."

"Relax. Use your charm." That damned honey dripped back into her voice. "It will all work out beautifully."

"We're here. She's always prompt." Wolfgang forced a smile, flinging himself out the door and up the steps.

The front door opened in its usual magical fashion. "How do you do it, Smythe? Do you realize I've only had to touch that door knocker once, in all the times I've been here?" He sailed past the red-faced butler. "Do you wait forever at the window, neglecting your other duties shamefully? Or are you truly clairvoyant?"

"Stop harassing him." Zel's husky alto floated down the staircase, followed by her lithe form wreathed in sea-green muslin. The beast trotted close behind.

"That animal is not coming with us." Wolfgang whistled softly. The dog bounded down the steps snatching the treat from his outstretched hand. "Never go anywhere without these gems."

"You're spoiling him."

"And you're lovely." He pulled her shawl off her arm, draping it over her nearly bare breasts and well-covered shoulders and arms. "But won't you be chilly tonight?"

"One must suffer for fashion." Zel frowned. "Can you see any bruises?"

"Nary a splotch of black or blue, only cream and sea foam." He grasped her elbow, nearly hurling her through the door. "Grandmama awaits." Smythe would faint dead away if he gave into impulse and swirled her into his arms, covering that frown with kisses.

Once Zel was settled in the coach beside Grandmama,

Wolfgang found himself completely ignored as the two women eagerly chatted up the blocks to Vauxhall Gardens.

As they left the carriage and strolled along the promenade to the grove, Wolfgang bent, lips near Zel's ear. "I have a treat for you. Do you know what the orchestra plays tonight?"

"I had not realized we came for the concert, but I assume it is the usual Handel or Haydn."

He smiled. "I'll keep the secret a bit longer. We'll take a supper box and have a few bites, then perhaps move closer to the orchestra when the music begins."

Conversation was light as they nibbled on ham, chicken, biscuits, and cheesecakes, washing it down with the pungent Vauxhall punch. Several of Grandmama's friends greeted them. No one behaved excessively friendly, but no one actively snubbed them either. The knot in Wolfgang's shoulders eased, until he noticed his aunt on a collision course with their table.

Aunt Dorothea held herself stiff and erect, a steel sword sheathed in gray silk, her handsome face set in hard, severe lines. Cousin Adam trotted dutifully a pace behind.

"Lady Darlington." Aunt Dorothea's voice tolled as she extended her hand. "Grizelda. Hardwicke." She stared across the table, clearly relieved the distance took away her decision of whether or not to touch hands with the pariahs. "Grizelda, you have met my son, Adam." Adam bowed slightly, his gaze fixed on Zel's chest.

"Yes, good evening, Mrs. Clayton." Zel nodded. Wolfgang frowned as she squirmed under Adam's continuing stare. "Mr. Clayton." He should advise her to bring back a few of her old, ugly but modest gowns, or he'd be forced to assault his cousin.

Adam seemed to feel Wolfgang's frown. He glanced up briefly, then refocused his eyes to the vicinity of Zel's shoulders. "Charmed, Miss Fleetwood."

Aunt Dorothea tapped her son's shoulder. "Adam."

"Would you join us for a spot of dinner, Dorothea?" Grandmama, ever gracious, indicated the empty seats at the table.

"Heavens, no." His aunt's laugh rang, hollowly. "We are meeting friends." Turning to her son, she traced the direction of his continued gaze. She glared at him. The little toad jumped and resumed his place behind her as she stalked past the row of tables.

Wolfgang watched them walk away, grumbling. "You know she never would have acknowledged us if I was not the master of her purse. So why ever would you ask them to join us?"

"Wolfie, she is your aunt." Grandmama scowled at him. "One should not alienate one's relations. Especially now when you need all the support you can get."

"They're no relations of yours, and I'll alienate whom I please." He softened his voice. "I'd rather they not ruin our evening."

"Is she so bad?" Zel looked from Wolfgang to his grandmother. "Your cousin seems harmless enough."

"Should I have begged him to stay?" Wolfgang tapped his foot against the table leg, watching the way the table shuddered with each tiny blow. "Did you like the way he ogled your chest?"

"Wolfgang!" Grandmama warned.

"Sorry." He held his tongue, following the wave of pink suffusing Zel's exposed skin, tapping the table a few more times with his toe. A faint squeaking rose up from the grove. "The orchestra is tuning up. Should we listen from here or find a spot in the trees a little closer?"

"I'd love to be close enough to hear without interference." Excitement hastened Zel's speech and shone in her eyes. "And I would like to watch the musicians at their art."

"You two walk down." Grandmama caught his eye. "I'll join a few of my friends and listen from here."

"Are you sure?" Zel hesitated.

"Yes, yes, now scoot along, dears."

They found a spot among the trees near enough to view the orchestra, far enough for a little privacy. He pulled her down beside him on a little stone bench, keeping her hand wedged between the crook of his elbow and his hand.

"Now, close your eyes," he whispered. "They are ready to begin. Tonight they play the musings of your demigod, Beethoven. Symphony number seven."

Wolfgang examined Zel's upturned face, lashes dark and thick against her pale cheeks. He felt her body recoil as the first notes lurched, then shimmered, through the twilit sky. A delicious shiver poured from her, coursing through him. She opened eyes, warm and liquid as a hot spring, parting her lips in a smile as ethereal and earthy as the notes alternately tickling and furrowing the air.

She leaned into him, her body swaying synchronistically with the movement of the music. Her dreamy little hum shadowed the melody line as it lyrically flitted, soared and plunged. He slipped his arm around her shoulders, pulling her against his chest, feeling the music flow through her as clearly as his ears heard its sound.

Wolfgang stirred as the last strains of the symphony's second movement faded into memory. Zel sat quietly but her body still vibrated with the evanescent tones. As a bell pealed, announcing the Cascade, Vauxhall's famous waterfall, he reluctantly straightened, not yet ready to remove his arm from her. "Would you—"

"Sshh."

He felt himself a pagan censured by a religious zealot.

Smiling, he brushed his cheek against her hair. It was no punishment to sit in silence, luxuriating in the softness of her body, the spicy scent of her hair. He shifted to see her face, surprised at the wet glitter in her eyes and the streaks down her cheeks. His finger swept away the tears. Her expression was blank. She had yet to reenter the real world, still inhabiting a magical realm of siren song and seraphim hymn.

If he kissed her now, he would breach all her defenses, touching the very core of her. Wolfgang held back, it would be an invasion. She was opened by the music—not by him. His ribs gripped his lungs so tightly he could scarcely breathe. Flames of hell, he longed for her in ways he'd never dreamed it was possible to want a woman. The yearning went deeper than he dared follow. If he didn't move or speak his chest would shatter.

"Marry me, Zel," he whispered, hoarsely.

"What?" She stared at him; the confusion in her eyes showed that his words brought her back from her enchanted world.

"Marry me."

"And we will travel off to Bedlam together." The touch of levity in her voice frightened him. She was not going to listen.

He twisted about, grasping her hands too tightly. "I'm serious, Zel. It would work, I know it would."

Her laughter slapped harshly at his ears. "You have gone totally mad."

"Perhaps I have." Wolfgang frowned into her lovely, now pinched, elfin face. "I'll get a special license and we can be wed by the day after tomorrow."

"Stop this now." She pushed him away, struggling to her feet. "You are acting the fool."

"No, for a change, I'm not." He hauled her back to the bench, arm circling her waist, mouth seeking hers.

Zel jerked her head about, leaving his kiss to land in her hair. "Stop this at once."

"Fine." He loosened his hold but still kept her firmly in place as he shifted his verbal attack. "Think about it, Zel, use your head. It's the perfect solution."

She snorted.

He ignored her. The first cannon volley was ineffective.

Time to switch to the sturdy, reliable infantry. "It would repair both our reputations. We would get on famously. And I wouldn't ask a lot. All I really need from you is to hostess my political dinners and share my bed, and of course the offshoot of that, provide me with an heir."

Zel stared at him, so still she didn't blink, eyes very dark in the fading light.

The devil and his cat, this was going badly. He swallowed and continued. "The rest of your life would be entirely your own to do with as you please. I promise I'll not interfere or make a nuisance of myself. I'll never make a single demand of you."

"Are you quite finished?" Her voice grated so low he could barely make out the words. "I must compliment you on your fine proposal. How could it fail to win a lady's hand?"

"Are you saying yes?" But he knew she was not. "I would ask for no foolish sentiment." Why in the name of Clootie did he say that? This was going downhill faster than a mudslide on a rain-soaked Spanish mountain pass.

"It seems I am not being clear." She tried again to pull away, but his arm stayed securely in place. "I am saying no, my lord."

"But you said women should insist on sensible rather than romantic marriages. I'll show you I can be sensible." He ran his free hand roughly through his hair. "Don't glare at me so. What do you want? A businesslike contractual arrangement, or me on bended knee vowing eternal devotion and fidelity?"

"I do not want you or marriage." Zel's voice crept up the scale. "I want nothing from you! Absolutely nothing!"

"You're being stupid and stubborn. You know this makes sense." Wolfgang intercepted her glance. "And you may try to deny it, but you want me in your goddamn bed!"

"You are the most arrogant, self-centered bore I have ever met." Satan's small clothes, she was hissing at him again, and this time he didn't like it. "I would sooner have a jackass in my bed."

"That's exactly what your blasted passions will get you!"

"My passions! What do you know about my passions?"

"Quite a lot, my dear." He bared his teeth. "I know you work so bloody hard to keep your passions in a neat little box, letting them out for an occasional tryst with Beethoven on the keyboards. And when you absolutely can't stop yourself, for a kiss with me."

"I will not listen to you." Zel pushed futilely on his chest. "And if you do not let me go, I will make a scene."

"Too late, we already have." Wolfgang pulled her closer. "You may try to smother that passion, but one day it will burst into flames and consume you. Let me help you harness the fires."

"Burst into flames, harness the fires—good God." She put her hands over her ears in a childish gesture. "I will listen to your ridiculous speech no longer. Take me home, now."

He stood, hauling her to her feet. "A most welcome idea. Come along."

She faltered. "What of Lady Darlington?"

"I'll return for her." He pulled her to the walk. "You wish to go home? Home it is. Never let it be said I displeased a lady."

The carriage ride seemed infinitely long and bumpy, but it was over before he could put together any coherent thoughts. The knots were back in his shoulders. He stared out the window, refusing to rub at them and let her see his discomfort.

Zel rose to let herself out, but his arm grasped her waist, drawing her taut body down to his. Wolfgang caught her cry with his lips. Hard and demanding. He felt her hesitation, not resistance, just a pause while her body warred with her stubborn mind. Her body easily won, his hand detected the softening as he traced the lines of her shoulder blades and spine. He deepened the kiss, pulling her into him with mouth, hands, and arms. She met and returned his fervor, her own arms locking about his neck, fingers tugging at his queue.

He pushed her away, laughing harshly at her startled expression. "Don't offer what you refuse to deliver. Keep your cold bed. Dry up like an old stick." He handed her out of the carriage, directing her up the stairs and past Smythe at the open front door. Watching her enter the hallway, he called after her rigid back. "Pleasant dreams, *Miss* Fleetwood."

Wolfgang threw himself into the coach, burying his head in his hands. Bride of the devil! Would he ever learn to use his head for more than a filler of hats? What a favorable taste he had given her of what it would be like to be his wife, allowing his anger and frustration to drive and excuse his rough actions toward her. He would not have her develop a fear of him. He wasn't like her father. She should know he'd never hurt her.

He'd lost this skirmish because of his own impulsiveness and idiotic lack of strategic planning. His forces may have been decimated and demoralized, but hers suffered a few losses too. And a good tactician knew when to retreat.

He would pull back, regroup, and examine his foe's strengths and weaknesses. Then he would plan a new campaign designed to exploit those weaknesses and circumvent those strengths. His enemy's strengths were numerous. She was indeed a worthy foe. But, praise Lucifer for that blessed weakness. Wolfgang stretched out on the squabs. He would hammer against it with his biggest cannons, his sharpest riflemen, and his most skillful swordsmen. The battle would be won, spoils to the victor.

CHAPTER 11

SCHERZO

A bright humorous musical piece
or movement in triple time

"MOUSE, go away." Zel pushed at the wet nose nestled in her palm. "I did not sleep well last night and I am in no mood to be up before noon." A warm, slobbery tongue slid up her arm. "Damn, Remus, go!"

She buried herself deep under the pillows and bedcovers, ignoring Remus's protesting whimper. That man had not only cost her a night's sleep, but even had her cursing at her dog. Was it any wonder she had determined never to marry? Her supposed friend decided he wanted her as a political hostess and brood mare. And as if that was not enough, he offered his services to help *her* harness *her* passions. When had her passions been the problem? She kept all her emotions nicely under control, unlike some people she could name. He was such a madman, he probably did murder half his family, as Robin claimed. She shook her head. No, Wolfgang might be a madman, a fool, and a rogue, but he wasn't a murderer.

Zel threw off the covers, flung herself out of the bed, and stomped to the armoire. She rubbed at her eyes. There would be no more sleep this morning, she might as well dress.

Call her a dried-up old stick, would he!

She yanked a gown from the cabinet and threw it over her shoulder. Not the green silk. Not the pale blue. The violet, no. She tossed clothing, shoes, and accessories about until Maggie scrambled into the room to rescue her wardrobe.

"Miss Zel, please." Maggie picked up a shoe and several pairs of stockings. "Let me help you choose a gown."

"Maybe I'll just stay in my night rail all day." Zel stepped back, surprised at the disarray on the floor. "Any will do."

She grabbed a chemise and morning gown and dressed impatiently, holding her tongue to avoid snapping at her blameless maid. As Maggie began braiding her hair a knock sounded at the door.

Aunt Diana stepped through the doorway, eyebrows raised as she surveyed the clothing-littered room. "Laundry day?"

"No." Zel's cheeks warmed. "I'm afraid I threw a little fit."

"A fit? You, dear?" Aunt Diana, looking amused, picked up a few gowns and laid them across a chair. "Did something happen you've . . . failed to tell me about?"

"Oh, I suppose there is no need to keep it a secret." Zel sighed loudly, anger not entirely diffused. "Northcliffe proposed last night."

"Oh, my dear, my dear. I am beside myself with amazement." Aunt Diana smiled broadly, matching a pair of stockings. "However did you . . . manage it? When is the happy event?"

"Stop! Are you mad too?" Zel twisted about, pulling the unfinished braid from Maggie's hands. "Whatever makes you think I accepted him?"

Smile fading, Aunt Diana smoothed a wrinkled gown. "But it's obvious there is, ah, something between the two of you."

"To what are you referring?" Zel looked from Maggie to her aunt, as Maggie grasped the escaping chignon.

"My dear Zel, everyone can see the attraction." Aunt Diana's smile returned as she took a seat on the ragged settee. "Northcliffe seems to have some tender feelings for you, and he's so handsome and virile."

"Virile, yes. Tender feelings, no." She snorted. "You would not think of tender feelings if you saw the way he mauls me when we are alone."

"Mauls you? Zel!" Aunt Diana spoke sharply. "What has been happening?"

"You would be surprised to know the liberties he takes, how he kisses and touches me." She jumped as Maggie rammed a hairpin into her neck.

"And you . . . you allow such liberties?" Her aunt watched her closely, eyes glassy with horror. "Grizelda Amadea Fleetwood, have you allowed yourself to be compromised?"

"Aunt Diana." The roiling in her stomach told Zel she should never have let the conversation take this turn. She lowered her voice. "It is not so bad as that."

"How long has this been going on?" Her aunt stood, pacing the small room from window to door, rattling on with uncharacteristic speed. "Why have you allowed it? This is not like you at all. Is not a virtuous woman's price above . . . oh, what's the name of that red stone?"

"Aunt Diana, I have not lost my virtue." Zel felt beleaguered and besieged. "Not totally. The stone is a ruby."

"Yes . . . price above rubies." Aunt Diana stopped pacing and glared at Zel. "You, missy, had better go running after that man and pray his offer still stands. Earls do not have to marry used goods."

"Used goods! I am *not* used goods."

"Used goods, tarnished goods. Whatever is happening between you and Northcliffe had better be put into a marriage bed. Now!" Aunt Diana stalked to the door, pausing with her hand on the latch. "Do not let your passions be your ruin."

"Passions? I—"

Aunt Diana interrupted. "I almost forgot, Emily Carland is downstairs." She pulled the door open and was halfway down the hall before Zel could finish her reply.

Zel sat in forced stillness while Maggie put the final touches to her toilette. "Thank you, Maggie." Her voice even, she stood and followed Aunt Diana. Emily would support her.

Aunt Diana preceded her into the drawing room by only minutes, but she had already pulled Emily aside, and sat, whispering in her ear. Both looked up guiltily when Zel entered the room.

Emily frowned, walking toward Zel, hands outstretched, searching her face. "Zel, your aunt claims you are compromised."

"Compromised?" Zel's voice rose to a shrill soprano, as she met Emily's narrowed brown eyes and clasped her small, plump hands. "I am not compromised. To allow a few private kisses and caresses does not mean I am compromised."

Emily took Zel's arm, leading her to a bright brocaded sofa. "Please calm down and consider this rationally."

"Calm down? I am calm." Zel glared at her petite friend and perched on the edge of the sofa. "I am always calm. Except when people drive me to distraction."

"Don't blindly refuse this marriage."

"I do not believe this." Zel sank into the cushions, groaning. "Two women opposed to marriage are trying to convince me to wed a reckless womanizer." She pushed away the teacup Aunt Diana tried to place in her hand. "You wish me to marry a man guaranteed to hurt me?"

Aunt Diana placed the teacup on a table and pulled a

chair close to the sofa. "I think you're wrong. He'll not intentionally hurt you. He's not like your father or my husband." She sat, leaning forward to take Zel's hand.

"Zel, you must listen. Not all men are cruel tyrants." Emily stroked her other hand. "Marriage need not be a prison. Many women find joy in the institution."

"I am not one of those women." Zel jerked her hands away, angry tears welling in her eyes. They were conspiring against her. "I never wished to marry, even when forced to for Robin."

"A woman of passion, such as you—"

"A woman of passion! What is wrong with everyone!" She lurched off the sofa, nearly overturning the tea table on her way to the door. "First Wolfgang, then Aunt Diana, and now you, Emily, all claiming I cannot control my passions." Zel knew she was shouting but she could not seem to lower her voice. She stood in the doorway and faced her accusers. "I would have you know, I am not a woman possessed of unruly passions. I have always lived a life of control and restraint, and will continue to do so." Zel blinked back the tears and, slowing her pace as much as humanly possible, strode down the hall.

Damn him! Damn them all! She would show them that Wolfgang's kisses and caresses meant nothing to her. She would never again yield to him only to be pushed away at his whim. She would never become a pawn to a man as her mother had.

As Robin said, Wolfgang was only interested in the hunt. He was like a cat with a mouse. After the mouse was caught the cat might toy with it a while but would eventually get bored, finish the kill, and move on to other entertainments. The marriage proposal was only another game in his repertoire to extend the time before ennui set in. And although she feared the passion and potential violence, she found there was something she feared more. His inevitable indifference and her resulting pain. She had allowed defenses, already chipped away by his outrageous yet boyish charm, to lower further, and he had slipped in with his tender ministrations. It was all just part of the game he played. Well, as of this moment her defenses were fortified, stronger than ever. He would not slip in again.

"WILL THE LIGHT of your life be here tonight?" The duke of Ridgemont's sculpted mouth was taut with suppressed humor.

Wolfgang growled at his friend, his mouth also tight, but not from holding back a smile. He leaned against a column in the theater box as he surveyed the noisy mob in the pit. "Grandmama promised, and when Grandmama promises, she delivers."

"But if they don't get here soon they'll miss the opening act." Rafael rubbed his chin thoughtfully. "Rather than offer for her again and risk another awful bumbling, why not have your grandmother propose for you? Zel likes her and—"

"Raf, I'm in no mood for your so-called humor." Wolfgang straightened, pulling on his waistcoat. "I've decided on a different strategy. When a frontal assault is repulsed, attack the flank."

"So, you've decided to get sneaky."

"I plan to show her that she can't live without me."

"And what manner of demonstration will do this?" Rafael stretched, pushing his chair farther to the back of the box, eyes never leaving Wolfgang.

"I'll appeal to her sensual nature." Wolfgang looked away, fingering the stone column dividing the boxes. "She wants me, and it's time she learned how much."

"Wolf, you're not going to seduce an unmarried virgin." Raf didn't question, he arrogantly ordered. "Forcing her into marriage will not set well with her. It could make your future together exceedingly dim."

"Give me credit for a little sense." He shifted his weight, watching the fashionables parade in and out of the theater boxes. "I won't take it that far, just enough to convince her she's too passionate to live her life without a man. This man."

"You're asking for trouble."

"I can handle it."

"Lord save us from a wolf on the prowl." Rafael laughed, indicating an opposing box. "And there's your she-wolf now, accompanied by the matriarch of the pack." He looked them over quizzically. "Do they coordinate their toilette? They look like they danced off the same necklace."

Wolfgang grimaced as the two tall, slender women dressed in complimentary shades of aquamarine spotted him. Grandmama nodded. Zel looked away, speaking to one of Grandmama's cronies. "They just know. I have a theory— they're twins accidentally born of different families in different generations."

"I've always wished your grandmama was a tad younger." Raf raised a sardonic brow. "Are you joining them now or during intermission?"

"I may as well face her now." He watched Zel continue to avoid his gaze.

Raf laughed. "One could never call you a coward."

Wolfgang made his way to his grandmother's box, the scowl on his face discouraging any greetings by acquaintances. If he behaved the perfect gentleman during the one-act play, perhaps he could convince her to walk out with him for refreshments.

Zel was as cool as expected, but did not complain verbally when he moved a chair to her side and engaged her in polite conversation. He kept his comments light and appropriate during the play, quite a feat, if he had to say so himself. Grandmama ignored them both, concentrating on the gossip of her friends.

Before the last words of the play were acted out, Wolfgang jumped to his feet, clasping Zel's hand in his. "We'll fetch refreshments."

Before Zel could refuse, Grandmama quickly added, "Yes, go dears, and bring me back a bit of punch."

"Come along then, Miss Fleetwood." He whisked her out into the foyer before she could change her mind, searching for a corner or anteroom where they could find some privacy.

Beelzebub's bootstraps! That wild shock of red hair waving in the crowd before them could only be his brother-in-law, Simon Bedford. He was bearing down on them with the subtlety of a Spanish bull with a matador's sword in his side. The man would not let go. Wolfgang almost wished for another challenge. He'd wing the cub and they could call it done. Simon could finish his grieving for his unworthy sister and get on with his life. He liked the boy and had a hard time believing he could plot a murder, but maybe he tired of Wolfgang's refusals to meet him with pistols at dawn and was willing to find his revenge where he could. Hellfire! Enough! He had another agenda tonight.

"My deceased wife's brother, again." He nodded in Simon's direction. "If you don't wish to serve as referee, we need to hide, quickly." He pulled her down the wide staircase, out the door, and past the Grecian columns decorating the exterior of the theater. They passed elaborately embellished courtesans, tawdry prostitutes, and other nearly invisible denizens of the street before he slid them both into a dark, empty doorway. He wedged her into the corner, blocking both her escape and the eyes of unwanted watchers with his body.

"Keep still, and no one will see you." He whispered into her hair, weaving one arm about her shoulder, the other about her waist. "Anyone who sees me will assume I'm confirming my evening's activities with a lady of the night."

"Was it necessary to come this far to avoid the confrontation?" Zel's breathless murmur tickled his neck. "Must you stand so near?"

"Yes, for your protection." Wolfgang chuckled softly, pressing into her until her full breasts crushed against his chest, and her long legs thrust into his thighs. "But to answer your first question. I confess to a degree of subterfuge. I did wish to avoid Simon, but I also wished to get you alone."

Zel stood so still, yet he could feel the quick thumping of her heart through the layers of their clothing. Her voice was firm and brave when she finally spoke. "Go ahead, kiss me, touch me. But I promise I will not respond this time."

" 'Cruelty, thy name is woman.' " He misquoted. "You do know how to hurt a man. But I'm not, tonight, bent on your seduction. I only wish to call in a favor."

"Favor?" Her back stiffened in his embrace. "You mean the favor I promised when you agreed to buy Robin's notes?"

Wolfgang rubbed at her back but she tensed more. "As I promised you, I won't ask what you cannot do. I only wish to spend time with you."

Even in the near darkness, he could see her eyes narrow as she lifted her head to peer up at him. "We spend too much time together now."

"A morning call here, a party there, a play whenever, a waltz almost never." He lowered his head, resting his chin on her shoulder, mouth at her neck. "Barely enough for more than a chance acquaintance. No, I want a week of your time."

"A week?" Zel brought her hands to his chest, a futile effort to put space between them. "We cannot be alone somewhere for a week."

"We needn't be alone." Wolfgang buried his nose in her hair, inhaling deeply of her so familiar spicy scent. "I have an invitation to a house party, two days hence, at the Staffords' country estate in Abingdon. I wish you to accompany me."

"A house party?" She sounded incredulous, clearly waiting for the catch. "Oh, *perfect.*" She tried to twist away. "Who would accept me at their house party? Few besides your grandmother's closest friends will even speak to me."

"The Staffords are part of a fast crowd." His lips brushed her hair. "They'll probably think you're my mistress. But unless we make love in the rose garden, they won't blink an eye."

Zel stiffened again, then sighed. "Are you sure my company is all you will ask of me? Can I trust you not to try to seduce me in the rose garden?"

"I don't care for roses. The thorns can interfere dreadfully." He frowned. Now he'd have to avoid flower gardens. "I'm asking you for a week, at a simple house party, spent wholly in my company."

She pounced, her hands fisting on his chest. "Wholly in your company? Am I then expected to occupy your bed and confirm everyone's opinions?"

He eased his hold on her and looked into her eyes, his jaw slack and eyes wide, feigning abject amazement. "My dear Miss Fleetwood, how you malign me. I told you, I wouldn't ask you to do anything that would cause you undue discomfort."

"So I may refuse your company?"

"Ugh!" Wolfgang groaned. "Another unkindness. I insist you spend your waking hours with me. But I give you full veto power over our activities." He raised her chin with his knuckle and watched her eyes, imagining how the gold specks would flash in stronger light. "You can do this. Or are you afraid?"

"I am not afraid of you." She met his smile with a scowl. "But what is the point?"

"Need there always be a point?"

She lowered her gaze, her fingers splayed over his waistcoat, her voice husky and soft. "I agree to the favor. What harm could a house party with the *fast* Staffords do? My reputation is already beyond repair."

Wolfgang filled his lungs and exhaled slowly. "I'll call for you in the morning at ten, in two days. Thank you."

An unreadable expression flitted over her face. "I prefer to meet you there."

"I'll send my traveling coach for you and your maid." He pinned her with a hard stare. "If you don't wish me to ride within, I'll play the part of outrider on Ari."

Zel nodded her consent.

"We'll return to the theater. Keep your head down till we get to the entry." Regretfully stepping back from her, he took her arm. "Grandmama will be fretting."

ZEL LEANED TOWARD the window of the plush coach, watching as smoky air and dingy buildings transformed into acre upon acre of storm-washed greenery and crisp, clean sunshine. Wolfgang rode close to the silver-and-black carriage. The ease with which he sat his mount, combined with a jacket the same hue as the horse's chestnut coat, gave him the air of a mythic centaur. His long, tapered fingers rested on the reins with a gentleness at war with the ready strength and power of his frame. She flushed when her eyes met the grin in his, knowing he was excessively pleased with her lengthy perusal. Zel quickly looked to Maggie, but his image remained fixed in her mind.

Tamping down the warmth rising through her body, she cleared her throat. "A week in his company! It will pass like this." She leaned forward and clapped her hands. "Like nothing."

Maggie sat opposite on the luxurious silver squabs, eyeing Zel dubiously. "Yes, Miss Zel, like nothing."

Zel snorted. "Oh, so you agree with everyone else?" The carriage hit a rut, throwing her back in the seat. "I cannot control myself? Ha! I will show you all. Woman of unharnessed passion! In a bloody pig's eye!"

Last evening's storm was only a vague recollection in the fluffy, scattered clouds overhead. The coach grew increasingly stuffy, but as hot and bored as she was, Zel would expire before she looked out again. She twitched around trying to get comfortable, finally throwing herself in a semirecline on the well-stuffed cushions.

"Maggie, if you tell me I should marry him, I shall scream."

"I—"

"Do not start with me. You know my feelings on marriage."

"Miss—"

"How you can possibly support the idea of marriage after what you have gone through, I cannot surmise." Zel's hand snaked unbidden to the black silk curtains, she paused then pulled them tightly shut. "My mother, my aunt, the women at the home, all victims of the unbridled passions of the male of the species."

"But—"

"Reckless, uncontrolled emotions culminate in violence."

"Not all—"

"Yes, all men, given the opportunity and motivation." Zel blinked, attempting to exorcise the visions of strong hands gently examining her for injury, long fingers stroking the pain from her head. She shook her head vigorously, freeing a few pins from the loose chignon, but the image persisted, followed by another image of her mother's hands, slight and pale. But the memories of being cared for by those hands were as fragile and faded as the hands themselves. Stronger were the remembrances of her own hands providing succor to the frail woman, battered of body and spirit. She swallowed a hard lump of anger, roundly berating herself for such feelings toward her mother. Her father, not her mother, was the deserving target of her ire. Or better yet she could aim a little fury at her tall, handsome nemesis. She glanced to the curtains. An excellent target, and well within range.

"And that man out there on the stallion, he is an example of the worst sort." Zel tightened her lips in smug satisfaction. "He is an undisciplined, voracious barbarian. Worse still, he finds his most deplorable traits to be humorous."

"Miss, you—"

"I do not find him humorous in the least." She bravely parted the curtains to face her foe. "I find him a pitiful creature. His persuasions will never prevail against my will." She watched instead the little white-haired valet who rode with surprising grace and stamina beside the centaur. The centaur, of course, spotted her and smiled.

The journey to Abingdon, including an overlong luncheon stop, continued in near silence, a silence that Zel felt compelled to breach only with an occasional heartfelt treatise on the character of the centaur, and her complete indifference to the beast. And if she cared to leave the curtains open to enjoy the view, it mattered little, as she showed the beast with a haughty nose in the air when he turned to smile at her.

Damn that crooked smile! It symbolized all his impossible attractions: the recklessness, the boyishness, the touch of danger, the humor, the sensuality, and the tenderness. All the things she desired and feared. She felt herself a swimmer, caught in a riptide, sure to drown if she allowed herself to be carried out to sea, equally sure to drown if she fought the tide and exhausted herself before she could make the safety of shore.

Zel leaned stiffly into the cushions, shutting her eyes tightly, like a child feigning sleep. She doggedly refused to move, despite the carriage seat's arrhythmic thumping against her tailbone and the perspiration pooling beneath her breasts.

Days rather than hours seemed to pass before the groom

helped her alight from the carriage in the Staffords' grace-fully curved drive. Wolfgang handed his mount over to a groom with barely a look in her direction, giving not the slightest indication of lending his assistance.

Zel took Maggie's arm, her long stride causing the little maid to run to keep pace. As she passed him, Wolfgang took a step toward her. He did not take her elbow but allowed her gown to slide over his outstretched leg. Zel suppressed an urge to stomp on his toes, an action sure to do damage to her slippered foot, while only scuffing the polish of his black riding boots. He followed her up the steps and into the elegant three-story half-timbered Queen Anne mansion, his step so close at her heels she feared he would tread on her hem.

She was introduced to the guests gathered in a large rose-and-beige drawing room. She knew few of the company, but the ubiquitous threesome of Newton, Melbourne, and Lady Horeton greeted her with mocking affability.

Zel took a seat by the window, scanning the room for Wolfgang from beneath her lashes. As she turned back to the doorway she found her face inches away from tan breeches and a chestnut jacket. Following the firm line of his chest upward, she met that unholy smile playing on his generous lips and crinkling his silver eyes. She hid the color rushing to her cheeks from him by twisting back to her hostess.

"Lady Stafford, your home is exquisite," she murmured, aware of the warmth of Wolfgang's body beside her chair. "I have always admired the Queen Anne style."

"I'll be happy to show you the house and grounds to-morrow, Miss Fleetwood." Lady Stafford's wrinkled face creased in pleasure. "Now I will have you and Northcliffe shown to your rooms where you may rest a bit before dress-ing for dinner." She nodded to the butler.

"Thank you, Lady Stafford." Wolfgang took several steps toward the door before swiveling back to Zel. "Coming, my dear?"

She frowned at him, but rose and accompanied him through the door, his arm close enough to rustle her sleeve. But still he failed to take her arm as they followed the butler to her room.

Before the evening ended Zel would have done anything to remove that exasperating grin from the infuriating man's face. Throughout dinner his knee bobbed precariously close to her leg. Again and again she could feel it brush against her skirts, but the anticipated pressure of a direct touch never came. He chatted to the woman on his left, smiling so amiably Zel found herself dreaming vividly of the pleasures of kicking his shin.

In the drawing room after dinner matters went rapidly from bad to worse. Whenever she turned he was there, a hair's breadth away. As she sat straight, refusing to acknowledge his presence, she felt his breath stir her hair, his heat penetrate her clothing, his long fingers curl round the arm of her chair. Finally, tired and frustrated, she addressed her hostess. "I am still fatigued from the journey. Thank you for your hospitality, but I believe I will retire early."

"Certainly, my dear," Lady Stafford gushed. "You must be rested for tomorrow's activities. We begin rehearsals for our theatrical after breakfast."

"I'd be pleased to escort you to your room." Wolfgang chirped in with obnoxious gallantry.

As she stood to take his arm, he bowed deeply, ignored her arm, and indicated the door. She smiled coldly and swept by him. What was wrong with the man? Did he fear she had the plague?

His footsteps kept pace with hers up the stairs. "I do hope you'll have a marvelous time, Miss Fleetwood. The company tonight was a bit dull, but the Staffords are known to run with the fast literary and theatrical crowd, so the usual collection of poets, actors, and musicians will surely arrive tomorrow and the tempo pick up accordingly."

"It sounds most amusing, my lord."

"You've started 'my lording' me again."

"And you are 'Miss Fleetwooding' me." Zel reached for the latch at her door. His body was so near, she reflexively leaned back, seeking the muscular warmth of his chest and arms. Stopping herself, she listened to the flow of his breathing, sure for a moment she also heard the pumping of his heart. She circled to face him. His eyes were hooded beneath his dark lashes, his mouth quirked at one corner. He lowered his head with painful slowness until his mouth hovered over hers.

Zel closed her eyes reveling in the anticipated pressure of his lips molding hers, the moisture of his tongue claiming hers. She opened her eyes to find his eyes on her mouth, yet his own mouth floated a tantalizing distance from her own dry lips, never touching, only teasing her with hot, brandy-scented breath.

She jerked away, desperate to be free of his fraudulent lure. Yanking at the latch, she strode into the room and slammed the door. She braced herself against the hard surface, whether to keep him out or herself in, she couldn't be sure. As his footsteps retreated down the hall Zel gasped in an unsteady breath.

What in the name of heaven was wrong with her? She seemed unable to control the slightest response around him. If she was not such a sensible woman, she would swear he was a sorcerer practicing his magic on her. She shivered, wrapping her arms about herself, holding on tight, warding off his spell.

"WAKE UP," Zel whispered, tapping Wolfgang on the forearm. His jaw hung slack, his head bobbed loosely on his neck, the arm on the sofa behind her, settled onto her back. He breathed slow and deep with a tiny rattle. He was going to snore.

"Wolfgang." She took careful aim with her elbow and rammed it into his ribs.

"Eeoww." He jumped awkwardly, slipping halfway off the sofa. Zel smiled, ignoring the stares of their fellow tortured listeners, watching as Wolfgang became aware of his surroundings and tried to inconspicuously resume his seat. "Vixen."

Her smile widened, the wretch deserved everything he got. "Stay awake, and listen."

He moaned softly. "Why are you punishing me?"

As if he did not know. She looked straight ahead, the smile still dancing on her lips. A little revenge tasted so sweet, and he was due much more. Having to listen to the history of waterways and canals in rural England, with the occasional help of a tap or prod from her, did not come near to evening the score. She met his eyes, raising her brows. "But you told me Lady Stafford had such interesting guests."

Moaning again, Wolfgang pulled his long frame erect, his hand brushing her shoulder as he draped his arm over the sofa.

The smile slid off her lips as she regarded him sourly. There was little of her he had not touched today. Those long wicked fingers, and other parts of his anatomy, had grazed, bumped, and slithered over her with most methodical chance. She had almost believed, at first, it was chance. Always in close proximity, partners at meals, audience in a tour for two of the Stafford mansion, ingenue lovers in the amateur theatricals, it was natural that they occasionally got in each other's way. But after she had lost count of how many times his thigh brushed her leg, his knuckles skimmed the outer curve of her breast, his hip nudged her bottom, his shoulder stroked her back, and his elbow prodded her stomach, she could no longer deny his intent.

Zel would gladly drown him in the nearest pond, or rush

back to London to avoid his continuing siege. But a bargain was a bargain, and she would never withdraw in defeat.

His lips were at her ear. "Let's get out of here. I'll agree to any other penance you demand." Wolfgang tucked his hand round her upper arm, pulling her to her feet and toward the door. Allowing herself to be removed, she ignored the sly smiles that accompanied them from the room. She had nothing to fear from either him or the gossips.

They made their way to a small salon at the far end of the wing. After seating Zel on a pastel green settee, he paced before her. "I hope you weren't enjoying that attack on the ears and mind. I assure you Lady Stafford normally does engage more entertaining guests."

"Oh, 'twas not so bad. Anyone with a little intelligence—"

"Are you saying I'm without intelligence?" Wolfgang whirled to face her, voice low and harsh. "Well, you wouldn't be the first or last."

"I never said—"

"I don't care what you damn well said. I can see the cogs turning in that bloody bluestocking mind of yours."

"Wolfgang, I—"

"You, my father, and all the cursed scholars." He leaned over her, eyes sparking like flint on steel. "I'm not stupid." He straightened, stalking to the small plastered fireplace.

Zel moved silently behind him, placing a hand on his shoulder. "Whatever is wrong?"

He shrugged her hand off, but she remained close at his back. When he finally spoke, his voice was soft, with an almost wistful quality to it. "Nothing. Old memories. I'm sorry, I don't know why I jumped on you."

She touched the sleek, black hair lying against his neck. He twisted, moving into her hand like a cat being petted. Lifting her fingers, she traced the bolt of silver at his temple, studying his rugged profile. "No one would call you anything less than brilliant. Your sharp humor, your grasp of philosophy and politics, your knowledge of music, all show the fine mind behind those inquisitive eyes and thoughtful brow." Her fingertips trailed across his forehead, outlining the arch of his eyebrows.

He turned fully to her, his chest grazing her breasts, his eyes glittering, hot and bright. "You wish to comfort me?"

Zel stepped back, lowering her hand to her side. "I . . ."

"You?" Wolfgang prompted, matching her step.

"I—" she took another step backward, sucking in a breath, "think you no longer need comforting."

He smiled, the dimple cutting his cheek, and edged his foot forward. "Oh, but I do."

She slid two more steps away from him, her back hitting the wall. "No . . ." She lurched toward the open room.

His hand shot out, meeting the wall above her shoulder. "Yes."

Zel leaned back, squarely braced where wall joined wall. His other hand stretched out, cornering her securely. He rolled into her, thighs, hips, stomach, and chest, slowly, gently pressing against the length of her. The tingle started at her toes, then followed the trail his body had blazed up her own. She swayed, her head suddenly light as the hot air balloons at Vauxhall Gardens. She was held suspended, tethered in her corner, elevated yet grounded by the hard warmth of his body against hers.

Wolfgang pulled away, the tether broken, but instead of floating free her balloon crashed to earth. Her back was not against the wall. She had been leaning into him so far that his sudden movement threatened to unbalance her. Zel flushed hot as she grasped his arms still braced at the wall beside her shoulders. His muscles bunched beneath her fingers as she fought to steady herself.

Only when her balance, if not her equilibrium, was secure did she dare to glance at his face. His grin widened as his tongue crept out to moisten his upper lip. Lord, if he did not look just like the cat who ate the canary.

"Thank you for the comforting, Gamine," he murmured, then he swung away from her and was gone.

As the door shut behind him, Zel seeped into a puddle on the floor, limbs thick and heavy as the densest Devonshire cream.

"Damn him."

CHAPTER 12

DITHYRAMB

A frenzied, passionate choric hymn
or dance in honor of the ancient
Greek god, Dionysus

THE BEGINNING of an excellent day. Wolfgang ran his tongue
over his lips and leaned back, as far as he could without
tipping, in the high-backed chair. Surveying the empty, sun-
streaked breakfast room, he spread jam over his biscuit, licking the excess off his knife. In fact, the last two days couldn't
have gone better. He'd soon have her lapping cream out of
the palm of his hand.

The first day it had nearly killed him to be constantly in
her company and not touch her. But he was amply rewarded
that night outside her bedchamber door. She'd looked at his
mouth as if it held such a rare and precious nectar she would
die for a sip. He bit into the biscuit, holding the morsel
motionless in his mouth, savoring the slow blending of butter, fruit, and bread before chewing thoroughly. It had taken
all his restraint, but he had touched her only with his eyes.

He licked the corners of his mouth. Satan's silk stockings, he could have sworn her lips swelled and reddened at
his visual caress.

And the second day. Wolfgang lifted his cup and let the coffee flow through his lips, the sweet, pale liquid gently scalding his tongue. He pressed the burning tip to the roof of his mouth. The "accidental" touching had her first confused, then angry, but lastly hungry. She had rubbed against his body as Hecate would rub against his leg when begging for a special tidbit of food. He would have been happy to find something to her tastes but instead stepped back letting her see the answering hunger in his eyes but allowing neither to gorge. The deliciousness of the eventual feast would grow in tandem with the craving. And he wanted her ravenous.

The only low point had been his tantrum over her slur of his intelligence. But it hadn't really been a slur. He had just been overly sensitive to an offhand remark. Or maybe he cared a little too much what she thought of him.

The door creaked and a sleek, sable-haired head popped in, hazel cat eyes blinking at him in surprise.

"Gamine, come in and have a bite." He smiled broadly as he met Zel at the door. "It seems we're the first up to enjoy this spread. I'll prepare you a plate." He took her hand before she could make good the escape he saw in the set lines of her face. Eyes never leaving hers, he raised her hand to his lips, stopping just before contact was made. Then quick as a snake strike he flicked out his tongue, tasting the back of her hand with its tip. She jerked free, anger and something else flashed molten gold in her eyes. Wolfgang's smile widened as he seated her next to his chair.

"What would you have, my dear?" He bowed as he waved a plate over the sideboard. "Before you is a magnificent breakfast array. Pastries, biscuits, eggs, bacon, and . . . ," he paused, sighing dramatically, "strawberries and clotted cream."

"I will have toast and coffee." Zel sat primly in her mahogany chair.

That stiff back, it was so encouraging. He clucked his tongue. "We've a busy day ahead, you must take proper sustenance, and the Miss Fleetwood I admire is nothing if not proper." He piled strawberries and cream on a plate, placing dry toast to the side, laying it before her with a flourish.

Zel looked at him with disgust. "I did not ask for strawberries."

Wolfgang snatched the toast, slathering it with butter and jam. He set the dripping bread back on her plate, deliberately licking the excess jam off the knife.

"You have the manners of a pig."

"Why, thank you, ma'am." He speared a cream-covered strawberry from her plate, slid it into his mouth, sighing more deeply than before. "Food fit for an emperor. Try one." He skewered another berry and popped it into her gaping mouth before she had time to object. He could almost see the thought cross her eyes that she would like to spit it out, but a lady would never display such ill manners at table. He watched her chew and swallow the delightful fruit as if it were a dry stalk of straw. By all the big devils and little demons, she was a stubborn wench.

"I said no berries." She eyed the toast, cut off a wedge, and tried to lift it as jam oozed over the edge. Catching a drip with his finger just as the toast entered her mouth, Wolfgang smeared the glob of jam over her lips. With careful precision he inserted his gooey finger into his own mouth, sucking it clean, while she dabbed at her lips with a fine linen napkin.

Zel stuck out her pointed chin. "Who let you out of the nursery, little man? You're not ready to dine with your elders."

He laughed, putting aside ideas of what he'd like to do with that chin and the ripe lips perched above it, contenting himself in watching her negotiate a truce with the sticky toast.

He poured her a cup of steaming coffee. "Cream?"

Zel nodded.

"Sugar?"

Again she nodded.

Wolfgang stirred. "I like it pale and sweet, too." He handed her the cup, studying her smooth white skin as she swirled the light brown liquid in the china cup. "I'll let you eat in peace if you'll do one thing."

"Oh?" She looked up, wary eyes half hidden under mahogany lashes.

"Feed me a strawberry smothered in cream, and I'll leave."

Zel reached for her fork.

"No, with your fingers."

"Fine." She gingerly pinched a strawberry between her thumb and finger, dipping it in the cream, then leaned toward him. He opened his mouth, eyes on the berry making its slow approach. As the berry passed his lips his teeth came down on her forefinger and thumb, trapping their tips in his mouth. Zel neither jerked free nor flinched, but closed her eyes when he relaxed the grip of his teeth, holding her only with his lips as he teased off every trace of clotted cream with his tongue.

ZEL ROUNDED THE CORNER, making her way down the western most wing of the monstrously huge mansion, scarcely believing she sought Wolfgang's company so soon after that strawberry breakfast. But they needed to rehearse. Though he may not care if they made fools of themselves in the performance tonight, she did. Every time she tried to trap him to read his lines he found a way to distract her, but not this time. The butler had looked at her strangely but admitted Lord Northcliffe's suite was the third on the right. She raised a hand to knock, stopping when she heard a cultured tenor voice read the closing lines to the play. Wolfgang's deep baritone repeated the lines, hesitating at one point until prompted by the higher voice.

"I believe you nearly have it, Captain. If we review again before dinner, you'll be ready."

"Thanks, Jenkins. What would I do without you? Now to find my ingenue lover."

The door opened before Zel could lower her hand.

"Speak of the devil." Wolfgang grinned, but he was unusually flushed. "Or should I say angel? What brings you to my door? I could dispense with Jenkins and devise a little tête-à-tête."

Jenkins hurriedly set down the play script. "Sorry, Miss Fleetwood." He nodded to her before moving from the sitting room to an adjoining room. Rank certainly had its privilege. An earl warranted a sumptuous suite, whereas a mere miss earned a single small bedchamber with her maid far away in the attic.

"I hope I did not disturb your rehearsal." She stared at Wolfgang, who looked like a boy caught with his hand in the candy jar. "We need to rehearse together."

"Most certainly, my dear. Jenkins was helping me learn my part." Color still high, he took her hand, twisting it palm up. Cupping it over his mouth, he breathed deeply onto the gloved skin. Warmth curled in her hand, then his lips were at her bare wrist, and although his mouth only grazed her flesh, his hot breath scorched her, moving in a searing trail up her forearm. He paused at the inner curve of her elbow, the pressure of his lips increasing until she felt her skin being pulled into his mouth. A tingling sensation pooled below her stomach.

Wolfgang smiled innocently and released her arm. "Have I set the mood adequately for our rehearsal, 'Angelica, my sweet young lover'?"

She willed the tingling to cease, quickly following his lead. "Indeed yes, 'Wilfred, my heart's delight.' "

"Let's move right into the final scene. The kiss cannot be perfect without practice."

"No. The ingenue kiss requires naive freshness." She had

grown wise to his tricks. "Rehearsal would destroy it entirely."

"I bow to greater experience." He bent slightly, but Zel saw the sudden silver spark in his eyes. "Miss Ingenue."

"Blast it all, Wolfgang, isn't it a bit early in the day for womanizing?"

Zel whirled about to face the gravelly voice, sucking in her breath at the sight of the man *filling* the doorway.

"Freddie!" Wolfgang answered in a low growl. *"This* is Miss Fleetwood."

"Oops." The man stepped into the room. Zel had never felt so small. He scanned her with eyes such a clear blue she half expected to see clouds scatter across them.

"This great oaf is Sir Frederick Ransley." Wolfgang glared at the big man. "My supposed friend."

Ransley bowed over Zel's hand, eyes still following her. "Charmed, ma'am."

"Sir Frederick." Zel returned his stare, studying his square sun-bronzed face.

Ransley still wore his travel-stained cloak about his massive frame, and his breathing was labored. "Wolf, I'm on my way through Abingdon to Cheltenham. I need to talk to you."

"What's in Cheltenham that has you in such a lather?" Wolfgang reached for the larger man's arm. "Have a seat, I'll ring for refreshments."

"We need to talk, and I need to be off quickly." Ransley eyed Zel again.

"I am past due for a promised game of battledore with Lady Stafford." Zel slipped toward the door. "Good day, gentlemen."

Wolfgang glanced rapidly from Ransley to Zel. Something was afoot between the two men, and although her curiosity was piqued, her presence was not wanted. She shut the door behind her, ignoring the urge to press her ear to the heavy wood, in what would probably be a futile attempt to eavesdrop.

WOLFGANG STRETCHED out full length on the blanket, watching the clouds sweep in and out of whimsical shapes. "Look, it's a berry tart." He pointed out the fluffy imitator.

"You have food on the brain." Zel laughed.

"Among other things." His eyes followed her hand as she raised a half-eaten sandwich to her lips. "Give me a bite."

"Get your own."

"I want a bite of yours."

She leaned toward him, sandwich in outstretched hand. "Here, finish it. I've had enough."

"Feed it to me." He enjoyed her blush, waiting for a sharp remark.

"Feed yourself." She abruptly laid the sandwich beside him. "Once bitten, twice shy. Besides, I wish to walk by the stream."

Wolfgang lowered his lids, listening to the rustle of her skirts as she stood and walked away. He'd let her get a head start then join her later for a private tryst by the water.

His shoulders and neck jerked, snapping him into sudden awareness. Damn, he'd dozed off. He sat, shaking off the fuzziness in his head. The sun shone warm on his face, his skin slightly damp beneath his clothing. He glanced about. Most of his fellow picnickers were still eating, so he hadn't slept long.

Wolfgang strolled with deliberate languor to the brook. No sign of Zel. Spotting some rocks and fallen logs upstream, he made his way along the bank. A smile tickled at his mouth as his foot struck a sky blue slipper. Blue stockings and a straw bonnet lay close by. He clambered over the logs, spying the matching blue of her gown dead ahead. Zel perched on a large flat boulder, skirts hitched to her knees, feet dangling in the clear water below.

He ducked behind the trees lining the brook, stealing along the bank to her side. Her face was tilted toward the sun, eyes closed, lips soft, relaxed. Her toes lightly tread the water, splashing it into sparkling droplets and ripples.

Slipping to the opposite side of the rock, Wolfgang stooped to the water, scooping the liquid in his palm. Zel turned to the sound and he flung the water into her face. She gasped, and skirts in hand, slid off the rock into the shallow stream, spattering water at him with her free hand.

He laughed at her futile efforts, tossing a double palmful of water at her chest, eyes following the wet trail as it ran over her breasts, the thin fabric of her bodice clinging like a second skin.

"You wish a battle?" She tucked the hem of her skirts into the sash tied high above her waist, and legs spread wide, beckoned him onward. After one long look from her bare calves to her disheveled hair, he stepped into the brook and flooded her with water. She desperately flung water back at him, but was soon soaked. Kicking a final stream in his direction, Zel turned and stumbled up the bank. A cry told him her tender feet were no match for the rocks and twigs. Wolfgang jumped the boulder and in two strides caught her up in his arms, carrying her to a sunbathed meadow, lowering her among grass and wild daisies.

"We need to dry off before going back." He spread out beside her, eyes riveted on the curves of her body so beautifully revealed by the wet gown. His eyes lowered, tracing the sleek lines of her still-bared calves. A spot of bright red grew between the toes of a long slender foot.

Wolfgang sat abruptly, grasping the chilled foot in his hands. "You've cut yourself." He pulled a damp handkerchief from a jacket pocket and wiped away the blood. "The wound is minor, Gamine. But one so injury prone as you should always keep a physician close at hand. At your service, again, my dear."

Zel pulled hesitantly, in a half-hearted attempt to free her foot from his clasp. "Stop, my foot is fine!"

He wrapped the handkerchief around her toes, but did not release her. With one hand firmly at her instep, his other hand stroked a line from heel to shapely calf.

"Wolfgang!" She warned, trying to sit, but he unbalanced her by lifting her leg higher, pushing her wet skirts up past her knees.

As his lips brushed her ankle and traced her graceful arch to her toes he could hear the harsh rasp of his own breath. He met her startled eyes, sparkling green and gold in the sunlight, and pulled away the handkerchief, touching his tongue to the dot of blood welling up between her smallest toes. It tasted of salt and copper. He took the tiny curved toe into his mouth, sucking gently, studying the texture with his tongue.

A faint giggle escaped her lips. "What are you doing?"

Wolfgang ran his tongue under her toe while his fingers grazed the soft flesh beneath her knee. Her giggle deepened as she wiggled free of his hold. He made no attempt to regain his grasp, watching her slither away. When she realized he was not pursuing, she stopped, yanking her skirts from her sash, modestly covering her legs. He smiled at the toes peeking out beneath the provocatively wet fabric.

"You stay over there." Zel shook her skirts, plucking a daisy and laying back in the grass. "My toes need no more of your attentions."

He chuckled, sidling closer, but settling a companionable distance from her. "Relax and enjoy the sunshine. We'll be sufficiently dry to join the others soon enough." He pulled off his soggy boots and jacket, then rolled onto his side watching as she smiled and raised the daisy to her nose. His plan of relentless attack and retreat had worked too well. She was securely caught in his sensual net, laughing over intimacies that only days ago would have shocked her. But he was just as securely caught.

Freddies's visit earlier today should have at least slowed this headlong pursuit. How could he think of wedding and bedding a woman when he might be murdered at any minute, and by her brother? But he could scarcely think of anything else.

Wolfgang closed his eyes. Freddie was on his way to Cheltenham to ferret out a lead on the suspected ringleader of the footpads. The suspect was a down-on-his-luck ex-dandy of the ton, now living at the nether edges of society. But Wolfgang didn't know him from Adam or Eve. Freddie surmised he must be a hired thug, likely to turn on his employer at a word of threat or a flash of gold. Employer! Damnation and the devil's tail, he prayed it wasn't Robin.

Lifting his lids a hair, he peeked at Zel. She was still lying on her back, a lazy smile playing about her lips, the daisy in her hand now bereft of most of its petals. Wolfgang stared in hopeless fascination, as the remaining petals drifted one by one onto her breasts and stomach. Brothers and murderers be consigned to hell, he would have her for his own.

"I'll go after them." Melbourne rose, brushing a wrinkle from his puce jacket, as he looked toward the stand of beech trees by the stream. "He thouldn't be alone with her for long, you know."

"Oh, Melbourne, don't be an idiot." Isadora allowed a touch of irritation to show on her face as she sipped her warming champagne. "She can take care of herself. Can't she, Newton?"

"An intelligent woman such as she can handle a man like Northcliffe." Newton's long, sensual face twisted in his semblance of a smile. "But we're nearby to help, if needed."

"Well." Melbourne straightened the rug, resuming his

seat. "I thuppothe you're right. It ith awfully gentlemanly of you to take an intereth."

Isadora smiled at the young fool. "Newton is nothing, if not a gentleman."

"Thank you, my dear." Newton smoothed his mustache, his faintly nasal tones deep and silky. "You would always recognize a gentleman, wouldn't you, dear Isadora?"

"That Northcliffe, he ain't no gentleman," Melbourne whined. "I don't underthtand what women thee in him."

"No, you wouldn't." Isadora laughed, patting Melbourne playfully on his padded shoulder. "Don't even try to understand, at least until your lunch is digested."

"Now, now, my dear," Newton murmured, then redirected his attention to Melbourne. "I believe what she means is you must leave the courting of Miss Fleetwood to Northcliffe."

Melbourne blushed. "But I wathn't——"

"Why, Jeremy, dearest." Isadora purred, "are you developing a tendre for her?"

Melbourne's color deepened. "Well, I . . ."

Her laughter pealed out. "Oh, this is rich."

"Isadora." Newton's warning came across clearly, but he pinned Melbourne with his cold dark eyes. "I do not want you to interfere with Northcliffe and Miss Fleetwood."

"But, I would thave her from more thcandal."

"No." Newton's harsh tone sent a pleasing little ripple of fear up Isadora's spine. Melbourne, uncharacteristically, was pushing too hard. A tiny twitch played at Newton's lips but he softened his tone. "You could be a great help if you'd keep an eye on our Miss Fleetwood. Be her little shadow and report back to me her every move."

"ANGELICA, light of my life, love of my heart." Wolfgang swooped down, pressing his knee to the floorboards of the makeshift stage, one hand on his heart, the other reaching out beseechingly. "Come away with me, tonight."

Zel raised a hand to her brow, turning dramatically to the audience. "Would that I could, but my life is not my own."

"You owe nothing to your evil uncle." Wolfgang stood, hauling her roughly to him. "Be my wife and he will command you no more."

"How can you want me?" She bowed her head, voice cracking, as rehearsed, in fear and grief. "What can I offer you?"

"Yourself." He lifted her face with gentle fingers at her chin. "All I ever wanted was you."

"Oh, Wilfred, my love." Zel collapsed into his arms.

He tilted her head, bringing his lips ever so slowly to hers, meeting her mouth with deliberate coolness and detachment. No burning press to mold and possess, instead he steeled his mind against thoughts of her, filling it with mathematics and . . . sheep. Yes, pages of meaningless numbers and worthless theorems and acres of smelly, noisy, stupid sheep.

Applause and laughter caught his ears. He drew away from Zel. She tripped slightly, but he took her hand, leading her in their curtsey and bow. "You missed your calling, Miss Fleetwood, your performance would put Mrs. Siddons to shame."

She laughed, but the forced sound did not hide the questions in her eyes. "And yours would dwarf Kemble's best, Northcliffe."

He guided her off the ballroom stage, and they strolled triumphantly through the congratulations of the milling guests.

Wolfgang filled a plate from a buffet supper laid out near the terrace doors. "It's too warm and crowded. Come with me." Balancing a bottle and the plate, he slipped his free fingers about hers, pulling her through the glass doors, across the garden. He tested a small door then drew her into an overgrown, moonlit conservatory. Seating her, he placed the food on a tiny table, drawing another chair close.

"A feast fit for a vagabond princess. No glasses, no silverware, only a shared plate in the moonlight."

Zel smiled warmly. "A vagabond princess and her wild gypsy lord."

He caught his breath, returning her smile, eyes caressing the pale loveliness of her face. "Gamine." He stopped, slowly exhaled, and centered himself, back on task. "Crab cake?"

Zel nodded, confusion reflected in her eyes as she took the fragrant morsel. Son of Satan, she might as well be confused. He certainly was. Wolfgang didn't understand what he felt for her. The desire was clear; he knew desire. But these other warm sensations in his chest and stomach when she was near or even when he thought of her . . . And those damnable urges to take her in his arms and just hold her, he couldn't fathom at all. The only emotions even approaching these were what he had felt for Gwen and what he felt for Grandmama. But he bloody well didn't see Zel as his sister or grandmother.

He shook his head and reached for another little seafood pattie. This whole business was entirely too strange and he wasn't at all sure he liked it, except when he touched her and looked into her eyes. Then and only then did it make any sense.

Wolfgang bit into the crab cake. The thought of spending a lifetime with her became more alluring every day. He admired her intelligence and humor. There was also a sense of stability and loyalty about her that somehow appealed to him. And of course the passion, which he knew would be expressed not only in sensuality but in a zest for life. There was something else, something in her eyes when she'd called him her wild gypsy, something beyond sex or companionship, something that he'd seen in her before, that nagged at the back of his mind and scared him silly. Beelzebub's boot-

black! If he continued in this vein, he'd soon be mistaken for
Byron or one of his romantic, poetic, idiotic set. He was best
off staying in the physical rather than the metaphysical
realm.

Wolfgang scooted his chair the remaining inches until
its arm touched the arm of Zel's chair. "Mushroom?" Plucking the pickled delicacy from the plate, he leaned over the
chair arm, ignoring Zel's hand, dangling the brown button
before her mouth. "Open up." Surprised at her obedience, he
paused a moment before sliding it into her waiting mouth.

He fed her cheese, dried fruits and tarts, delighted as she
popped a few tidbits in his mouth. She even guzzled champagne straight from the bottle. Finally she signaled him to
stop before he pushed a last apricot through her half-closed
lips.

"One more sip left." He handed her the bottle.

She raised it to her lips, clearly savoring the last gulp,
emitting a soft, ladylike burp as she lowered the bottle. "Pardon." She chuckled, low and musical.

"I'm appalled at your juvenile manners, Miss Fleetwood," Wolfgang teased, throwing this morning's words at
her. "Who let you out of the nursery?"

Zel stared at him, then let loose a full-bodied, rolling
laugh. He tossed back his head joining her laughter until his
stomach and jaw ached.

She wiped tears from the corners of her eyes, gazing at
him a little shyly, as if they had shared a deep intimacy.

He stood, trapping her feet between his, clasping the
arms of her chair. "Zel." He bent closer, perusing sea-green
eyes dazed with champagne, full lips moistened with food
and wine. This kiss would not be tempered by mathematics
or sheep.

Her mouth was soft and yielding. He explored the texture of her lips, slowly, from corner to corner. She pressed
harder, molding her lips to his. He flicked out his tongue.

Her mouth opened, tongue grazing his, boldly outlining his teeth and lips.

He held himself still, relishing the myriad textures of her mouth, the lingering bittersweet taste of the sparkling wine, and her ever-present gingerbread scent. As he edged back she leaned toward him, dragging his tongue into her mouth. With a shudder he gripped the chair arms, maintaining the distance between them with a force of will that surprised him.

Wolfgang withdrew again, and she followed, leading him further into the depths of sensation. Inch by inch he worked away from her, inch by inch she eased forward to keep him, until she was nearly out of the seat, refusing to sever the contact between them.

He jerked free, at the nether limits of his control, ready to dispatch his plans to the devil. Zel slumped back into the chair, eyeing him warily, a deep blush revealing her awareness of her role in the kiss.

Dropping into his own chair, putting more distance between them, Wolfgang focused on her hands as they curled in her lap. His strategy was working better than he ever dreamed. But could he maintain it until the battle was won?

JENKINS POLISHED off the remnants of his supper, continuing to study the tiny redhead across the table. Maggie, but what was her last name? Usually a lady's maid was called by her last name, but Maggie was always Maggie, most likely to keep that devil husband off her trail.

The captain hadn't said much about her after the day they'd run off the brute. Imagine attacking women in daylight on a city street. The man was an animal. Miss Fleetwood was taking care of the frightened little thing, and the captain kept an eye on her too. Even so he felt an old feeling begin to stir, a desire to protect, to hold her, cupped in his hand like some small flame-crested bird. He grinned. She was a bit like a bird, so petite with quick, graceful movements. But her plumage glowed brighter than the female of the bird species normally sported.

She'd smiled shyly at him a few times at meals or passing in the halls, but had scarcely uttered more than a handful of words. How could she be other than frightened of him? With her experience of men, and his own hideous face.

He'd looked up again and caught her soft green eyes on him. He flashed his toothy, white grin at her, and the corners of her mouth turned up, ever so slightly, before she looked away.

Lingering over a cup of tea after everyone had left, he considered approaches. What would not cause her to flutter away in panic? Jenkins pushed back his chair and stood, surprised to see her hovering, ready to flee, in the doorway.

"Would you care for a cup of tea, Maggie?" His voice sounded unnaturally loud in the deserted room. She would bolt.

"Yes, thank you." Maggie's voice trilled, barely more than a whisper.

He held out a chair across the corner from his, seating her with a flourish. "I believe you take your tea plain?"

"Yes, thank you." The words came out a little stronger, but this had the makings of a one-sided conversation.

Jenkins filled a cup for her and warmed his own, searching for a safe topic. "The Staffords have a lovely estate, though it's not as fine as Cliffehaven."

"Cliffehaven?" Her question moved a little above a murmur, some hope here.

"Yes, the captain's estate." He paused at her puzzled expression. "Excuse me, I rarely use his lordship's title. Cliffehaven is Lord Northcliffe's estate, by the sea. It is not your conventional country manor, but it is surprisingly beautiful in a wild kind of way. Suits the captain, it does."

Maggie sighed softly. "Perhaps I'll see it someday, if my mistress . . ."

"Yes, if your mistress?"

"I'm not the kind of servant to gossip, but . . ."

"But?" He coaxed.

"Oh, well, you are his valet and I am her maid, I suppose they have few secrets from us." She lifted her teacup with a delicate hand. The tiny hand that had gripped his in the coach after he had driven her husband away.

"No secrets."

A little storm passed over her brow and the words burst out. "Why can't they admit how they feel and just get married?"

"I think the captain made a few strategic mistakes, which instead of winning him the war served to heat up the battle."

"He doesn't seem a fool." Maggie was clearly more than a bit perturbed. "Why doesn't he patch it up?"

"I believe that is what he is doing."

"Well, it doesn't seem to be working." She tossed her head. "She complains of him more than ever."

"She does?"

Maggie gazed into the teacup so seriously, Jenkins wondered if she might be reading the leaves. "She does, but I wonder." She looked absently into his eyes. "I think she may be softening. Much as she complains, maybe she is truly enjoying this week. But she's still afraid."

"Afraid of the captain?" Jenkins stopped a laugh. "He is a dangerous man to some but tender as a lamb to her."

Now it was Maggie's turn to stifle a laugh. "A lamb? Lord Northcliffe?" She took another sip of tea, a frown pulling at those rosebud lips. "He may not be a lamb, but I believe he would not hurt her. Convincing her of that is another matter."

A chance to help the captain win his lady and spend more time in the company of this sweet creature. Wasn't he getting a bit too old for all of this? He looked at Maggie's winning little face. No, not too old at all. "Perhaps it is an undertaking we should try."

ZEL JERKED AWAKE, shivering convulsively, wiping the sheen of perspiration from her forehead and upper lip, her other hand reaching to her breast. It was covered by the fragile lawn of her night rail, the nipple beneath budded tight, the surrounding flesh swollen and tender. She blinked back the shadowed visions that flashed in her mind. Dream images of a shaggy-haired wolf stalking moonbeams, luminous silver eyes glowing hot in the dark, long tapering fingers stroking her bare, pale skin.

She cried out in near pain, dashing from the bed to the nightstand. With shaking hands Zel poured water into the basin and splashed the night-cooled liquid over her face and neck. Tearing at the ribbons, she yanked her night rail over her head. The sharp morning air hit her body hard as a fist, followed by the cold water she ruthlessly tossed over her shoulders and chest. Water and energy spent, gasping for breath, she stood, allowing the remaining skin-heated droplets to trickle down her, skating over her breasts, belly, and thighs in a soft caress.

Looking down at her wet body in the predawn light, Zel studied the well-known, yet suddenly strange, lines and curves. What did Wolfgang see when he looked at her? She had spent little of her life in the company of men other than her brother and father, and had encountered desire in a man's eyes only a handful of times before. She recognized it now. He liked what he saw, and he had certainly seen much more than he should.

Two tiny streams joined at the tip of her breast, dripping slowly off the puckered nub. He had suckled at that nub, drawing so hard she had felt strands of shimmering tension run through her torso, clenching together at the juncture of her thighs.

Zel followed the dribble of water as it hit her leg, streaking down her long thigh, skimming about her knee, racing across her shin and ankle to converge with the growing pool at her toes. She closed her eyes as the trickle of water filled her with memories of the brush of strong, slim fingers.

A large drop slipped between her breasts, sliding quickly across her flat stomach, hiding in the dark down at the base of her abdomen. A twin drop flowed the length of her spine, nestling between the curves of her derriere. Zel shuddered, skin suddenly hot where he had previously touched her only through layers of silk and lawn.

How would it feel to have his eyes, hands, and mouth on her naked flesh, everywhere? Leaving not a single inch bereft of his searing touch. Lord, she would never survive it. She would spontaneously burst into unquenchable flames. When she married him, he would make himself a widower on their wedding night. When she married him . . . not if, *when*.

Sighing, Zel reached for a drying cloth and rubbed her chilling skin briskly. She would marry him. She would share his bed, bear his children, host his political dinners, and pray like hell that she was not absorbed totally into his life, a pawn to his expectations and desires, with nothing left belonging to her.

She could no longer deny she wanted to be part of his life, to connect with him both in and out of the marriage bed. But she could not be the wife most men demanded. She could not compromise and compromise until she had sacrificed all that made her who she was, becoming a shell of a woman as her mother had. Wolfgang had told her in many ways that he respected her mind, admired her views, and supported her work. But marriage could change all that. Once she gave him legal rights over her, as her husband, he would own her as surely as he owned his phaeton and grays. Under the law she would cease to exist as a separate person, and any power she held would be that granted by him.

Shivering, suddenly very cold, Zel pulled on her robe,

belting it tightly. She was afraid. But she would say yes when he asked again. If he asked again. No, he would ask again, even if she had to hook him with a few of his own lures.

Her decision was made. She had known when he sucked her toe. She sat down hard on the stool before the dressing table. Damn, wasn't there something at least a little odd in that? The man sucked her toe, and did she push him away, strike him, or resist him in any way? No, she giggled. Giggled like a schoolgirl as he laid the final death blow to her defenses with that devilishly clever mouth of his.

CHAPTER 13

TOCCATA

A free form musical piece
with full chords, swift runs and lofty harmonies;
from the Italian "to touch"

"WHY THE DEVIL are you squinting so?" Wolfgang walked
Zel away from the open lawns to a hedge-shrouded bench to
await their next turns with the bow and arrow. "Where are
your spectacles?" He looked back toward the small group of
archers, barely visible through the thick greenery. "Is that
damn Melbourne following you again?"

Zel flopped onto the bench, pushing her hair back off
her brow. "I have not seen Lord Melbourne all morning, and
I can see well enough without my eyeglasses, thank you."

"Now that I think of it, I haven't seen your spectacles
since I returned them to you." He stood beside her, one foot
on the bench at her hip. "This vanity isn't like you, Zel."

She fixed a hard look on him. "It is not vanity."

"Then where are your spectacles?" He persisted. "I'll
send a footman for them."

"I have been unable to get new ones since the old ones
were broken." She looked at her hands. He followed her gaze,
watching as her long, slender fingers intertwined.

"But certainly it doesn't take that long to get new ones, or at least get the old ones repaired?" Wolfgang ran a knuckle along her jaw. "I don't mind if you're a little vain, you know, but it is important for you to see."

"I am not vain." Raising her eyes, she met his gaze squarely. "I cannot afford them. I spent all my extra money from my allowance for the rest of the year on frippery for my season."

"Are your finances that bad?"

Zel frowned at him. "You saw my accounts. You of all people should know how bad my finances are."

"Yes." He looked away. "My man of affairs handled that." He sat close to her, returning his gaze to her face. "I know you didn't spend large sums at the modistes or milliners. Your money went to merchants for food and household supplies and to your few servants to cover their wages, in advance."

"I covered necessary expenses first, of course, but I had a few coins left."

"How are they entered in your books?" He gripped her elbow.

She squirmed under his intense grasp and gaze. "Under miscellaneous personal expenses."

"No, I do remember enough to know that the only sizeable entries were the household accounts and wages." He levered her closer. "I should have put this together before. When I first met you, you were gowned in little better than rags. Now you have such a lovely, costly, albeit unusual wardrobe. Where did it come from, Zel?"

"A gentleman does not concern himself with the source of a lady's gowns or their cost." She tried to pull away.

Wolfgang clutched her other arm, hauling her nearly to his lap. "I'll ask what I please as your family's financial guardian. And I have the right to honest answers."

She gazed at him coldly, only the golden flames in her eyes reflecting her anger. "Do you think I stole them?"

"Zel, don't play with me. Are you protecting Robin again?"

"Damn." Zel's spine went limp as she slumped against him. He released her, wedging his arm around her shoulders instead.

"You need to tell me—" He stopped. Her shoulders were shaking. He lifted her face to his. God, the minx was laughing. "What, in Lucifer's name, is so funny?"

"I should have known . . . you suspect poor Robin," she blurted out between gales of laughter. "I thought you thought I . . . bloody thief."

Wolfgang shook her gently. "I'm sorry, I didn't think you a thief."

"You thought Robin . . . thief . . . I bought bargain thread, ribbon . . . raided aunt's attic . . . her coming out clothes." Her laughter rang so out of control she was coughing and hiccupping. "Nearly fifteen years old . . . you pompous . . . ass. Small wonder—" she choked, "Robin hates you."

He glared at her, giving her another little shake. "Stop this. Compose yourself."

Zel tried to stare him down, but dissolved into another wave of hilarity. ". . . see yourself . . . pompous ass."

Wolfgang watched the tears streaming down her cheeks. He was behaving like a pompous, overbearing, overprotective ass. And she was developing the language of a sailor. His lips twitched as he zeroed in on her, drawing her rapidly into his embrace. But the resistance he expected did not materialize, and the force of his attack laid them out on the hard bench.

He twisted about, sprawling her on top of him, taking her mouth deeply, fiercely, without gentle preliminaries, swallowing her hiccups and giggles. She wiggled, rubbing her hips into him, slipping her arms beneath his shoulders. He slid one leg over the backs of her knees, as his hand at her derriere pressed her into his arousal.

"Wolfgang," she whispered, burrowing into his chest.

By all the brimstone in hell, he'd like to yank up her skirts and bury himself so deep in her it would take an army of Welsh coal miners to dig him out. He choked back the growl rising in his throat, stilling his marauding mouth and hands. Why was it so damn difficult to keep to his plan? To give her just a taste and make her come for more. Around her he acted no better than a randy schoolboy out to tumble the nearest dairy maid. But he didn't want a quick tumble in the hay with Zel. He wanted her first time, their first time, to be a prelude to their life together, filled to overflowing with tenderness and ecstasy.

"Zel?" Wolfgang eased her off him, scrambling to his feet, reaching to pull her upright. She swayed slightly, as dazed as he at the sudden onset then abrupt interruption of passion. He brushed the wrinkles out of her skirt and pushed a few pins more securely into her hair. Half the house party thought they were having an affair. They didn't need to convince the other half. "You look a bit rumpled, but you'll do." He tugged at his jacket, smoothing the fabric over his chest. "Come, Gamine, squint all you wish, only please hit the target this time. We'll replace your spectacles when we're back in town."

SHE SHOULD HAVE brought her music. She would have remembered it if she hadn't been so furious with Aunt Diana and Emily and Wolfgang. Zel was never without it for so long, and now to be asked to perform and to depend on the taste of strangers. . . . She scattered another pile of sheet music.

Haydn, Handel, Clementi, Haydn, Purcell, Haydn. Wolfgang called this a fast crowd and not a Beethoven in the house. No, here . . . a sonata and another. She eagerly pulled the scores from the stack. *Pathétique* and *Appassionata*. "Oh, Lady Stafford, forgive my rash tongue, you are a saint among women," she murmured, settling the familiar music on the pianoforte. Either could be ready in the two days before the concert. More notice would have been nice but no longer necessary.

Pathétique she knew would play well to this audience. *Appassionata,* a more recent and challenging piece, might be doing it a bit strong. She spread out the former and eased into the first movement, soon absorbed by the relentlessly haunting melody. She stumbled over a few complicated sections, but halted to catch her breath only after the last note was played. With that breath came a well-known scent, an untamed smell of oak and birch, tall grass, horseflesh and saddle leather.

"I should have known to look for you here." His voice sounded just above her head.

"Have you been riding?" She pivoted around, scanning up his broad chest to the tanned, slightly flushed face.

"Yes." Wolfgang's eyes met hers, his tone accusatory. "I couldn't find you."

"I was meeting with Lady Stafford, planning the musicale." Zel matched his tone. "And if one is to do any accusing, it should be me. You regaled the lady with stories of my prodigious talent. She refused to hear my nays and placed me firmly in the program with nothing less than a sonata."

"Good, I'm proud of your talent." He folded his arms, looking very smug.

"You might have been embarrassed if I'd failed to find familiar music."

"But you must know many pieces by heart." He sat beside her on the bench.

"Shorter pieces, yes, but I rely on the score to prompt me on the longer pieces."

"What are your choices? I heard only the end of the one you were playing. Beethoven, I presume?"

Zel held up the music. "Both Beethoven. *Pathétique* or *Appassionata.*"

"Why, there's no choice." Wolfgang grinned. *"Appassionata* it must be."

"But I know *Pathétique* so well, it is nearly ready now."

"Play *Appassionata."* He clasped her hand. "For me."

"You'll have to promise to leave me alone then, for the rest of the afternoon today and several more hours in the morning and afternoon tomorrow."

"I suppose I can handle that." He sulked. "If I could have a few moments now, before you lose yourself in your rehearsal."

"Shall we move to the sofa?" She stood, taking his other hand to draw him up.

His eyes intent upon hers, he raised her hand to his lips and gently kissed each fingertip. "You're unlike any other woman I've known." He sat very close to her on the settee.

"Lady Stafford said the same thing." Zel grimaced. "But I do not believe she was being complimentary."

Wolfgang's eyes shuttered. "What did she say?"

She paused, then plunged in. "That I was nothing like your other women and certainly not like your wife."

"Damnation and demon spawn." He raked his fingers viciously through his hair, pulling free the already disordered queue. "I'm sorry. I wouldn't have you embarrassed for the world. But thank God you are nothing like Rosalind."

Zel's voice sounded tiny, even to her ears. "What was she like?"

"Where do I begin? Are you sure you really want to know?"

She nodded.

He jumped to his feet, stalking to the pianoforte, running his fingers roughly over the keys. "She was a whore. A bitch in heat." He smiled grimly at the shock on Zel's face. "I suppose it didn't start that way. At least I didn't know it from the start. I was just home from the Peninsula, my physical wounds barely healed, when Ridgemont persuaded me to forget my worries in the social whirl."

Wolfgang sat at the bench again, face to the pianoforte, back to Zel. "I met her at her come-out ball. She looked like a fairy princess. Tiny and delicately beautiful, face framed in a cloud of golden hair. She seemed all that was good and sweet. I was completely besotted." He swiveled, a hard, unseeing glare aimed at Zel. "I had to have her. I had nothing to offer but promises. I told her I would make a fortune for her no matter what it took. I'd become a pillar of the community. Everyone would look up to us.

"She had dozens of suitors, but I was the most obsessed. I never left her side at parties, never looked at another. I never did more than kiss her fingertips, I was so certain of her purity. She chose me." Wolfgang pushed off the bench, striding to the windows. "She insisted on a long engagement and the thrill of the hunt began to wane. I started to work, making good my promise of wealth, devoting myself to my properties and investments. I hadn't inherited the earldom, had no hope of doing so with so many in line before me, but I wasn't a pauper." He ran restless fingers over the lines dividing the panes of glass. "She complained that my adoration for her wavered. I tried to devote myself to her and my promises, feeling stretched to the limit, consoling myself that the wedding drew near and all would be well." He struck the window, the glass shook.

Zel dashed to him, enclosing his fist in both her hands. "If this is too difficult, you do not need to continue."

He looked at her queerly. "I want to tell you."

She guided him back to the settee. "Then sit with me." She opened his fist and twined her fingers with his.

"The wedding was a disaster. The bride was drunk and crude. The groom thought his disillusionment complete. But the illusion was to be shattered further. The bride wasn't a virgin and made no secret of the fact she had a string of lovers both before and during the engagement." He leaned into Zel, eyes focused on their hands. "I could have forgiven lovers before the engagement. I was certainly no saint. But

I'd been stupidly faithful to my betrothed and expected the same.

"During the wedding trip to the lake country she tried to convince me she was still my fairy princess, tried to rekindle my adoration. But it was gone. I could see too clearly behind the facade." Wolfgang squeezed Zel's hand.

"I realized I'd never loved her, never really knew her. I tried to bargain with her. I'd provide her with the wealth she craved in exchange for fidelity until she bore me a son, then she could do as she pleased." He stroked Zel's thumb, scratching his own finger with her nail. "She laughed in my face, and the minute we were back in town she took up with her former lovers, one of whom was Newton." He raised her hand to his cheek. "He's one of the men who cuckolded me and then blamed me for not making her happy. Maybe I didn't try enough, I don't know. I finally exiled her to a small family holding in Scotland, promising to divorce her if I found she was pregnant. She lashed out in fury, and word came she was bedding anything on two legs.

"I went to Scotland and told her I would begin divorce proceedings immediately. We fought bitterly and I left to spend the night at a local inn. The next morning she was found dead at the bottom of the stairs."

Zel gasped and pressed in close, kneading his hands.

"There was an inquest and I was cleared. She was seen alive by the servants after I left, and witnesses at the inn swore I was there all night." He raised his eyes, no longer trying to mask his pain. "But there were many who believed I killed her. I put my affairs in order and took off for the Orient before the dirt had settled on her grave, and didn't return until two years ago."

"My God, I am so sorry, Wolfgang." Zel released one of his hands, laying her fingers lightly over his cheek.

"Those years in the Orient probably saved my sanity." He breathed in deeply. "My father had been a missionary in the Far East before his marriage, and he brought home his

Chinese butler. Some of my earliest memories are of Mr. Yang and his friendship. He taught me his language and culture."

The faint stubble on his face scratched at her palm as he pushed his cheek into her hand. "With that kind of knowledge, I found I could make deals with a few renegade Chinese merchants in Singapore. Deals no other English barbarian had a chance at. I threw myself into trading. I was only trying to forget Rosalind, but made a tidy fortune in the process."

Wolfgang pulled her fingers to his lips, his shaky laugh warming her hand. "I didn't plan to burden you with my memories. Some wounds refuse to heal." He leaned forward, holding her hand to his chest. "It's been over five years, and I can't stop thinking I should have done something differently."

Zel put her free arm about his shoulders. "But you did not kill her, you cannot blame yourself."

"I was a fool. I should've seen her for what she was and never married her at all. She'd be alive now."

She smoothed the hair at his nape. He released her hand, arms circling around her waist. Wrapping her own arms about his neck, she pulled his head to her chest. "She made her choices. You made yours. What's done is done. What does it serve to torture yourself over the past?"

Wolfgang gripped her tighter. "I seem good at doing just that."

Zel gently massaged his shoulders and back. "Are you talking now about the deaths in the succession line?" She kept her tone light. "Surely you haven't found a way to blame yourself for those too?"

"Just hold me." His sigh shuddered through her body as he rubbed his cheek against her silk-covered breast, arms still clenched fast about her.

.   .   .

"I DON'T TRUST that man." Maggie looked into the kind, scarred face, seeking the reassuring bright blue eyes. "He and his friends watch Miss Zel all the time, follow her around. Jenkins, we need to do something about him."

"Maggie, I asked you to call me Marmeduke." He flashed his strangely perfect teeth, so at odds with the rest of his face. "The captain takes care of his own. There's no love lost between him and Newton, but your mistress won't be hurt."

"He makes me fretful." She leaned against the thick oak trunk, watching Newton enter the stables. "I suppose I worry too much, but I don't like the look of him or that Horeton woman either."

"Come walk a bit more." Marmeduke took her elbow. "You won't be needed for another hour or more."

Maggie sighed and followed his lead, wondering again why she felt so safe in this man's company. She barely knew him and she certainly could not be drawn to his looks. She peered up at him. He looked as if Miss Zel's dog had chewed on him more than a bit. But all those scars were somehow comforting. He'd smile at her with those amazing white teeth and the chill she'd lived with for years would suddenly lift. She wanted to know everything about him. "How long have you worked for Lord Northcliffe?"

"I worked for his family near as long as I can remember." He steered her along an overgrown path, away from the house. "His grandfather pulled me off the streets, gave me work in his stables. I was one of his Christian charities, but it saved my life even if not my soul. When the captain's father, a third son, mind you, married, I left with him to live on his wife's estate and run the stables there.

"Captain always adored horses. People used to say he was born astride a saddle, such a wild thing he was." Marmeduke held a willow branch aside for Maggie to pass. "After his sister died he didn't have anyone except the Chinese butler, myself, and his horses. He did make some friends at school, and later when they all bought their colors he asked me to go to the Peninsula as his batman. I thought it would be my last chance for adventure before sinking into old age." He laughed, a wonderfully warm sound. "But it sunk me good."

Maggie joined his laughter. "I wouldn't say you're sunk yet."

"I caught a rifle ball and came back in no condition to work the stables. Captain asked me to be his valet. I couldn't believe my ears, but when he sweetened the pot with a promise of my own horse, how could I refuse?" He stopped at a small lily-clogged pond. "I learned the job. It's easier than training horses at my age. I do it well. Now, tell me more about you."

"I've only worked for Miss Zel about a month." She meant to be evasive but suddenly wanted him to know the truth. He already knew most of it. "I ran away from my husband. You met him."

"Shall we sit?" Marmeduke had her settled on a bench beside him before she could reply. His voice when he spoke was hard. "I know. He beat you."

"I married young. My parents were pleased that a prosperous farmer would want me, with no dowry. The beatings didn't start right away but he controlled my every move, kept me away from my family and friends." She took a deep breath and continued. "The first time he hit me was after I smiled at a neighbor in church. The next day he tended my wounds and cried as he begged forgiveness. I wept with relief and forgave him.

"We repeated that little scene often but still I believed that each beating would be the last. It was years before I faced the fact I would die if I stayed. Then I ran away so many times it all blurs together." Maggie waved her hand, he took it, steadying it with his own firm grip. "He always found me and dragged me back. The beatings got worse. This last time I made it to London, and a woman on the streets told me about Miss Zel, who gave me a safe place to stay. Several days later when my injuries started to heal, she asked me to work for her."

Maggie turned, watching the sunlight glint off his thick, white hair. "I was afraid to say yes, even though I wanted the position more than anything. What did I know of being a lady's maid? But she didn't care. She took me in and Mrs. Stanfield's maid, Sally, taught me how to go on. Sometimes I think Miss Zel doesn't have a lot of need for a personal maid, but she lets me fuss over her and I help around the house too, same as Sally does. And you know, I have a knack for it too.

"I'd do anything for miss." She kept her tone light but didn't try to hide the tears in her eyes. "What other maid in London, or the world for that matter, has a mistress willing to battle a brute of a husband for her?"

"She's a true gem, a worthy mate for the captain."

"But is he worthy of her?" She queried half in jest, half in earnest.

"Aye, he surely is."

"ZEL? Where are you? Are you hiding from me?"

"Sssh." Zel beckoned him from a hedge off the moonlit terrace.

Wolfgang strode toward her, grin widening with every step. "Leading me on a merry chase?"

"No, I am avoiding Lord Newton." She frowned at his even, white teeth, as he laughed. How could he be in such high humor, playful and flirtatious, when just this afternoon he was clinging to her, near tears? She pulled him behind the hedge, groaning. "I let him connive a dance out of me, but I hate to have him touch me, and it's a waltz."

"By Satan's horns, ma'am, I never knew you to be such a craven coward."

"He refused to take no for an answer. He got Lady Stafford to put his name on my card."

"The scoundrel. Should I call him out, my lady?" He bowed over her hand.

Zel pulled away her hand. Wolfgang might be teasing her, but she decided it would be unwise to tell him how Lord Newton had crudely whispered to her that he was ready as soon as Northcliffe moved on. The last thing she wanted was for a duel to be fought over her. "There is something about him. I get little shivers down my spine whenever he is near."

Wolfgang raised his brows. "Should I be jealous?"

"Not those kind of shivers."

"Are there different kinds?"

"Of course. There are the bad kind that make one nervous." Zel walked along the path heading away from the terrace. "And the good kind that tickle."

She was not aware he was so close until his finger ran down the back of her neck, inducing a tiny tremor. His whisper feathered the hairs at her nape. "Which kind was that?"

"If you cannot guess, I'll never tell." Zel ducked away, straying farther down the path as the moon slid behind a cloud.

Wolfgang followed, only a step behind. "I think there might be a third kind." He clasped her arm firmly in his long fingers. "Hold still so I can demonstrate." He hauled her back against his chest, slipping an arm about her waist as he ran his lips ever so lightly up and down her neck. "Now, I'm not sure, you'll have to tell me. What kind of shiver was that?"

"Well . . ." She paused. "It did tickle my neck."

"Just your neck?"

"Yes."

His warm lips started at her ear, brushing moonbeam soft across the back of her neck to her shoulder, sliding the sleeve of her gown down her arm. "Now didn't that tickle go down your spine and end in a warm puddle right about here?" Wolfgang wedged a hand between them tracing a line lower and lower down the center of her back.

"No." Zel broke away, scurrying ever farther down the cobbled path, deeper into the garden.

His laughter echoed deep, rich, and very near. "Stop, I haven't finished my demonstration." He whipped her about so quickly she lost her balance. He joined her tumble into a fragrant flower bed, taking the force of the fall on his back, shifting her to his chest. She laughed and squirmed as he grazed her ribs and sides with his fingers. The laughter subsided as he rolled her to her back and slid on top of her. His body covered hers, heavy and warm, a blanket of flesh and muscle.

Zel felt oddly bare and cold when he pushed off her. She gazed into his face as he hovered over her, knees and lower legs braced along her hips and thighs, hands at her shoulders. The moonlight was filtered by the trees and flowering shrubbery, too dim to see his eyes clearly, but they seemed backlit, two glowing, silver half-moons surveying her face and form. A shiver coursed the length of her body as if he touched her everywhere at once. The scent of roses filled her nostrils as she watched the shimmering sphere in the sky above dip behind an oak branch. Closing her eyes, she pictured his mouth, hot and mobile, pressing to hers. As if in answer to that invitation his head lowered until his lips met the corner of her mouth.

Perched over her on all fours, he became a wild beast bent on devouring her with his feral mouth. He took her lower lip between his teeth, shaking it gently, releasing it to nibble a line along her upper lip, then following that line with the tip of his tongue. She stirred languidly as he nipped her lobe and laved the swirls of her ear. His mouth and teeth left a trail of little circlets of sensation down her throat, moving to her chest. He burrowed through the valley of her breasts, his chin pushing aside the fabric of her gown as he feasted on the narrow canyon's inner curves.

Wolfgang lifted his head abruptly, molten eyes on her half-bared breasts. Bending again, he licked her nipple through the thin silk of her gown. Zel shuddered violently as he nudged aside the cloth and took the puckered tip between his teeth, alternately nipping, licking, and suckling until she sighed in relief when he released the tortured flesh to torment its twin.

Slowly, he raised his head again, looking deeply into her eyes, a smile spreading from his silver eyes to his generous mouth. He barked out a rough laugh, arched his back, head high, and howled softly at the full moon.

She stared at him, dazed, for several moments, then answered his smile, whispering his name.

His laugh caressed her gently. "Demonstration complete, an undisputable shiver of the third kind."

"I DON'T UNDERSTAND why you are doing this." Isadora sounded like a truculent child. "He's such a fool over her you'll only force a marriage."

Newton circled her chair and gave her a scathing look. No wonder Northcliffe had thrown the woman over so quickly. Her charms were not sufficient to overcome the grasping, stupid, all-encompassing self-interest. "Do you think so?"

"She is a nobody, and not even that attractive."

"You gravely underestimate her attractions, my dear." He smiled, seating himself on the polished mahogany chair next to hers in the small salon.

She sniffed, her aristocratic nose lifted high. "She's pretty enough, I suppose, and her figure adequate. But she's an Amazon, entirely too tall and unfashionable."

"Not all men care that a woman be a slave to fashion. She is more than pretty and her figure is far beyond adequate." Newton scanned the length of Isadora, emphasizing her lack of height. "Many men like a tall woman. Those long legs. But there is more than appearance to consider."

Isadora frowned. "Men want a beautiful woman on their arm and in their bed."

"But to hold a man of intelligence, a woman must have more than the latest fashion plates up here." He leaned over, tapping lightly on her forehead.

"But men hate bluestockings." She seemed truly puzzled.

"Isadora, there's little more exciting than the surrender of a woman of intelligence, strong will, and fire." Pulling a cheroot out, he watched a glimmer of comprehension float over her eyes.

"Oh, I see, you are talking of the chase enhancing the eventual submission."

He lit the cheroot, drawing deeply of the smoke, exhaling slowly. "In part, dear Isadora, in part."

She turned her head to avoid his smoke. "But I still don't understand why you wish to force marriage."

"I don't believe I ever said I wished to force a marriage."

"Then what do you plan?"

"Do you wish Northcliffe happiness?"

"No, but what has that to do—"

Newton cut in. "I wish to muddy an already murky situation." He flicked the ash off the end of the long cheroot. "Northcliffe and his lady are always together and her brother's debts are paid, but I'm certain she is still a virgin."

"I don't understand," Isadora whined.

"Neither do I, my dear. That's the problem." He laughed sharply. "He could have her now, with or without marriage."

"Then wouldn't he be a fool to marry her?"

"That is the very question for which we will soon have an answer." Newton smiled thinly. "She's truly a woman on the verge. And your old lover is pushing her over the edge."

"How can you be so sure?" She pouted.

"After what I saw last night, I'm sure." He took another drag.

Isadora looked like one of those irritatingly eager little lap dogs. "What did you see?"

"Only a little tête-à-tête in the garden last night."

"Details, details!" Only her voyeurism could outdo her envy.

"Jealous, my dear? Do you still pine for the man?" He could never resist a dig at her vanity. Isadora couldn't bear to think a man could ever prefer another to her, while at the same time she wished all the details of his love-play with that other.

Isadora tossed her head arrogantly. "You know he threw me over. I don't care a lick for him anymore." Her eyes gleamed. "What did you see?"

"I don't gossip unduly about ladies, but even with my experience and jaded tastes, I was quite stimulated."

"So that explains your ardor last night."

"I suppose it does. There had to be some reason for it." Newton blew a smoke ring in her face. "My plan tonight requires your assistance. I need you to keep the good vicar entertained and at ready tonight, while I do the same with Lady Stafford."

"But, what do you think will happen?"

"Everything, my dear. Miss Fleetwood plays Beethoven at the musicale." He flicked ash at the hem of her skirts.

Isadora stood, shaking her gown. She frowned at him but held her grip on their conversation. "Oh, and what is the significance of that?"

"Watch Northcliffe while she plays. You'll see."

"Newton? Lady H?"

"Melbourne," Newton whispered. "That young pup with his calf love could ruin everything. Keep him occupied tonight too, if you have to sit on his lap. Better yet I'll give him a job to do. He can betray his love." He raised his voice as the young fop poked a pointed nose in the half-open doorway. "Melbourne, come join us. We were just speaking of your favorite subject."

"Ah? My favorite thubject?" Melbourne sauntered in, striking a pose at the window.

Newton blinked. Gads, he could be blinded by the way that bright purple ensemble reflected the sunlight. "Miss Fleetwood. She is snared in Northcliffe's net and we are desperately seeking the means to save her."

"We mutht protect her. How can I help?" Melbourne's face glowed with pathetic zeal.

"Could you keep a watch on them? Not too close, mind you," Newton warned. "Let me know if they leave together."

"Yeth, yeth, then what?"

"You may follow them, if you can do so discreetly. Then return to me with their whereabouts."

"And then?"

"I'll handle it from there. Don't look so crestfallen." Newton smiled grimly, restraining a laugh. "What happens next could be dangerous. Northcliffe's not a man to tangle with."

"But I would fight for her." Melbourne stood to his full height, straightening his cravat.

"You must stay away from Northcliffe, avoid injury." Newton exchanged a glance with Isadora. The idiot made her look a scholar. "You must be there to comfort her when all is done."

WOLFGANG CLOSED his eyes, willing them all away, but when he peeked, the crowd remained, eavesdropping on the music Zel played for him alone.

Appassionata. Beethoven was a man of the flesh. This piece combined with Zel's fire and physical nearness played on his senses with all the power and drive of her assault on the keys.

He brushed her arm as he reached to turn the page. She

smiled at him, the same sloe-eyed smile she'd given him last night in the garden. The smile that heated him from toes to fingertips. He'd come up in the world this week, almost equal to Beethoven in her passions. He grinned. Could he ask for more?

But the promise of something more lingered within the ocean of green in her eyes. A promise he'd seen before, never comprehending its full meaning. Now part of that meaning was clear. She was his. After her performance he would ask her to be his wife, and this time she would say yes. A damn good thing, at the rate things were going he'd never last the rest of the week. He'd convince her of the wisdom of a special license, waiting a month to read the banns would be unnecessary torture.

Wolfgang shoved his thoughts aside, allowing the music to pull him in, focusing on the complex piece flowing effortlessly from her long, nimble fingers. The forceful notes thundered against him like a fierce storm, and the soft notes enveloped him like sea mist at dawn.

Zel poked a discreet elbow in his ribs, and he roused himself from his trance long enough to turn the page and return her smile. He didn't make the best musician's assistant, but it was her fault. How could he concentrate on the little black marks on the sheet while she transformed them into a pure, seductive force that swirled about him with the danger of a hurricane?

He breathed a sigh of relief when the last tone reverberated through his chest. The physical and emotional effort of her playing left him unaccountably winded and sated, as if he had been caught completing an intimate act. He slipped his hand about her upper arm, penetrating her fever with a squeeze. "Make your curtsey and come with me. We need to talk."

She nodded as she accepted the applause. He guided her slowly from the gilt-and-cream music room, careful to blend well with the other guests adjourning to the drawing room and terrace, graciously accepting congratulations. Eventually they made their way down an empty hallway through a slightly ajar door into a small salon, lit only by the moonlight pouring through undraped French doors. He would convince her he was not like the other men in her life, then make his proposal.

Wolfgang inhaled abruptly, locking the door behind him. Turning to her, he started his speech on the exhale. "I hope you don't think me like your father—"

Zel cut in, placing her hands firmly on his shoulders. "I should hope not." She skimmed one hand around his neck, pulling him down to meet her lips.

"We need to talk," he breathed into her mouth.

Laughing, she captured his eyes as she momentarily freed his lips. "You talk too much, kiss me."

"Devil take us." He moaned, surrendering to the insistant pressure as her mouth molded to his. The proposal could wait, neither of them were going anywhere. Running his hands the length of her back, he crushed her breasts to him. As he backed her to an oversized sofa, he claimed leadership of the kiss, deepening it to taste the soft recesses of her mouth. He ran his fingers through her hair, scattering pins about them.

Her low laugh filled his ears as they tumbled onto the sofa. He shifted his weight, lying half on, half off her long slender body, patterning kisses across her eyes. Zel retaliated with lips skating along the line of his jaw, ending in hot circles in the whorls of his ear. Ah, the woman was a remarkably fast learner.

He yelped when she nipped too hard on his earlobe. Fire and brimstone, perhaps she needed to work a bit on finesse, but her fervor was all he could wish. Eagerly taking her mouth, he scraped his tongue along those sharp little teeth, while his fingers dislodged the smooth silk at her shoulders to expose the silkier skin beneath. He inhaled her scent and eased his lips slowly down her throat to nestle in the soft curve joining neck and bared shoulder. Her fingers wedged between them, working at the buttons of his waistcoat and the edges of his control.

Blood thundering in his ears, Wolfgang pressed his teeth softly into her throat as he lowered her bodice and chemise in one swift motion. She arched into his hand, transforming his light touch into a bold possession. He rasped out a breath, stroking the sleek mound, gently pinching and rolling the nipple between his thumb and forefinger. Her breath escaped in a purr as she tugged at his rumpled cravat. Jerking the offending neckcloth free, he gazed at her bared breasts, glowing with enticing perfection in the dim light. He lowered his head to the tight bud in his hand.

"Ah, Zel," he murmured, as he took the hardened nub into his mouth, tracing its pebbly texture with his tongue. Her hands continued their work at his chest, intent on releasing him from his shirt. Suckling and nibbling at her breasts, he studied the firm contours of her rib cage and the flat plane of her stomach with an unsteady hand while she desperately fought his shirt studs. He knew her success when her heartbeat raced and her fingers smoothed the hairs on his chest. Pulling his shirt wide, he clasped her to him, rubbing against her naked breasts, nipples hot and hard as glowing coals against his skin.

Whatever snippet of control Wolfgang had left snapped. He hauled her skirts up her legs. The skin above her stockings was soft and warm. He could lose himself forever in her endlessly long thighs. Her skirts edged farther upward, the prize within his grasp but for the flimsy barrier of her drawers. "Lucifer's inferno! I hate these things. Take them off."

Incredibly agreeable, Zel ripped at the tapes that fastened the offensive garment to her petticoat, her voice at his ear broken and husky. "Not so difficult."

With a growl he yanked the tubular pieces of cloth down and off her legs, tossing them over the back of the sofa. His fingers quickly refound her thighs, rubbing in ever wider circles until his knuckles brushed the curls at the juncture of her legs. Smiling at her rapid intake of breath, he outlined the soft triangle with the very tips of his fingers, finally skimming her tender cleft. He dipped a gentle finger into the folds, pleased with the moisture there and with the little whimpers his lips followed up her throat.

Wolfgang took her mouth roughly, plunging his tongue as deeply as he wished to plunge into that other passage. Her fingers tangled in his hair and her hips thrust into his hand, intensifying his touch, negating any thought he might have entertained to slow things down.

As he nipped at her lips, his restless hand wedged farther between her legs, massaging her swollen flesh until she writhed beneath him. With painstaking slowness, he eased one finger deep inside her. "Do you like that, Gamine?"

Her moan was the only affirmative he needed, and the lone finger sunk to the palm. She tightened around him and he tightened in painful response. Stroking rhythmically in and out with his finger, he circled his thumb around the centerpoint of her pleasure. His skin tingled when the first shiver slivered through her. Increasing the pace of his intimate caress, he whispered, "That's right, Zel, let it happen."

Wolfgang lifted his head, looking into her hazy, passion-drugged eyes, then bent to draw a taut nipple into his mouth, seizing it between his teeth, teasing it with his tongue.

Her body stiffened, rigid as stone, then with a cry, a shudder rushed through her he could feel down to his toenails. He clung to her, savoring her tremors of pleasure, relishing the depth of her response to him.

Nudging her legs farther apart with his knee, he unfastened his pantaloons with clumsy urgency. "Satan's horns! I can wait no longer," Wolfgang rasped. The moist warmth of her flesh, as he positioned himself, drew him inward. He stopped, breathing hard. If he didn't slow down he'd injure her and kill himself.

"We heard a cry. Is anyone hurt?"

Wolfgang raised to face the intruding voice. The cords of desire threading through him clenched into a heavy knot of dread.

Rector Nibbleton and Lady Stafford stood stiff as statues in the open French doors, moonlight casting their long shadows deep into the room.

BRAVURA

A musical passage requiring superior
agility and technical finesse

A CHILL SHIFTED over Zel as the last wave of pleasure
quivered through her. What was that strange voice and why
was Wolfgang mumbling unintelligible words in her ear?

"Please give us a moment to collect ourselves." He
seemed to be speaking to someone other than her. As he slid
part way off her, she could see two figures by the leaded glass
doors. They faced outward to where another person stood.

Wolfgang pushed up, fumbling with his pantaloons.
"Pull up your gown."

She stared at the dark hairs on his chest, hairs that moments before had tickled her breasts. He jerked her to her
feet, swatting down her skirts, yanking up her bodice. Zel
watched him button the studs of his shirt, his fingers trembling slightly, his mouth and eyes grim. "Straighten your
hair."

Patting the hair tumbling about her shoulders, she wondered where and when the hairpins had gone. She spotted
several on the settee, a few more on the floor. Lord, a drawer
leg. Snatching it up, she scanned the room for its other half.

Wolfgang saw it first, draped over a neighboring chair, and stuffed it into the waistcoat he was fastening. She was by his side in two strides. "I'll take that."

"No." He took the matching leg from her, adding it to his waistcoat. Pushing aside his hands, she grappled for the garment.

"Ahem."

Zel whirled to see the rector approaching, disapproval etched in his face. "Rector Nibbleton." Scarlet heat marched rapidly up her chest and neck to her hairline.

"Miss Fleetwood," the Rector began, his voice piercing as a steeple bell.

Wolfgang took her arm. "This is entirely my fault. Miss Fleetwood is blameless." He pinched her gently. "I set out to seduce her, but will do my duty as a gentleman and wed her as soon as arrangements can be made."

Zel sputtered, rising anger making her inarticulate.

"I'm sure you understand," Wolfgang continued smoothly, "that my betrothed and I need to speak privately."

"I will remain nearby, on the terrace," the Rector sniffed, escorting Lady Stafford through the French doors to join the third person standing in the shadows.

"Newton," Wolfgang gasped beside her. "Damn the man." He drew her down to face him on the settee, still warm from their aborted coupling. "Zel, I'm sorry it happened this way."

"Sorry!" She choked back a scream. "I will not be forced or tricked into marriage."

"You goddamn little fool." His voice was very quiet and harsh. "I didn't purposefully try to seduce you. I told the vicar that to protect you." His grasp on her arms was beginning to hurt. "Don't you understand this is now beyond your control?"

"No, we can—"

"By all the fires in hell, you make me wild." His hands tightened, then he suddenly relaxed his grip. "We can do nothing but marry and quickly. If we don't, you'll be ruined, completely, irretrievably. I won't allow that to happen."

Zel squirmed, unable to free herself from even his loosened grasp. "I can go to the country, live quietly, the gossip will die soon. I do not care what the ton thinks, anyway."

"I can't believe you are truly this naive." He eyed her coldly. "Everyone, not just the ton, will cut you now. You'll be labeled a whore. No one will receive you."

Her ribs contracted about her lungs, forcing the next words out in a gasp. "No! You are wrong. People who know me will not judge me so harshly."

"They'll judge you, and condemn you." His voice and eyes softened. "Zel, I know about this. I was a pariah after my wife's death, the subject of endless gossip and scorn." He released her arms, taking her hands in a gentle grasp. "For you it'll be worse. It's always worse for a woman. Think about what you've already endured."

"I can face it."

"The devil." Wolfgang dropped her hands and stood, one hand rubbing his brow. "Think. Think what Lady Stafford saw. Think what she will tell."

"But we . . ." She straightened her spine. "I mean . . . well, we did not finish."

"Zel, put the pieces together." He hovered over her. "You were on your back on this settee, skirts up to your hips, bodice down to your waist. I was on top of you with my shirt and pantaloons open. Lady Stafford doesn't even need to embellish."

"But you said this was a fast crowd." She looked up hopefully. "Surely they will not care—"

"Even the fast crowd draws the line somewhere." He frowned at her. "It just doesn't wash to be discovered by the local vicar making love on the sofa in your hostess's salon. The story will be spinning about London within hours. Your days of doing charity work will be over."

"Lord." Zel slumped into the cushions, head in hands, the reality of the situation hitting her like a blow.

Wolfgang slipped onto the settee, hands on her shoulders. "If we marry now, there will be some scandal, but it will die in time. I can absorb most of the blame. It's my fault anyway. I can't believe I allowed this to happen." He lifted her chin with his knuckle. "Hellfire, it may even clean up my reputation. People will say he seduced the sweet thing, but he did right by her, made a proper marriage of it."

She gave him a ghost of a smile, squaring her shoulders, still too dazed to think clearly. "What do we do from here?"

"Zel, this will work, I promise." He brushed his lips over her forehead. "I'm sorry, but believe me, I didn't plan things to happen this way. I lost my head."

Knowing he did not carry all the blame, she sighed, releasing some of her anger for him and replacing it with blame for herself. She didn't plan for things to happen this way either. "We both lost our heads."

"We'll ride this out together." Wolfgang traced the hollow of her cheek with his long fingers. "I'll head out on Ari at first light and put Rafael to work on a special license. Then I'll see my solicitor to draw up a settlement."

"Settlement?"

He took her hand. "Yes, I plan to settle an amount on you that will allow you complete financial independence if anything happens to me. I'll also provide you with a generous allowance."

Zel ran her thumb lightly over the back of his hand. "But you've already paid Robin's debts. And I do not even have a shilling for a dowry."

"Yes, *Robin's* debts. This settlement is for you. Maybe it can help you feel less trapped in this marriage."

"But—"

"I want to do this."

She met his eyes and nodded her assent.

"Good." He squeezed her fingers. "While I'm in London

I'll meet with your father and contact the other relations. You take the carriage to London then meet me at Cliffehaven."

"I suppose there will be enough time to gather my possessions and talk to Aunt Diana and my friend Emily?"

"Bring them with you, bring anyone you wish. Plan to be at Cliffehaven day after tomorrow, and we'll wed the following day. No, it's the Queen's Tea and Grandmama and Mother will have to be there, so the wedding will have to wait one more day."

"The Queen's Tea!" Zel rested her head wearily on his shoulder. The room seemed to be spinning, she felt dizzy from the speed with which this was happening. "Lord, every woman in London will be gossiping about us."

"Grandmama will defend us." He stroked her hair.

"Your family will be furious, put upon to produce a wedding with no advance warning."

Wolfgang groaned. "You'll have to meet my mother and older sister. Don't worry, Grandmama will take charge, keep them in line." His lips twitched. "She'd rebuild Prinny's Pavilion in a day if she thought it'd get me married. And she adores you."

"Your sister?"

"I have an older sister, a cold witch like my mother. Try to ignore her. Grandmama will help."

"She is a sweet old woman. What would we do without her?"

He laughed. The rector clucked at them. Wolfgang smiled at the rector good humoredly, then turned back to Zel. "Don't ever let her hear you call her old. But, she'll be beyond pleased that you'll be my wife."

"Wife," Zel mused, lifting her head to meet his eyes. "How strange it sounds."

"It won't be so bad." He fingered a stray lock of her hair. "Give it a chance, you'll come to like it."

* • • •

NEWTON SURVEYED the card room at Brooks's. A little early for the usual crowd, but a good enough time to start collecting on his wagers. He'd make a decent sum, too bad so few had been willing to bet against him. He pulled up a chair, settling himself down with a few regulars, Melbourne close at his elbow.

"Time to pay up, old fellows."

"Pay up?" Southerby cocked a grizzled brow.

"Northcliffe brought his fox to ground." Newton smiled smugly.

Melbourne sniffed. "Not right to bandy her name about."

"The bluestocking surrendered?" Rutherford boomed.

"Yes, but the hunter was caught in his own snare."

Southerby raised his other brow. "Do say more, Newton."

"Suffice it to say the pair were caught in flagrante delicto on the sofa of Lady Stafford's salon." Newton modulated his tone to be heard at the neighboring tables. "Northcliffe played the gentleman and offered for her. They'll be married within days at his main seat near Winchelsea."

"So the slippery snake is caught." Rutherford held his round stomach in and roared. "It's what he gets for dipping his quill in a chaste inkwell."

"Mith Fleetwood ith a lady," Melbourne interjected.

"Well, yes, she will be." Rutherford clapped Melbourne soundly on the back. "*Lady* Northcliffe, that is." He dissolved into another round of laughter while Melbourne grew steadily redder.

"I don't believe it. Mith Fleetwood would never . . ."

Newton smiled at his featherbrained minion. "I'm sorry to knock her off the pedestal, Melbourne, but you know I saw them with my own eyes."

"Better keep your tongue when Northcliffe's about,"

warned Southerby. "The man's a loose screw. Fought duels over a mistress or two and always wounded his man. Likely to kill over his wife."

"Never dueled over the first one." Rutherford piped in, dissolving into peals of laughter again. "Killed . . . her instead!"

Newton allowed a little smile to curve his lips. "North-cliffe doesn't know of the wagers?"

"No one breathed a word of them to him after one night when he got a mite testy over the gel's reputation." Southerby swallowed a healthy dose of port. "And the man never looks at the betting books."

"Well, I do watch the books, so pay up."

Rutherford grumbled. "I'm not sure I like this. Marrying her ain't the same as bedding her, you know."

"True, it often is not." Newton pulled out a cheroot. "But take it from me, in this case the bedding came first, even if it was on a sofa."

"IT MUST HAVE been built by a deranged fairy." Zel peered, transfixed, out the carriage window.

"Let me see." Emily pushed her aside, pressing her face to the glass. "Lud!"

"What in the world! Move!" Aunt Diana squeezed in. "Oh! I've never seen the like."

"Damn, Remus." Zel pushed the dog back to the floor.

"Watch your mouth, dear."

Zel jockeyed for a place at the window, completely entranced as the coach drew nearer the castle—no, manor—no, cottage—no, mansion, no—she hadn't the slightest idea what one would call Wolfgang's country home.

Cliffehaven was like a stew—separate pieces a cook would combine in a palate-pleasing conglomeration. At first sight she wasn't sure it worked, but as they progressed up the long drive suddenly it coalesced. The parts all came together and she liked the result.

It obviously began with an ancient castle, two towers still peaked near the center of the assemblage. Then every one hundred years, or thereabouts, someone must have gotten the urge to expand, and constructed an addition in the mode of the time. Not being an avid student of architecture, she didn't recognize all the styles, but she knew the stucco and timber of Tudor, the squared brick of Georgian, and the pillars of Palladian. And somehow they all gracefully, even playfully, intertwined, encircled by sections of formal and wild gardens.

"It suits him." Aunt Diana smiled.

"Who? Northcliffe?" Zel queried, scratching Mouse's ears.

"And I think it will suit you." Emily reclined on the cushions beside Zel.

Zel grimaced at her. "I admit it is intriguing. I shall enjoy exploring and learning architecture at the same time."

"I suppose you'll have some time to explore." Aunt Diana remained fixed to the window. "I wish you were taking a wedding trip. It would be a good way to, ah, solidify your marriage."

"I have work on Aquitaine House and Northcliffe has a bill in Parliament. We will return to London in a week or less." Zel pushed a few strands of hair off her brow. "Besides, I'm not sure either of us wants a great deal of time alone together."

"Zel Fleetwood, you can be such an idiot." Emily chuckled, rolling her eyes. "I think your husband-to-be will want to spend a great deal of time alone with you."

"Oh, that." Zel's neck and cheeks warmed while she buried her face in Remus's furry back.

"Don't sink this marriage before it has begun." Emily's tone turned serious. "Don't let your father kill it. You've already admitted to me you had decided to marry him before the incident. Give yourself a chance for some happiness."

"This just is not the way to start a marriage." Zel lifted her head, rubbing her temples vigorously. "I know Wolfgang is not like my father, but sometimes I cannot help being afraid."

Emily laid her hand on Zel's shoulder. "For once in your life, don't try to control everything. Let things happen."

"Control everything? I do not try to control everything."

"How can I say this?" Emily paused. "Think of marriage as playing a Beethoven sonata. There are strong elements of control and discipline, but there comes a point with the true artist when the music takes over, has a life of its own."

"I'm not sure how this applies to marriage?" Zel looked closely at her friend.

Emily gave her a quick hug, landing a kiss on her cheek. "Oh, Zel, for such an intelligent woman you can be so thickheaded. Just promise me you'll relax a little and at least not try to make the marriage fail."

"Come what may, we're here and with plenty of time to rest before dinner," Aunt Diana pronounced as the coach stopped before a wide, columned entryway. "Zel, hold that animal back. We can't have him assaulting a new relation. Speaking of relations, don't look now but there's an older female version of Northcliffe standing in the doorway."

"Northcliffe's aunt, Dorothea Clayton—" Zel began, but Remus decided the woman's plain pewter gown would look better with a paw print design and bounded up the stairs. Wolfgang's top-lofty aunt landed hard on her bottom before Zel pulled the hound off. "Forgive me . . ."

The butler Zel remembered from Wolfgang's town house bent to help the disgruntled lady to her feet, sneaking a wink at Zel. "At your service, m'lady."

"Oh, McDougall, do not rush it. I am not m'lady yet."

Remus licked the massive Scotsman's hand. "Thank God, he likes you. Could you take charge of him until we settle in?"

"With pleasure, m'lady." He waved footmen into motion to handle baggage, horses, and coaches, while he wedged his fingers firmly into Remus's collar.

"Upstart fortune hunter," Aunt Dorothea mumbled. "No better than she ought to be, already familiar with the butler."

Zel ignored the woman, concentrating on getting her small party, including the second coach containing Maggie, Sally, and Emily's maid, Pru, into the house.

Dorothea straightened, a sharp, hard laugh tearing from her throat. "Do not expect people to forget your scandalous behavior soon, and this too-hasty wedding. You were the talk of the Queen's Tea. Even Lady Darlington couldn't save you. Hardwicke should never have been made earl and you are certainly no countess." She turned abruptly and stalked up the stairs.

"Ignore her," McDougall advised. "You're welcome here. The captain will introduce you to the servants later. I told them what kind of lady their new mistress is."

"I am not sure if I should be pleased or dismayed."

"Pleased for sure, m'lady." The brazen fellow winked again and she felt strangely at ease. Wolfgang's retainers were not the conventional sort, but that didn't surprise her. "Aye, here's the captain now."

Zel whirled about as Wolfgang swung off his huge chestnut and raced up the stairs. He pulled her into his arms, kissing her firmly on the mouth, releasing her to address the broadly grinning McDougall. "Is Miss Fleetwood's party settling in?"

"Of course, Captain." McDougall sounded mildly insulted that his efficiency could be doubted.

"Where's Hecate? I think we need to carefully introduce her to that beast you're restraining." As if in response to the question, the big gray cat rounded the corner into the entryway. Wolfgang bent to pick up the animal, just as Mouse spotted her. The cat looked haughtily down at the hound, with unblinking yellow eyes. Remus whined, then sprang at cat and master. McDougall moved quickly, his hand at the collar firm. Mouse fell back exactly where he'd taken off.

Zel stroked the dog's head and neck. "No, the kitty is not for you."

Wolfgang chuckled. "Kitty? I don't believe Hecate's ever been called a kitty. She's rumbling fiercely as any lioness."

"I hoped at least one of them would be calm. She looks fine to me."

"She's ready, positively itching, for a fight. Every hair and claw is on end. This little sorceress likes her foes much bigger than herself, like another enchantress I could name." He smiled warmly and turned back to the butler. "Take Miss Fleetwood and her, er, dog to her room. I'll take Hecate to the library." He reached into his pocket, drawing out a small battered package, presenting it to Zel with a bow, his dimple flashing. "A little prenuptial gift. Open it upstairs."

Zel took the package, brushed her lips over his cheek, and dashed after the departing butler.

Her rooms suited her taste, done in emerald and sapphire tones, the furniture in cherry wood, everything massive but elegant. McDougall indicated her sitting room and dressing room, and the door adjoining the master's suite with a key in the lock.

"Tell Maggie to settle in before she attends me. I believe I will have a nap." She flung herself onto the curtained four-poster bed as McDougall stepped from the room.

Zel tore at the wrapping of the package and out spilled her drawers. Of all the nerve. Shaking them out, she caught a flash of light. She balanced the ring between her finger and thumb, watching as the brilliant marquis sapphire caught the rays of sunlight glinting through the window. A scrap of paper lay half-concealed inside the wrapping, the handwriting so neat and even she doubted it could be Wolfgang's.

"A relic of our unholy passion, surrounding a prayer for its endlessness. W."

She read the note again, aloud, laughter gurgling up from her throat. Maybe life with Wolfgang wouldn't be so bad. Then again . . . She sighed, slipping the ring on her finger.

"RUB A LITTLE oil in my shoulders, Maggie." Miss Zel sat straighter in the bath, as Maggie reached around her for the scented oil. "I feel tight all over."

"But the ceremony went well." Maggie pinched and stroked the tense muscles, relieved the deed was done, her mistress at last a married lady. Somehow she feared there'd be some last-minute mishap.

"The ceremony went smoothly enough. The breakfast, however, was a complete disaster." Miss Zel sighed, leaning into Maggie's hands. "I wish we could forego dinner, but it's a long ride back to London, so nearly everyone is staying tonight."

"What happened?"

"Wolfgang's aunt insulted me constantly, his cousin leered, his mother played queen, Aunt Diana dithered about, Father and Robin downed a cellarful of champagne, and," she paused for breath, "Wolfgang and his grandmama bristled and growled at everyone, hackles up like Remus looking for a battle." She splashed water on her chest and neck. "If it were not for Emily and Wolfgang's friends, Ridgemont and Ransley, I would have taken the first coach back to London."

Maggie jerked upright when the adjoining door opened. Lord Northcliffe stalked in, satin dressing gown draping bare legs and chest, looking for all the world like some reckless god come to earth, the kind in those Greek stories Miss Zel was forever reading.

"You may leave, Maggie." His voice was as hard as his handsome face.

"Yes, m'lord." She readied miss's towel and dressing gown, but his lordship was already shedding his robe and reaching for his new wife. Maggie dropped an oil bottle. The man wasn't wearing a stitch. And he seemed to have forgotten she was even in the room.

"I need to dry off, Wolfgang, I'm cold and wet."

Maggie scurried for the door.

"Fine, I'm hot and dry."

Water splashed as Maggie grasped the door latch. When she yanked the door wide a sizzle like bacon slapping a hot griddle hit her ears. Face burning, she stumbled through the door. A flash of gray whipped past her feet. She turned back toward the room, toppling on her knees as a solid form smacked her in the back, leaping over her shoulders.

"Remus," Maggie called, but the huge beast could no more hear her than sprout wings and fly.

Cat and dog barreled headlong for the two naked figures by the bed. "Lord." Maggie prayed for divine assistance and closed the door.

She stood motionless outside. His lordship swore fluently, Miss Zel's voice was a little softer, every other word either Wolfgang or Mouse. Glass broke, wood cracked. Maggie knocked tentatively at the door.

"Who the hell is it?" Lord Northcliffe was not a man she could easily approach at the best of moments.

"Do you need help?" Maggie inquired timidly.

The door flew open, his lordship had donned his robe, but failed to fasten it. She looked away as he barked, "Get someone, now!"

Maggie darted down the hall, and Jenkins and McDougall nearly ran her over at the stairs. "The animals . . . Miss Zel's room."

She followed them back down the hall, peeking around Jenkins through the open door. The room looked like a whirlwind had struck, chairs and tables overturned, bed drapes ripped, glass and crockery littering the floor. His lordship, dressing gown now securely tied, straddled Remus. That animal was still, finally recognizing a beast wilder than himself.

Miss Zel huddled in the bed, blankets pulled up over her bosom, clutching the cat to her chest with bare arms. Two sets of slanted eyes stared at Maggie, wide and unblinking.

"Straighten the furniture and get that glass up before someone's cut," his lordship snapped.

Miss coughed. Maggie looked up from the glass. Gracious, this was not a time to be laughing.

"What's so funny, Lady Northcliffe?" his lordship growled.

Miss's laughter rolled out. "I'm . . . sorry."

Lord Northcliffe climbed off the dog, motioning to Mc-Dougall. "Take this thing into my chambers." He pulled the cat from the giggling Miss Zel, placing the animal in Jenkins's arms. "Jenkins, join him, I'll be there shortly. We'll find a way to control these beasts or consign them to hell."

He sat on the bed beside Miss Zel as Maggie lowered her head, filling an unbroken vase with shattered glass. "The comedy is over, calm yourself."

"I'm sorry." Miss tried unsuccessfully to choke back more laughter. "You are so . . . funny."

"Me? Funny?" Maggie could hear the scowl, as he bit out the words. "Explain yourself, madam wife."

"Madam wife . . ." She was off on another peal. "If only you . . . see yourself."

"Satan's horns, I think the world was safer before I tried to thaw the ice maiden." He paused, then continued, his voice very low and controlled. "Go on, explain yourself."

"Well, first . . . you looked like a stallion." She stopped laughing. "Kind of magnificent, ah, ready to mount a mare."

Maggie gasped. "Miss Zel!"

"Miss Zel, indeed. Close your ears, Maggie, finish with that glass and leave." His voice dipped so low, Maggie had to strain to hear. "And that was funny?"

"No." Miss gulped. "It was more funny when you mounted Remus and wilted."

His lordship's tone fell even lower, rasping out roughly, "You are treading on dangerous ground."

"You said to explain."

"The devil save men from plain-spoken virgins." He tripped over Maggie's feet. "And their redheaded maids."

"Pardon, m'lord." But he was already through the connecting door, slamming it behind him.

Miss Zel sighed from the big bed. "Hand me my wrapper, Maggie."

Maggie winced at the bangs and crashes coming from the next room. "Seems they're tearing up his lordship's chambers now."

Her mistress slipped on the thin silk wrapper, a broad grin lighting her face. "Yes, it seems they are."

"SMILE," Zel hissed at him. "We barely made it through dinner, and your thundercloud attitude is not helping."

Wolfgang surveyed the unwanted guests milling about the informal salon, whispering through bared teeth. "Better?" He glared at his toadeating cousin who stood nearby, leering relentlessly at Zel. The idiot seemed to have no idea he was putting his life in danger.

Zel stared coolly at Wolfgang. Then she pulled away from him, turning to her new cousin, Adam.

Grasping her hand, Wolfgang replaced it at his elbow, his voice low. "We'll face this together. I need your restraint. Without it, I may do bodily injury to someone. I wasn't thinking when I had Raf and Freddie leave after the wedding breakfast. They could have at least sat on your father and my mother."

Zel's father chose that moment to appear and grab Wolfgang's hand, giving it a squeeze and shake while raising a champagne glass in his free hand. " 'Gratulations, old man. Glad to have you part of the family." He leaned his rounded belly forward, conspiratorially, not bothering to lower his voice. "Even if you had to get under her skirts to get her to the altar."

"Fleetwood." Wolfgang laid his warm hand over Zel's stiff, cold one at his elbow, his throat tight. "You will treat my wife with the respect due her."

Sir Edward's ruddy cheeks reddened more. "Don't get yourself in a snit. You know I respect the chit—"

"I am not a chit," Zel interrupted. "If I told you—"

"See, she don't respect me," Sir Edward whined.

"Champagne, cousin?" Adam smiled, placing a filled glass in Zel's hand, hovering too close to Zel on the other side, eyes again focused on the low décolletage of her pale green silk gown. Wolfgang felt another wave of anger stir in his chest. Satan's tail, he wasn't going to be a jealous husband, was he? Zel would have more sense than to conduct a flirtation with his foppish cousin. But they hadn't spoken about what marriage meant, about fidelity, commitment, children—all those damn things he didn't want to think about.

Drawing her away abruptly, rudely, from her father and Adam, he whispered, "I expect you to be faithful."

Zel jerked about, golden sparks flashing in her eyes. "Giving orders so soon, *my lord*."

"You promised only this morning to obey me."

She choked on her champagne.

"As I think on it now, you didn't say obey." He hauled her against him, breathing in her ear. "You mumbled that part."

"How could I agree to obey?" Her sweet smile contrasted with the flames still burning in her eyes. "That would be a lie."

Wolfgang smiled back. "You said love clearly enough."

A bright flush suffused her cheeks.

"No quick answer, my dear?" He widened his smile.

"Well." She collected herself. "I do care about you a tiny bit, so it's not such a big lie. And you have no room to taunt me. Even people outside the chapel heard you say . . ."

He used his most seductive tones on her. "Heard me say what, Gamine?"

"That part about, ah, with my body . . ." Zel stumbled over the words.

Wolfgang nodded, unwilling to help. "Yes?"

She blurted out, "With my body I thee worship."

"And that, if we can ever be alone, will be no lie." He greeted Zel's friend Emily, approaching on Robin's arm, with a full grin. Robin looked more than a little dog bit, and less than eager to converse with his new brother-in-law.

"Lies?" Emily teased, her dimples peeping out. "I hope you two are not starting your life together with lies."

"All lies . . ." Robin slurred, stepping his lanky frame up to Wolfgang, staring at him with bloodshot eyes. "You'll answer to me if you hurt her."

"We've been through this before, Robin." Wolfgang met his gaze sternly. "Don't make a fool of yourself. She's my wife now. I'll protect her as I deem necessary."

"Wolfgang, Robin." Zel tugged at Robin's sleeve. "Why must you two constantly posture and fight like a couple of roosters. I do not require protection."

Robin jerked his arm roughly from her grasp. "Buy my notes . . . she'd sleep with the devil—"

"Fleetwood." Wolfgang's low grumble penetrated the younger man's thick skull, and he closed his mouth with a sullen glare.

Zel turned to smile at Wolfgang's mother and sister, who had joined the growing circle. "Mrs. Hardwicke, how can I make these two behave?"

"You cannot." His mother, even from a half foot shorter,

seemed to look down her straight nose at her son, her voice calculated to freeze. "It seems as if my son has married into the perfect sort of family, for him."

Wolfgang's lovely sister smiled at him, her little shrew teeth showing. "Yes, dear brother, your new relations are certainly all *you* could ask them to be."

"Dearest daughter and granddaughter." Grandmama stepped to his side, her tone deceptively even, but her warning rang clear. "You should be considering an early bedtime, you have far to travel tomorrow and should get an early start."

"Oh, we thought we would stay a few days." His mother smiled, always eager to do battle with her own mother. "After all, this is the dear boy's first time inviting us to Cliffehaven."

"And the last," Wolfgang muttered under his breath.

"Then none of us shall wear out our welcome. The newlyweds need time alone." Grandmama signaled the footman for more champagne. "Diana, Dorothea, come join us to toast the bride and groom." She waited while the guests all gathered round, then raised her glass. "To Zel and Wolfgang, may this union bring them the happiness they deserve."

Aunt Dorothea pursed her lips, straightening a wrinkle from her gray skirts. "Yes, to the happiness they deserve." She sipped lightly from her glass.

"May the marriage be fertile." Sir Edward gulped down his drink and clapped Wolfgang's mother on her back. "As well it should be. Your lad is a potent, virile fellow and my Zel, though not a spring chick, won't be a shirker. Clever girl like her will get knocked up in no time. Probably already is."

"Edward!" Aunt Diana stared at her brother, coughing repeatedly. Then she turned to the rest of the company with a conciliatory smile. "Er, yes, wasn't it Shakespeare who said 'it is a wise father that begets his own child'?"

Wolfgang's sister gasped. "They shouldn't be let out in polite society."

His mother's glare alternated between Diana and Sir Edward.

Robin snorted.

Aunt Dorothea sniffed arrogantly. "Breeding will tell." She mumbled something, which Wolfgang couldn't catch, about a barnyard.

Emily Carland laughed so hard she spilled champagne down her watered-silk gown.

Grandmama took Diana's arm. "Yes, dear, I believe between Shakespeare and the Bible something like that was said."

Zel stood very still, her face pale. Wolfgang squeezed her arm gently. "I'll make our excuses." He turned to address the sniffing, snorting, laughing, glaring group. "My wife and I bid you farewell. We'll retire for the evening now and will not rise until after you have departed." He smiled an advance thanks to Grandmama and escorted his silent bride from the room. "And if they don't leave, I'll growl fiercely and chase them all out."

Zel smiled a little uncertainly at him as he directed her up the wide central staircase. "Beware of the Big Bad Earl."

He laughed. "The Big Bad Wolfgang." Slipping an arm around her shoulders, he lowered his voice seductively. "Now come into my chamber, little girl."

She batted her eyelashes, jumping quickly into his playful mood. "What a big house this is, I fear I may get lost."

"The better to keep you here, my dear." He chuckled, feeling better every inch he moved away from the menagerie downstairs. "Through here, little girl." He opened the door to his bedroom.

As he pushed her inside, she gasped coquettishly. "What a big room, it's far larger than mine."

"The better for our comfort, my dear."

She glanced at the bed on the far side of the room, her

tone a little higher. "And what a big bed, I think we could fit a small battalion on that."

Softly closing the door, he smiled broadly. "The better to please you in, my dear."

He watched as she reddened and looked away to the dog lounging in a large three-sided box lined with cushions and draped in blankets near the bed. Remus lifted his head and shifted his paws. Wolfgang put a hand out and the beast stilled.

With a self-satisfied smile, Wolfgang waved toward the opposite side of the bed. "The queen also has a throne." Hecate sat on a cushioned perch at the top of a tall carved armoire. Her yellow eyes surveyed the beings beneath her.

Zel laughed, a husky little rumble. "This is the product of all that noise earlier this afternoon?"

"Yes, a job well done, a situation well in hand." He clasped her shoulders, lowering his mouth to hers, meeting her lips with the lightest pressure. His fingers found the tiny pearl buttons at the back of her gown and slowly eased them one by one from the little loops that held them captive.

Zel's body pressed against his as she went up on her toes to better catch his lips. Her hands slid up his arms, across his shoulders. "What big shoulders you have."

"The better to hold you with, my dear. And now, little girl, I'm ready for a different game." Wolfgang pushed urgently at the sleeves of her gown. "I want to see and touch you, all of you." His lips traced the smooth line of her neck as gown, chemise, and petticoat slipped down, baring her chest and back to her hips. But the purr he heard was not Zel, and he felt her tense in his arms. He pulled back. "What's wrong, Gamine?"

He followed her eyes from Hecate to Remus. The cat's unblinking stare and the dog's liquid brown gaze never wavered from their master and mistress's embracing forms.

"They are watching us," Zel whispered.

He blew out the candle then hauled her in, tight to his body. "Satan's hairy toes! Close your eyes. Ignore them."

Zel's voice was tiny. "I cannot. I can still see their eyes, looking."

"The devil!" He freed Zel, stalking to the furry ball on the armoire. "You mind your own business, little witch. I have been celibate too damn long."

He strode across the room, grabbing the hound by the scruff of the neck. "And you, shaggy beast, if you interfere any more with the exercise of my husbandly rights, it's off to outer Mongolia with you."

Wolfgang released the dog and turned back to the bed, picking up his nearly naked wife, tossing her on top of the covers. A few good tugs and her gown and undergarments landed on the floor. Slippers and stockings followed in rapid order. Two sets of eyes, glowing in the darkness, watched as Wolfgang jerked the thin curtains around the massive four-poster.

He quickly shed his clothing. Remus growled a warning. Wolfgang bared his teeth, an answering growl rising from deep in his chest. The dog lowered his head, whimpering softly.

"It's bloody time you learned your place in this pack." He snarled between clenched teeth and made a dive, through the curtains, for the bed. "Zel? Where the hell are you?"

"Over here, this bed is too big."

"And dark. But don't worry, I'll find you." He pushed toward her voice, sighing as he felt her hands groping for him, moaning when her fingers grasped the perfect spot.

Her usually deep alto came out barely a squeak. "What a big—"

CHAPTER 15

COUNTERPOINT

The act of combining two independent
melodies into one harmonic structure in which
each reserves its own linear character

WOLFGANG CIRCLED her hand with his own before she could
jerk it away. "Ah, that's it."

"But—"

He smothered the rest of her words with his mouth,
using his free arm to gather her closer. Her hand clenched
tight over his erection. A moan of near pain escaped his lips.
Uncaring if he died of pleasure, he slid her hand slowly up
and down. Her fingers tensed, gripping him with an unbearable pressure.

"Mother of Lucifer!" He growled, moving her hand
faster.

"Am I hurting you?" Zel whispered, a quaver in her
voice.

"Killing me, more like."

She tried to yank her hand free and when he refused to
release her, she grasped him harder.

"Lakes of brimstone, woman!" Wolfgang hissed. "You'll
have me exploding and shaming myself before I've even

started on you." He caught his breath and pried her fingers loose, laying her hand safely on his chest. "I think we'll go about this differently."

Turning on his side and raising himself on his elbow, he searched for her face in the darkness. Unable to make out more than a vague outline of her head, he reached eager fingers for the likely location of her cheek.

"Ouch!"

"Devil it! I'm sorry." His skin heated. He was acting the veriest unschooled infant. What better way to start lovemaking than to poke his wife in the eye. "Did I hurt you?"

"Only a little." Zel giggled. "But if that is your idea of different, maybe we need to go back to the first plan."

"No." Wolfgang pulled her onto her side, wrapping his arms about her, allowing her laughter to infect him and ease his nerves. Nerves? Satan's short hairs! He *was* nervous. More nervous even than his first time behind the stables with that wild upstairs maid.

He wanted to please Zel. Hellfire, didn't he always wish to please his partners? But this went beyond a simple desire for mutual sexual pleasure. He expected more from their joining. But what? He was setting himself up for a major disappointment. Sex was sex. Still, he could use all his expertise to make this memorable for them both. As he nuzzled her neck, he considered the perfect beginning for the perfect night. "I know just the thing. And the third time *will* be the charm."

Zel skimmed her lips lightly over his face as if seeking his mouth. He stopped her search short, claiming her with a deep kiss, tasting her lips and tongue. She pressed herself to him so tightly he could define the contours of her breasts, ribs, and thighs. But he wasn't close enough. He clasped each mound of her firm, rounded bottom in a hand and pulled her into him, grinding his arousal into her smooth, flat abdomen.

This was not his plan at all. Wolfgang reluctantly freed

her mouth and kissed his way down to the pulse beating hard and fast along the column of her neck. He slipped over her collarbone and settled in at her breasts, burying his face in the soft valley. Her fingers fastened onto his shoulders.

Demon's fangs, he could lie like this forever. But there was so much more to explore. He circled a taut nipple with his tongue, then drew the bud slowly into his mouth, caressing the pebbled texture with his lips. The little moans bubbling up her throat stirred the blood already boiling through his veins. Abruptly abandoning her nipple, he laved a wet trail to her navel, dropping a kiss in its center.

He pushed Zel onto her back and nibbled at her hipbone. His teeth traced a jagged line down her outer thigh, stopping at her knee to scan her long, sleek body.

"Damnation!"

She jerked to awareness, her voice fuzzy and languorous. "What is it?"

"Those cursed animals. I want to see you."

Zel laughed shakily. "I think I'm glad you cannot."

He ran his teeth down her shin. "Then I'll just have to see you with my mouth."

She sighed as his tongue slivered up her calf and he bit at the tender skin behind her knee.

Wolfgang continued his path up her inner thigh, licking and sucking until he could feel little shivers run up from her toes.

Giving her no opportunity for counter or retreat, he launched his tongue into the soft, moist cleft at the juncture of her legs, seeking the core of her.

Her thighs clamped hard over his ears. "What are you doing?"

"As much as I love your thighs about my head, you're hurting my ears." Wolfgang pushed open her legs and darted back in.

Pulling at his hair, she protested again. "Stop, you can't do this."

He lifted his head. "But this is the something different I promised. Relax and enjoy it. If you make me stop I have no idea what I'll do next."

Zel released his hair and he returned to his ministrations. She lay very still for several moments, then the low moaning started again. He flicked his tongue rapidly over the center point of her pleasure, and her moaning grew louder. He eased a finger into her tight channel.

"Stop! You're killing me." Her fingers threaded roughly through his hair.

Wolfgang raised his head, gulping down a few steadying breaths, leaving his finger embedded deep within her. "Are you all right?"

"If you stop, I think I'll die." She tugged his head back down.

He stroked her with finger and tongue until she writhed and bucked, crying out for him to stop with every other breath. But when he paused for even a second, she gripped his hair so hard his scalp ached. The tension built rapidly to a breaking point, he could feel it in her rigid thighs, arched back, and clenched fingers. With a sharp shriek the shudder of release finally washed over her. Stunned, he reached down to touch himself, unsure of whether or not he too had climaxed.

"Thank God!" Wolfgang gasped, relieved to find himself still hard, urgent to take her and make her his. He lifted himself over her and plunged in to the hilt. Fires of Hades! She was so tight and hot! He would die of pleasure.

"You're hurting me." Zel's cry carried through the fog of exquisite agony surrounding him. She struggled against him.

"I'm sorry." Wedging his hands beneath her, he held her close. "Keep still, the pain will ease," he murmured into her ear, biting carefully on the lobe, then tracing the hollow of her cheek to her mouth. Gently he molded her lips to his, sharing the searing tenderness that so strangely tempered the passion. He had never been so lost in bliss, yet at the same time so aware of her, her pleasure and pain.

Zel began to relax. Wolfgang could feel the stiffness leave her muscles as the sweat broke out on his brow. A few more moments. He could hold out that long. Concentrating on the air entering and leaving his lungs, he kept himself motionless second after second. Finally he ran his hands up and down her back, starting to rotate his hips, ever so slowly, gradually stretching and opening her, tormenting himself. Her arms crept round his neck. He withdrew, hesitating, readying his reentry.

Jerking him back, she groaned. "No."

Wolfgang stopped, wishing he could see her eyes.

"Is it over?" she whispered so softly, he barely made out the words.

"No. Am I hurting you?"

"Only when you stop." Zel wrapped a leg around him, pinning him captive in the cradle of her hips.

"Satan, Lucifer, Beelzebub, and Clootie!" He dropped all pretense of control, pounding into her, stroke after stroke, trying to penetrate past her flesh, trying to bury himself so deep inside her that a part of him would never emerge. Zel cried out again and again, but he didn't stop, knowing she had ventured far beyond ordinary pain into the same realm of torturous ecstasy he inhabited. His shout of triumphant release mingled with her culminating scream.

Energy drained from his body with his seed, and he collapsed onto her warm softness, breathing in time with her rapidly beating heart.

Zel's voice rumbled faintly against his neck. "Am I still alive?"

Wolfgang chuckled. "I think so." The chuckle expanded in his chest to a full, boisterous laugh. Zel drew in a sharp breath, but when he rolled to his back and rocked her against his chest the laugh overtook her until she was shaking with mirth. He pulled her head to his for a grateful kiss. "But I'm not so sure about me."

"GRIZELDA AMADEA FLEETWOOD HARDWICKE is a screamer."

"Sshh." Zel listened for any sign of movement outside the bed curtains. "You'll wake the animals."

Wolfgang's voice lowered as his tongue circled another toe. "Zel Hardwicke is a screamer."

"I most certainly am not." Zel tried to pull her foot away.

"Are too." He grasped her ankle firmly, nibbling on the tiniest toe. "And I like it."

"Well then . . ." She paused to think of a good rejoinder. "Wolfgang John Wesley Hardwicke, Earl Northcliffe, is a toe sucker."

He released the toe, laughing deeply. "Aye, that I am." He gently bit her big toe. "But only if the toes are wickedly long and graceful and attached to the body of the new Countess Northcliffe."

"Have I been insulted? All you can find to praise is my toes." She pulled away, jerking the sheet up to her shoulders.

Wolfgang pushed the bed curtains slightly open, allowing in a ray of moonlight. Yanking the sheet down, he rolled her onto her back. "How can I praise what you hide?" He ran a finger slowly up her leg, over her hip and across her stomach. "Besides I can't decide what I like best." The finger circled her breast, as his warm, solid body slid over her. "Much as I admire your toes, they aren't in the running with your breasts and thighs." He pushed a lock of her hair behind her ear and licked the lobe. "But if I had to choose, I must admit a partiality to elfin ears." His tongue moved painstakingly up the outer shell. "These little points at the top of yours utterly demolish my self-control."

Her answering laugh disappeared into his kiss as he wrapped his arms about her, clasping her so tightly she feared her ribs would crack. If they did, it wouldn't matter a bit, as she planned to never leave his fierce embrace.

Zel planted kisses along his neck and he gradually loosened his hold, carrying her with him as he rolled to his back.

She pushed up on her elbow, her fingers tracing lazy circles around his chest, savoring the contrasting textures of crisp hair and soft skin overlaying steely muscle. He choked in a breath when her nail caught his tiny nipple. She giggled, pausing in her exploration. "It's funny how this is so small but it hardens like mine does."

Wolfgang took her hand, sucking on the fingertips. "Are you laughing at me again?"

"No." She thought through the act they had just completed. "But you must admit making love is a very strange thing."

"Strange?"

"Strange." She laughed again. "And funny."

"Damnation and the devil's tail, woman! You laugh at my body, then you laugh at my sexual performance." He ran a finger up her spine. "Do you wish to completely unman me?"

Zel wiggled against him, her body wedged to his hard, unyielding form. "Even if that were my aim, it's not working. I can feel something growing."

Wolfgang groaned, but his answering laughter permeated his voice. "Already?"

"Is it too soon?" She wiggled more.

"No, my little glutton, it's not too soon." He ran his hands down her back, cupping her bottom. "So, you still think it's funny?"

Sighing, she nipped at his shoulder. "From the ridiculous comes the sublime."

"I don't know about the ridiculous." Wolfgang rubbed against her belly. "But we could aspire to the sublime, reach for that ultimate shiver."

Zel pushed into the long-fingered hand that had drifted

between her legs, smiling at the rumble coming from his chest. "A shiver of the, which would it be, fourth kind?" With a bow of her back, she moved her mouth to his chest, nuzzling and seeking. Catching that tiny nipple between her lips, she teased it with her tongue, fascinated again by the reaction, wondering if he felt the little strings vibrating from the hardened tip to the juncture of his thighs. His moan told her he felt something akin to that delicate torture.

Arching her back more, she ran a curious hand down his ridged chest and flat stomach, skirting about the part she had earlier grasped so brazenly. His fingers pushed into her, stretching her, making her ready for the exquisite entry to come. The ache inside burned nigh to unbearable, heightened by the tenderness of flesh newly tested and stimulated.

She searched what she could reach of Wolfgang's hips and thighs and with a sigh slipped her hand between their bodies, returning to the object of her most avid curiosity. But this time she wouldn't squeeze him like a milkmaid at an udder. Instead she caressed him with a feather soft touch.

"Satan's small clothes!"

"Am I still being too rough? It's such a strange mixture of hard and soft." Zel whispered into his shoulder. "I'm not sure how to go about touching it."

"You're doing fine." His voice sounded low, raspy, as he ran his free hand through her hair, pulling her face back to his. "Only, you're calling me strange again."

"I'm sor—" His lips angled and pressed into hers. When his tongue caught hers, she realized the salty taste she had noticed on his tongue was her. She squirmed against his hand until his thumb rested on the amazingly sensitive little button of skin. That newly familiar tightening began deep in her abdomen, pulling at her until she felt drawn and taut as the strings of her pianoforte, and still he stroked her.

"Now," Zel breathed, releasing him and rolling to her back to give him access to her. "I want you to be part of me again."

Wolfgang wound an arm about her. "Then where are you going?" Not waiting for an answer, he drew her over his chest and glided into her slowly and smoothly. "Have you never wished to ride astride?"

The grip on her insides tightened as she pushed nearly upright, bracing herself, with hands splayed on his chest. "I think I like this." She moved her hips in a circular motion, grinning at his groan. "Yes, Mr. Centaur, I like this a lot."

"I could get quite used to this view." His hands edged up her sides to weigh her breasts in his palms, his thumbs teasing her erect nipples, his eyes absorbing her. "You have a perfect seat, ma'am, among other things. Can you go the distance?"

"Try me."

"Your wish is my command, Countess." He started out seductively slow, an easy walk along a path in a well-tended park. Yet as she adjusted to his smooth movements adding a few twists of her own, he shifted to a trot.

"Lord." Zel gasped, her whole insides clenched as if in the grasp of a giant fist. A fist that kept squeezing her, shaking her, pulling her away from the safety of the trail.

"Better than—" he muttered between quickening breaths, "—sidesaddle?"

Rational speech left her and she could only nod as Wolfgang moved into a canter, slapping her thighs softly against his chest and sides. He hauled her to his chest, claiming her lips with the same force he claimed the rest of her body.

"God, Wolf." Zel breathed into his mouth as they broke into a full gallop and his fingers slipped between them. She felt her body stumble and shake as she neared the precipice toward which this mad ride was headed.

"Now. With me," he whispered, harsh, ragged, pulling her screeching over the edge, dashing her senseless, shattering bone, nerve, and sinew.

"Good . . . Lord, Wolf." Zel slumped against him, conscious only of the rhythmic pulsing fanning from her core. She lay still, unable to move, unwilling to break their joining, contact more intimate than anything she would have imagined possible just days ago, leaving her open and vulnerable yet warm and content.

As Wolfgang's breathing slowly returned to normal, his unsteady hand threaded through her hair. "Centaurs are immortal, Gamine, but not deity."

She stirred, tickled by his chest hairs against her cheek. "What are you talking of now, you madman?"

"More insults! You call me god. You call me centaur. Now you call me madman." He tugged on her ear, playfully pinching the tip. "Which is it, elf?"

"I think you are a half-mad centaur." Zel laughed into his neck. "But if this gets any better, I fear I may begin to worship at your feet."

"DO YOU THINK we will ever get vouchers for Almack's?" Wolfgang watched Zel's shoulders jerk as he broke the silence.

Her eyes were wide when she looked up from the thin-sliced beef she'd been gradually slipping to the waiting hound. "Almack's?" She coughed. "Us?"

"Yes, us." He gestured to her plate. "Remus can go to the kitchen and get his own food. We'd do that stuffy, old assembly hall some good."

She smiled shyly. "Who would agree to sponsor us?"

"Lady Cowper owes me a favor." He grinned broadly before bathing a piece of crisp carrot in the tangy sauce and popping it into his mouth. "Plus she'll like you."

"I don't know." Lowering her eyes, she pushed a few peas around her plate. "We should let the gossip die down first. There is no hurry." She stabbed one of the elusive vegetables. "Besides, I am a little frightened to go."

"Frightened? Of Almack's?" He pushed back his chair, and in two strides shoved Remus aside and knelt beside her.

"You needn't be afraid of anything, Gamine. Together we can brave whatever the ton throws our way."

"I am not as brave as you."

"I disagree. I think you're fearless."

Zel looked at her hands. "I fear too many things."

He scanned her face, surprised at her confession. "You don't fear me, do you?"

She twisted away from him. "No, but it's so . . . awkward, facing you over the dinner table." Her fingers tensed around her fork. "After what we have done . . . to each other."

"Then perhaps in future we should arise earlier." Wolfgang eased the fork from her grip, rubbing her long slender fingers. "Then we can face each other over the breakfast table."

Zel's voice was tiny and low. "That won't help."

"I know what will." He clasped her hand and stood, pulling her from the table. "Let's get out of here. You haven't even seen the bay yet."

Unresisting, she followed him into the hall. "I can smell the sea air. How close are we?"

"It's just over the rise at the back of the house." Taking her elbow, he guided her down the hall and through a rear door. "We'll take the road winding through the tall hedgerow over there." He gestured toward a trail starting at the stables.

They walked in silence up the hill. Before reaching the crest, he turned her back toward the house. "I've always loved this place. Even as a child when I visited my grandfather here, I felt I belonged." He slipped his arm about her waist. "I never liked the old man, but Cliffehaven, with its scrambled architecture and the wild beauty of its setting, I always felt should be mine."

"It looks almost alive, glowing in the last rays of the sun." Zel smiled at him. "It is a stirring sight."

Wolfgang pulled her into him, nestling her backside

against him, feeling that odd childhood sense of belonging expand to include her. Breathing in deeply, he tried to contain the sudden shakiness in his chest, twisting the sigh into a little chuckle. "Ah, it is stirring." He turned her to face him. "But no more stirring than what I hold in my arms."

Her blush crept up her neck, spreading over her face.

"You're such an innocent." Wolfgang grazed her red cheeks with his knuckles.

"But I'm not anymore."

"You'll always retain that intriguing mix of naive miss and siren." He took her pointed elfin chin in his hand, looking deeply into her tip-tilted eyes. "I'll still be able to make you blush when you are five and seventy." He kissed her hard and quick. "And you'll still make me feel like a randy youth of twenty, when I should have one foot in the grave.

"Come, I'll show you the ocean before the sun is gone." Wolfgang whirled her about and towed her at a run to the top of the hill.

Zel stopped, breathing in gulps, surveying the high cliffs and rocky beach below. "It's splendid."

"There's a path down to the beach we can take another time, when we have more light." He slipped his arm around her, smiling broadly when she rested her head against his shoulder.

Wolfgang stood quietly, watching the waves crash against the rocky shore while the brisk wind whipped about their clothing and hair. He inhaled deeply of the mixed scent of sea air and spice. "You always smell of gingerbread, fresh out of the oven, but that comforting scent has become far more erotic to me than roses or lavender ever could."

A gust of wind threw her voice about his ears. "It's just my hair soap. I'm glad you like it." She sighed, wedging in tight against his chest, twining her arm about his waist. "Will your chef be insulted we left dinner so soon?"

"Mr. Nah has a pretty thick skin, but what did you think of his concoction?"

"I have never had anything like it before. But I liked it." Zel huddled closer. "We should have served it at our wedding dinner. It would have been a nice surprise."

"More than a surprise to some. Not all have an adventurous palate, Gamine. In fact, the English are notoriously unwilling to accept surprises at their dinner tables. Satan's sweetmeats! I didn't think of it, but one bite and mother and sister would never wish to visit again." Wolfgang sighed, brushing his cheek against her hair. "I'm glad that bizarre crew is gone. If ever we entertain it must be in secret. Unless every relative but Grandmama and your aunt are on a far isle of Scotland."

Zel laughed. The walk was a good idea. She'd begun to release a little of the stiffness, the embarrassment he hadn't been surprised to see follow the wild abandon of their wedding night. It would take her time to become comfortable with her own sensuality, and he hadn't helped matters by overdoing it. He should have been gentler, gone slower, reined himself in.

But Lucifer's chin whiskers, he had wanted her, wanted to lay claim to every inch of her. He smiled, last night had been worth the wait. Zel hadn't been at all shy, she had gone the distance, keeping up with him every step of the way. He kicked a stone over the cliff edge. Throughout the night and morning he had reached for her again and again. She hadn't hesitated, eagerly sharing her body with him.

"What are you smiling about now? My aunt, my brother, or my father?" A teasing tone accompanied Zel's wry smile.

"What about my mother, my aunt, or my cousin? If they weren't so blasted funny, I might have strangled one of them." He watched a bird soar overhead, a blur of movement in the darkening sky. "Fact is, I seriously considered a little murder. I already have the reputation, after all. But who would I start with and where would it end?"

Wolfgang frowned, resuming their former silence.

Where would it end? He felt so useless holed up in the country, but it was safer for himself and Zel. He should have waited until this was resolved to marry her, but he had pushed her until finally they had no choice. He had gotten what he wanted, but at what price?

He watched the gull circle the bay, skirting the rocks in a long, low glide. Spawn of the devil! If Robin was his villain it could tear them apart. In the end she would give her loyalty to her brother. Zel cared for him, he felt certain, especially after her acceptance of their forced marriage. But how could he ever compete against her brother? All the years she had spent loving and protecting the unworthy cur would clearly outweigh the short weeks since they met at the Selby's house party.

Robin could not be guilty. He wouldn't allow it. It was as simple as that. It must be Simon. He had motive enough to kill. The obsession with the death of his sister endured even after so many years. Or Newton. He would enjoy all the plotting and planning, whether he wished to kill or just harass. Or his cold aunt and toad of a cousin. They were greedy enough and lavished no love on the new earl. He twitched his shoulders restlessly. Worm of hell! Where were Raf and Freddie when he needed them?

Wolfgang laughed harshly, catching Zel's gaze as it lifted from the wave-thrashed beach to meet his eyes. His friends were loyally following orders and staying away from his honeymoon. He smiled thinly at her, wishing he dared to tell her everything, put that wise head to work on the mystery, put that compassionate heart to work on his worries. But Robin loomed between them, as tangible as if he were there, sharing their quiet walk.

"ARE YOU SURE we won't be missed, Marmeduke?"

"We could fall off the face of the earth and not be missed

by those two." Jenkins chuckled, flashing his perfect teeth at his companion.

Maggie smiled warmly, her red hair shooting off copper sparks in the sunshine. "If they continue to stay abed this late every morning they'll likely get bed sores."

"No." He took her hand, ignoring a rustling in the hedges, pulling her past the impossible topiary animals and evergreen turrets lining the side entrance to the Elizabethan wing. "I think you have to lie still more often for that."

"For shame," Maggie scolded. A week ago she would have expired of embarrassment at such a remark, but now her rosy lips parted in a sweet little pout. "Talking of your master so."

"He wouldn't blink an eye, and I for one am happy for the extra time we've had together these last few days."

"It's been like a storybook come true for me." Maggie smiled boldly, then shyly averted her eyes.

"For me too, princess."

"Princess. I'll be damned." Suddenly, a huge well-fleshed face loomed over them. "Caught you a fancy man, eh, Mags?"

"Ned!" she cried out, stepping in front of Jenkins, chin high. "What business have you here?"

"No business!" Jenkins moved beside her. "Remove yourself from Cliffehaven or you'll be arrested for trespass."

"Fancy man?" Ned laughed loudly. "My mistake. Not with that ugly face. Get out of my way. I'm here for my wife."

"How could you find me here?" Maggie stood her ground.

"Weren't too hard." Ned grasped her arm. "Everybody in town's talkin' about that wild mistress of yours and her new husband, the earl. The very ones I ran into in London."

Jenkins pushed Maggie behind him. "Leave now! She'll go nowhere with you."

"I say she'll come." Ned swung a beefy fist.

Jenkins dodged it easily. "Maggie, get back." He tugged up his sleeves. "The man needs to learn a lesson or two."

Ned drew back his arm, but Jenkins stepped out of range before the huge man could plant his next blow. The valet quickly jabbed the giant on a jowly cheek and circled wide.

"Marmeduke, take care."

"Marmeduke?" Ned bellowed, cheeks bright red. "That ain't no man's name." A fist glanced off his chest, as Jenkins landed a facer square onto Ned's nose. "Eeow, you mangy dog." He shook his head. Blood splattered on Jenkins's white vest and cravat.

Jenkins pranced around Maggie's husband, teeth bared. "A little harder isn't it, beating up a man?"

"Ain't none of your affair what I do with my wife." Ned growled, breathing hard.

"I've made it my affair." He continued to whirl about the big oaf.

"Oh! Please!" Maggie stepped between the two sparring men.

"No, Maggie!" Jenkins groped for her, off balance. Ned moved in with surprising speed, fist hammering into his mouth. He bent, spitting out the blood into his hand. Two hard little objects spewed out with the bright red liquid.

His teeth. The bastard had cost him his teeth.

Straightening, Jenkins held his fists high, pitching well-aimed blows in his opponent's face. Ned waved his arms about wildly, failing to connect a single punch.

Jenkins beat a rapid tattoo into Ned's jaw and cheek. He could see the man's eyes begin to glaze as he nailed a final blow to the chin, then watched the massive form crumble to the pebbled walk. "Get a few footmen and some rope. Quickly, Maggie." As she ran up the pathway he surveyed the giant brute laid out before him. If he had the money, he'd ship the beast off to the most untamed corner of the world.

"What did you bag, Jenkins? Looks like a big one." The captain was at his shoulder, dressing gown and hair flapping in the breeze. "Your mouth!"

"I'm fine. Sorry to get you up, Captain." He gestured to the recumbent form. "But Maggie's husband found us."

"You did good work, but I'm afraid a broken nose and a few bruises won't keep the man away." The captain pushed his hair off his brow. "Maybe I can pay him off."

"He doesn't deserve payment for his brutality."

"Do you want Maggie free and safe or her husband treated justly? Unless we intervene the courts will return her to him."

"I see your point, milord."

"Don't go getting all stiff and formal on me." The captain sat on a little stone bench. "Three letters should do it. One to Harcourt to book this fellow passage to the New World, on one of his fine frigates. The second to my agent in Canada to purchase a small farm." He stretched out long legs. "The third to the local magistrate swearing out a complaint for assault and theft."

Jenkins smiled. "I think that will hold him well and guarantee he won't return."

Three footmen emerged from the house following Maggie. Lady Zel dashed out behind them, trying to keep her dressing gown closed over bare legs, her ever-present wolfhound at her side.

"Zel, I asked you to stay inside." The captain frowned briefly at his wife, scanned the unconscious man on the ground, then turned to Maggie. "Maggie, I believe your husband has decided to become a Canadian."

. . .

"YOU'VE BEEN shamefully neglecting your other lover."

Zel nearly fell off Wolfgang's knee, spilling deep purple burgundy on his formerly immaculate cravat. "Lover?"

He took the wineglass from her hand, cuddling her closer. "Herr Beethoven, of course." She felt his lips on her ear. "You haven't time or stamina for a third." He licked at the tip.

She sighed. "I hope one day I will become accustomed to that wicked tongue of yours."

"Ma'am, I sincerely hope not."

And he deftly demonstrated some of the reasons why his hope was the more likely of the two. Zel wrapped her arms around him, responding warmly to the pressure of his lips on her mouth. But the warmth was not limited to her lips nor even her skin. It pervaded her entire being. She no longer felt embarrassment at the abandonment with which she gave herself to him. It seemed right, as if she belonged in his arms, in his bed, in his life.

She sighed, pushing him away. "We must stop for just a few minutes. I wish to talk seriously, Wolfgang."

He gave her the look of a boy who had lost his last plaything. "But I was being serious."

Zel pried off his arms and shifted onto the cushions of the settee beside him. "We've been married ten days now. I believe it is time to return to London."

"Is the honeymoon over already?"

"I hope not." She took his hand, squeezing his long fingers. "But the world goes on without us. I must attend to Aquitaine House and you have a bill in Parliament."

"Debate on that bill has begun." Wolfgang bit at her knuckles. "I do need to be there. I've won a few supporters but I need many more to give the bill a prayer. We should also appear at some of the fêtes honoring the return of the heroes."

"We shall take London by storm, Wolf." Zel laughed. "If anyone will receive us."

"People will receive us, elf. We're a nearly respectable married couple now. And not all political circles are such sticklers." He sucked on her thumb. "Look at Lady Holland, even a divorce couldn't destroy her. You'd like her and she you."

"If you are sure we would be accepted, I might enjoy a political dinner or two." His lips were soft and pliable around the knuckle of her thumb.

"Gossip dies quickly. Remember we're married. We are the earl and countess of Northcliffe, and we are very wealthy. Most of the ton will embrace us with open arms." Wolfgang stroked hermuslin-covered back. "And to play our parts, you must spend a little money, jewels, gowns, accessories."

"I do not need a lot."

"Zel, I have the money, the merchants and tradesmen need the work, and your aunt's castoffs are close to fifteen years old. Then there are your undergarments. They're so hideous I can't wait to get them off you."

"Maybe I shouldn't get any."

Wolfgang kissed her neck. "That would suit me just fine."

"I'm sure it would until I caught an inflammation of the lungs. Wolf, I've never spent freely. I do not know if I can."

"We'll find you a new and struggling, but clever, modiste, a brilliant jeweler with twenty children to support, and a war-wounded shoemaker. And just think of all you could buy for Aquitaine House." He fingered the neck of her gown. "Will that help you spend more freely?"

Chuckling, she trailed little kisses along his strong jaw line. "Indeed, my rich and gracious lord." She pulled the leather thong from his hair. "Shall we retire for the evening?"

"Are you hinting at something, Gamine? I had hoped you'd read aloud to me."

"Not hinting, demanding." Zel stood, hauling his unresisting form to his feet. "I don't wish to read tonight. Besides, you never take your turn."

His lips twitched. "Literature be damned. I have a sportin' wife. I'll find Hecate. You settle in Remus and I'll meet you upstairs in five minutes."

CHAPTER 16

STACCATO

Crisply cut short, disconnected;
from the Italian "to detach"

THE BOOK ROOM DOOR stood ajar. The rumble of masculine voices drifted into the hallway. Wolfgang was closeted with his secretary, as he had been on several occasions since their return to London the day before. Zel should leave and approach him later, but this matter concerned Mr. Radison too.

She silently pushed the door open and slipped through. Both men bent over the desk, Wolfgang's dark head with the silver flash a stark contrast to his secretary's shiny, pink dome fringed in light brown.

"Now these figures show the income from Cliffehaven over the last quarter." Radison's soft monotone droned, as his finger traced lines in a large open book. "This column is the outlay for improvements."

"Just tell me." Wolfgang's tone carried a sharp edge. "Am I laying out too much money or is the place turning a profit?"

"Captain," Radison responded patiently, "you asked me to show you—"

"I don't know why either of us bothers. We know it

looks little better than hen scratchings to me." He shoved the ledger at Radison and stood abruptly, almost toppling his chair. "Why I never get used to it——" He broke off, eyes on Zel in the doorway, a slow flush staining his neck and face.

"I, ah, needed to talk . . ." The words stumbled from her mouth.

"Radison, leave us." Wolfgang sank back into the chair, staring at a little carved centaur on the lacquer desk before him.

Looking at his unusually slumped shoulders, the pieces fell into place. She remembered only seeing him read once, that day shortly after they'd met, when she'd come upon him mumbling over a letter. Too aware of his physical presence at the time to note it, she now realized his low voice had stumbled, hesitated, and he'd quickly put up the letter as he became aware of her. And there were all the times he had avoided reading words or figures. He refused to look at the accounting of Robin's debts. He memorized the play at the Staffords' house party with Jenkins's assistance. The nights since their marriage when she read aloud, he wouldn't take a turn, flattering her with comments on how lovely her voice was and how he could listen to her for hours.

"I'm sorry, Wolfgang." Zel moved toward him.

"Why should you be sorry? It's my problem." He turned away, his fist tightening over the jade centaur. "The only thing you have to be sorry about is your marriage to an idiot."

"Do you think I have grounds for annulment?" she teased, astounded by the pain in his eyes when he whirled about to face her. Kneeling beside him, she took his hands in hers. "I'm sorry, that was a cruel joke."

"I don't know what made me think I could keep it from you." Wolfgang's eyes were directed at their joined hands.

"There is no need to keep it from me." She stroked his

tapered fingers. "Maybe I could help, I have tutored several women who had difficulty with reading and mathematics."

"What's wrong is beyond mere difficulty. I've had these problems all my life." He slumped into the silk-and-lacquer chair. "Mathematics may as well be Egyptian hieroglyphics, and the written word is little better. Reading aloud is the only way I can concentrate enough to follow the words at all, and even then they dance about the page and my attention wanders."

"Did no one try to help you?"

"My father and all my teachers and tutors tried to beat it into me. I was called wild, undisciplined, even evil." He raised his head, voice a faint whisper, but his eyes did not meet hers. "My father, the genius religious scholar, hated me. He couldn't believe he spawned an imbecile. He ridiculed and abused me. I only wanted to please him." Wolfgang twisted, pulling at her fingers. "I tried, but I could barely sit still in my chair, I couldn't attend to my work for more than minutes at a time. And it made little sense when I did attend anyway."

"You are not an imbecile, far from it," Zel tried to reassure him, but he continued as if he hadn't heard her.

"I was always in one scrape or another. Even now I act before I think." He laughed harshly. "You know that better than most." He weakly attempted to push her away as she rose and planted herself firmly on the arm of his chair. "I should have stayed in the army. That was the only place my recklessness has ever been appreciated. You get medals for it, plus I understood the maps and strategy and I always had aides to read the orders. If it wasn't for all that damned getting shot at." His eyes darkened. "And watching my men die."

She stared at him, unsure of how to respond. "It must have been horrible."

Wolfgang shrugged and turned away.

Zel tried to keep her voice light, but she felt a dull ache

in her chest for the pain of the little boy and the man. "How did you survive all those years of school, even university?"

"It's funny I even wished to stay—but horrible as it was, it was preferable to home." Wolfgang sat erect; his hand moving restlessly over her back. "I never would have survived if not for Raf and Freddie. They supported me through everything. They read my lessons to me and luckily most exams were oral." He tugged at her chignon. "I could have become an adequate student, except for my continuing scrapes. But all that only confirmed Father's opinion that I was wild and undisciplined and a cheat besides."

"Your father was the fool."

"Perhaps." He eased the pins from her hair, threading his hands through the thick mass.

Zel ran a finger over his lips, sliding off the chair arm into his lap, resting her head against his shoulder. "He must have been, because you are not."

"Fool or no, are you sorry you married me? Do you wish you'd braved the scandal?"

"No, Wolfgang." She shifted her head to kiss his jaw. "And I had decided to marry you before we were discovered."

He took her chin in hand, probing her eyes with his silver gaze. "That's why you took it so well. You never said a word."

"I had only just decided." Zel looked away, suddenly shy. "And I was waiting for you to ask again."

Wolfgang hugged her to him, laughing into her hair. "I would have asked you, but you kissed me and the next thing I knew we had an audience to our little scene on the settee." His inhalation was ragged. "What changed your mind? Did you decide I might be different from the other men in your life?"

"I think you are not at all like my father, uncle, Maggie's husband, or those men who drive their wives to Aquitaine House."

"Thank you." He gently kissed her eyes and cheeks. "Now what did you need to talk to me about?"

"I hate to bring it up now. I don't wish to burden you with my worries."

"If my burdens are yours, then yours are mine." He twined a finger in the loose hair at her ear. "Tell me, Gamine."

Zel hesitated, cleared her throat, and coughed it out. "It's Robin."

"What now?"

"I think he's drinking more and has new gambling debts."

"I'll chain him to his bed. I can put it out that if anyone accepts his notes, they'll answer to me."

Before she could answer, the door swung wide. Sir Frederick Ransley ducked through the opening, hair windblown, boots and breeches spattered with mud.

"Lucifer and the hounds of hell! Freddie! What are you doing here?"

Zel squirmed to free herself, but Wolfgang held on tighter.

Ransley scowled at her, obviously displeased, but with her perch on Wolfgang's lap, her loosened hair, or her mere presence, she couldn't tell. "I need to talk with you, Wolf."

"Talk away."

The giant of a man looked pointedly at Zel. "Alone."

Wolfgang smiled. "You can speak freely before my wife."

"Alone, Wolf."

"I need to meet with the housekeeper." Zel slid from Wolfgang's arms. "Sir Frederick." She nodded and quickly left the room, shutting the door quietly behind her.

"YOUR RUDENESS is overwhelming." Wolfgang stood, staring at the closed door before turning to scan his friend's rough face. "Should I call you out for insulting Zel or listen to the seemingly important news you have to impart?"

"Wolf, you won't like what I have to say." Ransley loosened his already sloppy cravat and unbuttoned his waistcoat. "Blast, but I have to say it."

"It couldn't be so important you can't have a drink first. You look like you could use it." Wolfgang opened a corner cabinet, withdrawing a decanter of liquor and two glasses. He poured healthy doses, handing one to Freddie, setting the other glass and decanter before him on the desk. "Sit and drink."

Freddie pulled up a chair directly across the desk from Wolfgang. "I'm not sure where to start." He took a large gulp of the amber liquid. "You know we had word that a John Pettibone had been acting the part of a footpad."

"Yes, get on with it." Wolfgang flopped into his chair.

"We've been questioning Pettibone's friends and relations." Freddie took another swallow. "I returned from Pettibone's father's estate in Cheltenham, then met with Raf."

"It's not like you to be so long-winded. Cut to the chase." Wolfgang sipped the spirits and coughed. Whiskey! Satan's starched neckcloth. Where was his brandy? Who put this nasty stuff in his liquor cabinet?

"Pettibone's bragging corresponds directly with the attacks on you—the two footpad incidents and the shooting in the park. He was in town on all three occasions."

Wolfgang stood, pushing back his chair. "But I don't even know the man. What does he have against me?"

"Nothing, but he is indebted to someone who does have a grudge." Freddie paused, examining his now empty glass. "Pettibone hangs about with a young crowd of drinkers and gamblers. He owes everyone money, but his creditors won't go for blood while his father lives."

"Enough, Freddie!" Wolfgang slammed his glass on the desk, spilling the pale liquid on the smooth lacquered surface. "Just tell me. It's Robin."

"It's Robin Fleetwood."

"Satan's body, Lucifer's blood." He collapsed into his chair. "Flames of hell."

"I'm sorry, Wolf." Freddie poured more whiskey. "I wish it were otherwise, but Fleetwood and Pettibone have been comrades in cards and cups for years."

"That could be coincidence." He threw back a portion of the rank drink. It took some of his throat with it going down.

"No, there's more." Freddie toyed with his disheveled cravat. "Fleetwood held some of Pettibone's numerous IOUs. When Fleetwood was on the road to debtor's prison he fought bitterly with Pettibone, trying to convince him to borrow from his wealthy father. But Pettibone's father has all but disinherited his son, and Pettibone couldn't risk word of more debts reaching the old man. Also there are stories about that Pettibone has played at highwayman and footpad in the past."

Wolfgang ran a finger through the little puddle of spilled liquor. "Sounds a bit farfetched—"

"I thought so too, at first." Freddie cut in. "But I found another footpad who admitted he was hired by Pettibone. I agreed not to prosecute him in exchange for information—"

"Just say it, Freddie." Wolfgang downed his whiskey and poured another glass. At this rate they'd be three sheets to the wind before the conversation reached its ugly conclusion.

"The man said Pettibone complained of being blackmailed to do the deeds by a supposed friend."

Wolfgang groaned, gulping more whiskey.

"I'm not through yet. Word in the clubs has it that Fleetwood still thinks you fleeced him and seduced his sister. Plus your hold on his purse strings is tight as a death grip."

"The first attack on me occurred the night following the fight at Maven's." The whiskey still burned a little on his raw throat, but it wasn't too bad. He could get used to it. "For some reason Robin decided I cheated him out of his money and knocked him out for good measure. Maybe he was too drunk to remember correctly. That night was the first time I saw Zel."

"If he disliked you enough to attack you then, your subsequent involvement with his sister could only have made matters worse."

Wolfgang felt a bit fuzzy, the damn whiskey was already going to his head and he didn't feel any better. "But there hasn't been an attack since I paid his debts."

"Not yet. After the last failed attack and after the debts were paid, Pettibone told his hired henchmen they'd have to try again." Freddie poured more whiskey in both their glasses. "What else, besides revenge, does he have to gain by your death?"

"The marriage settlements." Wolfgang rubbed his eyes but it didn't clear his vision. "Mephistopheles, that's not promising. He may think to get his hands on Zel's widow's portion."

"How large are the settlements?"

"Most of my unentailed estate."

"Gads, man, most of London would kill you for that fortune." Ransley yanked on his cravat. "But Wolf, there's more. Raf heard at Brooks's that Fleetwood was looking through the betting books and found some wagers regarding you and his sister."

Wolfgang flew out of the chair, bumping against the desk. "He can't blame me for those fools who bet on anything."

"Ah, but there's the problem, several entries were signed with your initials, WJWH."

"By the devil, you know I never even look at those books."

"But Fleetwood doesn't know that and he was furious." Freddie examined the half-empty decanter. "He was heard muttering 'Northcliffe's a dead man.' You're in danger. We should move for his arrest."

"No!" Wolfgang shouted over the din in his ears. His head felt light, his vision clouded. He eased back into the chair, head lowered, crouching there, bringing his hands over his face.

"Wolf?" Freddie was at his side, a large hand resting on his shoulder.

"I—I'm fine . . ." he stammered. "Give me a minute." Arrest Robin? God in heaven, Lucifer in hell. Freddie had no idea what he asked. It would destroy everything he had with Zel, everything they could have. Their marriage would be over. He took a deep, rattling breath, lifting his head. "Freddie, I admit it doesn't look good for my brother-in-law." He took another breath. "Will Pettibone testify against him?"

"That's a problem." Freddie resumed his seat and polished off another glass. "We can't find the man."

Wolfgang's half-suppressed sigh was answered by a tightening around his friend's mouth. "Are you interested in preserving your own life? Or would you prefer to be shot or bludgeoned to death? Perhaps poison is more to your liking?"

"Of course I don't wish to be murdered." He twisted the stopper around the mouth of the cut-glass decanter, nearly oversetting it. "Not the most heartening news . . . to discover my mortal enemy is my wife's brother."

"If you won't put the man away, what are you going to do?" Freddie poured still another drink and eyed Wolfgang skeptically.

"I don't know . . . for right now, I could use another drink." He held a shaky glass out for Freddie to fill.

"You need to hire a runner to watch young Fleetwood and a few more brawny footmen to keep an eye on you."

"It won't do any good." The Scottish whiskey flowed roughly down his throat. "He runs tame in my house."

"Then rein him in." Freddie's voice rumbled in his ears.

"And what do I tell Zel?" His tongue was thickening.

"Tell her the truth."

"The truth?" Wolfgang laughed. "What the hell do you know 'bout women?"

"SIR FREDERICK?" Zel watched Wolfgang's huge friend start up the stairs, a familiar human bundle draped over his shoulder. "Wolfgang?"

"He's had a bit too much whiskey." Ransley carried Wolfgang's sizable frame as if it were no bigger than a child's. "I thought I'd take him to his room."

"Ze . . . e . . . el." Wolfgang, barely conscious, sounded out her name into Ransley's back.

She stepped behind Ransley and found Wolfgang's head buried in the bigger man's jacket. "We're putting you to bed."

"Only if . . . you come with me." He turned his head, trying to smile. "Gam . . . ine."

Zel stepped past Ransley and his boneless burden, leading the way up the stairs into Wolfgang's chambers. "Lay him on the bed. We can manage to undress him without calling Jenkins." She pushed aside the silk bed hangings.

"Sorry, Lady Northcliffe, he doesn't usually drink much." Ransley frowned apologetically. "He tried to keep up with me."

"Bed . . . time?" Wolfgang settled into the Chinese embroidered cushions scattered on the bed as Zel bent over him, pulling off his loosened cravat. "Shouldn't we wait . . . Freddie leaves?"

"Your friend is helping me." Zel started on the shirt buttons. His jacket was long gone, the waistcoat already opened.

"We need . . . help?"

"You are in no shape to do anything but sleep." She

turned to the silent man standing beside the bed. "Sir Frederick, can you lift him a bit so I can take off his waistcoat and shirt?"

As Ransley shifted Wolfgang to a sitting position, Zel slipped off the clothing, baring his chest. Wolfgang shivered when her hand attacked the fastenings to his pantaloons. He snaked an arm about her waist. "Eager wench . . . kiss me."

Zel batted his arm away. "Stop it." He grinned crookedly and allowed her, with Ransley's help, to remove his pantaloons and smallclothes. He pushed away the nightshirt she attempted to pull over his head, face scrunched like a defiant boy's.

As she tried to pull the bedclothes over him, he hauled her in close. "Stay . . . Freddie, go."

"Sir Frederick, thank you." Zel nodded as the hastily departing figure bowed slightly, then closed the door behind him.

Wolfgang sighed, cuddling against her, his head at her breast. He smelled. Not his usual aroma of horses, leather, and trees, not even his occasional sweet brandy smell, but a sour, overpowering odor. Like her father. Whiskey.

Grunting, hands at his chest, she tried to push him away. His arms tightened about her. "Need you . . . Zel."

She stilled, his words echoing in her ears, whiskey smell forgotten. Her hands curled over his shoulders and neck, fingers stroking his loosened hair. A painful swelling grew in her chest. She wanted to keep him in her arms, protect him from all the past hurts, his deceased father and all those horrible tutors and teachers. To tell him again and again, until he believed it, that he was bright and quick, that his mind was superior, that he had nothing to be ashamed of. And since when did a politician need to read or write? They all had secretaries to do that.

This must be what a cat, lioness or tabby, felt when her kittens were threatened. This was something like what she felt for her brother. But it was different, and not because she had feelings for Wolfgang that were in no way sisterly. She protected and sheltered Robin, gave love and compassion knowing there would be no return, knowing that his taking was her only reward. Wolfgang gave, drew out, then filled needs in her she hadn't known existed. He satisfied her physically, of that there was no doubt. And he made her laugh. But he also gave her respect, admiration, and trust. She never doubted for a minute that he saw she had a mind and expected her to use it. Maybe they could build a marriage with a kind of partnership she had never believed possible.

Zel held him secured at her breast, his breath warm through the thin muslin of her gown, his chest rising and falling evenly against her stomach and abdomen.

She had never seen him drunk, never seen him drink more than a couple of brandies in a night. Somehow it touched rather than disgusted her, not like her father's drinking at all. It brought to mind a boy experimenting with adulthood, stealing his father's whiskey. But there was more, a less familiar dark undercurrent, a frightened, vulnerable man beneath the rebellious boy.

Pulling him closer, wishing to share his fears, she whispered into his soft, black hair, "God, how I love you."

WOLFGANG BLINKED, but the sunlight glaring through the crack in the curtains wouldn't go away.

What in Satan's name had he been thinking last night? Whiskey. He'd sooner drink spirits of turpentine. The stuff must have been his grandfather's. And keeping up with Freddie? He hadn't attempted that stunt since Cambridge.

He stretched a tentative arm across the bed. No Zel. He frowned at the empty pillow, remembering how she'd held him close, stroking his hair. Then when she was sure he slept she whispered those ever so faint words, "I love you."

She loved him.

How the devil was he supposed to feel about that? Shouldn't he be happy? It was what he wanted. Then why did he feel like someone had blown a hole through his chest?

How could he build a life with the sister of the man who wanted him dead? The man he should transport or hang. Wolfgang sat up in bed, pain vaulting through his head in relentless waves. Zel would never believe Robin guilty, she would support him to the ends of the earth. Her capacity for loyalty and commitment to Robin was boundless and blind. She might whisper words of love when she thought her husband slept, but that could never compare to the years of almost motherly devotion to her brother. How could less than two months stand up to over twenty years?

Wolfgang had hoped even if Robin was guilty that the payment of his debts would defuse his anger. He stood, holding on to his pounding head. But the debts were not the entire problem. Robin had also been suspicious of Wolfgang's intentions toward Zel, and for good reason. Now Zel said Robin was drinking and gaming again, and Freddie had some story about wagers at Brooks's. Zel couldn't know anything about the wagers or he would have heard.

He rang hard on the bell for Jenkins. Damnation and the bottomless pit! He couldn't tell Zel the truth. He wouldn't have Robin arrested, yet, but if there was another attempt on his life, his hand would be forced. Meanwhile he'd wait around to see if he was shot, stabbed, bludgeoned, or poisoned.

Rubbing his forehead, he tried to focus his thoughts. What of Zel's safety? She'd jump in to protect him if he were attacked, and Robin's inept assassins could injure her again. He couldn't win. If he arrested Robin, he'd lose Zel. If he did nothing, both of them could be killed.

There had to be a better answer. He could send her to the country. Wolfgang laughed bitterly. Zel had business at Aquitaine House and was not a woman who would blindly obey her husband anyway. Nor would he want her to be. But he could stay away from her, keeping the danger to himself. They could stay in London but go nowhere together. He should not share her meals. He would even have to avoid her bed. She'd be safe, he'd go mad. God, it couldn't be so difficult, most of the ton lived that way. It would also prepare him for the nightmare to come when he had to arrest Robin.

Impatiently Wolfgang endured Jenkins's attendance to his dress, gratefully drinking the nasty concoction his invaluable valet had learned to make on the Peninsula.

As he eased himself down the stairs, he heard the stately strains of Handel on the ancient harpsichord. Much better hangover accompaniment than Beethoven or that other fellow, Bach.

He walked into the room, standing quietly behind her. Zel stopped, bending until her forehead rested dischordantly on the keys.

"Zel?" He slid beside her on the bench. "What is it?"

She sat upright, slowly, eyes overly bright, voice faint through clenched teeth. "It's that damn time of month."

"Why are you playing?" Not waiting for an answer, he took her arm, leading her from the room. "Upstairs you go, to bed."

On the stairs to her room he sent a young housemaid scurrying for tea. He helped her out of her morning gown, into a silk wrapper, then tucked her under the bedclothes.

"Can you do the Chinese pressure that helped so much before?" She looked up at him, face drawn, lips pinched and white around the edges, eyes wide with shy trust and need. He felt like a gaoler in charge of his own hanging. He could choose his own noose now, or wait for the more deadly one to come when she turned to Robin—and away from him.

"I can't. I have an appointment." His voice rang hollow, harsh. He pressed his dry lips lightly on her forehead. "Take some laudanum."

He walked away, her brittle gasp cracking over him.

Nearly upending the tea tray Maggie carried into the room, he hurried to escape what he would now see in Zel's eyes. She might come to hate him, but she'd be safe.

"IF YOUR DARLING captain doesn't mend his ways, and quick, I swear I'll shoot him with his own dueling pistols." Maggie's anger at his lordship spilled over onto his blameless valet.

"Now, Maggie." Marmeduke soothed, handing her into his little sitting room. "I think you know this is not like him."

"I don't know if it's like him or not." Maggie tossed her head, feeling guilty for snapping at Marmeduke for the earl's misdeeds. "But I won't have him breaking her heart."

"He's hurting too." Marmeduke pulled out a chair.

She frowned at him, placing herself carefully on the indicated seat. "But he's doing the hurting."

"Now, don't frown at me." He settled a matching chair across from hers. "I don't control the man."

"I'm sorry." She gave him an apologetic smile. "If only he spent some time with her."

"A man doesn't live in his wife's pocket."

"I know." She sighed. "In the country they were always together. Her bedchamber was used only as a dressing room. Now, after little over a fortnight of marriage, they are on their way to becoming another cold, fashionable union. Couldn't you try to talk with him?"

"What about her?"

"I have talked to her." Maggie smoothed her gown. "Lady Zel is mystified by his coolness and I tell you she is hurt."

"I've seen him act this way in Spain, the night before a big battle."

"But what big battle is he facing here?"

"I know little and what I do know I'm not at liberty to

share, even with you." Marmeduke stood, turning from her. "The captain and his lady must live out their own lives. I believe he will come about eventually."

"I'm sorry." Maggie rose to stand beside him. "I am being quite the gossip. I hate to see her unhappy, especially when she was so afraid of marriage. And if he doesn't come about soon, it will be too late to regain her trust."

"And what of your happiness, princess?" He took her tiny hand in his. "Have you found some contentment with Ned on his way to the New World?"

"I feel a sense of lightness." She looked at their joined hands. "A lifting of a large burden."

"He was a big man." Marmeduke smiled at her chuckle. "If you can fun about it, you must be healing."

"I believe I am. With him really gone, I am."

He brought her hand to his mouth, his lips warm and firm against her knuckles. "I'm happy for you."

"It was due to you." Maggie's gaze followed the rough lines of his face.

"It wasn't just me." Marmeduke's vivid eyes caught hers in a look so tender her breath stopped in her chest. "But there is nothing I would rather do than be of service to you."

She couldn't draw her eyes away from his, couldn't think of a word to say. So she stood there, for how long she didn't know, probably looking for all the world like a dying fish with her mouth gaping, her eyes wide and unblinking.

Marmeduke gave her fingers a little squeeze, his face solemn, scarred lips a steady line across his face. His other hand grazed her jaw, fingertips resting under her chin. "May I kiss you, Maggie?"

The breath rushed from her lungs and her eyelids closed. Her lips still refused to function. She nodded and waited. His lips were as warm on her mouth as they had been on her hand, but now she could taste and smell just a hint of tea and honey. The tip of her tongue eased out of her mouth to sample more of that comforting taste.

His hands dropped, abandoning her hand and chin. The sense of loss must have shown when her eyes flew open, for with a groan, Marmeduke wrapped his arms about her completely. He pulled her against his chest, lips pressing to hers. She found comfort in his embrace, but there was more. The bitter fear and loneliness she had lived with for so many years seemed to fade, nudged aside by the sweetness of his kiss.

He released her lips, keeping her nestled in his arms, her head at his shoulder. Maggie held on to him, and that feeling of warmth and safety, tea-with-honey comfort, spiked with just a splash of the finest aged spirits.

ZEL THREW HERSELF onto an overstuffed sofa, wiping her brow with a less than adequate lace handkerchief. "This thing is worthless. I suppose real ladies don't perspire."

Emily flopped down beside her. "You don't need to do this, Zel. Your husband would give you the money to hire a regular housekeeper, in fact a whole army of servants, for Aquitaine House. We could use more footmen for everyone's safety and you could spend your time organizing, writing, fund raising. Any of the things you prefer to housekeeping and do much better."

"I've already spent my allowance on furnishings and supplies. I will not ask him for more." She looked about the large high-ceilinged room. The old stone house was shaping up nicely. It hadn't looked like much when they started the repairs and cleaning months ago, but now one wing was filling with women and this wing would soon be ready for habitation. "Besides, it will feel good to go home bone tired tonight."

"Zel, what is wrong?" Emily grasped her arm, refusing to let her turn away. "You've been mooning about for days now. Is something amiss between you and Northcliffe?"

"Why should anything be amiss? After all, we are newlyweds." Zel stared stubbornly ahead. If she looked into Emily's sympathetic eyes, she'd explode into tears.

"You're a horrible liar." Emily threaded an arm around her shoulders. "Spill it out."

"I will not cry." Zel blinked back the tears and let her anger rise in her throat. "He may not beat me, but he's as big a fool as any man alive."

"I see marriage has not altered your opinions." Emily gave her a little squeeze. "I should be happy for that, but I had hoped it would alter your too-firm hold on your emotions."

"It did. And my emotions were stomped into the ground." If she could keep her back stiff and her face tight with anger, the burning moisture at the back of her eyes wouldn't flow.

Emily rubbed at the back of her head in tiny circles, almost the way Wolfgang had, what seemed ages ago, and then refused to do only a se'ennight before. The tears seeped out between Zel's tightly closed lids. "Damn him."

"There's nothing wrong with being angry or sad or both."

Zel swallowed a sob, but her voice cracked. "You told me it was good to feel . . . well, I followed your advice. I handed him my heart . . . he threw it out with the rest of the refuse."

"I thought he cared for you." Emily clasped her hand. "How could that change days after marriage?"

"I foolishly told him I loved him. I thought he was asleep or I never would have said it." Zel stood and walked to the window, staring at the traffic parading up and down the busy Kensington Street. "He never asked for my love, clearly it was not what he wanted of me. We would both be happier now if I had just become his mistress."

"Zel Fleetwood!" Emily jumped to her feet, glaring at her friend, adding almost as an afterthought, "Hardwicke."

"I don't mean that, Emily. I could never live that way." She rubbed her eyes. The tears had stopped, dried up, absorbed by the arid hollowness inside. "If only I hadn't started to believe . . ."

"HAVE YOU EVER seen a longer face?"

"Only on his horse."

"I've had enough of your clever repartee." Wolfgang threw down his cards, glaring first at his friends, then in general about the shabby tavern. "And I'm bored to tears of this inane card game."

The duke of Ridgemont lifted his eyebrows to their huge comrade seated across the table. "Freddie, we need to find a way to amuse the man. He's bored with boxing, shooting, cards, drinking, theater, opera, driving, racing, and the conquering heroes' return. Lord, he's a hero himself with a string of ribbons and medals, even if his daring military exploits were years ago. But he's bored with that, too. What's left?"

"Hunting." Sir Frederick Ransley added his favorite. "But this wolf has never been keen on the hunt."

"He just prefers hunting two-legged creatures. That's it. Fornicating! His specialty. It's off to the Wilson sisters' for us." Rafael laughed at the scowl on Wolfgang's face. "With all these late nights with the boys, Wolf, you must be in need."

Wolfgang lurched to his feet, leaning over the plain, sturdy table, hands braced on the edges. "Lucifer's hairy back! Raf, keep your bloody nose out of my affairs."

Raf didn't move, but looked coolly into Wolfgang's face. "But, my dear Wolf, that is precisely the problem. You have no affairs into which I may stick my nose."

"And I won't."

"So, the rake becomes the faithful husband." Rafael dramatically wiped his eyes with his handkerchief. "I've seen it before, but it's still a mournful sight."

"A faithful husband, if I have a marriage left." Wolfgang flopped back into his seat.

Frederick eyed him over the rim of his glass. "You won't have a marriage left if you never see your wife."

"Or, if I have to hang her brother or ship him off to Australia," Wolfgang murmured.

"Not *if* you have to, Wolf, but when." Raf leaned back in his chair, tucking the handkerchief back into his waistcoat. "You're foolishly endangering yourself by refusing to act."

"We've bowed to your wishes, but if you don't do something soon, one of us will." Freddie gulped down his whiskey.

"Stay out of it." Wolfgang growled. "I'll do what I need to do."

"But *you* are doing nothing." Raf, as usual, was not about to let him off the hook. "As your friends we are obligated—"

"You are obligated to do nothing, unless I ask you. And I'm not asking."

"You're taking no action to save your life." Rafael poured himself a drink of brandy, motioning to Wolfgang, who shook his head. "You're not drinking, you're not gambling, you're not bedding your wife or anyone else. Jesu, don't say you're preparing to take religious orders. My heart couldn't bear it."

"You didn't mention Freddie's second favorite pastime, tavern brawls." Wolfgang glanced from Raf to a couple of rough characters across the whitewashed room, harassing a pretty barmaid. "A sport I'm dangerously close to initiating. We could get it going then slip out before much damage is done."

Rubbing his knuckles enthusiastically, Freddie permitted a rare smile to creep over his face. "I haven't indulged in months. The innkeeper won't mind, if we reimburse him handsomely for the usual broken chairs and crockery."

"Count me out of your infantile games." Rafael stood to leave. "But don't let my opinion stop you, Wolf. Your old cuts and bruises are healed, so if you think a few more injuries will cure your foul humor and ease your boredom, do it."

CHAPTER 17

FUGUE

A musical composition designed for
a number of instruments or voices in which one
or two themes are announced in one voice and
developed by successively entering and continuously
interweaving voice parts

"HOLD ON TO REMUS, that's Dorothea dead ahead." Grandmama Darlington waved long fingers at a clump of elms farther down the muddy Hyde Park trail. "She's seen us, there's no escape."

"Steady boy." Zel smiled at the elderly woman, grabbing the rope tied loosely around the dog's neck with one hand, her other hand latched on to the fur along his spine. "I don't know what it is, but he cannot resist jumping on her every time he sees her."

"The dog can be a bounder. But I can't say as I blame him."

"Lucretia! You sound as bad as your grandson."

"Oh, Diana, we all know the woman is a loose screw." Grandmama tapped Remus on the hind quarters. "Now sit!"

Aunt Dorothea stormed forward, Cousin Adam in her wake. The deep scowl on her face made it clear she greeted them against her wishes. "Lady Darlington, Mrs. Stanfield, Grizelda."

Adam tipped his hat, offering a shallow bow. "Ladies. I'm surprised to see you out braving the mud."

"The park is still recovering from the parades." Aunt Diana smiled. "But we couldn't resist the sunshine."

"I need to see Hardwicke." Aunt Dorothea lowered her nose enough to see over it, glaring at Zel. "Where is your husband?"

"I haven't the foggiest notion." Tamping down her irritation and a desire to correct the woman's refusal to use Wolfgang's title, Zel looked into the narrowed brown eyes. "I am not his keeper."

"Did I say he needed one?" Dorothea's shrill voice drew the stares of nearby walkers and riders. "I would never say it, although everyone knows he does. His wife could use one, too."

"Now, Mrs. Clayton——"

"So, Mrs. Diana Ninnyhammer Stanfield, you wish to come to the rescue of your wanton niece and her rakehell husband?"

"Dorothea!" Grandmama's voice tightened in warning.

Aunt Dorothea paid no heed. "If your grandson didn't hold the purse strings, I would shun the lot of you."

"Now, now." Aunt Diana laid out her most conciliatory tone. "Don't throw the first stone unless you live in a glass house."

Dorothea glared at her, then turned her hard eyes back to quell Zel's smile. "Have your husband call on me, immediately!" She clasped Adam's arm, striding away on the tree-lined path.

"I think I would rather have her snub me." Zel watched her retreating back in confusion. "I never know what she's about."

"If she can't show a little more restraint, Wolfgang

could make her allowance contingent on her permanent removal to a remote country estate. You shouldn't have to deal with her insults." Grandmama pulled Zel's hand from its grip on Mouse's fur and turned the small party to a narrow side trail. "Perhaps we can finish our walk in peace."

"Despite the early hour we seem doomed to run into everyone we know." Aunt Diana pointed to a horseman rounding the next corner before them. "Isn't that Northcliffe's big friend?"

Zel yanked a flower off a rhododendron bush and surveyed the enormous man on an equally enormous mount, remembering the last time she saw him. She tore at a petal. The night the blossoming intimacy of her marriage had withered at her premature declaration. A bud cut too soon to open. "It's Ransley." Her skin heated. "And Wolfgang's right behind him."

The two men smoothly guided their horses to the little group of women. Ransley nodded while Wolfgang ran a finger across the brim of his hat. "Such a charming bevy of spring flowers."

Zel forced a smile and stared. Wolfgang's face was a panorama of cuts and bruises, from a slightly swollen split on his lower lip, through a purplish blotch on his cheek, to a small, scabbing gash above his eye. Ransley looked no better, with a black eye and bruised jaw. She trapped her tongue between her teeth to keep in the questions.

Grandmama had no such compunctions, berating the adult males in her most scolding tone. "You two are worse than a couple of overgrown schoolboys. Were you brawling?"

Wolfgang looked sheepishly at his hands. "We were defending a lady's honor."

Ransley coughed and directed his gaze down the path.

"Couldn't Ridgemont stop you this time?"

"He didn't try, Grandmama. Said it would do me good, and it did." Wolfgang grinned, then grimaced when his lip split further and a drop of blood dripped down his chin. He impatiently wiped it away with his fist. "For a while."

"Dismount and walk with us a bit, dear."

Zel studiously avoided the silvery gaze she knew focused on her. She couldn't face another rejection.

"No." Wolfgang hesitated, then continued in a stronger voice, "Freddie and I have business."

Ransley glanced from Wolfgang to Zel, catching Zel's eyes with a look she couldn't decipher. "Wolf, we don't—"

"Yes, we do." Wolfgang turned his horse, covering half the path before Ransley frowned apologetically and followed.

"A TOAST to a job well done." Newton raised his glass in salute to his coconspirator. "If I must say so myself."

"Are we finished with them?" Isadora raised her glass in response and sipped at the deep burgundy.

"Never say we're finished." Scanning Isadora's seldom-used library, Newton allowed a hint of a smile to touch his lips. "But I am satisfied, for the moment. The forced marriage seems to have done the trick. Lady Northcliffe is looking frightfully downcast. Northcliffe is seen frequently on the town, but never in the company of his bride. And best of all, he doesn't seem at all his usual self. So quiet and glum." He stretched out on the small sofa. "It's delightful."

"I'm happy you are so pleased."

"The bloom is off the rose." Sitting up straight, he looked pointedly at Isadora's pout. "Why the big lip?"

"Wolfgang may be free, but he shows absolutely no interest in me." The pout grew.

"You've approached him already? Have you no subtlety, woman?" And no brains, he completed silently.

A touch of pink passed over Isadora's cheeks. The jade could still blush! "I put myself in his way and he acted like I didn't exist."

"Isadora, Isadora. How can you be such a fool? Listen to

and heed the master." Swirling his wine in the goblet, he stood over her to further make his point. "You must proceed slowly in these matters. Cultivate and groom your quarry. Be kind and sympathetic. Let him cry on your shoulder. Then make certain you're there when he's ready to succumb."

"And you are the expert." She tossed her golden head. "Watch me."

"Watch you? What do you have planned?"

"Northcliffe's lady will be in my bed. Not in days, I'm not a fool like you. But mark my words and watch. She'll be my mistress. Northcliffe will be cuckolded, again."

Isadora stared at him, taking an unusually long time to find her voice. "You would throw me over for that creature?"

Newton surveyed her slowly from bottom to top. "Yes, I would." At her strangled gasp, he continued, "You'd throw me over for Northcliffe, given half a chance."

"My God! You are both animalth. Viciouth animalth." Melbourne stood in the doorway, face flushed, hands fisted at his sides. His speech included both people in the room, but his accusing eyes focused on Newton.

"Now, Melbourne. We were only playing a little trick on the newlyweds." Newton waved the younger man into the room, but Melbourne stood there stiffly, ignoring Newton's summons.

"I may not be the motht intelligent man on earth, Newton, but I am not deaf. I heard you clearly." Melbourne took a deep breath. "It wathn't tho bad when I thought we were trying to thave Mith—Lady Northcliffe from a man tho unworthy of her. But I won't be party to a plan to hand her over to *you*."

Newton stared at Melbourne, astonished at Melbourne's reaction. "Jeremy, I had no idea you cared so much. Lord, I've never heard you string so many words together." He moved towards the door. "I won't deny it. We used you."

Melbourne looked close to tears. "Thank you for not lying further. I am leaving thoon for my country houthe."

"Perhaps I may visit you there." Newton nodded his head, surprised at the note of pleading in his own voice.

"I think not." Melbourne made a shallow bow to Isadora, as he backed out of the doorway. "Good day, ma'am. I may thee you briefly at the Whiltonth' before I go."

"MAGGIE?" Jenkins had waited nearly an hour in his sitting room to share tea with the tiny maid and finally, in desperation, poked his nose into Lady Zel's room.

"What are you doing here?" Maggie emerged from the Chinese silk bed hangings, the rich color battling violently with the fire red of her hair.

"The tea is cold."

"Oh, Marmeduke, forgive me." The corners of her mouth turned down as she tied a curtain securely to the wall fastening. "I've been so distracted, I completely forgot."

"Worrying about your mistress?" He slipped into the room, feeling a sense of trepidation as he breached the forbidden domain. Neither the captain nor his lady had given orders against his entrance, but a valet simply did not enter milady's chambers.

Maggie beckoned him forward, moving with silent efficiency about the room, clutter becoming order beneath her hands. "Don't just stand there, shut the door behind you."

Jenkins complied, surveying the clothes-strewn chamber. "I had no idea Lady Z was so, ah, disorganized."

"She isn't normally this messy."

"Another sin to lay at the captain's feet?" Jenkins picked up a few gowns off a chair and handed them to Maggie. The sheer night rail he surreptitiously returned to the chair.

Maggie hid a smile under her slender fingers. "I'm tired of worrying about his sins and her sorrows. I've never seen two such intelligent people behave like such idiots." She took his hand, dragging him to the door. "Let's forget them for a few minutes."

They stole from the room, down the staircase, finding a little-used salon. Jenkins squeezed her fingers as he settled beside her on the low settee. "What if we're discovered?"

Her laugh was clear and high as a silver sleigh bell. She didn't laugh near enough. "And what would we do if we were? Have a rushed marriage as our employers did?"

"Our situation is not quite so compromising." Jenkins felt heat stealing up his face. He hadn't blushed since he was a child. Maybe not even then. But her words so reflected his thoughts, he felt disconcerted. "And how would you feel if that were to happen?"

She looked into his eyes as if she sought the answer to his question there. "I'm not sure what you mean?"

"I know this is too soon, but an old fool is the worst fool." Breathing deeply, he took her other hand. "Maggie, will you marry me?" He waved away her reply. "Don't answer yet. I don't have much to offer, only a few rooms, my horse, and some savings. But all I have or ever hope to have is yours."

"Oh, Marmeduke, I could never receive a sweeter offer, but—"

"But, no. I'm not suitable husband material. I am too old, too ugly, too poor—"

"Ssshh, you are not so old. You are rich and beautiful in everything that matters." She gently squeezed his hands. "But you forget, I'm already married."

"I don't care." And as he gazed into the vibrant green eyes shining up at him, he truly didn't care about anything but her. Ned no longer existed as far as he was concerned. They would work out whatever they needed to work out.

"And everyone knows servants don't marry."

"Captain and Lady Z won't care, in fact they would be the first to rejoice in our happiness." Jenkins raised her hand to his lips, savoring each dainty finger in turn. "I don't have a ring for such a pretty hand, but I've kept this as a symbol of my vow to always love and protect you. I would like you to have it." He reached into his pocket and handed her a delicate chased-silver snuff box. Then he smiled, his white-toothed smile no longer perfect with the conspicuous gap in the top front teeth.

Maggie opened the box. Resting on a swatch of black felt were two well-polished white teeth.

He accepted her smiling yes with his lips, her sweetness so much more than he ever believed life would give him.

"Zel! I'm surprised my Wolfie let you out of the house in that gown." Lady Darlington scanned her, frowning.

"Your Wolfie has no say over my wardrobe." Zel pulled the flimsy shawl tighter over her shoulders and chest. "He did ask me to purchase new clothing, but Emily helped me shop. Wolfgang hasn't even seen any of the gowns yet."

"The cut is flattering on your tall, slender figure, and I'm pleased you haven't added all those flounces and frills so many young ladies favor." Lady Darlington plucked at the skirts of Zel's gown. "But I've never seen you in anything cut so low. The men will do nothing but stare at your bosom."

"Lady Darlington—"

"No, dear, I told you to call me Grandmama."

"Well, then, Grandmama." Zel took the older woman's hand and tucked it in her arm, exiting the house for the waiting carriage. "The men at the ball will have better things to do than stare at my bosom."

"Zel, how little you know of the men of the ton." She gave Zel's arm a little squeeze. "I wish that husband of yours was with us. He has been conspicuous in his absence these last days, and now the season is nearly over."

"He has been busy with politics. The vote on his bill is tomorrow." Zel handed Grandmama to the footman, who assisted her into the coach. "I fear I run a poor second."

"I don't understand him, even if he is my grandson. A

new bride should not be second to politics." She settled on the squabs as Zel ascended into the coach. "I'll talk with the boy."

"No, you will not." Zel sat beside her, arranging her skirts. "It's fitting he have an occupation important to him."

"I'll abide by your wishes, but I'm not happy. I hoped you two would have a marriage different than most of the ton."

So had she. Zel gazed out the window onto the dark London streets. At Cliffehaven Wolfgang had been so charming and passionate, almost loving. She had believed the marriage could work. But after their arrival in town he drew away from her. After *I love you* had escaped unbidden from her lips. He hadn't answered, made no perceptible response, but he was clearly unhappy, even angry, to have such an unfashionably emotional wife. He had never asked for her love, never offered his.

The long line of carriages delivering guests to the Whiltons' ball moved torturously slow. It seemed hours before they pulled up to the grand town house. As they alighted from the coach at the long staircase, Robin darted out of the crowd, grasped her arm, and drew her up to the reception line. Zel twisted to take Grandmama's arm, hissing at Robin. "Slower, please, and take Lady Darlington's arm."

"Why should I take *his* grandmother's arm?" Robin's quick glance at the woman across from Zel showed his cold eyes and tight mouth. "You have her arm, you keep it."

"Robin," she whispered, "Lady Darlington is now my grandmother too. I will not have you be rude to her."

"Fine." He grunted, stepping around Zel and placing both ladies' hands at his elbows. "Don't expect me to eat supper with you, I'll be in the card room."

"Lady Darlington, you have met my ill-mannered brother, Robin." Zel glared at her dark-haired brother, aware of the smell of alcohol on his breath. "I would prefer you not gamble."

"I'll do as I please, neither you nor your husband is my keeper." He guided them smoothly into the reception line.

"Young man, show your sister respect." Grandmama rapped his leg with her cane.

He made no response, but frowned at the Whiltons and their plump little debutante daughter.

"And where is your handsome husband, Lady Northcliffe?" Lady Whilton's little eyes pried in unison with her words.

"He has important business in Parliament tomorrow, Lady Whilton, and sends his regrets." A feeling hit her that she would be repeating this line all night. Many sets of feminine eyes would tell her the merry dance was over. The chase had been prolonged, but she tumbled like all the rest and with much less discretion. She may have won the title, but she could not keep him any more than they could.

Straightening her shoulders, she raised her chin and smiled at the wide-eyed Whilton daughter. "Lady Cecile, I hope your come-out is all you dreamed it would be."

Zel had ceased to be amazed at the way the ton now received her. Certainly there were sidelong glances, whispers, and pointed comments, but few cut her directly. Wolfgang was right, as a wealthy, married countess she would have to dance naked on the Covent Garden stage to earn complete censure, and even then some would probably look aside and call her eccentric. Tonight she pasted on her best smile, determined to secure more patronage for Aquitaine House.

"Ah, Simon, old chum." Robin squeezed her fingers, dragging her toward a familiar red-haired man. "Come meet my dear sister, Lady Northcliffe. Zel, this is Simon Bedford." Robin grinned with a flash of exaggerated puzzlement. "Demmed if I know if he's a relation to you or not. You were almost introduced several weeks ago at some gathering. He's brother to Northcliffe's deceased first wife, Rosalind Bedford Hardwicke."

"Simon." Grandmama nodded a curt greeting.

"Mr. Bedford." Zel extended a tentative hand.

Bedford looked at her hand, his face white, eyes narrowed. "Where is your husband, Lady Northcliffe?"

She repeated Wolfgang's excuses, but Bedford barely attended to her after learning Wolfgang was not at the ball.

"Fleetwood, I'll be in the card room. Lady Darlington, Lady Northcliffe." Bedford ran cold eyes over Zel, turned on his heel, and strode across the crowded room.

Robin bid a curt dismissal and followed after Bedford.

Zel, trying for a measure of normalcy, danced two sets with men she had met at that first, fateful house party, her thoughts flickering back to the masquerade ball. Even then she had been falling in love with Wolfgang, for as flirtatious as she'd felt that night, her response to his touch signaled a deeper longing. A longing she fought to keep penned in, under control. But it had broken through as if it had a life of its own.

Throwing herself on a settee beside Grandmama on Matron's Row, she refused the next set, sending the prospective partner instead for punch.

"Are you finally convinced you are a success, Zel?"

"I had supposed I would be snubbed by everyone." She fanned herself, stirring the hot humid air of the ballroom. "The last week has convinced me that no one has forgotten my indiscretions, but neither will they make a big to-do of them."

"Now all we need do is bring that foolish boy around." Grandmama patted her hand. "And get you with child, then life will be sunshine."

"Here comes a little cloudburst." Zel indicated the approaching gray-clad figure of Wolfgang's aunt.

"Grizelda, Lady Darlington." Aunt Dorothea's bell tones tolled.

"Cousin, m'lady." Cousin Adam peeked around his mother, peering down Zel's neckline as usual.

"Where is Hardwicke?" Aunt Dorothea scanned the room, a little scowl pinching her lips.

Zel repeated her husband's excuses, unable to hide a blush under Aunt Dorothea's speculative gaze.

Dorothea laughed, high and shrill. "Ah, he has already done his duty, and now abandons his bride?"

"Whatever do you mean?" Zel blurted out, wishing at the gleam in the woman's eye that she'd held her tongue.

"Are you pregnant?" Aunt Dorothea surveyed her coldly.

Gasping, Zel glanced about to ensure no one had overheard. "I am barely married. It is much too soon to even consider."

Aunt Dorothea sniffed. "Let us hope so." She took her son's arm. "Save a dance for Adam. After supper."

Cousin Adam bowed. "Servant. Cousin, Lady Darlington."

"I expect to be the first to know when you are increasing, Grizelda. I'll not take it kindly if you are hiding it from me." She turned, dragging her son off in the train of her skirts.

Speechless, Zel looked at Grandmama, not knowing whether she should laugh or scream. "And she has the nerve to criticize Aunt Diana?"

"The woman's always been a little off. She'd take the earldom if she could." Grandmama coughed into her handkerchief. "Ignore her. She's harmless as long as she gets her allowance."

Successfully avoiding relatives and other mortal enemies through supper gave Zel confidence the evening would progress favorably. But her luck did not hold. It was all she could do not to hide under the settee as she watched that fearsome threesome of Lady Horeton, Newton, and Melbourne stalk toward her. Of course, one could scarcely call Melbourne, who followed a pace behind, an unusual scowl on his face, fearsome unless one feared kittens. But the other two were predators, ready to feed on whatever hapless victim couldn't escape their clutches.

Newton bowed low before her, pressing his lips to her knuckles a moment longer than proper. "Lady Northcliffe, you are in excessive looks tonight." His eyes traveled slowly up her body. "I do not see your husband in attendance."

"No, my grandson is engaged in Parliamentary business." Grandmama rescued Zel from another explanation, then turned to the petite blonde. "Lady Horeton."

"Good evening, Lady Darlington and Grizelda. I feel I may continue to call you that, we have so much in common." She purred, her delicate head tilted at its most flattering angle.

"Indeed, *Lady* Horeton, I am certain we must." Zel's own husky tones were near a growl. "If we could only discover what."

"Touché, Lady Northcliffe." A hint of warmth glinted beneath Newton's cold eyes.

"Mith Fleet—pardon, Lady Northcliffe." Melbourne stumbled over himself reaching for her hand. "Would you . . . ah . . ."

"What my shy friend is asking is that you honor him with a dance, after this set with me." Newton glanced swiftly at his friend then back to Zel as he took her arm. Melbourne glared as Newton led her onto the floor to the strains of a waltz.

Too late to back out, she faced her partner, ignoring that unpleasant little shiver running down her spine. As he placed a hand at her waist, moving into the gracefully swaying crowd, she forced herself to relax. "You are an excellent dancer, my lord."

"No, my dear, any grace lies totally with my partner.

You should be enjoying the ball with your new husband."
Newton pulled her close to swirl about another couple encroaching on their space. "The man shows the best of taste in
selecting his brides but then hideously ignores them as one
would an ordinary mistress when the gleam of newness wears
off."

"THANK YOU, McDougall." Zel stepped through the entryway, pausing to look at her reflection in the lacquer-framed
mirror hanging accusingly at the foot of the staircase. The
gleam of newness. Had it worn off so soon for Wolfgang,
before it could grow into something stronger, more lasting,
as it had for her?

Wolfgang hadn't touched her in well over a week, other
than a formal hand at her arm or a tiny half kiss on her brow
that he seemed to regret afterward. She expected understanding when her courses began, but his passion before had not
prepared her for this long abstinence. Over and over she tried
to convince herself he waited politely, but she knew it wasn't
true. He was not a man to wait politely for anything he
desired. And he knew her pain only lasted a few days. Now
she could no longer deny that his withdrawal was complete.

Little more than a se'ennight to undo all they had
started to build. And a lifetime to live as strangers.

Zel shook herself, rubbing at her burning eyes. All they
started to build. What a fool she was. They had met only
two months ago. What time had there been to build anything but false dreams? He was nothing but a stranger. A
stranger to whom she had mistakenly confessed her love.

Wearily, she climbed the stairs, mentally preparing herself for a restless night. As she turned toward her room she
heard a rustling. She looked down the dimly lit hallway to
the service stairway but saw nothing.

Pausing at Wolfgang's door, she searched herself for a

modicum of courage. She stepped to the door, pausing again, placing her hand on the warm carved wood. Her forehead lowered of its own volition to rest on the smooth surface. With a deep breath, she reached for the latch.

Smoke!

Zel flung open the door, coughing over the outrush of heat and dark smoke.

"Wolfgang!"

The window drapes were solid flame. The bed curtains flickered and sparked with burgeoning fire.

"Help! God, someone help!" She choked. "It's fire!"

On leaden legs, she waded through the smoke to the bed. Hauling the counterpane off the huge bed, she groped for him, barely making out his shape in the thick darkness. She pulled at his ankles, fingers sliding down his feet. His body refused to move. Her hands edged farther up his legs but there was nothing to hold on to, nothing to grasp.

Perspiration dripped down her spine and pooled beneath her breasts as she tugged at his legs, dragging him in excruciatingly slow inches.

"Wake up! Dear God, wake up! You're too damn heavy." Her voice screeched. "Help! Please!"

Gasping out the smoke invading her lungs, Zel grabbed his knees. Her muscles bunched as she strained, chest tight, throat seared by smoke and heat. With a tremendous heave, she yanked his naked form to the floor.

"Wolfgang!" Sobbing, she struck sparks away from his chest. "I can't do this." But she again gripped his knees in her arms, jerking him in short stops and starts along the deep carpet pile.

"Lady Z!" The tenor voice was a balm to her ears. Firm hands moved her aside. Jenkins and McDougall carried Wolfgang from the room. Servants rushed in with rugs and buckets of water to battle the flames.

Zel backed into the hallway, collapsing against the wall,

watching helplessly as Wolfgang's unconscious body disappeared down the stairs. She coughed, a ragged croak from deep in her lungs, feeling the tears flooding her cheeks and the tremor convulsing her body, afraid to stay where she stood but more afraid to follow down the staircase.

CHAPTER 18

CADENZA

A flourish in a solo piece near
the end of a cadence or movement

"I KNOW I didn't leave a candle burning too close to the curtains." Wolfgang's words rasped against his abraded throat as he surveyed the blackened bed. He stole a glance at Zel's tight profile. His wife's courage had saved his life. And he'd been right to stay away from her. If she'd been sleeping with him, they both would have died. "I put out the candles before retiring."

"Then what—" Zel interrupted herself. "Wolfgang, I heard a noise in the hall before I smelled smoke. Do you suppose—"

He took her by the shoulders, turning her from the charred and sodden mess. "No, I don't suppose."

"But, Wolf, you've been attacked before."

"My dear, footpads and thieves don't set housefires."

To touch her, to look so deeply into the golden flames floating in her sea-green eyes, was a mistake. The elegant evening gown draping her slender form was torn and soiled beyond repair. One side of her head remained elaborately coiffed, the other side was a tangle of wild curls. He yearned to pull her to the wet carpet beneath them and take her amid the ashes, water, and lingering smoke. To brand her forever as his. To sear their lives irrevocably together with the fire of their passion.

Make love to her tonight and arrest Robin tomorrow. His hand was forced, as he feared it would be. Robin's mad pursuit of revenge endangered others, including his own sister.

Wolfgang released her, whirling away, banging his leg against a heavy, mahogany table. His dressing gown caught. Yanking the cloth free, he ran his hand over the rough edge of the table. A tiny piece of fabric fell into his fingers, a soft shimmering swatch of gray.

"What is it?" Zel was back at his side, so close even the smell of burnt wood and cloth could not overpower her cinnamon-nutmeg scent.

"Nothing." He dropped the small fabric triangle. "Only an old table tearing up my servants' livery. I'll have McDougall see to it when the rest of the room is repaired." Wolfgang stretched his stiff shoulders. "We need to find other beds for the night. Even your chambers will reek of smoke."

She twined a long, slender arm about his neck. "One bed. Stay with me tonight."

He inhaled deeply, lungs raw, more scorched by her nearness than the flames from which she'd pulled him.

Zel didn't wait for an answer, just took his hand and a candelabra and gently drew him through the door and down the hall. Desire swirled through him. He couldn't fight anymore. He'd take tonight, take her love, and force himself to forget how much greater the pain would be when she turned from him.

"This way. There isn't a room ready and the smoke won't be as bad downstairs." Wolfgang guided her down the stairs, opening the first door off the landing. Scooping Zel up into his arms, he strode into his book room, elbowing the door closed behind them. He took the candle from her and deposited it on a corner table. A smile brushed her lips as he pushed aside ledgers, papers, and the little jade centaur and sat her down on the massive lacquer desk.

Wolfgang ran his fingers over the smoke and water stains on the delicate silk of her gown, then reverently removed the ruined garment and underclothes. Leaning over her, he traced a smudgy line of soot down her jaw, throat, and breast to where the gray ash ended in clean, white skin inches above an invitingly peaked nipple. Groaning his surrender, he ripped open his dressing gown and pressed his bare chest to hers, the coolness of her skin singeing his flesh. Sliding her closer, arms around her shoulders, he parted her thighs with his hips.

Satan's horns, the days of abstinence had fanned the flame of his need for her so high he feared he might do her harm in his haste. Gulping in breath after breath of cool night air, he steadied himself.

"Are you ill?" She broke his grip, hands braced against his shoulders. "You must rest. I heard that smoke can damage—"

Pulling her back to him, Wolfgang smothered her protest with his mouth.

Zel pushed off his chest. "Let me send for a doctor."

"No!" He wrapped her arms around his neck, holding her hands at his nape. "I don't need a doctor." He shifted his head. "Look at me."

Her eyes glowed molten in the flickering candlelight, seeming to look for something in his eyes. He lowered his lids, breath caught in his throat. "I need you."

She put a hand to each side of his head, drawing him back within range of her lips. But he moved more quickly, taking her full lower lip between his teeth, hard enough to leave an imprint when he abandoned the lip to thrust his tongue deep into her mouth. Slipping his hand between them, he found her heated core.

"You're ready," he whispered, adjusting his hips to prepare for entry. "And the devil only knows I am."

Wolfgang moved against her, slowing himself, stirring the embers, allowing the hot spots to spark and flare. But Zel, clearly impatient with gentleness and caution, arched to him, grasping his hips, pulling him roughly into her, incinerating his pretense at control.

Plunging to the hilt, he reached deeper and deeper inside her with each wild stroke. Like kindling offered to a bonfire, he burned hot and fast, oblivious to her response until her cry intermingled with his shout, reverberating in his ears. He fell against her, spent, reduced to a clump of lambent cinders.

"REMUS! Mouse!" Zel strode from the breakfast room down the hallway shouting into the open doorways. "Where is that damn dog? Did someone let him out earlier this morning? He never misses his bacon."

"Lady Zel!" Maggie's high shriek came from the library. "He's here. Oh, God!"

Zel rushed through the imposing, dark room, pushing aside the goddess Kali and her many arms to kneel by Maggie. Her hand brushed over the dog's back, as her head went to his chest. His heart beat slowly. His lungs unsteadily filled and emptied.

A sickly sweet smell curled about her nostrils. Laudanum. "He's been drugged." She laid her cheek against his closed eyes.

"Drugged? Remus?" Maggie's incredulous voice echoed her own thoughts. "Who would want to hurt him?"

"Who . . ." Zel stroked the shaggy coat. He whimpered, eyes fluttering open. She hugged the limp form to her. "Mouse! Oh, you big, silly thing."

"Is he coming around?"

Zel ruffled the hair over his eyes. "He's tough. He'll recover." She stood slowly. "But why give a dog laudanum?"

The fire! She tried to breathe through the growing constriction in her chest. Wolfgang! He could still be in danger. Lifting her skirts, she ran up the stairs, barreling through his dressing room door.

"Madam?" He smiled at her coolly as Jenkins made the finishing touches to his smoke-scented toilette.

"Wolfgang." Zel tried to steady herself and ignore the distance he was re-erecting between them. She had awakened with surprise earlier this morning in a strange bed devoid of his presence, only his scent and the indentation in the bed where he had lain lingered to remind her of the night they'd shared. Quickly donning the dressing gown he left draped over a chair, she had dashed eagerly down the hall into his chambers. His icy rebuff as she interrupted his bath had felt like a slap to the face. How could he make love to her with such a wildfire combination of passion and tenderness last night and push her away only hours later?

Now, ready for his coldness, she tossed back her head and met his eyes. "Someone is trying to kill you."

"Me, my dear?" He waved Jenkins away.

"Remus was dosed with laudanum last night." She watched Jenkins close the door behind him and continued, "Someone set that fire last night and knew they had to get Remus out of the way to do it."

A steel spark briefly flickered in his eyes, before he smiled again and patted her hand. "That hound of yours must have raided the housekeeper's medical supplies."

"You aren't telling me everything." She eyed him warily. "It's more than the fire. How could I be such an idiot? The wound at the first house party. The cut on your head after we returned to London. The footpads, if that's what they were, outside your home." She touched the scab on his lip. "The new scratches and bruises and now the fire."

"Zel—"

"Don't 'Zel' me." Her voice moving rapidly up the scale, she shook his arm. "What in God's name is going on?"

Pulling free of her, he threw himself onto a silk-cushioned settee, his tone tight and so low she could barely make out the words. "There is nothing you need to know."

"Someone is trying to kill you. And you decide not to tell your wife."

"Lucifer's spawn! I'll take care of this myself." His cool look faded as the anger spread across his face.

"I thought we were a partnership." A matching heat burned a trail up her chest, neck and cheeks.

"Some things are none of your bloody business." His voice flared.

"Attacks on my goddamn husband *are* my bloody business."

Wolfgang lurched to his feet, bending over her until his face was only inches from hers. "Hold your tongue, madam wife!"

Icy fingers of anger and fear gripped her spine, but she held her ground. "I'll say what I bloody well please, *my lord.*"

He grasped her shoulders, the thunder in his voice echoing the storm brewing in his eyes. "You'll keep that sharp little nose out of things that don't concern you."

"Now we get at the truth." She scowled back at him. "You're no different from any other man. You spout a few words of equality to hook me, but when it comes down to reality you treat me worse than a child—either keep me in the dark at arm's length or threaten me."

Squeezing her shoulders, he lowered his voice. "You don't have a clue what you're talking about."

"I know only too well what you're about." Zel wiggled under his grip. "You are hurting me."

"Sit down and listen." Wolfgang released her.

Unbalanced, she sprawled onto the settee, glaring at him. "Your most obedient audience, sirrah."

"Goddammit! I'm sorry!" He raged, towering over her, fists clenched at his sides.

"A damn shouted apology doesn't count."

The effort he made to control his anger showed clearly in his tense jaw and slivered eyes. "Zel, I am sorry. There are things I wish I could tell you." He ran his hands roughly over his face. "But I can't."

Zel made no effort to lower her own voice. "Keep your secrets—"

"Please, Zel . . ." He leaned toward her, hand extended.

She crossed her arms beneath her breasts, ignoring his outstretched hand. It would be easy to surrender to his touch, to forget herself in his big warm body. She couldn't set aside the rift between them, wouldn't allow herself to forget that he might now be giving her access to his body, but other than a crack in the doorway last night, he was still denying her his heart and mind. "You make choices that keep us apart."

"Would that I had choices." He sank onto the settee beside her, staring into her eyes as if to read her soul.

Closing her eyes, she shook her head fiercely. "No, I don't believe that." Zel felt him move toward her and tore open her eyes, jumping up from the settee. "Don't touch me again."

She looked back from the doorway, feeling the pain in his eyes deep in the pit of her own stomach. But she knew he wouldn't reveal the cause of that pain, couldn't ask her to share it, and didn't know that sharing it, no matter what it was, would hurt her far less than this damnable estrangement.

Shutting the door softly behind her, she stood, silent and still, waiting for him to come to her. But there was no sound from the adjoining room. Zel felt as helpless as she had trying to pull him from the fire. She could not control then whether he lived or died any more than she could now change his unwillingness to bridge the distance between them.

"GO GET HER, McDougall, or I will."

"Mr. Fleetwood, I believe she is resting."

"She never rests during the day, get her."

"Robin, I'm here." Zel stood at the top of the steps. "You do not need to disturb the entire house. Come up to the drawing room." She smiled as Robin took the steps two at a time. "Eager to see me, dear brother?"

"Heard about the fire. Are you all right?" At her nod he grabbed her arm, pulling her urgently down the hall. "I need to talk to you."

Zel called behind her as they entered the gold-and-green room. "McDougall, send up some tea."

"Need something stronger. Brandy, McDougall."

"Tea, McDougall."

"Fine, I'll drink your damn tea."

"Come in. Sit down." Indicating a chair, she dropped onto the silk-and-teak ottoman beside it. "What has you so upset?"

He sat stiffly, running his slender fingers through a lock of hair hanging over his ear. "Don't know why you ever got involved with that man."

"Robinson Fleetwood, you drag me in here because you need to speak to me and all you wish to do is complain about my husband?" Zel yanked at his cravat when he tried to stand. "If you have something more to say, then say it."

"Let go, you're ruining my Waterfall."

"You are becoming a fop." She released the neckcloth, and Robin flopped back into the chair.

"You are a cruel taskmaster." He put his hands protectively over his cravat. "I'll tell all. Don't mangle my linen."

"Here is your reprieve now. Saved by McDougall's efficiency." She turned to the maid hovering in the doorway.

"Pay no mind to us, Polly. Bring in the tea and you may leave."

With the tea steeping on an inlaid teakwood table, Zel returned her attention to her brother. "Speak up."

"It's that devil, Northcliffe—"

"Robin!"

"He's a rotter."

"I won't listen to any more name calling and innuendo." Zel tried to catch his eyes. After her fight with Wolfgang only hours before, she was in no mood to listen to Robin's complaints and gossip. "Can you not try to get along with Wolfgang? He is trying to be a friend, even an older brother, to you."

"Don't trust him." Robin fingered the disheveled neckcloth. "I can show you good reason why you shouldn't either."

"More stories about his deceased wife or relations?"

"No, this concerns you directly."

She sighed, resting her elbow on the arm of his chair. "I'm listening."

"Friend invited me to Brooks's—"

She cut in, temper piqued. "Robinson, are you gambling?"

"This was days ago. Besides I'm not playing deep." He touched her arm lightly. "Northcliffe is."

"Wolfgang rarely gambles, deep or otherwise."

"Call it deep when he's playing with your reputation and affections." Robin's full mouth was tight and grim.

Zel stretched her arm out, plucking at his sleeve. "I don't understand."

"At Brooks's I ran into an old gaming comrade I was certain owed me money on a horse race. When he disputed the date and the participants, I thought I could prove it in the betting books." He paused. "Give me some tea. My throat is dry."

She poured two cups of tea, adding the preferred amounts of cream to each, waiting for him to continue.

Robin took a sip of the hot liquid. "I came across a wager. It was dated right after that first house party you went to, Lady Selby's. Aunt Diana's friend." He sipped more tea. "You know, where you met *him.*"

"And the wager?"

"It said, 'Match all comers. Earl of N. will bed Miss F. before the season is out.' And it was signed 'WJWH'."

She sucked in a breath with a soft, sibilant hiss. "No."

"Zel, I saw the entry myself."

"It must be a coincidence." She tried to slow her speech. "It does not mean anything, it's only initials."

"I'm sorry, Zel, but it fits too well." Frowning, Robin set down his tea. "He is the earl of N. You are Miss F. And his full name is Wolfgang John Wesley Hardwicke, WJWH. There couldn't be any other men at Brooks's with exactly that title and those initials. The timing is right. And it explains why he continued to pursue you despite your rebuffs."

"But he doesn't need the money." Zel rapidly stirred her cooling tea.

"For most of us hardened gamblers, wagering has little to do with the money." He pushed a shaggy brown lock off his brow. "It's the excitement, the ups and downs, the risk of losing, the challenge of winning, playing against impossible odds because that next big win must be right around the corner. You couldn't understand it, unless you've been caught up in it."

"Maybe I do understand." She took a deep breath and swallowed a little tea. "I still don't understand why Wolf—"

"Zel, they don't come any wilder than your husband." Robin rubbed her hand. "He's a gambler, along with everything else. Thrives on risks, the pursuit of that impossible challenge. Bet my next year's allowance on it. He's reckless and he doesn't think or care about anyone but himself."

She laid her cup on the low table, lowering her eyes. "But I thought he cared about me, at least a little."

"Cares about his own pleasures." He stirred in the chair. "Would a man who really cared about you have so little regard for your reputation and sensibilities? From the start he's only cared about getting under your skirts."

"Robin!" She fastened a hard look on him, her voice sharp. "He paid your debts and married me."

"What does marriage mean to him? Just that you were harder to get than the others, and there have been and will be many others. But the gambler doesn't mind losses as long as he gets that big win in the end. And he won. He got what he wanted." Robin pushed back his chair and stood. "How long before he gets restless and moves on to the next challenge? And the man has a temper, so what happens if you cross him?"

"Robin, enough!" Zel clasped his arm. "Why did you wait to tell me this?" She eyed him warily. "And why tell me now?"

"Wish you were half as suspicious of him as you are of me." He turned to the door.

"Robin, I want an answer." Her grip tightened on his arm.

He glanced at her then looked down at her hand. "Didn't want you to know I'd been in the clubs."

"I knew you'd been gambling." She sighed. "But why were you so insistent on telling me now?"

"Because he's making you miserable." Robin shook off her hand. "He's no good. I don't want you around him. Leave him."

Zel stared at him. "I'm not leaving my husband."

"He'll only hurt you. Has already. You're a fool to stay."

"Why am I even listening to you?" Zel stopped, steadying her voice. "My relationship with my husband isn't your concern."

"Just think about it." His eyes never left hers as he backed out the door. "And take care."

Think about it! As if she could do anything else. Zel lurched off the ottoman and paced to the fireplace. Could Wolfgang truly have wagered on her virtue? Was the entire courtship, irregular as it was, only a ploy to get her into his bed to satisfy a bet? a ploy accidently ending in marriage? a marriage he could then disregard at will?

Zel had no doubts that in the beginning his plans did not include marriage. But the night at Vauxhall Gardens. The impetuous proposal. That had seemed sincere. Confused, maddening, but sincere. So sincere as to terrify her. And the second house party, had his aim been only seduction? A seduction that erroneously went public?

It would be so much easier if Wolfgang was a stolid, slow, predictable man. She'd be sure of his mind, his motivations. Sighing deeply, she stared into the empty hearth. But then none of this would be happening because she was drawn to the very things that frightened and frustrated her. His mercurial temperament, his reckless charm, and his unpredictability.

She gripped the high mantel edge hard between the heel of her hand and fingers. The whole thing made no sense. Her sane, sensible approach to life was a tree uprooted in a windstorm. A windstorm with an earl's coronet and quicksilver eyes. What had Robin said? How long before he got restless? Zel rubbed at her temples. Maybe he already was. Last night he had been afire with passion. She smiled grimly. After she forced him to bed her. Now she paid the price for it as they moved further apart.

What would happen when she crossed him? A windstorm might be exhilarating, but should she tame it—or ride it out? And more to the point, would he even let her try?

The old helpless feelings came roaring back. So much lay out of her control—the fire, the estrangement, the assaults on Wolfgang, and now these bloody wagers! What had ever made her dream she could meet a man like him head-on and not be washed away by the storm?

She tried again to rub the pain away, but a new thought came whipping through the haze in her head. Robin had been so public about his dislike for her husband. Wolfgang must think Robin was behind the attempts on his life! No, he couldn't think that. But it fit, God, it fit only too well. It would explain Wolf's silence and anger, maybe even the distance he placed between them. He was wrong. But he'd never let her close enough to convince him.

A BLOODY IDIOT. That's what he was. Wolfgang barely noticed the familiar rows of houses and businesses as the carriage headed home through the fine drizzle. The first real chance at giving tenants some power in government and he'd scuttled it with that rider. Satan's tail! He had worked so hard at getting support. Many of the lords liked to think they still lived in feudal times with serfs and slaves farming their lands. Convincing them of the wisdom of giving their tenants even a minuscule amount of control over their own lives had been like pulling firmly rooted teeth.

He'd bargained with some, smooth talked others, and terrorized the rest with tales of the French Revolution, building a mixed bag of supporters. Then he added that last-minute clause with the kiss-of-death word, *widows*.

He was blind to even consider for one second that the gentlemen of the House of Lords would allow a widow or any woman any kind of vote, even a proxy vote. Wolfgang tapped absently on the windowpane, forcing a droplet of rain on a downward path. He hadn't been thinking clearly, focusing on currying Zel's favor not on what constituted a viable bill. Maybe in some distant future, Zel's ideas of equality for women could be presented without ridicule, but not in 1814 England.

Sighing deeply, he realized the idiotic thing about today's fiasco was the idea that his tilt at windmills would have any effect on his marriage. The hard truth remained the same. For his safety and hers, he would have Robin arrested. Even if Wolfgang could become an overnight hero of women, loyalties such as Zel's were not easily swayed. He knew she'd do anything for her brother. Robin had made it clear at the wedding that the night Zel had come to ask Wolfgang for payment of the gambling debts, she was prepared to offer herself, to become the mistress of the man believed responsible for a good portion of their problems. Sleep with the devil, Robin had said. And in his own eagerness to make her indebted to him, Wolfgang had prevented her offer. He brushed a speck of lint off his blue superfine jacket. Events could have progressed very differently, but somehow the end result would be the same. Robin would emerge the victor.

The carriage stopped before the front entrance to Hardwicke Hall. He fought an urge to order the coachman to drive his horses hard and fast in any direction away from London. Exhaling loudly, he stretched his legs and jumped down to the walk. Maybe he could hide in his book room for a few hours, work on his courage and face her at dinner. They would both be more civilized over a meal.

The book room door stood slightly ajar. He slipped in, quietly shutting the door behind him.

"Trying to avoid me?" Zel sat, dwarfed by the big leather chair at the desk, her spectacle lenses glinting in the few rays of sunlight filtering through the clouds.

"Perhaps." He picked up the little centaur and settled on the edge of the desk, looking down at her. "Did you wish to see me?"

She shifted position several times before blurting out, "Are you a gambler?"

He stared at her, jerked to full attention by her unexpected inquiry.

"I asked you a question. Could you have the decency to

answer?" Her usually melodious voice grated, high and scratchy.

"You know I gamble occasionally, but I've never considered myself a gambler."

Zel straightened in the chair. "Then why did you place a wager on me?"

Wolfgang reached for her reflexively. She lurched back, out of his reach, the chair legs rasping on the hard wood floor. "A wager on you? What are you talking about?"

"Robin found it in the betting books at Brooks's, so you needn't play the innocent." She held her chin stubbornly high but couldn't erase the tiny quiver of her lips.

"I don't use the books." He squeezed the jade beast in his fist. "And no one would make entries in my name."

She met his eyes. "Surely you remember the wager you made shortly after the Selby's house party. It was initialed WJWH. You took on all comers, claiming you would bed me before the season was out."

Wolfgang could feel his skin getting hotter, his chest constricting, painfully. He took a long, slow breath. "Do you believe I would do such a thing?"

"It makes perfect sense." Zel dropped her eyes. "The challenge of openly seducing an innocent woman who wanted nothing to do with men was too enticing for you to pass up."

He took another deep breath, but it didn't steady him at all. "Fiends from hell! I kept your brother out of debtors' prison and saved you from marriage to an old lecher."

"And then proceeded to seduce me anyway."

"I wasn't trying to seduce you."

"Then what was that week in the country about?"

Wolfgang returned the statue to the desk. "I wanted to show you how sensual you were, and that you couldn't live your life without expressing that side of your nature."

The pink flush on her cheeks shifted to a deep red, an angry red. "Were you trying to make me a whore?"

"You're twisting everything I say. I thought I could get you to marry me. To explore your sensuality only with me."

"That part certainly wor—"

"I didn't plan to have our hostess and the minister find us. I didn't plan for things to go so far." He jumped off the desk, pacing to the window. "I've told you all this before. I thought you believed me."

"I did. Then."

"But now you believe Robin over me."

"Robin has no reason to lie to me."

Wolfgang slammed his hand to the windowsill. "He has every reason to lie."

"Explain yourself."

Now it would all come out and Robin owned her unyielding support. "Your brother is trying to kill me." He turned to see the expression on her face. It was blank, totally blank.

Zel stood, slowly. "I knew it! I knew you thought that!"

"Whatever you think you know, please just sit and listen." He kept his voice even and stalked back to the desk. "You were right last night, I was keeping secrets." He shoved papers aside and sat on the desk, directly before her. "The attempts on my life have been conclusively linked to your brother." He lifted a hand to silence her. "Please wait. Let me have my say. Robin still blames me for his losses and the attack on him at Maven's. He is convinced I seduced you and forced you into marriage. He still thinks I killed my first wife and most of my relatives. And he believes I wagered on your virtue. If I were your brother, I'd want to kill me too."

Wolfgang leaned forward, trying desperately to read the thoughts sweeping over her face. "Do you believe all that, too? No, don't answer. I'd rather not know. There's more. Robin has threatened me within hearing of others. He was in town at the time of each attack. We have proof the leader of the attacks is a friend of his who owes him money. Everything points to Robin. He probably told you about the wagers to get you safely away before his next inept attempt kills you too." He sighed. "I planned to tell you all this and then have Robin arrested."

She stared at him. "I don't believe any of this."

He laughed harshly. "That's certainly no surprise to me."

"You're wrong. Robin is not guilty of attempted murder." Her voice rose in volume and pitch. "Why couldn't you tell me of your suspicions earlier? We could have—"

"We could have done nothing. I knew you'd never believe it, so what would be the point?" He watched the pulse beat at her neck, the pulse he loved to kiss when it throbbed with passion.

"We could have talked it over—"

"Zel, there was nothing to talk over. If you knew how I agonized over this." He gripped the edge of the desk to stop from reaching for her. If only she would say she believed him, supported him, understood his fears and reluctance. But he knew those words would not pass her lips. This scene was playing out exactly as he predicted it would. He had felled himself with his own inevitable decision. And now lay bleeding at her feet.

"It's someone else. Show me the evidence. We can—"

"Lucifer's blood! It's over." He stood, sending papers flying. "He'll be in jail tomorrow."

"Wolfgang, you cannot do this." Zel grabbed at his arm.

"It's done." He jerked away, but caught her eyes as he shot the last bullet straight to his own heart. "I nearly forgot to tell you, my bill failed. I stupidly added a rider on proxy votes for widows, and the lords made their disapproval clear."

"Wolfgang—"

He cut her off. "Don't say more. I'll only regret it. I didn't expect anything to be otherwise. Robin is your brother. I'm an unwanted husband. But I had to draw the line at letting him kill me when he also endangered you."

He reached the door in two strides. "I'll move out as soon as I can secure an appropriate town house. Meanwhile I'll stay at the club."

"What in God's name are you saying?"

Wolfgang didn't look at her, he couldn't. "I'm sorry as hell for everything." He yanked open the door, but shut gently behind him as he whispered it, "Sorry as hell."

His hand went to his chest as he raced down the steps, the pain so intense he could have sworn he'd been pierced by his own sharp words. He looked at his fingers, surprised to find them free of blood.

CHAPTER 19

CRESCENDO

*An increase, by degree, in the intensity of sound
in a musical passage, the peak of that increase*

ZEL WATCHED out her bedroom window as a thin line of
drizzle collected on a leaf, gradually weighing it down until
it tipped and the water ran onto the sill.

Her throat felt dry and tight. She made a little choking
sound, trying to swallow a lump the size of an orange.

She and Wolfgang had sparred since they met, yet she
had always felt a measure of safety with him. Something
inside her had whispered that this was a man who would not
hurt her. But now the old fears were rearing their ugly heads.
Zel laid her palm against the window. They had never
fought with such cold anger before. She'd felt fear, blind,
frozen fear. Fear that worsened the more his voice lowered
and his manner calmed.

Lord, she could barely remember what they fought
about. Her forehead rested against the cool glass. It started
when she confronted him on the wagers. With the clarity of
hindsight she knew despite his faults and wildness he'd never
make such a bet.

And Robin. Robin could not be guilty. He wasn't capable of murder. She could eventually convince Wolfgang of that. Perhaps she needed to allow him and Robin to work it out themselves.

And the bill. Zel breathed onto the windowpane and absently drew designs with her finger in the foggy glass. She never asked Wolfgang to risk his bill with that rider. She, of all people, knew it would mean death to his bill. What he'd done was rather sweet. But sweetness and politics didn't mix.

The garden beneath her lay sheathed in the gray of twilight. Shivering, Zel turned inward to the darkening, unseasonably chilly room. She didn't know what a marriage was. Didn't know how two people came together to build a life, to be a family. She had lived with the domination of her father and the capitulation of her mother and had tried to choose independence for herself. But she had never been truly independent. She had always been bound by her commitment to Robin.

Now she was tied by her marriage vows to Wolfgang, her vows and her love. Zel bent before the flickering fire, jabbing at it with the heavy iron poker. There must be a way to work through the barriers that kept them apart. To stop him from pulling away. To make him understand. To compromise without losing herself. To create that partnership where two could be one and still remain two.

Now she felt fuzzy and dull. She had to get away. It wouldn't be running away, just time to think things through. Remaining at Hardwicke Hall would be a constant reminder of Wolfgang's refusal to stay and fight it out with her.

Did he blame her for what he saw as Robin's treachery? Shaking the thought loose, she walked to the door. She had all the pieces now. She would put them together and somehow know what to do. Wolfgang was clearly in pain too. And that gave her hope.

Zel rang resolutely for Maggie. The first decision was made. She would be on her way to Cliffehaven within the

hour. But what if he got angry about her leaving and followed? She needed time to herself.

Sitting at her writing desk, she pulled out paper and
quill and penned him a brief note. Let him think she hied off
to Moreton-in-Marsh. It would earn her a few days. If he
even noticed she was gone.

HIS SOLES BURNED like the fires of hell and probably looked
like raw meat. Mephistopheles, London was big, especially
when surveyed on foot.

Wolfgang yawned for the hundredth time that morning,
cursing at the hard, too-short bed at Brooks's, calling himself
all manner of stubborn asses. He should have stayed home
last night and fought it out with Zel. But even the worst
battles on the Peninsula had not frightened him half as much
as facing her. He regretted not telling her earlier about
Robin, but how could he have done otherwise?

Shaking the rain off his jacket, he watched the lazy flow
of the Thames. Little by little she had learned his secrets,
learned of his cruel, hate-filled father, his whore of a first
wife, even his own stupidity. She learned of his old pain and
his world hadn't fallen apart. He'd been so frightened and
angry when he finally told her about Robin. But her reaction
was nothing compared to what he imagined. She'd even
guessed his suspicions, yet he'd fled in terror before giving
himself a chance to see that maybe all was not lost.

He was tired of walking, tired of hiding, tired of being
afraid of pain. It was time to stop being the first to run away.
Time to stay and fight and take the risk that she might leave
him. Raggedly drawing in the damp air, he turned back
toward home. He would tell her everything he knew about
the attempts on his life. He would reveal himself completely
to her, even telling her what he'd never spoken aloud, the
truth about his sister, Gwen. Although the gnawing in his
chest had a heaviness to it, his feet felt a little lighter.

In a matter of minutes he arrived at his door. He clasped McDougall's arm as the brawny Scotsman opened the door. "Where is she, my friend?"

"Lady Z is not at home, m'lord."

Wolfgang swallowed the hard lump in his throat, muttering, "The devil, just as I get up my courage."

"M'lord?" McDougall displayed an unusual coolness.

"Stop the formality. When will she be back?"

"I'm sorry, I don't know, m'lord."

"Lucifer's misbegotten. If you say m'lord one more time, I'll plant a facer so hard you'll land in the next block." Wolfgang started up the stairs, then paused. "Where did she go?"

"I don't know that either, Captain."

"Then what the hell do you know?"

"She left last night with a portmanteau, Maggie, a coachman, and a groom, with no word of where was she bound." McDougall met his eyes squarely. "I took the liberty of sending two additional men after her. None have returned."

"Bloody—" He took the stairs in several leaps. "Jenkins!"

He nearly tripped over Jenkins, bent down on hands and knees by the dressing room doorway, in the smoke-scented bedroom. "What are you doing?"

"Captain, did you see this?" Jenkins held aloft a triangle of dirty cloth.

Wolfgang took the scrap from him. "That table is tearing up more livery." He moved to toss it in the fireplace.

"Wait." Jenkins watched the fabric fall to the floor.

"It's just a torn scrap of livery."

"It felt like fine silk."

Wolfgang rapped the offending table. "I didn't come looking for you to discuss livery. Where is she?"

"Lady Z?"

"Yes, Lady Z." Wolfgang warily eyed his little valet. "Don't be evasive."

Jenkins's tenor voice articulated very softly, "There's a letter on your writing table."

Wolfgang strode to the table, Jenkins close behind. Ripping open the note, he saw his name glaring at him from the top of the page, but the rest of the words swam before his eyes. Lowering his lids he took a deep breath and tried to slow his racing thoughts. When he opened his eyes the words continued their mad dance across the page. In frustration he tore the letter into tiny bits, tossing the jagged fragments into the fireplace. He looked stubbornly into Jenkins's questioning eyes. "She must be at Cliffehaven by now."

Jenkins looked to the coals in the fireplace where the letter was now only a wisp of smoke. "She said she went to Cliffehaven? Funny, Maggie wouldn't tell me. Does she wish you to follow?"

"I don't care what she wishes. I'm going after her." He kicked at the table leg. "Why did she leave?"

"You are asking me?"

"Yes, I'm asking you!" He kicked the table leg a little harder. "Was she angry?"

"Not noticeably angry. Quieter than usual. And very pale." Jenkins's bright eyes never left Wolfgang's.

"I'm taking Ari. Pack me a bag. Take the coach and meet me there."

"How long a stay should I plan for, Captain?"

"Damned if I know." With a flicker of his old grin, Wolfgang strode through the door. "She may throw me out tonight."

The grin faded as he made his way to the stables, becoming a grimace as he saddled Ari. "Well, old boy, it's on the wet side for a hard ride, and our reception is bound to be icy." He stroked the horse's chestnut neck and mounted. "Satan's nosehairs, I hope it's only anger I have to deal with, not fear or disgust."

• • •

WOLFGANG STOOD, hand at the doorjamb, watching as Zel pounded on the pianoforte, striking the keys hard enough to break a string.

By the devil's cloven hoof. It was that damned courage thing again. He'd arrived at Cliffehaven nearly an hour ago, first cleaning off the mud, then hiding away in his study, refusing to search for her until the music drew him out. The music that by its deafening thunder made it clear she knew of his arrival. If he wasn't going to face her, he might as well turn tail and ride back to London. Drawing in a slow, deep breath, he pulled the door wide and strode in.

Her back faced him but her stiff spine told him she sensed his presence. The notes pealed out loud and harsh. One step tentatively followed another until he reached her side. He scanned her profile, the delicate lines were drawn with fatigue.

"How did you get here so quickly?" She didn't move, her voice so soft he could scarcely make out the words.

"I came as soon as I got your note."

The music abruptly stopped. Zel turned slowly on the stool, eyes narrowed, searching his face. "My note?"

"Yes. And I've come to beard the dragon in her den."

Her lips pulled tight. "I'm so fearsome?"

Dropping to both knees before her, he reached vainly for her hands, fingers clutching the skirts of her gown. "I'm tired, Zel. I rode here fueled by anger and fear. But they've burnt out and now I don't know what to do." He bowed his head, forehead resting on her thigh. "What do I do, Gamine? What do we do?"

He felt her long slender fingers hesitate, then weave gently through his hair. "I wish I knew."

"Why did you leave me?" His voice came out barely a whisper, muffled by her muslin skirts.

"I think you have it wrong." She laughed, low and brittle. "You left me."

"I went to the club because I didn't know what else to do." Wolfgang knelt, motionless, lest she remove her hand. "I was afraid."

Her hand stilled, then pulled a few locks of hair loose from his leather-bound queue. "You do make me sound a dragon."

"And I a most reluctant Saint George, come to assault you with more horrors from my past." He raised his head, grasping her fingers as they trailed over his forehead. "I don't want to run anymore. I need to tell you . . ." Pausing, he searched her face, seeking just a hint of warmth.

"I'm listening." The lines around her mouth softened.

"I've never told anyone." He ran her fingertips over his lips as if that would free his speech. "I was eight years old and Gwen, my sister, was nearly six. It was August, hot and dry. We escaped our tutor, the local vicar, and ran all the way to the lake." He closed his eyes, the scene still so vivid he could see the overbright green of the trees, smell the musty odor of the water. "We stripped down in seconds. The water felt so cool. She swam out further and further, daring me to follow. Not one to be beaten by a slip of a girl, I dared her to race me to the stump on the other side." He settled his weight on his heels. "I was nearly there when I realized there was no sound of splashing behind me."

Wolfgang opened his eyes, reaching for her other hand. She locked her fingers in his. "I dove for her again and again. I would have drowned looking for her, but a groom sent to find us pulled me out. I was carried back to the house while the search for her continued." He brushed their joined hands over his cheek. "My mother told me the next morning she was dead. I was locked in my room for days, maybe weeks. No one visited except Mr. Yang, father's butler. He brought up my meals and wash water, but wasn't allowed to stay.

When I was finally released the funeral had long since passed."

His head felt light, his knees a little wobbly. Lowering himself to sit on the carpet, he still clutched Zel's hands, but looked away from the tears in her eyes. "I sought out my father, to tell him I would die if it would bring her back. His fist cracked into my jaw before I could utter a word." Wolfgang laughed bitterly. "Funny thing, I almost died from that beating, but she still didn't come back."

Zel's thumb rubbed little circles into his palm. "You didn't kill her."

"I was responsible for her."

"You were eight years old." Zel's husky alto flowed balmlike over him. "You may have blamed yourself then, but can't you see now that a child is not responsible for another child?"

He shook his head stubbornly, fighting her soothing tones. "I never should have let her swim so far."

Zel squeezed his fingers. "I blamed myself for years when my mother died. Tortured myself with thoughts of what I could have done differently."

"But you were a—"

"Yes, I was a child." She leaned forward, dusting his brow with cool lips. "Let go of it, Wolfgang."

"But she left me, you left me. Everyone leaves." His voice was less than a whisper, little more than a breath. "I don't deserve to have anyone care about me. So I learned to leave first."

"Wolfgang, I didn't leave you." She rested her cheek at his temple. "I only needed a little time alone."

"You left me for Robin."

"I did not leave you for Robin. You pushed me away." She frowned, pulling a hand free.

"I understand, Zel. You have ties to Robin. Your loyalty is to him." Wolfgang held tight to her remaining hand, trying desperately to remain calm.

"You speak like I need to make a choice between you."

"Your choice is already made. I know. But I have no choice." He looked at her hand, willing her to understand. "I have to arrest him."

Zel jerked loose her other hand, standing suddenly, toppling the stool. "You're being an idiot. Robin isn't guilty."

He winced under the blow. "Yes, I may be stupid—"

She interrupted, hovering over him. "I'm sorry, Wolfgang. You know I didn't mean that, you're not stupid. But you're wrong about Robin."

"I wish to God I was."

"Tell me everything. It must be someone else."

"Zel, no. Not now. I can't deal with it now." He rose, righting the stool. "And it'll make no difference."

"You stubborn, arrogant fool. I have a right to know." She faced him, hands on hips, nostrils flared, anger supplanting compassion.

Wolfgang sat on the stool, drawing close to the keyboard. "No. There's nothing you can do."

"This isn't over."

"I know." Fingering through the notes of a ballad, he listened as her footsteps exited the room and receded down the hall. Remarkable how well he'd managed that encounter. He might as well have handed Zel to Robin on a platter.

The white keys blurred. He picked out another melody, a popular tavern song, solemnly humming along with the rollicking tune. He'd not give in, turn tail and run. Whether he deserved her or not, he wouldn't let her abandon him without a fight.

There was nothing he could do to save Gwen, to stop his father's hatred, to warm his cold mother, or to make his first wife faithful. Those losses were in the past, memories he would no longer allow to hurt him.

Ignoring a flurry of noises coming from the hall, he played another verse of the song. Zel could hurt him. He had been certain she would. But maybe he was wrong. Maybe the love he had unknowingly watched grow in her eyes, the love she had named only when sure he couldn't hear, would be enough.

A footstep sounded in the doorway, he turned eagerly, ready to kiss away Zel's frown. "Aunt Dorothea? What—?"

"Arthur, shut the door." Aunt Dorothea watched Wolfgang closely as the thin man behind her quietly shut the door.

Wolfgang stood, eyeing her warily. "Aunt—"

"Stay where you are, *nephew*." His aunt reached into a large reticule, withdrawing a well-polished dueling pistol. The thin man, whom he now recognized as her butler, Arthur Martindale, turned, holding its twin.

"What in the name of Satan?" He took a step toward her.

"Stop." She motioned to the sofa with the gun. "Sit down." She edged closer to Martindale as Wolfgang slowly lowered himself onto the sofa. "Arthur, don't take your eyes off him for a moment."

"I don't under—"

"You don't understand. No one understands. No one ever understands." She laughed shrilly. "You never suspected me, a woman, did you? You've led a charmed existence, but the fifth time will break the spell. I won't fail this time."

"I don't believe this." Wolfgang leaned forward in the sofa, hands braced to stand. She aimed the pistol barrel at his chest. "You plan to shoot me in my own home?"

"I am a good shot, but I'm not a fool." She smiled queerly. "You're going to have a carriage accident on the cliff road into town. The rain has stopped but it's wet and dangerous, and you are a very reckless man."

"But why?" He shifted position on the sofa, eyeing the two guns pointed at him. "What do you have to gain, but a little money? Very little in fact, as the estate follows the male line and will revert to the crown if I die, and my personal fortune is willed to my wife."

Aunt Dorothea's features softened, a muted light gleamed in her eyes. "I will be earl of Northcliffe. Not you or some whelp gotten off that Fleetwood woman."

He choked back a laugh. "You can't be an earl. You can't even be a countess."

"You think because I'm a woman, I can't be earl?" The bell tones of her voice rang hollowly.

"We both know even your son can't inherit."

"But the male line will be gone. You are the last." She waved the gun at him. "I will petition the prince regent for my son or myself."

"You're insane." He paused, watching her hand tighten around the pistol. "Prinny will never agree. You don't have enough money to pay his price."

"But I will."

"I told you, my fortune goes—" Wolfgang clenched his hands together into one fist. "My God, you're going to kill her too!"

"You've given me no choice. You've given her your money and your seed."

"She's not carrying my child!"

Dorothea's voice cracked. "Don't lie to me. One of your maids told Arthur you two copulate like rabbits. She's pregnant. I can see it in her eyes."

"You're mad—"

"Shut up!" She waived the gun wildly.

He needed to calm her or she'd shoot him before he could formulate a plan of escape. "How did you know to find us here?"

"Arthur saw Grizelda leave last night and as he was discovering her whereabouts this morning you followed after her. You have made it so easy."

"Your plan will never work. Give it up and I'll see you're not hanged." He shifted his hands.

She glared at him. "I am firstborn. I have influence. It is

my right. You and all the others stood in my way. But not anymore."

"Oh, God." He buried his head in his hands, finally realizing the enormity of her madness. "You killed them all, every bloody male in the line—your father, your brothers, and your nephew. All for something you can never have."

"I can and will have the earldom." She screeched, then lowered her voice. "I didn't kill my father. As for the rest, they were a worthless, stupid lot and didn't deserve the title. Your father was the only one with a brain in his head and he wasted it on God and religion. But I would have killed him too, if he hadn't had the good sense to die on his own years ago.

"You were supposed to be blamed for the deaths and hanged." She jerked her head toward the butler. "We are wasting time. Get Grizelda. I want to set up well before dark."

The door swung open, Zel and Remus swept into the room. "You stopped playing and I heard voices . . ." When she saw Aunt Dorothea and the pistol, she stopped, hand buried in the shaggy hair at the dog's neck. "What—"

"Grizelda, dear, how convenient." Aunt Dorothea directed the pistol at Zel. "Sorry I can't greet you properly. Sit over there and keep that dog with you." She indicated the pianoforte stool. "You are just in time to take a carriage ride."

Wolfgang lurched to his feet. "You—"

"Sit down." Aunt Dorothea growled. "Or she'll take a bullet now."

He sat rigidly on the edge of the sofa. "Leave her out of this."

Zel stared from Aunt Dorothea to Wolfgang, taking a step toward Wolfgang. "What—"

"Silence! Sit down. Now!" Aunt Dorothea hissed, eyes returning to Wolfgang only after Zel settled herself on the stool. "There will be no heir."

Wolfgang tried to catch Zel's eye, but she stared straight ahead, seemingly mesmerized by the pistol in his aunt's hand. Glancing surreptitiously around the room, he looked for anything usable as a weapon. The fireplace pokers were too far. The vase too small to do any damage. He needed to keep her talking while he worked on a plan. "You hired Pettibone."

"Pettibone." She laughed scornfully. "He was a big mistake. A friend of Adam's, owed him money. He played at footpad and highwayman to pay his debts. But the man's a fool. Much better to do the job myself."

"You set the fire." Zel's voice registered her incredulity. She seemed in shock, gripping Remus's neck like a lifeline. "That was you in the hallway."

"It would have worked, but you came home too early." Dorothea's laugh grated against Wolfgang's teeth. "Or perhaps I was the one too early." She waved the pistol. "It's time to go. The carriages should be out front by now. I took the liberty of ordering yours, along with your cloaks." She tucked the pistol into the folds of her silver silk gown.

"You'll never pull this off." Wolfgang stood at the motion of Martindale's weapon. "My staff know you're here."

"The story will go that I followed you into town in my carriage, but got frightened by the bad road and turned back." She bared her teeth in a parody of a grin. "We will wait and wait in vain for your return. Your crushed carriage and broken bodies will be found tomorrow."

Movement exploded at his side. He whirled about to watch Remus leap through the air and Zel hurl the pianoforte stool. Remus hit the butler square in the chest. Both bodies toppled to the floor, the pistol clattering harmlessly under a chair. A fraction of a second later the stool slammed into Aunt Dorothea's left shoulder. Her gun went off. Wolfgang dove over a table and connected with a thud to his aunt's midsection. She crumbled under him as he wrenched the pistol free.

Footmen and maids scrambled into the room. Wolfgang stood, jerking his aunt up with him, shoving her toward the nearest footman, his voice a tight growl coming from deep in his chest. "Tie her hands and watch her." He pointed another footman toward Martindale. "Pull the dog off him and tie him too. When they're secured send for the local constabulary." He looked about the room, a frisson of fear crawling up his spine. "Zel?"

A faint moan came from beside the pianoforte. Hurling aside a footman and chair, he knelt at her side. Scarcely breathing, Wolfgang ripped the bloody cloth from her shoulder. He yanked off his cravat and swabbed at the wound. The bullet had struck her upper arm. He probed the wound with his fingers. Trying to raise up on her elbows, Zel moaned again. Remus nudged Wolfgang, whimpering softly.

Wolfgang scooped Zel up, holding her tight against his chest. Striding through the door, he shouted over his shoulder. "Send a maid with hot water, clean cloths, and whiskey. Now! Get the doctor!"

The stairs disappeared two at a time under his feet. He kicked open the door to his chambers and laid her on the bed. The blood-soaked fabric of her gown and shift tore easily beneath his hands. He slid off her slippers and pulled the bedclothes over her chest. She stirred as he reexamined the wound.

"Wolfgang. I—"

"Sshh, don't try to talk, Gamine." He brushed a finger over her lips. "I'll take care of you. I think the bullet did little more than nick the skin. It will heal well."

Two young women brought in the supplies and set them on a table. He nodded a thanks to the departing maids and took a cloth, dipping it in the water. Holding her steady with his free hand, he gently washed the blood from her arm and shoulder.

"You're a brave woman." Wolfgang rinsed the cloth and dabbed more at her pale skin, trying to ignore her grimace of pain. "But foolish. You could have been killed. You did choose a better weapon this time. A stool can do more damage than a reticule or umbrella."

"I save your damned life," Zel muttered between gritted teeth, "and you call me foolish and complain about my choice of weapons?"

"Forgive me." He placed a light kiss on her tight lips. "And thank you, madam wife. But if you ever scare me again like that, I'll shoot you myself."

Zel smiled gamely, but her bottom lip trembled.

"I'm going to pour whiskey on the wound—"

"Whiskey? No, you are not."

"I've seen field doctors do it, and there seems to be less fever." Wolfgang lowered the bedcovers and lifted her, placing a cloth beneath her. "This is going to hurt like hell."

She cried out and stiffened as the amber fluid trailed down her shoulder, arm, and breast. Watching the tears squeeze out from between her clenched lashes, he felt a swelling in his chest. He pressed a square of cotton cloth to the still bleeding injury, then raised the whiskey bottle to her lips. "Drink a little."

Coughing down a mouthful of whiskey, she pushed the bottle away. "It's horrible, why does anyone drink it?"

"It is bad, but it has a few medicinal uses, elf." Wolfgang tried to hide the shaking of his hands as he set down the whiskey bottle. Sitting beside her on the bed, he drew her slender form carefully into his arms, keeping the compress firm against her arm. "I could use some myself, but I need a clear head."

Wolfgang sucked in a breath, burying his face in her hair. "When I saw you lying on the floor, your shoulder and chest drenched in blood, I was so afraid." He ran his lips over her eyes, tasting the salty liquid still clinging to her lashes. "So afraid of losing you. I've been afraid from the start of losing you." He stroked her hair. "I wanted your love but barely believed it was real, let alone something that would last. I never knew what it meant to have a family's love. Only my sister." His grip on Zel tightened. "My sister was an angel, much too sweet for me."

"You can't blame yourself for her death." Zel's voice resonated soft and low in his ear.

"I know, I was a child." Wolfgang pulled away slightly, kissing the tip of her nose, looking into the mossy depths of her eyes. "I *was* a child." He sighed, stretching in surprise at the sudden lightness of his shoulders.

"You told me you loved me the night Robin's guilt seemed inevitable. I knew in a contest with him, I'd never win." He leaned back into the pillows, keeping her secure in his arms. "I pulled away first, in part to protect you, but also to protect me from the pain that would come when you left me for him."

"Wolfgang, I do love you." She nuzzled her head against his chest. "There is and was no contest. Robin is my brother, not my child. And I am your wife."

"You are my wife, Gamine." He swallowed. "I want everything you have to give me."

Zel's head jerked up. "Everything?" Her eyes met his, laughter there under the tears.

"You minx. I'm trying to be serious."

"Then just tell me you love me."

"It started the night you blackened my eye." He laughed at her puzzled look. "I just couldn't resist trying to dig out the passionate woman from beneath that mountain of self-control."

She smiled and burrowed in closer. "Had I known the effect of that blow, I would have blackened your other eye and broken your nose and saved us all this doubt and misery. But I'm still waiting."

Wolfgang gently freed himself, pushing her back onto the pillows, studying her arm. "It's still bleeding, but not as much. I'll wrap it until the doctor comes." He daubed away the blood and began to wind the cloth around her arm, soundlessly mouthing the words she waited to hear. "I love you."

Zel winced. "Gently. You're hurting me."

"Then I won't say it again." Wolfgang grinned down at her.

"You had better say it again, in fact daily." Her eyes followed his hands as he finished wrapping her arm. "My life seemed so under control, before I met you. But I had bound myself up so tightly with fear I was ready to explode.

"I didn't leave you last night. I came home to decide how to change you to make our marriage work." Zel settled deeper into the pillows. "But I discovered my choices were already made. You're part of my life. I want you with all the surprises and uncertainties." She smiled a little crookedly. "And speaking of surprises, my note said I was on my way to Moreton-in-Marsh."

Wolfgang stared at her. "I was so upset when I discovered you'd gone, I couldn't have read that letter to save my life. But I was sure you would have headed for Cliffehaven."

"Wolfgang, your problem may have saved your life." She drew him down beside her. "If you had read my letter you would have gone to Moreton-in-Marsh and Remus and I wouldn't have been there when your aunt followed."

"Then you don't care so much that you're saddled with an idiot?"

"If you call yourself that again, you may see a little violence in this marriage after all, when I wring your neck." She reached for his neck with her uninjured arm. "What can I do to convince you of all the brilliance contained within that thick skull of yours?"

Wolfgang pulled her fingers to his lips. "We'll make a pact. Every day after I tell you how much I love you, you tell me that you fell in love with me because of my keen mind. Give it about ten years or so and I might even believe you."

"You'd better believe me much sooner than ten years,

you stubborn man, for I do love your mind as well as all your other parts."

"Praise the devil for those parts." He stretched out beside her. "If it hadn't been for the demands of some of those parts, our stubborn minds would have kept us apart." He tugged gently at a long sable curl resting above her breast. "Were we such fools? Fighting against the inevitable? I yield to the decisions of the body and the heart. After all, don't they say that when a wolf finds his mate he is mated for life?"

POSTLUDE

A closing piece of music

FREDDIE NEARLY SMILED as Zel entered Cliffehaven's spacious music room, surprise evident on her face. She looked over the assorted guests, eyes lighting accusingly on Wolf. "I thought we were to have an intimate evening at home."

Wolf grinned at her, totally unrepentant. "I must have gotten it reversed. I meant an evening at home with our intimates."

But Zel was already off, receiving birthday hugs and kisses from her friends, her aunt, and Wolf's grandmother. Freddie stood near the pianoforte, keeping back from the crush.

Rafael held Zel overly long until Wolf frowned at his friend and pried him loose. Snatching one last kiss, Raf smiled at the couple. *"Bonne Anniversaire."* The man would be trying to spark the tempers of his friends when the three of them were seventy.

Freddie stepped forward, taking her hand, gently squeezing her fingers. "We're not intruding, are we?"

"Of course not." Her lips curved softly. "I would only,

just once, like to venture a guess on what my husband has planned, and be right."

Wolf took her arm, still careful of the wound, which nearly a month after the shooting, must be healed. "Gifts and champagne before dinner. My gift first." He led her to a draped object on a table beside the pianoforte. "Pull the cloth."

Zel dramatically swirled off the square of fabric, revealing a large bust of a man as rough looking as Freddie himself.

Wolf swept his arm over the statue. "Behold, my rival, Herr Beethoven. Carved in the finest Italian marble, he shall reside in my music room, where I can keep a sharp eye on him and my wife."

His wife laughed, taking her husband by the shoulders, kissing him on the mouth, long and deep. Freddie looked away.

"I say, how disgusting. A married couple kissing in public." Freddie smiled at the half-serious grimace that accompanied Raf's comments.

"You remaining bachelors are just frightened, Ridgemont. It always happens when one of your number happily succumbs." Lady Darlington took Zel's elbow, guiding her to a settee. "Come sit with me, I have a gift for you too, maybe not as spectacular as the maestro, but something I want you to have."

"You can't challenge me and run away, Lady D." Raf pulled up a chair next to them. "I'm not afraid of marriage. In fact I'll probably leg-shackle myself within the next year or two." His mouth curled into that smile women forever swooned over. "I'm looking for a sweet, young thing, fresh out of the schoolroom. One I can mold into the perfect duchess."

Zel's little friend, Mrs. Carland, took the bait. "Ridgemont, your ideas on women belong in the Dark Ages." Taking the chair near Raf, she turned to the innocent Freddie, nailing him with a superior look. "Ransley, I assume your philosophy must be prehistoric."

"Mrs. Carland." Freddie lowered his eyes to her, matching her stare. "I assure you, I hold women in the highest regard. But I'd certainly never be fool enough to marry one again."

Wolf chuckled. "I said the same thing myself." He plopped down at Zel's feet as Lady Darlington pinned an heirloom sapphire brooch to Zel's bodice. "Changed my tune, but then I got the best of the lot."

"As did I." Zel stroked Wolf's hair, twining her fingers in the narrow silver streak.

"I don't believe my stomach can bear more of this." Raf withdrew his enameled snuff box from his waistcoat. "Nasty habit, I know, but easier on the digestion than love." He took a pinch, wiping the excess off his fingers with a handkerchief. "Speaking of nasty things, where is your dear Aunt Dorothea?"

Wolf sighed. "I suppose someone had to bring her up. Aunt Dorothea and her faithful butler, Martindale, are even now sailing for Australia. She was still demanding everyone call her the earl of Northcliffe as she boarded." He took Zel's hand and rubbed it along his jaw. "Maybe I should have put her in an asylum, but I couldn't bring myself to do it. Somehow Botany Bay, tough as it's reputed to be, seemed kinder."

"Martindale will care for her," Zel continued. "Pettibone hasn't surfaced, but Wolfgang's certain he has no stake in finishing the job. Cousin Adam appears adrift. He had no part in it, never suspected her, as close as they were. I think he may eventually join her in Australia."

"Where is young Fleetwood, and does he know the whole of it?" Freddie tried to keep his inquiry innocuous.

"No need for discretion, Freddie. Everyone knows Robin was the major suspect at one time." Wolf rose slowly and walked to the window. "Robin was furious when he found out, took off for Moreton-in-Marsh to get away from me.

Zel's father followed." The smile he directed at Zel and her aunt seemed a bit tentative. "I'm happy my wife and Diana are still speaking to me."

"Robin needs time to sulk. And Father will be back begging for money." Zel went to him, placing her arm about his waist. "It's all behind us now."

"Not quite." Rafael tucked his snuff box back into his pocket. "What did you do about that betting book wager?"

Lady Darlington tapped Raf's shoe with her ebony cane, but her eyes followed her grandson. "Who was it?"

"Wilmington John Wilborn Hawthorne, Lord Newton." Wolf draped his arm over Zel's shoulders. "As long as I've known the man, I had no idea our initials were identical."

"Newton has thrust himself forward as your rival since we were all schoolboys." Raf stuffed his handkerchief in the pocket beside the snuff box.

"Hawthorne," Zel's aunt mumbled. "A veritable thorn in the side."

Lady Darlington laughed politely.

Zel smiled indulgently at her aunt and turned to Wolf. "We should have known it was him. Whenever anything bad happened, he was there."

"I've taken care of him." Wolf pulled Zel closer.

"Wolfgang!" Lady Darlington and Zel's voices rose in tandem. Lady Darlington stared at her grandson. "What did you do?"

Freddie suppressed a cough as Wolf played his innocent routine to the hilt, complete with boyish grin. "You two, yes, Zel and Grandmama, are overly suspicious. I did nothing but threaten to reveal a little secret should he ever bother Zel again."

Zel twisted beneath his arm. "What secret?"

"A secret's not a secret if everyone knows it." Wolf lightly brushed her hair with his lips. "It's Newton's secret, not mine. You know you share mine."

She smiled up at him, then snuggled into his side.

Freddie felt the corners of his mouth creaking upward, he was getting as maudlin as the rest. This love stuff must be dangerous, even contagious. No, Hélène had inoculated him against love as surely as that new vaccine protected him from smallpox. He watched as Wolf's huge gray cat, Hecate, sauntered into the room, beelining for the newest item. She jumped onto the table, sniffing suspiciously at the marble bust.

Zel's wolfhound stood in the doorway, surveying the room. He stretched taller than his already generous height when he spotted the cat. Freddie watched helplessly as the dog's muscles bunched and he sprang across the room, aimed straight at Beethoven and the feline. Hecate eyed the hound and at the last possible moment hopped lightly to the floor. The dog crashed, sending statue and table flying.

"Mary Magdelene's bloomers!" Freddie's chin must have dropped to his chest as he watched Zel, cursing vigorously, dash after the offending pets.

"By all the saints of hell, you are a bad dog, Remus!" She grasped the hound by the scruff of his neck, guiding his unresisting form to a waiting footman.

"Hecate! You devil's familiar!" She hissed, diving for the cat, catching the furry mass squarely around the chest. "Out! You damned troublemaker." She dropped the cat into the hall, shut the door behind her and dusted off her hands.

Freddie glanced around the room. With the exception of one, the inhabitants stood in stunned silence. The exception was the virago's husband.

Wolf's lips twitched and his shoulders shook as he dissolved into laughter.

Zel strode to the fallen Beethoven. Lifting the heavy statue, she angrily displayed the chipped nose. "Those beasts destroyed it. Beethoven is ruined."

Rafael laughed, a harsh bark. "Wolf, you need to control your pets and your wife. At least get her to mind her language." He raised a pale eyebrow. "The chit's bound to embarrass you before the ton."

"Embarrass *me?*" Wolf's grin spread the width of his face. "Don't be a pompous ass. And the proper term is 'woman,' not 'chit.'"

Wolf took the statue from Zel's arms, righting the table and placing the bust on top. "He looks good with a little less nose." He nuzzled Zel's loosened hair. "And mind your own business, Ridgemont. I like my animals and my woman a bit on the wild side."

You won't want to miss the next
irresistible historical romance from

REBECCA KELLEY

"I go where I please."

"No. You go where I please." Tarrant's big hand
engulfed her shoulder. . . . Rina showed her
teeth, ready to meet Tarrant head to head and beat
him at this own game. He would learn that any
attempt to control her was in vain. She would find
Papa without his help and she would gain her own
independence. But Tarrant had already lost interest
in her, staring vacantly at something up the street.
His face went slack then froze into a hard, brittle
mask that would surely crack if she dared to touch
it. She followed his line of sight, and stumbled. . . . A woman who could be her twin stood
beside a shop door, her gaze locked on Tarrant, a
cold smile on her pouting lips.

A passionate Beauty and the Beast tale of
Victorian England . . . with a twist.

Coming in Summer 1999 from Bantam Books.

AUTHOR'S NOTE

Johann Sebastian Bach, as indicated in *The Wedding Chase,* was all but unknown in Europe during the Regency period. During his lifetime (1685–1750) he was acclaimed as a musician but few of his compositions were performed. Felix Mendelssohn discovered *St. Matthew Passion* through his great aunt and conducted an enthusiastically received performance in Berlin during March of 1829. Bach's works then began to be published and played throughout Europe.

Beethoven's Seventh Symphony would not have been played in Vauxhall Gardens in the spring of 1814, although it was completed in 1812. But it is my favorite piece of music and its sheer beauty never fails to bring tears to my eyes. I couldn't resist using it for a pivotal scene in the book.

Rebecca Kelley lives in Oregon with her husband, children, cat, and dog. She has worked for years counseling criminal offenders, so one would naturally assume she'd be writing contemporary suspense. But, no, she prefers her fictional thrills firmly fixed in the 1800s or earlier.

Cursed with an irreverent sense of humor, Rebecca allows nothing past her without a gentle poke in the ribs, or, if more deserving, a less-than-gentle kick in the shins.

When time permits, she centers herself creating masks, vases, and jewelry from clay and metal.

Rebecca loves romance because where else can you meet such fascinating men and courageous women?

After years of verbally revising books, movies, plays, and TV shows, Rebecca returns to her early love of writing with her first novel, *The Wedding Chase*.

A deeply enthralling, richly romantic novel of
passion and adventure . . .

A Rose in Winter

by Shana Abé

When Lady Solange's ruthless father threatened the
life of her true love, Damon Wolf, she agreed to
turn him away and to marry another. For nine long years,
she has lived a nightmare, wed to a handsome lord with a
soul of darkest evil. Just as she is poised to make her escape, Damon suddenly appears at the castle gate. Gone is
the gentle hero of her childhood, replaced by a fiercely attractive, thunderously angry knight, who has never forgiven her betrayal. Convincing Damon to escort her to
safety will take all Solange's ingenuity. But the real challenge lies in breaching the walls that Damon has built between them. ___57787-5 $5.50/$7.50 Canada